AN ANCIENT CURSE.

FORBIDDEN LOVE.

AND A HEART STRONG ENOUGH
TO CONQUER THE GOD OF DEATH.

BRIDE OF THE CORPSE KING

EMILY SHORE

BRIDE OF THE CORPSE KING

Copyright © 2021 Emily Shore
EMILYBETHSHORE.INFO

All rights reserved. No part of this publication may be reproduced, distributed, or transmitted in any form or by any means, including photocopying, recording, or other electronic or mechanical methods, without the prior written permission of the publisher, except in the case of brief quotations embodied in critical reviews and certain other noncommercial uses permitted by copyright law.

This book is a work of fiction. Names, characters, places, and incidents are either products of the author's imagination or are used fictitiously. Any resemblance to actual persons, living, dead or otherwise, events, or locales is entirely coincidental.

Cover and Interior Design by We Got You Covered Book Design
WWW.WEGOTYOUCOVEREDBOOKDESIGN.COM

CONTENT WARNING

Bride of the Corpse King began as a New Adult fantasy but evolved to include more adult content, including trauma-overcoming themes. My book hits on deep subjects and includes sexual scenes woven through beauty and emotion. As I aim to reach older teens through this, I've still showcased a strong, sex-positive and body-positive heroine who challenges toxic authority figures and fights for her freedom even with her own sweat, blood, and pain. But as an abuse survivor, I wish you to be aware of some darker subject matter and care for your mental well-being. Please enjoy the steamier scenes, especially toward the end!

The Corpse King became my greatest challenge. Allysteir is a powerful character, traumatized by his past demons and pain. At heart, he is a romantic and a drama queen with the best intentions. Don't let his behavioral shift shut you down as he punishes himself worse and undergoes a trial of penance and redemption. Ultimately, redemption and rebirth are the two strongest themes of this book.

OTHER WORKS BY EMILY SHORE

POST 2020 AUTHOR JOURNEY:

The Twisted Myths Series

Bride of the Corpse King — Book One on Kindle Vella

Hell's Angel Series

Bride of Lucifer: Hell on Earth — Book One on Kindle Vella (Coming to KU/Paperback October. Read **Author's Note** for how you can get a **Signed** Paperback Copy)

Bride of Lucifer: The Bride Trials — Book Two on Kindle Vella (Coming to KU/Paperback October. Read **Author's Note** for how you can get a **Signed** Paperback Copy)

Bride of the Shifter King — Companion Book in the Hell's Angel Universe (Coming to KU/Paperback November/December. Read **Author's Note** for how you can get a **Signed** Paperback Copy)

PRE 2020 AUTHOR JOURNEY:

The Uncaged Series

The Aviary — Book One
The Garden - Book Two

The Temple - Book Three
The Temple Twins — Book Four
The Aquarium - Book Five

The Roseblood Series

Roseblood — Book One
Silhouette — Book Two
Requiem — Book Three
Sanctuary — Book Four
Roseborn — Book Five (WIP)

The Flesh and Ash Series

Flesher — Book One
Flesher: Resurrection — Book Two (WIP)

PLAYLIST

Isla's Theme Song: "Undo" by Nightcore

Allysteir aka the Corpse King's Theme Song: "Hate Me" by Eurielle/Nightcore Cover

Aryahn Kryach's Theme Song: "Persephone" by Tamino

Theme Song for All Three: "Lovely" by Billie Eilish and Khalid — Cover by Lauren Babic and Jordan Radvansky

Allysteir and Finleigh's Theme Song: "Far Across the Land" by Eurielle

GENERAL SONGS:

"City of the Dead" by Eurielle

"Zombie" by the Cranberries — Nightcore Cover

"All the King's Horses" by Karmina

"O' Death" by Jen Titus from *Supernatural*

"My Love Will Never Die" by Claire Wyndham

"Lullaby of Woe" by Ashley Serena

"Poets of the Fall" by Carnival of Rust

"Sally's Song and Corpse Bride Medley" by Trickywi

"Dear Agony" by Breaking Benjamin

"Kiss My Eyes and Lay Me to Sleep" by Afi

"Hymn for the Missing" and "Pieces" by Red

"Safe and Sound" by Taylor Swift (feat. The Civil Wars)

"Anthem of Our Dying Day" by Story of the Year

"Broken Pieces" by Apocalyptica feat. Lacey Sturm

"Enchanting Songs for a Witch — Folk/Pagan Songs" by Yuecubed

"If It Means a Lot to You" by A Day to Remember

"Savage Daughter" by Sarah Hester

DEDICATION

This is honestly dedicated to the 2021 version of Emily Shore.

Shortly after finding her voice in late 2020 and coming out as bisexual, 2021 Emily embarked on what she never knew was the hardest and darkest year of her life. From April-December, writing this book gave Emily what she needed to keep going, keep working, keep breathing amidst the worst health, mental health, and family trials ever. She poured her heart and soul and essence into this book. It became a true labor of love. Blood and tears were shed.

2022 Emily couldn't be prouder of her 2021 self and how hard she worked through her darkest trials and still managed to finish this book from April-December while beginning another and editing multiple works to get them onto Kindle Vella.

2022 EMILY TO 2021 EMILY:

Hush now and lay down your head,
No more courage and no more dread
Rainbows is our word for a bright new year
Colors and silver linings as the darkness disappears...

To learn more about my journey AND how you may receive a **signed** paperback copy of one of my latest books, please read the **Author's Note** at the end of the book.

GLOSSARY OF TERMS

Talahn-Feylan — The Land of the Feyal-Ithydeir

Nathyan Ghyeal — The White Ladies — Five Mountains with the City of the Dead/Underworld at their center. (Note: My Underworld borders the traditional versions of the Underworld. Nathyan Ghyeal is the entrance to the true realm of the spirits. Celtic lore and setting inspired Nathyan Ghyeal.)

Feyal-Ithydeir — Civil and sane flesh-eaters

Eth-gharym aka refters — Mad flesh-eaters aka zombies

Mathyr — Mother

Fathyr — Father

Nighyans — Young women

Scyan — A type of Celtic dagger

Wisp-Shee — Fae Folk

Sythe — Vampire

Eylfe — Elf

Shifters — All animal form shifters

Inker — Witch

Blue-Skin — Mer-Folk

Ban-Sythe — Banshee

www.samaiya.com

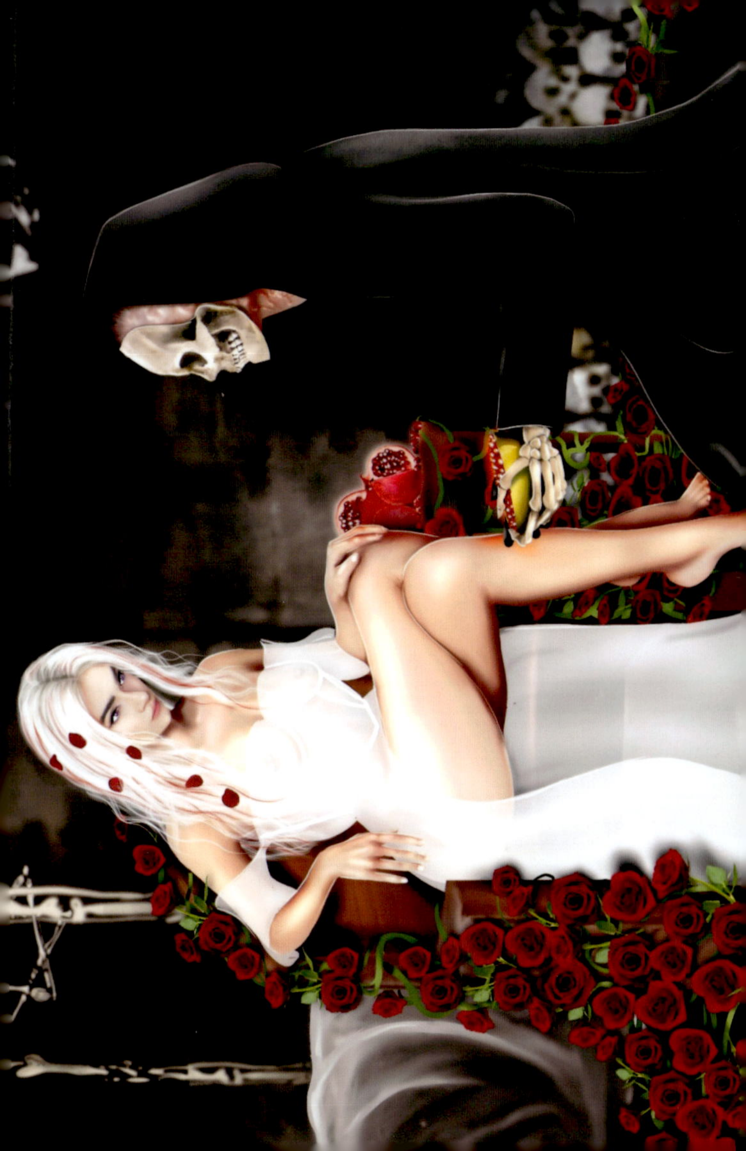

Thank you for your review! Follow me for more are opportunities!

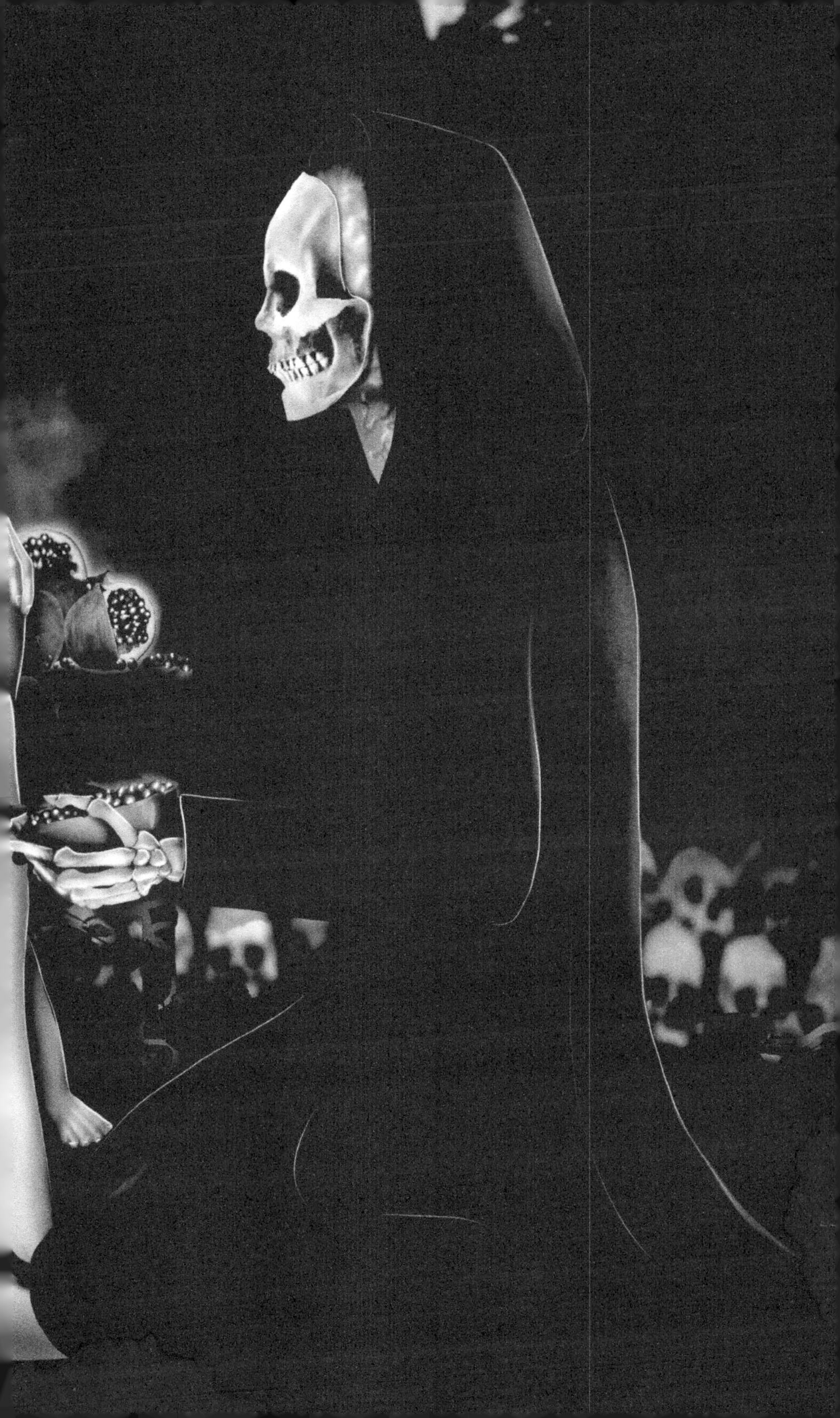

Underneath the mountains so lonely and deep
The Corpse King closes his eyes to sleep
With black shroud and bones for hands
His rotted shade flies 'cross the land

After sun has fallen and dusk is nigh
Listen for his shadow lullaby
He brings death to the roses as he seeks
The souls of the old, the wild, and the weak

Fret not, my child and close your eyes
Dream of sweet heather and butterflies
I will lament when your body first bleeds
And pray over bones and pomegranate seeds

The Corpse King accepts the curse of Death
So dance the night away at his Feast of Flesh
And there I will weep knowing you cannot hide
For he'll take you to be his maidyan bride

~A MOTHER'S SONG FOR HER DAUGHTER~

ONE

THE FEAST OF FLESH

ISLA

The Corpse King needs a new bride.

With the knowledge chilling my spine, I hand my sealed summons to the flesh-master, push my shoulders back, and set my jaw, praying he won't realize it's forged. Forging an elder's summons could land me in an Ithydeir prison. Sneaking into the King's Underworld to enter the Bone Games would land me in much worse. If I get caught.

After the master inspects the elder seal, he pinches his lips, scrutinizing me. I raise my chin, neck regal-high. Around his throat dangling from a leather cord is a proud wishbone: a gift inherited from an ancestor, no doubt. I sigh longingly at the beautiful piece which could pay off months' worth of my family's debt. Half consider swiping it, but it's too risky.

Stop staring, I chastise myself and lift my eyes to the flesh-master's. Provided that weasel-faced Ganyx gave me accurate information, I'll walk away with enough rare bones to fund the farm for the next year.

"Quite a summons for a girl from the humble homestead of Cock-

Cross," remarks the flesh-master, chuckling at the name of our little farming town famed for its rooster bones. I almost chuckle, too until he opens his mouth, jagged teeth flashing.

Biting a groan from his intimidation tactic, I ball my clammy hands into fists to prevent them from shaking and stare him down, daring him to try and claim me. Those teeth and their keen claws are the differences between us and the elite Feyal-Ithydeir—the flesh-eaters.

And only the elders may practice bone magic. I resist the urge to squeeze my shoulders because I've forged the highest elder's seal. Since my father has dealt with Elder Kanat in the past, it was familiar.

Pressing my determined lips together, I weave the truth into my response with an edge to my voice as I lie through my teeth, "Yes, I traveled all day to answer Elder Kanat's summons. I'm certain he wishes to finish his cases and join the festivities."

Tonight is the Feast of Flesh. I won't get another chance.

Mathyr's tears when I'd dragged my bleeding father back home still haunt me. I stiffen, remembering how I'd stabbed my scyan into the ethgharym, damned, crazed refters after one had sunk its teeth into Fathyr's shoulder. Sucking refter venom from his flesh was not on my to-do list two nights ago. Thanks to the mender, he will live, but menders are expensive.

I have no choice but to play the Bone Games.

As if testing me, the flesh-master's eyes drift across my young and unmarked flesh. I tense. An unclaimed and unescorted human girl is a high target at the Corpse King's nationwide masked ball, especially when he's invited all races to his Citadel of Bones.

He's desperate for a new bride. Tonight is the last opportunity for the King to appease the God of Death: Aryahn Kryach. Feathery ice crawls along my flesh. The last thing I must ever be is a Feyal-bride.

Behind me, an impatient Wisp-Shee hisses, baring her pointed teeth. She spreads her translucent wings to intimidate, but with gold-lined veins and edges decorated in gemstone flecks, she doesn't intimidate much. Instead, I smirk and hiss, wagging my mother's iron charm around my neck in a warning: iron is deadly to the Shee. She wrinkles her nose but steps back. Yes, I'm unescorted but never defenseless. I grin from the cold metal of my scyan kissing my inner thigh beneath my gown. After a lifetime of slaying refters, I'm prepared for any Shee or their Sythe cousins who may plunge their fangs or teeth into my blood. Or Shifters. Or Inker magic and Eylfe allure. This is foolhardy at best. Lethal at worst.

Turning to the flesh-master, grateful for the stench of human flesh on his breath from a recent feeding, I tighten my muscles. Many humans will meet their future claimers who will mark them at the Bite Offering tonight.

If I don't succeed at the Bone Games, my bride status is a guarantee. Ganyx' snake-like tongue has promised ten times the winnings at the Bone Games. I must win or our family's farms, our home will be forfeit, and I'll be married off to a Cock-Cross Ithydeir.

Relieved when the flesh-master juts the summons into my hands and jerks on a rope to open the gates, I beat a hasty retreat inside. The cavern ceiling welcomes me into its shadow. I suck a brazen breath, gazing at the hundreds who await passage to the Citadel of Bones. On the Feast of Flesh, the royals welcome human citizens inside the collective five mountains: Nathyan Ghyeal: the White Ladies with the formidable Citadel deep beneath their center. The Underworld. Most humans have escorts.

Utter darkness, save for the flickering firelight of torches on the far sides of the train platform, embraces me. The God of Death's shade power eclipses this Underworld, his spirit hunting for maidyans.

At the base of my spine, my Nether-mark chafes. I clamp my fingers into my gown, resisting the urge to scratch the ghost brand, which has haunted my back since I was discovered on the border of the Void: the cursed spirit realm. The endless boundary between all countries and the god Isles.

The line moves. Bone trains transport hundreds of citizens to the Citadel. I will be next. A Feyal-Ithydeir or informal Ith, as we humans dub them, eyes me from the side, perusing my flesh. I refuse to meet his gaze which would welcome his interest. If any Ith taste my blood, they would not appreciate the flavor. Thanks to my Nether mark, I'm certain I would taste like a refter. Nothing but black mania, doom, wrath, and death... even if I shine on the outside.

Thankfully, human flesh is prized, cherished in Talahn-Feylan. Unless it's a powerful elder, the Ith do not concern me.

"Isla!" a familiar voice shrieks my name, and I spin, almost bumping noses with Franzyna. Garbed in an emerald, glittery gown hugging her slender figure and complimenting her auburn hair, Franzyna embraces me. Her warm, ruby lips settling on my cheek prompt a rush of blood to my pale cheeks.

"Slantya, Franzy," I informally greet my friend who didn't need to forge her invitation to reach the head of the line.

"I didn't know if you were going to make it. Isla, are you sure about—"

I kiss her, claiming Franzy's lips and the familiar taste of cinnamon and sugar from her father's vessel-imported sweets. She sighs into my mouth, welcoming my kiss. As a trader's daughter, Franzy has spent much of her youth with me while our parents haggled over prices. Last year, we snuck into the Feast of Flesh and drank a whole bottle of Sythe wine in one night. We woke naked and tangled in each other's arms the next morning. Ever since, we've danced around our mutual attraction.

"I'm doing this, Franzy. But you shouldn't come," I whisper, squeezing her hand. "Go enjoy the festival."

"Not a chance. I'd never let you go alone. You look lovely," she changes the subject, admiring me, clasping my hands. "Are you wearing your mother's wedding gown?" Her warm, amber eyes survey the pix-spun lace along the off-the-shoulder sleeves at my elbows and the translucent gown embroidered with pearls and feathers.

I touch my waist where the gown's snugger thanks to my more generous curves. And my love of honey shortbread. "Mathyr let me wear it tonight," I boast and fold my hand into Franzy's. "It's so low-cut, it's almost obscene!" Which may come in handy at the Bone Games.

Franzy giggles. "I love it. You will taunt the Ith lords with your ample bosom all Cock-Cross girls dream of having."

"Yes, and my bountiful thighs." I roll my eyes but stroke Franzy's tawny gold arm. "I look like an angyl goddess, don't I?"

"Isla!" she squeals, quick to shush me. It's blasphemy to speak of the ancient angyls. Her words lower to a seductive murmur to tickle the hairs on the back of my neck and rouse my Nether-mark's heat when she leans in to add, "It brings out the hellfire in your hair."

Since the day we met, Franzy has claimed the sunset red streaks in my pearlescent hair are Void-born. And I must have inherited the silver from the angyls of Eyleanan. After all, Mathyr and Fathyr named me after the gods' celestial Isle realms…after they found me curled in their garden with corpus roses growing all around me and refter bites sprinkled across my flesh. The bites healed…but not the Nether-mark.

"You're the one who plays with fire, Franzy," I taunt her, reminding her of the time she nearly incinerated my kitchen.

Franzy scrunches her nose, bristling. "One time, Isla." Suffice to say, I'll do all the cooking when we're married.

As we approach the platform to await the next bone cargo train, I coil my arm around my friend's and assure her, "After the Bone Games, I promise we will amorously dance the night away. As long as we don't catch the eye of the Corpse King." I stick out my tongue.

Franzy clutches the back of my neck, whispering the eerie nursery rhyme of our childhood.

"Corpse King, Corpse King, he's coming for his bride
Corpse King, Corpse King, all you virgin nighyans hide
He'll steal your bones to make his brew
And your heart will taste so sweet in his stew
Corpse King, Corpse King, to him we give him laud
Corpse King, Corpse King, he who quells the gods
He'll carry you off to his cold and lonely bed
He'll eat your soul until you're all but dead!"

"Yes, unless I'm the Mallyach-Ender!" I dare to whisper.

Franzy covers my mouth with her hands, spinning her head, eyes wide and frightened as a creature caught in a hunter's gaze. As if waiting for the gods to annihilate me for breathing the possibility of a curse-ender!

Fire and ice from my Nether-mark cloy my spine. A heavy pang in my chest at the thought of all the King's dead brides. How he bears the gods' Curse...

I'll be damned if Franzy and I ever become a bride. She is an obvious choice: full of youthful innocence, of passion with her near-gold eyes and vivacious curls. I would be a scarred consolation prize with my calloused farm hands and firm, muscled limbs and too-plump thighs. And the Nether-mark. I shiver. If an elder discovers the sacrilegious brand, it will guarantee a death sentence by burning.

But as long as it doesn't betray me tonight, the mark will help me win the Bone Games and save my family.

On the train, Franzy fidgets, staring at a famed locale: the tombs of our former kings and queens. Elevated to a lofty status due to the God of Death's Curse, their tombs are architectural feats encased and guarded by fallen dragyn rib cages. Ripples of awe overwhelm the slowing train. All fawn over the City of Tombs.

The train descends, stopping at different points along the route to the Citadel. Franzy marvels at the shrine of the gods where elders perform bone rituals. I wrinkle my nose. Yes, I'm grateful for the King who carries the Curse. Otherwise, the gods would play with the races and vomit hundreds of refters from the Void onto our lands as they did in ancient times. But I don't care for the elders who trade their magic to needy humans...like my family.

Once the herald announces the Hall of Heroes, Franzy and I make our way off the train.

"This is exciting!" she squeals, gesturing to the catacombs housing the greatest Ith warriors who felled the refter outbreaks in past wars. Or defended Talahn-Feyal against the Sythe, shifters, and Shee. Impressed, I grin but glimpse at the crude map sketch on the blackwood bark from Ganyx detailing the Hollows—old ruins from an ancient city where the Bone Games are held.

"Later, we'll visit Queen Scathyk's tomb," promises Franzy, hinting at my favorite famed warrioress: the Scarlet Scathyk who trained all her warriors in the art of battle. And sexual pleasure.

I sigh. "What I wouldn't give to be a born-Ith. I'd steal one of her bones, grind it, and ingest it and have as much power as her."

"Oh, you already have a warrior spirit, Isla," Franzy denies.

"Maybe if I was an Ith," I point out. Despite how the Ith turn humans over time thanks to their venom, transformed humans don't gain the same strength or power as the born Ithydeir race.

Franzy clings to my arm as we proceed through convoluted halls and passages. We arrive at the great arch marking the end of the Hall of Heroes. Restricted territory. From the twinkling light of the scintillating stalactites far above our heads, I squint and survey a steep staircase descending to a bridge leading to the Hollows. First, I retrieve my scyan, persuade Franzy, "Last chance to go back."

She shakes her head, though fear creases the skin around her eyes. Better not to argue, I heave a sigh and hope this sketch is accurate. The last thing we want is to find ourselves lost underneath the mountains. Slow and quiet, we descend. The lower we go, the more smoke drifts from torches beyond the bridge, indicating we are going in the correct direction.

At the staircase base, I freeze in my tracks while Franzy shrieks and buries her head in my shoulder.

"It's all right..." I soothe her and myself in a way.

Chills like winter tears travel my flesh at the sight of the ruined corpses dangling from bone trees—an ominous warning as to what happens to humans who consume spirit-matter, who practice bone magic.

My Nether-mark lashes heat at my spine: a reminder of why I could suck the refter venom from Fathyr's flesh. I am immune.

I have to credit the Bone Games masters on their ironic yet cunning location marked by the damned dead.

"Come on," I assure her, tugging her toward the bridge.

"Isla..." Franzy whispers, leaning closer, gripping my arm. "The flowers are following you again."

What? "Ugh," I groan, tipping my head because it's the last thing I need. The corpus roses, aptly named from their inner petals forming the image of a skull, shoot through the bridge cracks. Their crimson blooms are drawn to my Nether-mark. I should have prepared for this with the essence of Aryahn Kryach wafting all over the catacombs.

"Away with you, my adorable beasts," I order, waving to the flowers who lower their heads, pouting. I smirk.

As a child whenever the Nether-mark would call me, tempting me to enter the dark death valley of the Void. Bound to my emotions, the roses would grow, offer me hope, an anchor.

Distracted by the blossoms, I don't register the danger until my Nether-mark pierces my spine with an icy needle-like burst. I recognize the warning, grip my scyan. The familiar white shape staggers out of the darkness, growling—crazed and animalistic. It thrashes its withered head, sharpened teeth snapping to bite Franzy. She screams.

My muscles quiver. I raise my lethal blade and hurl it at the refter's heart. The creature freezes, its teeth an inch from Franzy's throat. With a screech, it drops, skull fracturing before a sprig of corpus roses grows through its eyes, its black blood drowning rose thorns. I sigh in relief.

Franzy rushes to me and crashes against my body, burying her face in my shoulder. "Warrior's spirit." She sniffs and peers at me, tears glistening in her eyes. "Remember when we were nine and the refters came while we played near your mother's garden?" I smile at the memory, shake my head. "You grabbed your father's pitchfork. You didn't care how much blood you got on your skirts. I thought you were ready to step into the Nether-Void itself and invade the realm of the gods!"

I roll my eyes with a breathy laugh. "Yes. I'll come with fire and blood and a host of flowers to intimidate them." I gesture to the roses, narrowing my eyes, curious. Never have so many grown, save for the time I ended up in my given-parents' garden.

Franzy leans over, plucks a few blooms around the fallen refter, and embeds them in my hair, fixing them to the combs holding my silver strands. "There, you'll win the Bone Games with your beauty alone. You're practically glowing."

I beam at her, wishing we had more time, but I remember my purpose in descending into the Underworld and grasp Franzy's hand so we may embark along the arched passageway to the old, ruined manor in the Hollows—a perfect location.

Once we push the heavy blackwood door with its spectral-like glow to come face to face with two overseers pinning a middle-aged man to the ground while another carves his hand bones from his flesh, I have no doubt neither my beauty nor my roses will help me.

Only my Nether-mark.

Whimpering, Franzy hides behind my body, avoiding the violence. I swallow a knot in my throat and drag her away from the screaming man.

Stacked in a great circle are several tables with the champion's in the center. Countless players stoop their heads low over the boards. The outer tables hold the meagerest of winnings—ones no better than the cock bones swarming the fields of my home. A thousand would never pay off our debt.

"This is no place for little unmarked girls," barks an overseer lingering near an outer table, words hurling at us.

Ignoring the intimidating sparrow skull necklace dangling around the overseer's bulky throat, I forsake Franzy and march to him to proclaim,

"Ganyx sent me. I'm here to enter."

"Coin or bone," he demands the entry payment with a sneer.

The fee is a fraction of our debt and the reason I allowed Franzy to come: her coin. I slam the fee into his open palm, steel my spine, and narrow my determined eyes. All I need is to get to the champion's table, to best the victor, and claim the rarest bones pillaged from a warrior or monarch. I don't care as long as they prevent me from becoming a Feyal-bride.

However, the elites love to cheat. *Try and cheat my Nether-mark, you bone-spiked bastards!*

After the overseer accepts my payment and snorts, he juts a thick finger to the first table with mere chicken bones as the prize. Once I reach the center, I will achieve human bones.

Hoping the roses don't rear their corpus heads, I slide into the seat across a wizened old man, bordering on emaciated. With his rotted teeth and sunken-in cheeks, he reminds me of a refter. Broken knuckles and stumps for fingers. A bone powder addict.

Remorse twinges inside me as I move my first piece on the board because once I win, the overseers will beat him. It takes all of a few moves, and the man licks his withered lips, swallowing tight, eyes watering.

When the overseer yanks him by his gnarled hair, I proclaim, "Stop!" Before either may protest, I sigh, remove a comb from my hair, and thrust it toward the overseer. "The payment is small. This should suffice."

The old man whimpers. The overseer pauses and inserts my heirloom comb laden with dragon-scale gems in his mouth to bite and determine its authenticity. He grunts acceptance. Deeper remorse engulfs my chest because I've granted the addict at least ten more games, feeding his gambling. But I couldn't be responsible for his beating.

Franzy's eyes are glassy as she gazes at me, her smile faint. It was her comb. Thankfully she offers a feeble nod. I move to the next table.

It's going to be a long night.

TWO
I SWEAR I WILL NEVER TAKE ANOTHER BRIDE

ALLYSTEIR

I open Finleigh's supple mouth beneath my ruined one and pray to the gods.

Let it be her, please...

Her fingers struggle with my robes, desiring more, but I clasp her wrists and nudge them to each side to love her slow. No one has ever beheld my entire body, but Finleigh alone has viewed my true face.

Hope tortures me as my hunger deepens: an inferno smoldering to the region of my body which never decays thanks to Aryahn Kryach's cruel fuckery. A malevolent twist. For centuries, the gods' sick tricks and disturbed machinations have plagued the races of Talahn-Feyhran. I've simply chosen to accept their Curse so my people do not as all kings before me.

Finleigh. My fair-haired hero. It has to be a sign. Her eyes treasure my true face beyond my rotted corpse. After she's received my cadaverous hands cherishing her body until my member throbs with need and she weeps from pleasure, I pause from her sweet mouth to stare at her, to capture this memory: the honey gold of her hair like the angyls to mirror her skin, the deep midwinter blue of her eyes which enraptured mine from the beginning, her mouth swollen from my deformed half, her cheeks flushed with lust, her perfect small breasts with rouged buds—ripe and puckered—the soft panes of her flattened stomach leading to narrow but round hips, her lithe thighs spreading to welcome me. All her flushed bride heat yearning to receive me.

Her generous warmth nourishes my heart, engulfs me. I don't deserve her.

She whispers my name like a prayer, closes her eyes, and urges me in a promise, in a vow.

Despite how many times I've dissuaded her, resisted her, battled her, damn-near chased her away, Finleigh has accepted the risk. And once a bride accepts, nothing can be done. Kryach will have his fun. While I hover above my wife, his spirit lingers in my veins, in my blood, his essence hovering in my mind—invisible eyes observing, burning into my back. Ever he haunts these moments: the specter God of Death. My spine bristles with the knowledge, but I banish the thought of him and focus on my bride.

Kissing Finleigh again, tasting her sweet succulence, I ease inside her slower than an isle of ice. She stiffens, unleashing a whimper. Halfway in, I pause, careful and cautious.

I cup her forehead with my cadaverous hand. "Do you want me to stop, Finny?" I murmur her nickname, tender, granting her ample time to change her mind.

She shakes her head, dips her hand into my robe, and cups my skeletal hip, urging. "Please, Allysteir," she begs.

My member pulses, pained, prepared to abandon control. Determined to move slow, I thrust deeper into her heat and trail my ravaged lips along her cheek, her jaw, her throat, her collarbone, lower. Her moan undoes me, triggering my swifter thrust. She closes her eyes, throws her head back, and clenches her sex around me.

Our eyes lock. Hers have turned to midnight blue storms, deep and pleading for more.

At last, I sink as deep into her as possible. Eyes never fleeing, I whisper her name in a petition as our pleasures unite, as she grips my hip and screams to the Isles, then falls against our bed.

Before her eyes turn to mine, void of anything but a swirling, gray, dark as smoke and shadows, I know.

Gritting my teeth, breaking one, I punch my fist to the bedpost, careless of how the phalanges fracture and tumble to the floor. Kryach's laugh echoes in my mind but can't snuff Finleigh's animalistic growls or her teeth snapping as she thrashes. Her soul, her spirit hovers in the air—only visible to me and Kryach. I capture the memory, but he confiscates her spirit, reaps it, and leaves me alone with her scent—the aftermath of her flesh, the memory of her fingertips cradling my face.

After ordering a steward to remove my former bride, whom I will deal with later, I tear my robe and snarl at my reflection in the mirror, my renewed flesh. Finleigh has paid with her soul to buy me another cursed year of restoration...before I waste away. The cycle has renewed. For we are all god-pawns in their twisted games.

Guilt-ridden, I ball my restored hand into a fist and punch the mirror until it shatters and my knuckles bleed.

No, I refuse to be a pawn. Nor subject another woman to this hell. Even if it damns us all.

"Kryach!" I snarl at my reflection, at the shadowy sneer greeting me, "I swear I will never take another bride!"

Picking up the open-skull goblet, I rub my thumb along one of its star-gems, eye my gruesome reflection in the stone, and tip it without another thought. I inhale, savoring the Sythe blood burning my throat cavity on its way, droplets spilling from my flesh gaps and onto my nether-spider-silk robes. The same robes Aydon will don in my stead tonight along with the refter-tooth crown and nether-bone mask. Even if it's been in my family for generations, I loathe the crown: a mockery of all past royal brides.

Wincing, I banish memories of Finleigh, of all my brides' names, and turn to the mirror. Despite the ivory frame and its glassy wholeness, my reflection is broken. Tonight marks one year without a bride. And five hundred years of this Curse. Five hundred years of breaking my oath.

I open my robe to my chest, to the ribcage protruding from the flesh.

"Torturing yourself again, eh brother?" Aydon mocks, striding toward me.

I sneer at his reflection, at his brow lifting before shifting my robes over my corpse. "By all means, make yourself at home, Aydon. And your jokes still aren't funny," I remind him and make my way to the table, bones rattling as I grip the Sythe-blood decanter and slug its contents.

"Oh, that hurts, Ally. Seriously, you wound me," he ridicules, digging the blade in while following me to our family portrait tapestry positioned above my bed: an intricate labyrinth of painted bones and teeth.

"You're just sore because I did what you didn't have the balls to," I scoff and curl half my upper lip back since two can play at that game. As usual, Aydon remains stoic, ever the political master even with his own brother, but his jaw hardens and his arms tighten from the reference of his sterility. Another curse of Kryach's. I am the true King. The line must continue through me, through my future bride. If she exists.

"At least I can fuck a woman more than once," he boasts as if he's checkmated me with all his philandering of humans and Ithydeir alike.

If Mathyr heard us, she'd smack the backs of our heads for our brotherly battle. No, only Aydon, considering she would likely sever my skull from its bone stem. And however it won't kill me, it is a headache to reposition. I smirk from my warped humor.

"What do you want, Aydon?" I demand and stray past him to rifle through my wardrobe for a fresh set of leather gloves. Tonight, I discard the ones spiked with bone armor. No need to draw attention to myself. I choose simple black ones.

"I came for a fresh robe."

I snort at the obvious lie. Aydon is far too careful with our spider-silk robes. My prim and proper half-brother born with a silver-bone spoon in his mouth unlike me: the younger bastard-born Queen's son—a result of her affair with our father's cousin. After Fathyr learned of the affair, he threw his cousin into the Nether Void. The end of it until eight months later when I showed up. Not like he could execute her as she was the one bride in a century who'd survived the curse. Everything changed when the Corpse King died.

"Mathyr sent you, didn't she?" I mutter and dig through my wardrobe, cursing when I hit my elbow against the door, dislocating my arm. I blow wind through my nostrils. More irritating compared to my decaying self—apart from my fucking cock, of course. Kryach's damned morbid humor.

"Seriously, Ally." Aydon shoves his way into the wardrobe and tugs on my arm, setting it in place. A too common occurrence. "If you didn't spend all your time on your little projects or let a servant clean this room, you wouldn't have trouble locating a simple mask." He fetches the bone hunter mask from a back ledge and hands it to me.

"You didn't come here to criticize my lack of organizational skills or my desire for privacy. Tell me Mathyr's message."

Heaving a sigh and leaning against the wardrobe, Aydon waves a hand to me. "It's the Feast of Flesh tonight."

Yes, the masked ball is Aydon's little joke, one he believed I'd appreciate. But it's the first time he's opened the Feast to all the nations across Talahn-Feyhran. Such pageantry I will never condone when our race is the most openly mocked. And ironically, the most feared. But Aydon always hopes to curry favor with the other royals. In the past, I've played along with his desire for spectacle, to display me before the privileged classes as a reminder of the burden the royals have carried for them—a reminder of what will happen if the gods are not satisfied.

And one High God who always haunts me.

After positioning the mask over my face, I grunt and wander to the bed to retrieve the ascot draped over its edge. "What of it?"

"I've agreed to your incognito desires tonight, Ally. But you will be present for the Offering later. And the supper following. The royal representatives will remain with us for a month, and I intend to make the most of their presence. We're all in this together."

Snorting again, I lift the edge of the mask up to bare the worst side of my face in a not-so-subtle "fuck off".

A heavy sigh escapes my brother's mouth, and he drags a hand through his polished, black curls: a contrast to my hair bound low past my neck, grayer than dead flowers. Hmm, I'll have to remember dead flowers for my next little *pursuit* as my brother dubs them. After looping the ascot around my blotted throat, I down the remaining blood wine and sigh to the numbness rippling through my walking cadaver.

"By the gods, Ally, you can't keep going on like this!" Aydon throws his hands in the air and marches to me. "You're half a bag of bones already. Mathyr is worried for you. And me."

"We both know you don't give a damn about me, brother. As long as I come to your political parties, show off my pretty skull, and play nice with the other monarchs who smile at our faces but curse us behind our backs. What was it the Blood Queen called us in her last Marking Ceremony? Oh, right...refter-fleshies." I sneer at the derogatory term for the Feyal-Ithydeir—the likening of our clans to the cannibalistic refters who originated from the Nether-Void and plague our lands.

"Oh, like you buying her peoples' blood on the Nether market?" he thwarts with a redundant argument.

I snarl through the mask and swallow hard, refraining from cracking my knuckles or grinding my teeth. A prisoner walking on eggshells in the cage of my own wrecked body, I must take the utmost precautions or I'll lose a tooth...or a phalange.

"You know why they're here." Aydon drops his hands to his sides, a heavy sigh loosening from his mouth. "The Nether-Void grows closer to all our kingdoms. Other territories are suffering the repercussions. It's time for you to take a new bride."

I flare my nostrils and hiss in rebellion. My brother knows I've vowed to never take a new bride, but he's right. Aydon's always right. It's why he makes a good stand-in king behind my mask. While I bear the God of Death's Curse and his games—the true crown—Aydon bears the politics I despise.

"Unless you'd prefer to doom our race, of course," he adds his wry humor and cups my shoulder, light through my robe. His deep-set eyes crease, his flawless cobalt irises brewing with dark shadows as he lowers his voice, "I can't change the past, Ally. But do not damn our land due to your torment. Take a bride tonight. Bite her at the Offering. And bring her to the supper so the royals can be at ease. It's the right decision, and we both know it."

He squeezes my shoulder and departs. I gaze at my mask in the mirror off to my right. Once I'm alone, the deathly specter flees the cavities of my being to appear in the reflection to taunt me. A raw ache, the bitter pain of my past pierces my heart as Kryach's spirit whispers to me, curses me for waiting this long. Hungry, he gnashes his teeth, launching black arrowed shadows to lash my chest which nearly rocks me to my knees.

My shoulders sink. Tonight, I must give him the blood of my new bride or all of Talahn-Feyal will pay the price. How many times since Finleigh have I vowed never to take one? Too many to count, but their names never leave me.

I breathe a deep sigh. No, my land does not deserve to be damned.

But I do.

THREE

THE ELDER'S PRICE

ISLA

The gold-lacquered jawbone forms a crude necklace around the fydthell champion's neck as he moves his pieces. I avoid the sight and pay attention to the game. No, my Nether-mark. Fire clawing at my spine is my warning: a sign of an impending attack. Ice alerts me it's safe to move my pieces. The mark has brought me this far.

After hours of playing, my lids are heavy, and my rump aches. By now, the festival has commenced, and I promised to drink wine and dance with Franzy.

My fingers tremble as I prepare to move my king through the clear path. Around me, the heavy breaths of the failed players warm the air along with the meager candlelight in the underground chamber. One figure tarries in the far back. My spine prickles at the dark cowl obscuring his face. Motionless as a statue, he observes the champion's table. Out of the corner of my eye, Franzy gazes at me, knotting her fingers, hopeful. No fire sparks my skin. The champion, with bone hoops piercing the nipples of his barren chest and navel, grins at me, a twisted, daring leer.

A soft snowfall lingers on my spine, no inferno. Oh, he's bluffing, but I mask my grin behind faux fear of trembling lips.

I don't hesitate. Confident, I slide my king forward.

The champion's eyes widen the moment my king arrives at the other end of the board, and our audience cheers, deafening. Disbelief clouds his face. Relief sinks my shoulders. He will honor the games because it is the Talahn-Feyal way. Even in illegal sport, we honor ancestral bones. He reluctantly surrenders the prize: a velvet satchel bearing the victor bones. Franzy's black market trader friend will know what to do.

"Care for another game, little Cock-Cross girl?" the champion tempts me, brows bobbing.

I smirk to one side and shake my head, taking Franzy's hands. "As *cocksure* of myself as I am, I have a festival to get to."

No sooner do I speak the words than the blackwood door crashes to the ground. Chaos erupts from the elder guild soldiers mobbing the chamber with skull insignias etched onto their armor. Panic spears my spine. Countless players knock over tables, scattering lamps to the floor, and scramble for the passage exits leading to deeper avenues of the mountains. Fire catches onto the blackwood. It flares to provide a flaming net barrier. Adrenaline courses into my blood, thrashing pain in my chest.

Grabbing Franzy's wrist, I gather my gown ends, leap over a fallen table, and haul her toward the far-left passage. Soldiers pursue us as we weave around the Hollows old manor. We won't get far…at least not without a diversion. Dizzy with the realization, I thrust the bone pouch into Franzy's hands before she can protest, grip her cheek, and command in a low whisper, "Run. Hide the bones. I'll meet you in the dance hall."

"But—"

I kiss her, then shove her down the dark alley to the bridge leading back to the Hall of Heroes. "I promised you I'd dance the night away with you. I'm counting on you, Franzy. My family needs those bones. Go! I'll be fine." And I will. With no bones in my possession, the most I should get is a sharp reprimand, a warning. Perhaps a small fine. But Franzy is underage. She can't be here.

I turn and flee, moving as fast as my legs can carry me...back to the manor entrance while Franzy dashes to the bridge. Heat from my Nethermark rears, pulses along my spine. Closer to the soldiers who surround me, but all I care about are the gaps between them, gaps betraying Franzy who scurries across the bridge and ascends the staircase.

Relieved, I shift my eyes upward in a silent prayer of thanks. Meanwhile, the soldiers force me to my knees before the kindled inferno of the Hollows manor. Smoke blows around me. Strands of silver hair eclipse my eyes, breaking my vision into pieces, but I recognize the cowled figure moving through the smoke toward me— the one studying me earlier.

"Lift her," he directs the soldiers in a low voice.

Where are all the other players? Am I the only one caught? Something tightens behind my ribcage. Swallowing the dry lump in my throat when the soldiers haul me to my feet, I take a deep breath while my beastly mark scalds my flesh as if sensing a powerful presence.

Too much power for the transgression of an underground fydthell game.

The figure creeps his fingers, laden with bone rings, to his cowl. Cold sweat coats my hands and the back of my neck. The rich scent of incense and lantern oil cloys the air from his robes.

As soon as he removes the cowl, my heart plunges into my stomach.

Tremors assail my body, my breath rasps, and I squeeze my eyes shut, wishing I could deny whom I've seen. The Ith man casts the outer robe aside to reveal his inner ones as red as pomegranate seeds. A status symbol of the highest Feyal-Ithydeir elder: Elder Kanat.

I lower my head in a respectful albeit feeble bow.

He is younger than expected, but I'd wager no less than ten years my senior. Woven into his long, dark braid are colorfully-painted wishbones. The most powerful elder. Will he detect my Void scar and call for my public burning or throw me to the Void, to the eth-gharym? I wince at my earliest childhood memories, of refters who'd sunk their teeth into my flesh. I'd survived them, run from them, and plunged into my Fathyr and Mathyr's garden, growing corpus roses to lap the blood streaming down my skin.

I will not survive Elder Kanat.

Upon his approach, I dip my head, grateful for my silver-white hair shrouding my face. My lips tremble when Elder Kanat's fingers settle beneath my chin. The Nether-mark responds with a surge of frost to nullify the flames while the Elder's fingers heat my skin.

"Isla Adayra," Elder Kanat greets me while raising my chin to his eyes. The flames from the burning Hollows catch the irises: they are deep and verdant green, contrasting the Underworld's decay. The black veins in his fair skin remind me of spider silk strands—a sign of the bone magic coursing through him.

"H-how do you know my name?" I force the dry words in a croak.

He grins and thumbs my chin, revealing, "A bone-ritual. A mere test if someone forges my summons."

My knees weaken. *A fool, Isla! A desperate fool.* I gasp for air while vines and leaves tickle my naked legs beneath my gown. *Not now!* I strive to quell the corpus roses growing through the stony ground.

"Your father, Iayn, speaks highly of his accepted daughter," continues Elder Kanat, pacing before me, his boots trampling unaware upon the rosebuds. Yes...Fathyr and Mathyr accepted me into their family, and this is how I repay them.

"Please, Elder Kanat, I can explain—" I pronounce, lifting my neck where his eyes linger upon my arched throat.

"Tsk, tsk, tsk, Isla," he clicks his teeth, inhales me through his long, curved nose, and sets his proud, thin jaw. His voice darkens in a chastisement, "This is a disappointment but one I may forgive, given your family's deep misfortune. Hard-working and valued citizens such as yours pay the price for the King's rebellious testing of the gods."

More roses grow, curling toward the limbs of the soldiers surrounding me. *No*...I close my eyes, wishing them away, but once I open them, more vines and thorns shoot through the cracks.

Elder Kanat taps my cheek, summoning me. His eyes narrow, more vulpine than I'd first registered, causing me to lean further away. His fingers traverse my cheek, but I ban the internal shiver from the intimate action. And how he's insulted the Corpse King...even if all of Talahn-Feyal know the Void encroaches closer, spitting out refters like the ones who attacked my father.

Elder Kanat tilts his head toward me, fingers descending to my chin. Whichever soldiers don't surround me tend to the Hollows fire which silhouettes the elder, making him more specter than Ith.

My breath hitches in my throat when he trails those fingers to my hair, lighting on my comb. "I am willing to grant your family leniency, Isla Adayra."

Relieved, I sigh until suspicion rouses gooseflesh as the feverish glint appears in Elder Kanat's eyes. They voyage across the bare flesh of my upper chest and shoulders thanks to my angyl-feathered gown. *Oh, no... he can't mean!*

"You will present yourself to me at the Bite Offering tonight," Elder Kanat defines.

The Nether-mark chafes my back again. *No!* I've worked hard to stay under the radar, beyond any Feyal-Ithydeir's eyes. Keeping to my family's farm and our animals and flowers. Franzy and I have spent years planning...tonight was my one transgression, my desperate blunder.

By whatever power I cannot fathom, more corpus roses rear their heads. Behind the soldiers, they've grown to half the length of the Ith warrior bodies.

"Please, Elder Kanat," I press, treading on dangerous ground. "I am not a consort. I would—"

"*Isla!*" Elder Kanat blows a huffed breath through his nose. I clamp my mouth shut, understanding the grievance I've committed. As the highest Elder, Kanat holds the King's favor and could order my execution for my protest. But he must already hold a number of flesh consorts. Why should he bother with a mere Cock-Cross orphan girl? And a recent felon!

Still, I am bold enough to meet the dark forest of his eyes when he informs me, "Your fathyr and I are good friends despite his lower station. Rest assured, I have had my eye on you for some time. Once I learned of your forging my seal, I came immediately. Rest assured, the promise of your flesh will not only cancel your family's debt but assure their comfort, given its...current state of honor," dictates Elder Kanat, knuckles brushing lower to my neckline.

I swallow a lump in my throat. Curse my *well-endowed* breasts.

"I am prepared to elevate my proposal." Elder Kanat's eyes burn against mine, and I bite a whimper and strengthen my quivering insides when he captures my palm and raises my body to stand, lifts my knuckles to his mouth. "I have never taken a Feyal-bride. You will be my first."

A Feyal-bride!

My gut clenches from the deep gravity of his proposal. He will welcome me into his court for my flesh servitude while offering me his home, his possessions, his vow, his...*bed*. An honor reserved for noble court humans. Humans never serve elders other than as flesh-consorts.

The nether-mark lashes the base of my spine in warning. Fear races through my body faster than a fueled flame. Elder Kanat is well known throughout the land for his favor with the gods and his worship of sacred tradition. If he'd merely offered a flesh-consort proposal, I could hide the shadow-scar. But the moment he takes me to his bed and discovers my Nether-mark, he will have me burned before the entire kingdom.

Or worse...cast me into the Void!

Hundreds of skull eyes from the inner rosebuds stare at me from beyond the soldiers and the elder oblivious to their presence. Each thorn is a deadly weapon the size of my hand. I hold my breath, praying no soldier turns. While I may not understand where this floral power comes from, this is my only chance.

Elder Kanat opens my hand and places...*oh, gods!*...a small chest vertebra bone in my palm. Symbolic of the strength of males and females standing together in companionship. I whimper. This is a deeper weight: I will be expected to bear his Ith children. "I look forward to biting you tonight, Isla Adayra."

The chest vertebra is heavier than a crypt. I freeze when Elder Kanat's mouth settles upon mine—hotter than a flaming altar, tongue probing

27

the seam of my lips. My limbs tingle. My chest tightens, heart faltering. Opening my mouth and tasting me deeper, Kanat tugs my flushed body to his. The Nether-mark scalds my back. I whimper into his mouth which only encourages him. Some deep part of me wants to surrender. As Franzy stated, I have a warrior's spirit. If anyone can wage this siege, it's me.

Beyond my family loyalty and the honor of the highest elder choosing me, a hunger stalks my blood, my heart. A fiery hunger I have suppressed for many years other than the few times I've shared with Franzy. But this can't be the fate the gods have transcribed for me. Unless my life has been a curse—a cruel, twisted joke of demons and angyls.

I am caught between a mountain and the hardest of places.

The Nether-mark sears my back as if pleading with me for self-preservation, for escape. Elder Kanat mistakes my moan for desire. His knuckles brush along my neckline, skimming the upper swell of my breasts as if testing my flesh for where he desires to bite me. I open my eyes, gazing beyond him and the soldiers to the skull roses which lunge—my floral warriors.

Once Elder Kanat angles his head to the side to deepen the kiss, and his hand winds around my waist, I break from his mouth, shove the chest vertebra into his hands, and gasp through parted, swollen lips, "No! I can't. I *won't!*"

Without another word, I nod my consent to the roses. They attack. Hundreds of thorns spear the soldiers, and they crash to their knees. Before the elder seizes me, I turn and flee faster than a blackwing flying from a nether-storm.

As I deviate through darker passages leading to deep avenues unknown, Elder Kanat roars behind me, "Bring her back!"

FOUR

THE DAMSEL IN DISTRESS

ALLYSTEIR

Underneath my robe, I conceal the skull parietal bone—a twin half to Aydon's—the sole indication of my identity. Other than everything beneath my robes, of course. Considering how many masked revelers have donned my appearance tonight, I don't stand out. Soon, my brother will arrive to sit on the throne, escorted by the elders and our most ruthless soldiers because Aydon will never spare finery.

At times, I wish a human would volunteer as Feyal-bride of the Corpse King and spare me the headache of choosing. It's only happened once and for good reason. Not that the kingdom knows the gritty details. Save for me and another.

One Ithydeir passes me, commending me on my costume, and peeling back his mask to exhibit his elaborate makeup. Once he's out of earshot, I snort. No amount of makeup could mimic the gruesomeness of my face, of the gods', of Kryach's curse.

"Would you care to dance, rygh airychdeil?" requests an auburn-haired girl in an emerald gown, lighting her hands on my glove.

By now, I've mastered the art of not recoiling despite the pain. At first, I consider stalking away and disappearing amidst all the masked imitations. This whole evening is a mockery of myself. If it were simply our Ithydeir race and prized humans, I could stomach it, but with the other races...

"I have a feeling this will be a night none will forget," she leans in and whispers her warm breath in my ear. I inhale her feminine scent: an alluring but common heather.

Dismissing her prior claim of "handsome king", I ease my gloved hand around her waist, draw the young lady close to my robed frame, and dip my head to study her eyes: a warm amber. Her boldness to approach a Feyal-Ithydeir and request a dance at the Feast of Flesh is commendable. There is strength in her eyes. In our past, only the strongest bride souls have withstood the curse of the gods...like my mother. Could this girl be the one?

As she squeezes my good hand and leans in, her ambrosia drifts across my face, and my disturbed member throbs. If the rest of my form wasn't decaying, it would be natural.

"Who will the Corpse King choose tonight, I wonder?" she hums as I coast her along the floor, careful to keep a wide berth between myself and others. Upon reaching middle age of my longer royal lifespan, I learned the art of balancing with weighted boots for my skeletal feet.

I contemplate Aydon's words. And the encroaching Void. If I don't take a bride soon, Kryach will send more refters to invade our lands. More blood will be shed. More human lives lost. While Aydon bears the political responsibility, of dispatching warriors to deal with such threats, the ultimate responsibility is mine...and my future bride's. We both pay a price unless...

"What is your name, fair maidyan?" I ask, evading a nearby Ithydeir and her unmarked human.

"Franzyna Mordhya." Her amber eyes catch the chandelier light above us to gleam like fire. "My father is a trader, and he named me after a small island in the realm of the shifters. I live up to its wild meaning every day," she expresses, tossing her flaming curls back. Yes, this girl's spirit may carry the power to thwart Kryach.

"And how old are you, Franzyna Mordhya?"

She parts her lips but pauses and licks them, hesitating. I've lived long enough to sniff out a lie, but she lowers her chin and purses her lips.

"Seventeen, my ithylaird," she confesses, addressing me in the formal term of the court, of all noble Ithydeir.

I stop in my tracks, raise her knuckles to my mouth concealed beneath the mask, offer her a peck, and turn, disappearing between a sea of citizens before she can balk. Yes, I am King. Such laws do not apply to myself, but I will not take an underage bride. Franzyna deserves to enjoy this night and the remaining year of her childhood without the weight of death upon her soul.

Slipping into a side hallway branching from the main court, I make my way through one of the narrower and darker passages leading away from the Citadel. When we were young, Aydon and I would explore the countless labyrinthine mountain passageways and use them to escape our lessons...before he got older and stuffier. Head too filled with politics and court proceedings and economic disparities of varying regions and gods if I know what else. Since I turned fifteen, I've spent most days hiding from court and keeping myself as pieced together as possible.

After wandering a few ascending passages, I round the corner and pause in my tracks, huffing at the sound of flapping wings behind me.

Without turning, I cross my arms over my chest and scoff, "Aryuhdair...I was wondering if you would swoop in for a visit tonight."

Other than his obvious presence, the low growl assures me he still hasn't earned his right to fly. Probably never will, considering the gods love any excuse to delegate tasks. The fallen angyl strides past me, brushing my body with a tattered, flightless wing. In the cavern's darkness, the gold chains binding his wrists gleam with celestial Isle-power.

"You're playing with fire, Allysteir," he warns, blowing smoke through his nostrils. The powerful talons on his feet echo off the walls.

I shrug. "Tried. Didn't stick. Apparently, my bones can't burn, but it took time for the skin to grow back." I recall the memory of my suicide attempt following the death of my twenty-seventh bride. By now, I've tried everything from leaping off the Raven Skull bluffs to drowning myself in the Bone Sea. Nothing works.

The gold tattoos beneath Aryuhdair's angelic flesh shift—a sign and seal of the gods' connection, of their messages transcribed into his body. "It's been a year. Kryach met with his fellow higher gods," he informs me as if I didn't already know. As if Kryach hasn't invaded my waking and sleeping thoughts, a relentless Death hound. "Provided you take a bride tonight and bite her, they will stem the tide of the Void from Talahn-Feyhran, the other territories. If not—"

"Now, don't *fly* off in a rage, Aryuhdair." I saunter forward, adjusting my robes, tightening my gloves, and ignoring the incensed plumage of smoke drifting around me. "It is the Feast of Flesh after all. A night where anything is possible!" I boast and adjust my mask. "Perhaps I need not choose a bride tonight. Perhaps...she will come to me."

"You have until dawn to bite a new bride," the angel dictates through gritted teeth, wincing from the raving celestial ink. "A year to consummate the marriage unless she chooses the risk sooner. Do not test the gods' generosity, Allysteir. You've been warned."

"You know how much I love to wing it, Aryuhdair." I lift my mask and wink. The fallen angyl winces, but I have no pity. Yes, the gods have damned us both, but I don't act like a morally superior messenger. Nor do I enjoy Kryach's spirit housed in my being, a parasite feeding on my soul. I chose this fate, not for rebellion's sake.

But Aryuhdair is right about one thing: I am testing the gods, Kryach. If I don't bite a human woman by dawn, one option is left: open war. My people left to the mercy of the Void and its army of waiting refters. It will spread to other regions which is the biggest reason all other royals are present...save for the bird and dragyn kingdoms, of course. And the northern and uncursed Blue-Skin fjord lands.

"Always a pleasure, Allysteir."

When I turn to make a last smart remark, the fallen angyl is gone. Dismissing the encounter, I press onward, forsaking the distant cheers as the minstrels make speeches, telling tales of our long and proud history to entertain the other monarchs. I don't have the stomach for it, not with the other royals. I'll return after the Feast commences...after Aydon arrives to take *my* throne.

For now, I make my way to the sub-passages between Guild levels. Few travel the Skull Ruins where urban legends abound regarding their history. Here, I may always find a few moments of peace and quiet.

The ruins remind me of catacombs, except no tombs shelter skeletons. Nothing but skulls forming a series of winding walls and pillars, statues, stairways, and floors. A mystery my ancestors never transcribed.

I crawl my gloved fingers across a nearby wall, stroking the remains, sensing the intricate energy of their powerhouse. Such essences remain undisturbed since only the most powerful of elders or royals may remove a skull from these walls: a rare occurrence.

Leaning against a nearby pillar, I close my eyes and touch my mask—a mimicry of my ruinous face. In these sacred moments, I'm tempting fate, angering Kryach because I left the presence of much flesh. His shadow feasts on my heart. I cringe as he stalks my mind with memories of my past brides of five hundred years. I roar inside our collective mental stream, wishing I could ban the devil and his arrogant taunts of how he's feasted on hundreds of my brides' blood and souls.

As he will again.

Perhaps I should consider Aydon's tactic: select the loudest and most abrasive bride, fuck her, and be done with it. Let the cycle renew. Why should I care when she will forget? In the moment I spill my seed into her, it won't matter. Kryach always wins.

Death laughs last.

Loud voices from the stairway to my right interrupt my musings. Should have known more tourists would flood these halls during the Feast of Flesh. *Damn Aydon and his flamboyance.*

When I prepare to escape the oncoming revelers and regain my solitude, a ripple of white feathers greets the corner of my eye. Turning, I appraise the growing lace and pearls, the translucent fabric revealing the shapely body of a young woman. A tad plumper than average, but I love a little extra flesh. The sight of her exposed neck, shoulders, chest, and arms are a feast for the eyes...and the upper slopes of her generous breasts. A wonder she can even run in such a gown.

Not that I take more than a glance of her frenzied state and the shadows of several men pursuing her. Since I linger behind the pillar, she doesn't notice me when she pauses to remove her lace shoes before tossing them down the opposite hallway. *Hmm...*I smirk.

Silent, I observe as she scurries away, corpus roses falling from her hair as it escapes her braids in a silver flurry—crackling flames woven into the flurry. The shoes were an apt ruse since the lead guard gestures most of his men in the opposite direction, spilling deeper into the ruins while he and two others follow the one where the girl fled.

It leads to a dead end.

FIVE
I VOLUNTEER TO BE BRIDE OF THE CORPSE KING!

ISLA

When my body slams into a wall of skulls, all my hopes of escape shatter. Cornered in this hollowed-out room, I spin to face Elder Kanat's sentries. Gasping and shaking, I close my eyes when the nether-mark chafes my flesh again. Foolish. He won't forgive this transgression. Any chance I had of helping my family is gone.

Damn those refters. Damn our debt. And damn Ganyx and his weasel-face and bird-beak nose and snake-like tongue! Damn that bad-to-the-bone elder most!

"Come with us now, little dove." Kanat's chief sentry approaches, flanked by two others. As he enters the hollow, he tenses, neck muscles bulging, straining the bone collar around his throat. It signifies his protector status—a personal warrior for the elders but with as much training as the King's soldiers. "No more chances to fly. Elder Kanat will not be kept waiting."

Yes, I'm certain he loves the idea of jumping *my* bones. Over my dead body.

Licking my lips, I press my back against the skulls until the bones bruise my flesh. No possible way around the sentries close to the exit.

Nearing me, the chief sentry raises his hands donned in bone-armor gloves with sharpened claws. My breath bursts as the mark wreaks havoc on my back, but gooseflesh prickles my naked arms as he advances, glove extending. I slam my eyes shut, panting.

"Shh...don't struggle. We don't want your sweet flesh spoiled for the Bite Offering."

I've soothed the frightened animals on our farm, pacified them with a tender caress and soft words before chopping off their heads to be used as meat. Now, I am one. The sentry's claws close around my arm. Elder Kanat will have me whipped before the Offering. Once he discovers my mark, he'll throw me into the Void and wash his hands of me. Or a public burning.

At the last second, I dig the nail into my coffin by reaching between my thighs for my scyan, my lethal blade. The Ith sentry opens his mouth and steps back, astonished. I narrow my eyes to deadly slits. Adrenaline sprints in my blood. The penalty for a human attacking an Ith is death. Nothing to lose, I'd sooner die at the hands of these soldiers than accept Elder Kanat's mark. Or invite his lascivious gaze upon my body on our wedding night. Nor will I allow him to punish my family with my execution. I close my eyes and suck in a deep breath, prepared to launch.

The sentry's claws retreat. When I open my eyes, I nearly scream. Instead, I bite my tongue, drawing blood. Skulls, dozens of ancient skulls, hover around the room—ripped from the walls. Stupefied, the sentries open their mouths, eyes fixed on the skulls dancing in the air.

"Come now, gentlemen," a rich baritone croons to the sentries.

"Whatever bone of contention this lovely, young nighyan may have with the Guild, surely it does not merit such unpleasantness."

Oh, I love his voice!

The chief sentry draws his sword and barks to the masked invader, "The girl owes a flesh debt to Elder Kanat."

"Hmm...yes, the elder is still no better than a dog with a bone."

Wide-eyed, dumbfounded, I gape at the masked man as he casually twirls the skulls following his deprecatory insult.

"Show your face!" demands the chief sentry, eyes wavering.

"I'd rather not," the man responds and flexes his gloves. The skulls waltz in the air, casting bone dust onto my skin. My lungs constrict from the air I'm holding. How does he wield such power?

"So be it!" The sentry charges.

The skulls attack.

I leap into the corner in the nick of time. Several skulls strike their target, driving the sentry to the ground. His head crashes against the wall—eyes rolling to their ceilings. Knocked unconscious. Frozen from fear or awe, I grate my nails into the skulls behind me as the other sentries run only for skulls to batter them. Most skulls shatter, but by the time the soldiers lay motionless on the ground, several still remain in the air. Their vacant, black-holed eyes face me. I blink, searching the darkness for an elder or potentially a bone seer, but no seer has been discovered in five centuries.

As my eyes center on the dark-robed, masked man lingering in the opening, the skulls fall, crashing to the ground. I flinch at the clatter of the bones and shrink when one rolls to tumble against my foot. Arms protecting my chest, I root my gaze on the figure, on the robes shifting to the side as he leans over. He collapses. Not wasting another moment,

I leap over the fallen chief sentry and cracked skulls and bone pieces, rushing to kneel before the figure.

I chew on my lower lip, debating, eyes flitting to the hall. "Just go, Isla," I urge myself in a desperate whisper because more soldiers could barge in at any moment.

But my gut clenches, my heart assaults the sheltering framework of my ribcage with need to learn my masked guardian's identity...for more reasons than one. Throughout my life, the Nether-mark has haunted my spine with its fire and ice...*until now*. Reaching behind me, I touch the puckered flesh, but it's subdued, peaceful, quiet. Never this quiet. Its shadow energy hums beneath my skin, but no pain engulfs my back.

Instead, deep shades abound, soothing my flesh.

Who is this man?

Lips parted, I gaze at my liberator and touch his chest. Garbed head to toe to mimic the Corpse King for this ceremonious night, the figure must be a seer. But my eyes lower to the significant bone dangling from a simple leather cord around his neck, and I cover my mouth to cage my gasp.

The parietal skull bone. The symbol of royalty. The Crown.

Fingers trembling, heart pounding in my ears, I slowly peel the mask to expose the face. I bite my tongue hard to cage the scream in my throat and taste blood.

It's the Corpse King. The King of the Underworld housing the God of Death himself...has saved me.

Fetching my gown ends, I scramble to the stairway, snatch my shoes,

and escape the Skull Ruins before other soldiers find me. Franzy's song echoes in my mind as I hurry to catch the Citadel train:
He'll carry you off to his cold and lonely bed
He'll eat your soul until you're all but dead...

The train doors open. I slip into a seat at the far end, scooting low when several Elder Guild soldiers embark onto the platform. I try to banish the memory of his face: a living refter as the legends describe. Half-refter. Rot had spared part of his face, unblemished. A beautiful half.

I knead my fingers into my head, cursing my curiosity, my longing, my...desire.

Nothing but the scent of decay follows him.

But he was nothing like the children's songs or legends. Yes, he wears the God of Death; the one who purges souls. Not to mention the Curse—how Kryach requires the blood and flesh and souls of virgin brides. But the Ith man in the ruins, the man who mocked an elder and defended me from the soldiers was nothing like the Corpse King stories of all Talahn-Feyhran history.

He is my enemy. The enemy of all virgin nighyans.

The soldiers are too late. The train departs, bound for the Citadel but takes the scenic route past the elder shrines. While passengers fixate on the spectacular Citadel with its ancient towers of fused obsidian and bones, the King's face haunts me. Flutters cluster in my stomach. A smirk tugs at my lips while my core heats from the memory of his sweet mockery of Elder Kanat, how he'd taunted the sentries.

Those lingering shades...

A burn tethers my cheeks, mimicking the growing flush of the Nethermark. As soon as I'd left his side, it flared to life. Perhaps too much death exists within the Corpse King, it nullifies my mark. All I know is

I did not fear him, nor his face. I didn't fly. Or fight.

What in hellfire am I thinking? I cover my flushed face with my hands, wishing I could deny this, but I can't. And what does it matter? Like I'd acknowledged, I have nothing to lose. Elder Kanat won't stop his pursuit. Only one being has authority over him.

The irony. Perhaps the safest place for me is with *death*.

In the center of the Great Hall is the Cryth River. The "Shivering" River, Cryth is the coldest river in all Talahn-Feyal. The Corpse King's River with its headwaters bordering the King's immense dais leading to his throne of bones—only accessible by boat. The same river which flows from the Citadel and to the Sea of Bones as all rivers underneath the White Ladies lead to the Sea. Somewhere within its vast expanse, the Cryth River bears a direct doorway to the Nether-Void.

All know to stay clear of Death's dark waters.

At the Great Hall entrance, I face the masses, throngs of merrymakers from every Talahn-Feyhran region. But despite numerous Corpse King imitations whirling past me, each race gathers in herds from predatory and elite Wisp-Shee—defined by their decorative and deadly razored wings fluttering among the dancers along with their close cousins: the Sythe. Tempting their circles are our Feyal-Ithydeir and their human claims. The Eylves remain closer to the dais, exhibiting their unparalleled beauty. Shifters huddle near the shadows while the blue-skins in their rolling-water chairs linger near the fountains. The inkers mingle.

From each side of the room, several Guild soldiers search the crowd. Of course, it didn't take long for Elder Kanat's orders to spread to the

Citadel. No doubt he's used bone magic to further the message. I can't imagine why the highest elder in the land desires me. Yes, my breasts are bounteous, but they're not worth this much trouble...are they?

I'm scrambling. Scatter-brained, I plunge into the mass hoard, aware of the danger...how any Shee or Sythe could sink their teeth into me. An Inker could inject their witch-light into my eyes to beguile me. A Shifter could carry me off.

When the music fades, all races in the hall freeze, the trumpet silencing chatter to announce the Corpse King's arrival. Everyone parts as is custom. A third of races on one side of the Cryth River, the rest on the other where I am.

All but the royals gathered at the long table of skulls erected upon the King's lower dais kneel before him...including me. I am only one row behind the river which serves as a shimmering aisle where the King's boat proceeds. I strain my neck over the wings of two Shee to glimpse the King's long fyhada with its impressive curves sailing the river on its way to berth at the dais—escorted by countless sentries and elders, including Elder Kanat whose smaller Elder craft follows the King's.

I squeeze my shoulders and avert my gaze, but it's too late. Curse my silver-flame hair. No more than a hundred feet away, Kanat's eyes lock onto mine. He simpers, his expression turning predatory. I swallow, and the Nether-mark injects its flames into my spine.

He won't do anything until the King takes the throne. As his vessel passes, I narrow my eyes toward the dais where the King wears his elaborate bone and refter-toothed crown and a bone-armor suit. Curious. He wasn't wearing them in the Skull Ruins.

The river procession concludes. Each vessel releases to a docking point beyond the Great Hall, not to interfere with the King's spectacle. Once he greets the other race monarchs, the Corpse King lowers himself onto the throne with the elders and his bone warriors flanking him.

All rise. The music resumes.

Soldiers advance toward me. But I ball my hands into fists, nails scraping my flesh. Because while the Corpse King has authority over Elder Kanat, this will be *my* ultimate power.

Only one girl has ever volunteered as a bride tribute. But if I'm going to go down, I'm going to do it in a blaze of glory!

More Guild soldiers close in, barely a few feet behind me.

Before the crowds fill the riversides, I collect my gown ends, run past bodies, and say a silent prayer, holding fast to the memory of the King in the Skull Ruins. The Nether-mark erupts fire and ice into my back, but I don't stop.

I plunge into the Cryth River.

Its icy arms stab into me, deep and swallowing. But I rise to the surface where crowds scream, gasp, voices shocked from the interruption to their festivities. Ignoring the onlookers, I haul my body through the cold water. My teeth chatter. The Shivering River's chilled fingers claw through my blood. No, they close around my ankles, my wrists, and my throat.

They drag me under.

Screams penetrate the watery veil from beyond the surface. Once I open my eyes, it's my turn to scream. Panic vaults pain in my chest. Too much air escapes my lungs in frantic bubbles. Dozens of incandescent eyes gleam all around me, shining like silver fire. Colder than winter bones, their ghostly forms surround me. I thrash my head, understanding the danger of the Cryth River, why it is this cold.

These are spirits. Lost souls lingering in the doorway to the Nether-

Void.

The fatal spirits pull me lower, deeper, into water as black as a closed coffin. Those silver flame eyes haunt me. Determined to make me one of them. *Hmm*...I consider how beautiful my body will appear once it surfaces. Lips blue as a plague. Hair of fire and ice. Skin of white roses. Perhaps, the spirits will take my clothes. Quite a scandal it would create! I giggle more bubbles.

Before my eyes may close, before I accept the bitter touch of Aryahn Kryach's shadows to hook my soul into the Nether-Void, a streak of blue shimmers past. All at once, the spirits thrust me *higher*. Mad, delirious, certain I must be hallucinating, I cough, swallowing water, but the spirits don't stop. They propel me through the dark river until the light of hundreds of chandeliers blurs through the water to assault my vision. My body charges into the air and collapses upon a hard surface. On my hands and knees, I peer through my soaked strands: the spirits have dropped me onto the lowest step of the dais.

The crowds' voices gasp, astonished while the monarchs flick their confounded gazes to the water-logged and wild human girl with water sluicing off her body and splattering the velvet as she boldly tears toward the throne. The King's warriors raise their bone-swords at the unlawful action and potential threat. I crash my knees to the dais before the throne. And lift my head to gaze at the Corpse mask concealing his face.

Incensed, Elder Kanat bares his teeth, but it's too late.

Heartbeat exploding and sending seismic waves into my body until all my limbs shudder, I grin, triumphant, and open my mouth to proclaim my dying anthem, "I volunteer to be Bride of the Corpse King!"

SIX

THE VIRGINITY TEST

ALLYSTEIR

"Where the damned devil is my mother-fucking brother?!" Aydon rants from the secondary hall, pacing such a rampage, he will wear a hole in the marble. He's removed my horn and tooth crown, his outer robes, and the corpse mask to the blackwood table in the center of the room.

Head pounding from my confrontation in the Skull Ruins, I snort and make my appearance from the back passage. "Blood and bones, Aydon! I assure you I've never fucked a mother in my life," I chide him as he marches toward me in a fury. "Unlike *your* anything-goes palette, it's one-night virgins for me."

Eyes aflame, veins twitching, Aydon demands, "Where have you been?"

Rolling my eyes, I stride past him, curling my lip at Elder Kanat lingering in the corner of the room and speaking in hushed tones to the lower elders. "Rescuing a little dove lost in the Skull Ruins." I wipe bone dust from my shroud, succeeding in my corpse hand shedding. Always making a mess as Aydon claims.

"And while *you* were bird-watching, I was experiencing history in the making," my brother says and follows me to the blackwood table before the lesser dais to fetch the flask of Shee wine. Not as spicy or effective as Sythe wine, but it will ease this ailing headache. At least my skull is intact thanks to my robes cushioning my fall.

"Oh, tell me, whatever could it be, Aydon?" I don't hide my sarcasm while removing the cork with my teeth and spitting it to the floor. Swallowing a long draught, I click my bony fingers along the table, appreciating their musical thuds. "The Shee and Sythe aligned to battle the shifters? Or did the Blue-Skin monarch welcome the Eylfe king's advances for the first time?"

Aydon hunches, pounds his fist on the table an inch from mine. I sneer, remembering our younger years when he'd purposefully knock into me. A game for his flouncy noble friends who'd predicted which bones would fall first to collect the winnings.

"For all we know, you could be fucking a mother by the next fortnight," Aydon says and rubs a hand down his face, straightening.

Our eyes drift to Elder Kanat who breaks from the others to approach us. "Your highness..." he bows, hand upon his breast—too exaggerative considering our *tumultuous* relationship.

"Good to see your hair grew back, Kanat," I leer, preening inside, remembering the last time I upset one of his rituals. Bringing an ancestral skeleton to dancing life before his altar was worth him dropping the candle and burning the shrine to the ground. A bonus along with scorching half his braid.

Ever stuffy and superior, Kanat maintains his stoicism and continues, "I strongly advise against this, Your Majesty."

I flick my eyes to Aydon for an explanation. All I want is to sink into the chair and drink this full flask, but I suspect it wouldn't last. Sitting and standing require nimble effort to preserve my form.

Aydon's eyes bore onto mine like icy barbs as he reveals, "For the first time in over five hundred years, a girl has volunteered for the bridal path."

"What?!"

"You've received a proposal, Allysteir," Aydon sighs and swears under his breath.

My bones rattle at the announcement which Elder Kanat confirms, voice strained, "Your Highness, we know nothing of—"

"Where is she?" I bark, scanning the bone warriors flanking the sides of the room and the elders mulling about like confused mice.

"In the Great Hall guarded by our soldiers," reveals Aydon. "Pretty, pale thing must be shaking in her slippers and undoubtedly regretting her impetuous and foolish decision."

Without another word, I move toward the heavy, velvet curtains shielding the secondary hall from the Great one. Aydon and Kanat follow close on my heels.

"I know a little of this girl and her background, Lord Allysteir," Kanat pursues me. "She is no bride, I assure you. Nothing but a Cock-Cross farm girl who smells of animals, manure, and refter blood. And one with recent transgressions of sacrilege. For all we know, her soul could be marred, and the eth-gharym could have claimed her. This girl could bring ruin to the crown, Your Majesty. And anger the gods!"

"Quite an impressive feat for a mere Cock-Cross farm girl," I retort and ease a hand to the velvet curtain, brushing it aside to afford me a glimpse of the Great Hall. "Bloody angyls and blessed demons!" I exclaim, breath heaving. If it isn't my damsel in distress, my little dove from the Skull Ruins.

"What?" Aydon approaches on my right to study the scene.

A deep chortle rolls from my throat as I declare, "Yes, I'm certain her slippers will fly right off at any moment on account of how much she's *shaking*, brother."

Kanat takes my left side, and we observe my little dove who, in spite of the guards providing a formidable net around her, swings her hips to the minstrels' mirthful music. If I could beam, I would. Her eyes catch the firelight as they had in the ruins, but they're no longer wide with the raging fear she showed as cornered prey. A warmth lurks to quell the chronic pain inside my miserable body when surveying her carefree gaiety, how she tempts the monarchs by twirling around the skull table reserved for Aydon's infernal supper meetings. Her damp pix-spun gown's sleeves have slipped lower from the curve of her shoulders to exhibit nearly half her opulent breasts.

Kryach's breath grows heavier in my mind. Not uncommon, but a deeper hunger persists, tugs at my being. I dismiss it since the Bite Offering will soon commence.

"Such a provocative, disgusting display." Kanat curls his lip back in revulsion, prompting my insides to further warm. "She bears the sign of hellfire in her hair."

Awed, I shake my head when my brazen girl blows the lustful Sythe Queen a kiss and resumes her twirling while sovereign, soldier, servant, and citizen's eyes stalk her. Aydon lowers the curtain and concentrates on the elder who rambles his religiosity.

"I guarantee you, Your Highnesses, this is no pure virgin nighyan. Kryach demands a *clean* soul," Kanat reminds me, voice bordering on a low threat. Damned if I don't yearn to burn every strand of his polished boned braid for him to weep over the loss. Probably host a funeral in its shorn honor.

"Please, Lord Allysteir," the Elder urges me, his verdant eyes bold enough to meet mine. "Give this stained one to me. She can be my consort, and I will purify her soul when I bite her at the Offering and cleanse her body when I take her flesh."

I swallow hard, repulsed. While this busty bride tribute shines with passion I haven't witnessed since Finleigh, who possessed a different sort, I've wedded enough brides to understand it has no bearing on their souls...or their blissful sex. The gods are nothing more than greedy monsters with voracious appetites for blood, beauty, and passion. And Kanat is no better.

Injecting the shadow essence of Aryahn Kryach into my vocal cords, I welcome the smoke hinting of blood fire curling from my mouth. However I loathe this display, it is necessary, and I love when the elder squirms to my decree, "She. Is. *Mine.*"

Kanat recoils, stepping back, avoiding my eyes which have turned black and hollow as the Void. Pain thunders through my body from Kryach's presence, but it can't compare to the torment in my heart because I am as much a monster for what I've done, for what I will do again.

"Enough!" Mathyr's sharp voice pierces from the passage on the opposite side of the room.

I draw Kryach back into my being but don't permit the blood fire to fade from my eyes. Mathyr sways toward us, garbed in her finest fire-jewel and pix-spun tulle and lace gown, bodice decorated in diamond-encrusted overlapping bones to compliment her crown of woven gold-lacquered wishbones. Obvious where Aydon gets his vainglory.

"Mathyr..." Aydon bows his head in and fetches her hand to rub his mouth across her knuckles. Always her favorite son, I sneer.

"Allysteir," Mathyr barely acknowledges me.

"Fashionably late as usual, Mathyr," I snort and note the crimson rosebuds woven through her full bun with a refter tooth fused into each petal.

"A steward alerted me of the startling turn of events. The whole court is in a stir. I spent a few minutes observing this potential bride and must agree with Elder Kanat." She gestures to the elder, and I refrain from clenching my teeth and breathe smoke through my nostrils instead. I don't give a damn what Kanat wants. I recognize the carnal glint in his eyes. The elder who takes more bitten consorts than any other but claims such piety and superiority for having never taken a bride.

"We will put it to a test," Aydon interjects with his political dexterity. "A simple pelvic bone rite to test her virginity will suffice."

"Yes," Mathyr agrees and narrows her stormy eyes upon me, nearly matching the inferno in mine. "I will assist in the ritual," she hints, and I grunt in distaste over the loathsome but necessary procedure to sate the gods and elders. Kryach will not welcome any "impurity" even if I could care less what has penetrated this little dove. Not since I admired her chucking her slippers to one hall. Perhaps it was her audacity at running from Elder Kanat in the first place. And when she pulled her scyan from her generous thighs and threatened an Ithydeir soldier with it, I knew I'd risk all manner of broken bones to assist her.

"*All* the elders will preside over the rite," I insist. Kanat shifts uncomfortably, but I won't have him taint the results in any way.

When Mathyr and Aydon agree and Kanat nods in reluctance, I sniff, shake out my robes, and proceed to the blackwood table where I fit Aydon's prior mask to my face and don the accursed crown. "Well? What are you waiting for? Go fetch my bride."

SEVEN
THE BLOOD QUEEN

ISLA

My breasts are half out of my gown. I'm fair breathless, but I can't stop twirling. As if pure Death courses through my veins, igniting my blood with fire. If it's my last night, I may as well eat, drink, sing, and by gods, I will dance!

I steal black death roses wherever I spin, tuck them into my hair and between my cleavage, crush others and scatter their plum-fragranced petals to the air. The Sythe Queen's eyes follow me as I dance around the skull table. The Blood Queen. I can't deny how undeniably erotic she is with her gown hugging her body in a scarlet cascade and its plunging neckline to expose much of her golden breasts—the bodice coated in rubies and thorns. Her lips remind me of plum roses occasionally baring the tiny saber fangs. Golden lust kindles her luminescent eyes while her hair falls like a roseate raiment. I blow her a kiss, blushing from her smirk and how her eyes roam my body. All the royals are individualistically beautiful.

Once I circle the table, countless Ith weave their hands around my waists, tongues salivating over the first tribute bride in centuries, but not one would ever dare to claim the Corpse King's possible intended. He still hasn't come for me.

A familiar pair of hands capture my waist, A warm and human and very soft cheek presses to mine. "Isla! What in Talahn-Feyhran were you thinking?" Franzy whispers wild against my ear, her voice carrying over the music.

"Oh, dance with me, my sweetheart. Tonight, I will away to a cold and lonely bed where he'll feast on my soul till I'm all but dead!"

Franzy seizes my face and needles her amber eyes onto mine. "My mind is a'mince, Isla!"

"And I'm off my head…" I purr in her ear and press my lips to hers, tasting the sweet, fruit wine from her tongue. Can she taste the Sythe wine on mine? When I'm full of drink, it's the only time my Nethermark dulls.

"Ye're out face!" she shouts of my full-intoxication, flustered when I twirl and kiss her again, hands groping with her gown.

"Come, we promised to dance the night away." I grip her hand, leading her through the crowds. We lose the soldiers and bustle down a dark passage.

"Isla, I—" Franzy squeaks, but I press her against the wall, mold my mouth to hers, and thrust my hips toward her pelvis.

It doesn't take long for her to bow to my prowess, for her lips to part. I moan, loving the taste of simple, honeyed wine on her tongue. Heat buds between my thighs, heart forging a blazing path out of my ribcage. Her hands stray to my waist, but I seize them and pin them above her head, savoring her adorable groan as she arches her neck to welcome my lips on her throat.

"Oh, gods! Oh, Kryach!" Franzy slurs when I trail my tongue along her throat and lower.

I smirk and murmur against her skin, "He will steal my soul soon, my bonnya sweet. But you'll always have my heart."

A draught sweeps my back.

Without hesitation, I spin and use my body as a barrier, a shield between her and the shifters who close in. My gaze darts between them. I shiver at the sight of the fleshy crown one wears: the beta Prince to the alpha Emperor! Younger, more muscled but not as skilled as the warrior alpha well known for his lion prowess, the beta Prince is here to make a point, to play me as a pawn in his game to achieve notoriety in his ranks.

Still, I'd be a fool to underestimate the Shifter with his dark stubble of a beard, his carmine pupils—dilated to hunger—, his rippled muscles, and bristles of short fur and claws he may extend at any time.

He clicks his teeth and opens his mouth. "The first tribute in centuries." He approaches me. Franzy trembles and whimpers behind me as I stare him down and wrinkle my nose. "Hmm...do you taste as arousing as you smell, little korye?"

Despite the beads of sweat gathering on my brow, I disguise my fear behind my rage and dare them, "Why don't you come and discover for yourself? Just let her go. She is far too sweet, no?" I divert them, prepared to shove Franzy down the hallway.

The Prince lifts a hand in dismissal, granting me my desire. Before Franzy can protest, I command against her mouth in a whisper, "Go or I swear to Kryach, I will use my bone barb on you instead of them." I wink at her, gesturing to the barb I retrieve from my cleavage. A worthy weapon for shifters.

Franzy gathers her gown skirts and skitters away because she will always resort to flight while my spirit always battles. *Little fire blossom,* Fathyr would call me. Petals of flame, nectar of poison. The girl with hellfire and heaven's light in her hair and death's Nether-mark upon her back. It flames. It blazes along my spine, but my ignited temper matches it.

The shifters charge with their lightning speed and superior muscles and knock the barb from my hands and slam my arms above my head. In the wake of the Prince licking his hot tongue down my throat to my breasts, I don't break. I seethe and jam my kneecap into his balls, earning a growl and a prompt strike from his hand.

"Where are those bright eyes now?" he mocks and nips my jaw. I hiss.

I spit in his face, and the Prince grips my throat in a direct threat, extending his face into a dominant wolf muzzle.

Fear plagues my body. The Nether-mark runs cold, penetrating my spine with familiar ice bursts. My limbs quiver. I buckle, but the Prince holds me, claws digging into my gown, lacerating my thigh, drawing blood.

"Mmm..." he leans in and growls low, savoring my fear, his muzzle nudging my cheek. I cringe and hold back bile when his hot tongue lashes at my mouth, forcing its way past my lips. "Little flower, I will pluck her petals and bite her before the Corpse King may sink his teeth into her. And all will know I am true alpha!"

Shifters would attempt as bold a statement as marking the Corpse King's future bride. I am nothing more than a pawn and a pleasure. Proof when he grips the edges of my gown and bunches them above my hips.

I gulp the urge to protest, to whimper, to show any weakness. They will always use weakness against you. They will use it as a fucking sword to draw your blood, to pierce your heart. You must always wear your skin as armor, kindle fire in your veins, and forge an iron ribcage to protect your weakest and ficklest of muscles.

But when the Prince palms my maidyan mound through my underclothes, I lick my lips, knuckles whitening, shaking uncontrollably. I close my eyes and brace myself because I want to curl on the floor, but the last thing I will do is surrender without a fight. When he retains his man shape, opens my lips, and dips a finger beneath the line of the fabric, I bite his lower lip as hard as I possibly can. He howls and tries to pull away.

Oh, no, you don't!

Blood fills my mouth, but I hold on, and something *fleshy* tears. The next I know, the Prince jerks away. His Shifter men weaken their hold on my wrists as they gape at their noble who wails and holds his bleeding lip. Disgusted, I chuck the fleshy piece lodged in my teeth and retch Sythe wine onto the two shifters on my left who release my wrists.

Blood rushing to my ears, I fall to my knees, but it doesn't take long for the Prince to recover. As he stalks to me, all fur and lust and fury, I curl into a ball and cover my head, prepared for a brutal and bloody bite. But his darkened shadow retreats.

"Prince Carsten, tsk, tsk, tsk..." A voice of silk and smoke, of blood rubies and dark roses, of shade dreams and lustful fangs, quells the moments of fire and rage. "You still pick battles with lionesses. To your own demise."

I peek through my hair strands. There she is! Arrayed in her seductive glory, her gown of scarlet beauty, the Sythe Queen sways past Carsten and slides a hand along the side of her body to rest on her prominent hip as sharp as a diamond. With her deadly barrier of a body between

Carsten and myself, she peers at me, eyes wandering in a glimpse. "People are looking for you, little lioness," she directs before turning to the Prince who gnashes his teeth.

"This is none of your business, Narcyssa!" he fumes, lower lip still bleeding. Half a lower lip now. I purse my own, wishing I could rid my tongue of his taste.

She rolls her eyes, tossing her fiery hair back. "If Alpha Drakos is impatient, it is *my* business. Such moods, when left to fester, will lead your Emperor to prickle. And then, it's my sythes against your shifters. And more fur is always shed than fangs." Queen Narcyssa slides her confident fingers, enthroned in lace gloves armored with trophy fangs, along Carsten's bare arm and to his pelvis, causing his muscles to bulge and his breath to pant as she finishes, "Besides, you know I am willing to offer you a pocket of heat to rival this little maidyan's. Heat which will accept your *wolf* member, Carsten."

"Give me your word in blood!" Carsten growls.

If I'd blinked, I'd have missed Narcyssa piercing her wrist with her fang, leeching blood through the lace to the fair skin mirroring it. The Shifter Prince extends his muzzle and lowers his massive tongue to nuzzle her wrist in a lash of a bargain. As soon as he's finished, he clenches his fists, hurls a growl at me, and departs with his shifters.

I don't rise. Instead, I wait for Narcyssa to charge for me, and sink her fangs into my naked throat. What astonishes me is when she heaves a sigh, wipes her hands, and turns to lower one palm to me. "Come, little lioness. I believe Lord Allysteir is finally ready to meet with you."

EIGHT
I LIKE HER.

ALLYSTEIR

Despite slashed portions of her gown, blood traces on her low neckline, bruises prowling her wrists, and the scent of Shifter fur all over her skin, my little dove's eyes have not lost their radiance, their rapture. First, I center my gaze on Mathyr who nods from my right-hand side. Her eyes flick to Aydon standing behind the girl along with the guards flanking her.

"The Shifter Prince..." Aydon merely states. I tense, caging a snarl at the mention of Carsten. "It seems our tribute survived an attack mostly unscathed."

I'll deal with the beta later.

The girl doesn't react or respond to Aydon's statement. Nor does she shift within the Ithydeir shadows. When I advance toward her with the scarlet-robed elders trailing in my wake like pumping hearts prepared to bleed in service to Kryach, she does not lower her chin.

Once my shadow engulfs the girl, and she lifts her head, posture as sovereign as an Isle-goddess, Kryach's spirit stalks my mind, breathing her scent through my nostrils.

Hmm...he inhales, cherishing the black death rose perfume, the fading fragrance of lust and Sythe wine, and the pungent aftermath of violence. *Her blood and flesh will be a glorious feast, Allysteir,* he coos to me, salivating, thirsting for her more than any past bride.

I narrow my eyes upon my little dove, waiting for her to shrink, to sink to her knees, anything but her high chin with her proud throat exposed like a beauteous offering.

"Kneel and pay homage to him who bears the God of Death!" Aydon barks the command behind her.

Not only does the girl *not* kneel, instead she squares her shoulders and steps toward me. Steadfast, her eyes brandish brutality with enough power to rival mine: a deep violet—the color of nightshade flowers.

"Lord Allysteir," she dares to address me, a strong and beautiful soprano lilt. Mathyr and Aydon drop their jaws, but my heartbeat quickens in admiration. "While anyone would be a fool to offend Aryahn Kryach, I believe *you* are in *my* debt as it is nearly the Bite Offering when all know I have signed my *death* warrant by volunteering to be your bride."

On all sides, the elders seethe from the girl's defiance, Mathyr and Aydon argue, the soldiers grip their swords, Kryach pants with unbridled craving. But I simper behind my corpse mask, appreciating this showdown. Damn, this will be difficult.

I like her. I fucking like her.

I raise a gloved hand to silence the group, carefully curve and settle my hand beneath the girl's chin and lower my head to inquire, "What is your name?"

"Isla Adayra," she pronounces, lashes lowering in a sultry invitation.

My throat grows thick with her name's celestial sound. Before anyone interjects, I brush my glove across her cheek—so fair, perhaps her skin will erupt with moonlight—and dictate, "You are correct, Isla Adayra. I am in your debt. But before I may add my signature to your bridal death warrant, you must understand the necessity of a certain...trial."

Elder Kanat bristles next to me, and Isla does not miss the gesture. "A virginity test," the elder dictates pointedly.

Her chuckle is the fluttering of silvery wings before she declares, "How interesting, considering I was snowy enough for you to claim me as a Feyal-bride not an hour ago."

The elders hurl outraged accusations at my intended, at Kanat, their voices overlapping like a gaggle of strutting peacocks. Isla merely crosses her arms over her chest which plumps her breasts. Elder cheeks redden to her growing cleavage, but someone must intervene as I'm tempted to sink my teeth into this hot-blooded fire flower's beguiling throat... careless whether she's a saint or strumpet.

Ever the political mastermind, Aydon approaches the girl and lights a hand on the center of her back, fingers traipsing across her hair. I growl low from his invasion. He flicks his eyes up, surprised by my action. I can't blame him, considering I've never shown this intensity of possession. But as I'd clarified before Elder Kanat: she is mine.

Ours...Kryach reminds me, his breath a deathly poison in my mind. I wince but cannot rebel. Always resigned to my fate, this curse I've accepted. Nor will it be the first time I sate him with blood but wait as long as possible for a bride's flesh. Isla will challenge me more than any other.

"This is not an offense against your honor, tribute Adayra," Aydon addresses her, his blue eyes pacifying her. Her shoulders sink, though she maintains crossed arms. Yes, my damned brother has that effect: a silk-wrapped venomous snake. "It is the first time such a thing has happened in centuries. Please forgive the bluntness of our questions and subsequent trial: are you a virgin?"

Easing a sigh, Isla turns her chin back to me, taps a finger to her bare arm, and responds, "I am not unfamiliar with the pleasurable throes of blissful climax, but I have never once been penetrated by a man's anything whether his tongue, mouth, fingers, nor a thick and rigid cock."

My chortling snort is drowned out by the elders' shocked gasps and yelps. Aydon kneads his brow while Mathyr stiffens, eyes wide. Isla simply shrugs as if to say, "what can you expect from a Cock-Cross girl?"

Fuck. Kryach latches onto my lust, driving it onward till my damned member responds, but I don't betray myself, grateful for my robes.

"Your Majesty, please!" Elder Kanat interjects, needling his eyes onto my bride. "Let us proceed with the test and reveal what a petulant tramp this girl is. Surely she must be a trickster aligned with our enemies. How convenient she escaped the guardian detail only to survive an attack of four shifters, including the vigorous wolf Prince."

"Yes, these introductions have finalized," Mathyr commands, stepping forward, her voice harder than winter bones. "I will accompany Isla Adayra to the garderobe where we may commence the procedure, provided she accepts." Her war smoke-gray eyes burrow onto Isla's, forceful enough to cow her sons into submission but not my little dove.

"What must I do?" she wonders.

Elder Kanat deepens his voice, an arrogant smirk pressing his lips, "We require a single tear, a drop of blood, and a lock of hair…from your *nether* regions."

Isla stiffens but raises her chin and offers a curt nod. "I accept."

Mathyr takes her wrist, prepared to escort her to the garderobe, but Isla reaches out and seizes my robe sleeve. I cringe from the infraction, wondering if she senses my forearm bone through the heavy robes, but if she does, she doesn't indicate, nor draws her hand away.

Instead, her eyes confess glassy desperation, prompting my blood to quicken in my veins. Her chest hitches, and she requests, "Will you come with me?"

My first instinct is to part my lips in shock, but I must battle a groan because I'm weary of the elders' condescending, too-moral outrage.

Mathyr tightens her hold on Isla's wrist, protesting, "Have you no shame, you uncivil and insolent nighyan?"

It's the first time my little dove lowers her chin, not in shame but in defeat and resignation, but tears glisten in her eyes. I've beheld enough brides on the wedding night to recognize when one is on the fringe of hyperventilating. Isla Adayra has willingly thrown herself at death's door. The armor around my heart weakens. I'll be damned if I leave her to face my she-wolf of a mother alone.

Before the Queen may drag her away, I assume Isla's other hand to declare, "Wait!" Ignoring the elders behind me, I cling to the flicker of light returning to my little dove's eyes and continue, "As uncouth and untraditional this may be, I will accompany you and remain with you for the procedure. We will erect a sheet to provide a barrier."

Isla releases a long breath and bows her head for the first time. "Thank you, thank you...Your Highness."

Between her double statement and how her eyes glaze across mine in a naked moment of vulnerability, I recognize she's thanking me not only for this small mercy but also the Skull Ruins. Fuck! She knows it was me. Could she possibly have seen me? My face? I can only hope she assumed my identity on account of my power and the parietal skull bone. Regardless, Kryach cackles and foams at the mouth inside my mind.

Damn you, Kryach! Damn you to the deepest pit of the Void! I rage but receive nothing but laughter in return. Because he knows...my armor has shattered. My feeble heart has fallen for Isla Adayra.

And I will ruin her heart as I've ruined all others.

NINE
THE QUEEN'S TEST

ISLA

The Corpse King does not release my hand, and I could die from gratitude.

The moment the Nether-mark had licked flames along my spine at one touch of the Queen, I knew I could not withstand this trial alone. Everything has changed overnight. The Sythe wine has depleted from my blood, and I must save what little courage I have for the Bite Offering. But whenever Allysteir is close, the mark stills to a warm quietude as if I'm sinking into a tepid bath.

I hope he understands I was thanking him for saving my life... as I've volunteered to save everyone in Talahn-Feyal. While I may have been perfectly content marrying my childhood love and spending the rest of our lives discussing trade and farming agreements while slaying the occasional refter with our nights spent in each other's arms as we grew fat and old and wrinkly and ever rich without the burden of children, I cannot complain over this fate. As Franzy told me on the train: I have a warrior's spirit. I may never achieve the notoriety of the Scarlet Scathyk, but my name will be writ into the history books of Talahn-Feyal. The bones of a common Cock-Cross girl will slumber in the tombs of the great kings and queens under the mountains.

I hold to the image when the Corpse King and his mother escort me into the garderobe. Similar to a parlor with an adjoining room of individual lavatory stalls. Considering all we have is a simple ditch on our farm's edge, the fine room is a worthy comfort for this oncoming trial.

"Lie down on the divan," the Queen directs me, gesturing to the backless furniture.

I swallow any flustered gasps and slowly move toward the ornate divan with its legs constructed of iron-fused bones fused. What surprises me is how Allysteir does not release my hand but remains close until I've settled onto the divan with my back slightly arched.

"Allysteir, fetch the tapestry behind you and fix it to the hooks in the ceiling," his mother orders, voice stern as an arrow, but he nods and releases my hand to obey her.

The tapestry settles against my waist, acting as the perfect barrier since Allysteir remains at the head of the divan close to my hair. The fabric is heavy from the gold-spun thread, velvet, and teeth depicting a battle. I can't help but smile at the legendary siege of Scarlet Scathyk, taking comfort in the portrait. Little flutters cluster in my belly. I blush at Scathyk's story: part history part legend of when she and her devoted soldiers engaged in a week-long siege against the Shee forces who invaded Talahn-Feyal, aiming to take her Dyn Kylverock Castle. I'll never forget the legend of how she tore off countless Shee wings, hung them upon her naked body, and paraded herself in such glory on the highest balustrade to divert the main forces while her men used their underground tunnels in a surprise attack to crush the unsuspecting army from behind.

"Spread your thighs wide. We will do the hard part first," the Queen commands from the divan's end. For some reason, I can't recall her name. Her fire-jewels catch the dim light of the lanterns in the room, casting ominous shadows upon her face.

I purse my lips and do as she directs but cringe...until Allysteir settles his gloves on each side of my head, hushing my tears and the Nether-mark with the breath of shadow curling upon my brow through the corpse mask. Closing my eyes, I bite my lower lip, warding off any instincts to tremble. The image of Scathyk with her sword raised high to the heavens and her breasts on full and glorious display above the translucent wings of the Shee bolsters me. I grin at the same time the Queen lifts my gown ends and positions it above my hips, prompting a rush of cool air.

Allysteir cocks his head. His corpse mask is a hollow imitation and can't compare to his true face's macabre beauty. But I won't urge him to show me since he doesn't know what I did in the Skull Ruins. I would never reveal the secret. No, I want to earn it, earn his trust. If the Corpse King can trust me—marked by refters and by the Void—if he can respect me, perhaps I may survive this Curse's cycle. After all, I respected him the moment I removed his mask.

Because I love nothing more than one who defies every legend spoken of them.

First, the Queen slides my lower undergarments until they arrive at my spread ankles, then casts them to the floor, leaving my lower half fully exposed to her eye. Upon hearing her gown sway back and forth, I crane my neck to the side, peeking beyond the edge of the tapestry, wincing because she is studying my sex too much. I sigh, relieved when Allysteir catches it with his gloved thumb. I smile because his phalange bone hints beneath the glove.

His presence must be the only reason the corpus roses do not grow, do not follow me.

I arch my back more when the Queen massages the upper slopes of my mound, her nails curling into my darker pubic hairs, though she truly has no need. I'd prefer her to pluck the strands to their roots than this anticipation. But I smile at Scathyk's bountiful breasts. No, mine cannot vie with hers. Or her flat stomach pane.

"Why are you smiling?" Allysteir's voice catches me by surprise, and I blush.

I nod to the tapestry. "She is my favorite legend." I inhale when the Queen's fingers descend, dangerously close to the center of my feminine pleasure...to my rosy nub.

"She is mine as well," he responds, his breath cool and abating across my brow.

"Oh!" I stiffen at the sudden lash of pain when the Queen plucks my pubic hairs and places them on the nearby end table. "Why?" I ask him, wondering why she doesn't fetch my undergarment.

"She possessed the courage I never have held," he dictates, and I notice his jaw steeling below his mask.

"Forgive me, My Lord, but I know one must *accept* Kryach's curse and spirit. That is no mere feat. It requires great courage...perhaps the greatest."

He snorts, surprising me with the sudden vehemence within his fingers curving into my skull. "Or great foolery. Or surrender because there was little other choice."

"Perhaps you may share with me sometime..." I trail off, too bold. Like Fathyr always warned me about my spirit...it could rival an unbroken mare.

"Perhaps." He offers no promises.

I cringe when the Queen pricks my finger and squeezes to loose a drop of blood into a prepared, glass vial. Allysteir's fingers do not retreat from the sides of my face when she lowers her lips to my ear and murmurs, "I have my own test, little tribute," she hints, her breath warm, her tone too-hinting. But unlike her son, she wears no mask. Her agenda is plain. She *hates* me. Is it because I am not worthy of her son? "It will aid in releasing her required tear."

"Mathyr..." Allysteir's voice darkens.

"Oh!" I moan when her fingers nudge my sex, parting my folds. "What are you—"

"She is moist and ripe, my son," the Queen retorts from beyond the tapestry.

My thighs and ankles quiver when she taunts my center by nudging my swelling rosebud, causing me to arch, eyes glistening. I buck. Hard. Clench my thighs. But the Queen pins them, her diamond-studded nails raking my skin.

"Stop!" demands the King, rising, body tensing, but his hands do not retreat from my cheeks.

"Why?" his mother challenges. My cheeks burn as she plunges two fingers into my inner chamber. "We must know if she is a fertile bride. One who will bear you a strong son able to free you from the Curse and assume the next mantle for Aryahn Kryach."

Oh, gods! I whimper when she adds another finger and plunges deeper.

"Gryzelda!" he exclaims her name, the essence of the Death God injecting into his voice, the shadows spiraling past the tapestry to threaten his mother.

No... I grip his sleeve and thrash my head. "Please, Allysteir..." I wince again, slamming my eyes shut when his mother rubs my clitoris in a frenzy and injects another finger. "I can take it," I assure him. When I deadpan with the Queen's eyes, I know she would prefer me to fight, struggle. *Do your worst*, I almost dare, but press my lips, narrow my eyes to deadly slits. They speak fathoms.

Everything in me screams to wage a war, but I can take whatever this Queen, this Gryzelda—a name of grey battle—throws my way. I will not balk. I will not weaken. And if I climax, I won't be ashamed. My eyes do not forsake the Corpse King's.

When the Queen has the audacity to add a final finger and curve them deep in my sex, I shriek from the irresistible climax. Aware of my body, I don't deny the lightning feathers titillating my spine to tingle my flesh. But I keep my eyes on Scathyk, on mine and the Corpse King's legend love, on his brow pressed to mine, his breath a fatal vapor on my face.

Queen Gryzelda does not hesitate to meet my eyes at the height of my climax. I battle a whimper when she raises her fingers to her mouth to suck my fluids before she replaces my undergarments without wiping the dampness out of spite. I sigh when she collects the tear from my cheeks, and nods, taking her leave to give the offerings to the elders. The King growls at her, shadows billowing a warning upon her departure.

Allysteir sighs and grips the tapestry, flinging it to the floor as if it's no more than a handkerchief. Cheeks flushed, I bite my lower lip and arch my neck when he eases my gown back over my spread legs and offers me his gloved hand.

Accepting, I wobble to my feet, legs trembling in the aftermath from the Queen mother's hands. The King catches me before my knees buckle. He apologizes, his breath an icy draught along my ear. "My mother can be—"

"A bitch?"

"I was going to say contentious, but your term is more appropriate."

"Lord Allsyteir..." I lower my head, recognizing how I insulted his mother. How he could have me executed for such a transgression and choose another bride. Perhaps she had her reasons aside from hatred. Or not...

Goosebumps or maybe tingles grow along my flesh when he curls his gloved fingers to my cheek and shakes his head. "No, Isla. You have nothing to apologize for. I love your sharp tongue and you should never soften it...not before me."

I smile. And I...I might *trust* him.

TEN
THE BITE OFFERING

ALLYSTEIR

Damn, I love her blushing cheeks and when she bites her lower lip. My cock throbs from her arousal. I cherish her moans from her climax despite it coming from my mother's *ministrations*. Yes, I have pleasured many a bride before I fucked them and collected their moans, their shrieks, their blissful wails. But never before has my mother inflicted her torture.

Yes, Isla will overshadow her Queenship. Mathyr was the first in centuries' worth of brides. Five hundred and twenty years ago—four years before my birth—Mathyr was one of only nine brides in our centuries-long history to ever survive Aryahn Kryach. No, she could not defeat him, but her soul was strong enough, he could only consume a portion. And left a bitter, jealous shrew shell.

As Isla rights herself, I curl my lip beyond my bone mask from the memory of the night I accepted the Curse of Aryahn Kryach because I'd sooner have welcomed the God of Death if it meant I could keep my art and give the "crown" to Aydon who was birthed for it. And because there was no other choice.

But Isla...oh hellfire, she will be my death! Thanks to my mother's damned actions, her nipples are erect through her gown's thin lace. It takes all my resolve not to petition her, to *beg* her to allow me to tear it from her frame, rip off my mask, and bury my face into her bosom to taste those sweet, ripe fruited seeds.

When the moment comes, when I fuck her, if her eyes open, if they open to no soul, I swear I will march right into the Void and storm the Isle gates themselves!

I sigh because I've said the same thing of a hundred brides of my past, but instead, I carry their weight of a thousand corpses upon my unworthy soul. I cannot hope Isla will be any different, though I love her more passionately, more ardently than all the others, save one. Knots form in my tongue. My heartbeat thrashes.

I must keep her at bay. Because for some reason, this sweet girl, this... my dark rose welcomes a walking corpse! *It's not love*, I deny. Some perverted, fading syndrome as a result of my saving her in the Skull Ruins. She is the same as all the others. If not..., I will have no choice.

Krayk purrs low in my mind, his essence infesting my heart with its icy thorns. *Show her, Allysteir. Show her how she will never love the one who wears the God of Death. Show her she is no better than the others. Even if she survives as your mother did, she will* never *break my Curse! She is nothing more than a fragile fire flower.*

Gods damn him!

I escort Isla to the secondary hall. Where the devil is Aydon? My brother should be here to witness the elders perform the bone rite. It takes all my strength to withstand Isla's closeness when she sidles her warm flesh against my non-skeletal side, stirring my member.

I rivet my gaze on the elders and not her. I focus on the pelvic bone they place on the altar, the pomegranate seeds as a symbol of fertility, the vial housing her blood, the other...her tear. Careless if I break one, I grit my teeth when Mathyr casts Isla's pubic hairs to the altar, and the elders chant.

I have my own ritual...far more powerful than those religious fools. It requires a closer kinship to Kryach, but it is worth it to thwart any deception from Kanat. I speak it within the inner vessels of my mind, summoning the God of Death's power.

Take this rite upon my heart
And grant me power beyond their dark arts
Grant your shadow upon the maidyan fair
And reap the truth of what she hath shared...

They light the altar on fire.

Isla flinches, but I meet her eyes, to study the fire catching their violet royalty. Something like immortality, like the breath of angyls and the venom of demons, grows within her eyes—a blessing and a curse more powerful than any rite or ritual and dare I consider...more powerful than Kryach himself. Within the never-solace of my mind, Kryach roars...a foreign sound, strange and beautiful, it summons an emotion I've not had since before I accepted the Curse over five hundred years ago: hope.

Once the offerings upon the altar burn away, leaving a revelatory message of ash, the elders nod to each other, turn, and bow their heads. Elder Kanat wrinkles his nose in disgust.

The elders reveal what Kryach already has. "Isla Aydara is a pure virgin."

And I do the unthinkable: I lift the edge of my mask so it nudges the passage above my upper lip. I lean in to arrest Isla by the waist, lower my head to hers, and capture her mouth with my ruinous one. Praying she will accept the kiss.

Oh, gods, she does!

Despite my swollen mouth on one side and the non-existent flesh on the opposite betraying sharp teeth to graze the right-hand side of her supple mouth, Isla welcomes me. Kryach is strangely silent when I kiss my bride—when I taste her essence. Oh Voids-damn me, she tastes more exquisite than I could have ever predicted! Wine and moon-lily juice and salt from her tears.

Heat plagues my form, rouses my cock to prod my heavy robs. My hands long to voyage lower, to those full breasts, to nuzzle my rotted mouth across her ripened buds. To worship between her thighs. Revere all her flesh.

Her moan is the signal to help me pull away, and I command the onlookers, "Commence the Bite Offering!"

Not once do I part from my to-be bride. It's enough to scrutinize her swollen lips, how she bites the lower one, how her cheeks flush. It's enough to capture the sight of her watery eyes and her panting breath.

By our wedding night, I will destroy everything. With Kryach, I will destroy any promptings of love, of desire. I will break her heart, spend a year piecing it back together, only to fuck her. And the moment I do, I will shatter her entire being.

Because I am a monster who dreams of beauty. Nothing more than a vessel of the God of Death who steals all beauty for himself.

I will do this for Talahn-Feyal. I pay the price for the majority, but my brides pay the deepest.

In full surrender, I lead my future bride-to-be onto the dais before the masses and the monarchs who will witness the engagement ceremony. The noble Feyal-Ithydeir are there, but when Aydon strides past me with a girl I recognize from an earlier dance, Isla gasps and covers her mouth—stunned at my older brother and his chosen Feyal-bride.

"Not Franzy," she breathes, her eyes misting.

Clearly, my intended bride knows this girl, a girl who has not come of age—doesn't matter to my bastard brother I have never managed to control.

When her chest lurches, her fingers curl toward the amber-eyed girl dressed in green, I collect my future bride and stay her hands. Shake my head. By law, my brother holds enough power to take whom he chooses. Except, in this case, the position where he places this Franzy before him reveals she has volunteered...as my Isla has.

Two solitary tears tumble down my intended's fair cheeks. This pain, I cannot spare my dark rose. If I could, I'd devour her tears, but it would not ease her heart. Still, her strength dumbfounds me when she squares her shoulders and assumes her place of prominence on the dais where bone warriors surround us. My mother lowers herself onto the iron throne behind us while Aydon shifts his ember-eyed Feyal-bride-to-be before him a few paces from myself.

Dozens of menders wait on all sides of the dais. Prepared to heal our humans, they will leave nothing but one bite mark as a first-claim scar. If she has prepared for the scar, I wonder what Isla will think of it. Will she itch and curse it as some past brides?

All other Feyal-Ithydeir congregate on either side of the Cryth River with their claimed humans facing the onlooking crowd. At the table of skulls, the foreign sovereigns await the ceremony, but never could they truly appreciate it. Nor the Sythe or Shee who feed on human blood.

Flesh is deeper than blood. Flesh is what we cherish and treasure above all. Every bit is sacred. A stain so deep for any Feyal-Ithydeir to ever bite a human without their consent. Deeper for rape. The punishment is severe unless you're a damned elder...

As head Elder, Kanat preaches the sanctimonious words to usher in the Bite Offering.

"Reap the curse from our breast, oh God of Death
Be satisfied with their pure blood and breath
Cleanse the darkness from our souls and our hands
And release the Void from our holy heartland
Grant us a year of honeyed fruit and sweet milk
Dreams of ripened flesh, full wombs, and soft silk
Accept this truth of teeth and rid us of refter blights
As our Feyal-Ithydeir open their mouths to solemnly bite..."

By the light of a thousand torches, the humans arch their necks in a formal offering, but Isla is different. Her fingers curl to my mask, longing but with no demand to remove the bone imitation. No, she merely wants me to know:

I see you, Allysteir.

Somehow, I resist the urge to seethe because Kryach curls his Death-shadows all over the edges of her body. She shivers, but her eyes do not descend to the shadows. No, she simply fixes them on the mockery skull holes as if perceiving my true cadaverous orbs.

So sweet, Allysteir, whispers Kryach in the dark solace of my mind. *Not a dove at all.*

No, she is the essence of corpus roses infecting my nostrils. I narrow my eyes, bewildered by the flowers upon her gown. I don't remember their presence. But I'm not an expert in floral matters. All I know is she reminds me of them: these corpus roses. A beauty of contrasts: of life and death, fire and ice, eyes of sweet dreams, and tongue of sharp silver.

Our dark rose, hints Kryach in a carnal whisper.

This is mine! I thwart him, wishing I could banish his spirit from this moment. *She is* mine!

The scent of blood permeates the air, rousing my desire for her flesh—as fair and soft as swans down. Kryach laughs as I lower my calamitous lips to Isla's neck where the curve meets the line of her shoulder.

First, I rub my mouth in a tender boon of a kiss—my offering—wishing this was as far as I could take it because I would give my flesh-lust and starve myself if it meant I could spare her the God of Death's shadow.

Isla leans her neck further. Her pulse thrums through her milky, moonlight flesh with her tempting blood like liquid rubies. In the background, countless humans moan and wail, succumbing to the Bite Offering, welcoming the scars.

"Allysteir," she breathes a whisper, prompting me to complete the ceremony.

I lean in, murmur hinting words against her ear, "More than my teeth, my little dove, my...dark rose," I add because Kryach is more discerning than I. "More than your blood."

Out of all the brides I have ever brushed my teeth across, Isla is the first who does not hold her breath.

She gasps when I suck her neck in a precursor of a warning. She clings to my robes, disturbing my balance, but I hold strong. "I've been bitten before," she whispers a fatal secret, and by gods, it stirs my soul's hunger, my heart's permission to plunge my teeth into her neck and welcome her cry. Not a scream.

Bloody angyls and blessed demons!—she tastes of the sweetest pomegranates. In the past, I've kept my first bites brief and gifted Kryach with a mere few drops to sate his lust. Not this time. Pulse panting with need in my throat, I sink my teeth. Her fingers grip my robes, her back pressed so deep against my skeletal chest which somehow bears her weight.

Kryach's spirit dives into her flesh, stabbing into her blood. For the first time in the history of the Bite Offering, his spirit trespasses beyond the boundaries of my body.

I cannot stop. Obsessive, I suck my dark rose's flesh, her sweet essence because something else lingers within her beguiling blood. It reminds me of Isle-fire: a glimmer of the gods' dwelling place. A passion I never could have predicted.

I slide my hand around her waist, coasting to settle my glove beneath her bust, longing to palm her generous, warm flesh. Her moans are a seductive symphony. Once I trespass on the boundary of drinking beyond my fill, I retract my teeth. The menders move in, but I don't forsake her. Isla whimpers as I rub my lips dripping with the juice of her blood along her lily-white skin until I arrive at her lips. To my astonishment, she accepts my kiss. She welcomes my taste, the taste of her own blood, her flesh.

The God of Death feasts on her blood while I feast on her succulent lips. Once he moans—his first ever moan—I break from her flesh with her blood trickling from my keen teeth, and gaze through the mask at her eyes of royal wine, of deep violet.

She whispers, "I am yours, Corpse King!"

Damn it, I descend! I return to her flesh, savoring her scream as I dive deeper, harder than ever because she is my breath, my blood, my flesh, my home, my fucking bones.

Above all, she is *mine*...

ELEVEN

"I AM THE CORPUS ROSE WHO HAUNTS HIM..."

ISLA

I would be a fool to deny the pain.

It's like a thousand burning corpus rose thorns have burrowed into my neck. With the shadows of Kryach's spirit winnowing along my curves in a bare brush of Death, it triggers countless memories from my childhood, from the night I fled the orphanage and carried myself to the Void border. In the greatest of ironies, I felt safe there.

Allysteir's teeth do not bite like refters. Not animalistic instinct razing my flesh and bone. No, the King savors, lapping my blood, my flesh caught between his teeth as he devours longer and deeper; he craves, demands, and entreats me.

I am the corpus rose who follows him, who haunts him.

When he penetrates me raw and hard, I scream but wage a siege against my rising tears because the last thing I want is for him to pull away. Not with his hand embracing my waist on the undersides of my breasts and rousing the heat between my thighs. Not with his sharp, breathless pants and quickening pulse nearly thundering in my ears.

Hundreds of eyes rivet their gaze upon us, but the King's cadaverous face clouds my vision—the face in the Skull Ruins. Someday, I will tell him *after* I've earned his trust. My flesh tingles with the thought.

Dizzy from his feasting, I crumble in his arms, knees buckling, vision blurring. Still, I smile because his teeth linger, mouth sucking and culling as much as he dares because he understands my strength. And it must mean one thing: he trusts me.

Oh, gods!

The moment Kryach's dark spirit shrouds my body in shadowy ice, Allysteir jerks back and thrusts me toward the closest mender. Unlike the rest, it requires more than one to heal my flesh. While the other Ith retreat with their healed human-chosens, including Prince Aydon and Franzy, Allysteir remains close while menders tend to me. They rub bone powder into my wounds, speak healing rites upon my flesh, but their words are distant and subdued as gray fog.

Kryach's spirit whispers upon my body—a dark caress of a lullaby. Despite his voicelessness, his deathly stroke assures me of how pleased he is with my blood and flesh. How he longs for more. A hollowness invades my stomach.

He'll eat your soul until you're all but dead...

For the first time, I whimper and shed a tear because Allysteir has become his mask. He does not look at me. He stands with his side facing me. My heart plummets to my stomach.

Look at me! I want to plead, but my breath is faint—winded from the bone powder knitting my flesh, sealing the wound until a cold eternity of teeth-scar remains.

Once the Bite Offering concludes, soldiers usher me into the secondary hall where Allysteir, Aydon and Franzy, Queen Gryzelda, and the elders wait, discussing political matters involving the other races. Allysteir barely acknowledges me, and I wish I could say the same for his mother whose sharpened eyes scrutinize me along with the elders, including Kanat. His eyes linger on my fresh scar and my lips.

Aydon steps toward me. I struggle to contain myself because Franzy lingers on his right-hand side, leaning on him for support with her raw bite mark. Her face is more blanched than usual, but her eyes have not lost their amber luster. My gut clenches in remorse and guilt because I promised her we would never become Feyal-brides. And now, we are brides to brothers. One who is the most powerful in Talahn-Feyal. My fingers quiver to touch her, to embrace her. But my knees are too weak from fatigue after the first bite.

Before I fall, the Prince assumes my hand and brushes his mouth across my knuckles, his eyes as blue as Wisp-Shee jewels shimmering across mine. "Well met and welcome, Lady Isla Adayra of Cock Cross to our Underworld. I wish you prosperity and many fruitful years as Queen of Talahn-Feyal." Yes, because my lifespan will be longer now as a Feyal-bride.

I nod, accepting his formality. I may not be well-versed in history, but it's common knowledge the last volunteering tribute was a well-bred girl from a noble court family.

"Thank you, Lord Aydon, but if you will excuse me…" I bow my head to him before turning to Franzy. And however untraditional, I can't help but throw my arms around my friend and press my lips to her cheek while fresh tears glisten in my eyes. "Franzy, I'm so—"

The last thing I expect is for her to shove me away. I taper my brows, confused because she lifts her chin, eyes tightening as her lips flatten before she acknowledges, "A pleasure to see you again, my friend. It will be an honor to attend your impending nuptials," she finishes, eyes roaming to Allysteir's mask.

I understand. She doesn't know what happened after she fled the Hollows. She doesn't know what happened in the Skull Ruins. I can't fault Franzy for feeling betrayed after all our years of planning, all our dreams and goals which have turned to cold ash. Soon, I must get her alone and explain. She will understand. I must find a way to get her out of the Citadel of Bones to escape this fate. I purse my lips because a fleeting thought has me wondering if she desires this, considering she volunteered. She remains close to Aydon's side. After all, the Feyal-bride of a Prince is far better than wedding a Cock-Cross girl with no dowry apart from a mountain of debt.

A sudden thought has my chest lurching. My family, Mathyr and Fathyr...I glance at Allysteir, yearning to ask what will become of them, but all he does is waver near the blackwood table where he snatches a flask of Shee-wine and downs it in one gulp.

While stroking Franzy's curls, Aydon continues where my friend left off, "Yes, we all await the wedding of the first common girl who has ever volunteered. The wedding will commence by the next full moon with the Adayra family in attendance, but we will have the royal supper within the next hour as the festivities continue. Until then, our Feyal-maids will accompany you to the bridal chambers and prepare you for the feast." He gestures to the nearby maids garbed in the Citadel skull insignia.

My heart leaps at the chance to be alone with Franzy until Queen Gryzelda steps toward me to announce, "I will accompany Allysteir's bride-to-be to her chambers and preside over her preparation. There is much I wish to discuss with her."

The color drains from my face, but when I turn to the King, he grunts and downs more wine. Remembering my last encounter with Gryzelda, I fortify myself. I wear the King's mark. She will not discover a mere Cock-Cross girl.

Now, I am the future Queen of the Underworld.

"These will be your private chambers until your wedding night," Queen Gryzelda informs me and pushes open double doors of fused iron, bone, and gold—ones I assume protected through bone rites.

Undone by the lavish suite which could house ten of my old bedrooms, I gush at the surroundings. In the center against the back wall is the massive bed with its canopy posts sculpted from the finest ivory. The domed ceiling depicts murals of past princesses while a ledge nudging multiple arched windows overlooks a Citadel courtyard with gardens and fountains. I touch the stained glass and smile at the gardens until my heart aches with the memory of home, of our farm gardens.

Once the Queen snorts, annoyed by my delay, she grips my elbow, tugs me to the opposite side of the room, and directs the Feyal-maids to escort me down a winding wrought-iron staircase. She follows. I swallow knots of apprehension from her shoes echoing behind me as we descend until the temperature lowers, prompting my gooseflesh.

The staircase ends before a room similar to the garderobe, except this is clearly a bathhouse. Beyond its walls, the inner mountain wind whips across the Citadel, chilling me through the chinks in the stone. Steam rises from the water of the generous hollowed-out bath.

Under the Queen's careful inspection, the maids remove my mother's wedding gown and strip me bare. I manage to keep my hands behind my back to hide my Nether-mark and in a firm voice, I command them, "You will wash any blood and soil from my gown and return it to me once it's clean. If any pix-spun thread is torn or feather is missing, I will know." I won't, but it's enough to divert the maids from my mark before they urge me into the steaming spring water of these lower chambers.

I lower myself under the feverish water laced with bone powder and other minerals to purify my flesh. I wonder if my corpus roses will grow to impart their oil. When I emerge, I come face to face with the Queen who holds a scrub brush and bar of soap. All the maids have departed. We are alone.

From the bench with her gown cascading along the floor in a pool of lace and flame jewels, she inspects me from head to toe with her dark eyes like autumn storms. I don't shrink. Not even when she bids me in a stern order, "Turn around."

With a reluctant sigh, I do as she commands, strengthening my heart's fortress. The Queen will have her say. First, she scrubs the moon-like strands of my hair. The pungent scent of honey lotus engulfs my nostrils.

"You think me cruel," she says, making her way to my ends while dragging one finger along my spine. I'm grateful the water conceals my Nether-mark because her finger rouses its fire. I tremble as she returns to the brush. "I am cruel. But I apologize for my actions earlier. It was my desperate attempt to dissuade you and intimidate you to withdraw your proposal."

I angle my neck so my chin lines with my shoulder and ask her, "Why? The Corpse King hadn't chosen a bride. You should thank me."

She wrenches my hair back and seethes, "Delusions of grandeur. Is this all a desperate suicide attempt? Mark your common name in our history books and your spirit reaps the glory? Rest assured, while our pages may care, Aryahn Kryach will not."

I gulp and squeeze my eyes, tears threatening to spill. Death's presence haunts my flesh, stalking me after Allysteir reaped my blood and flesh. Kryach desired everything.

"You are right, my Lady Queen," I croak, confirming her accuracy. "The gods never care." We are all their playthings. And she has felt Kryach's spirit.

Gryzelda's eyes bore into mine, and she loosens her hold. Thanks to my arched neck, the bath chamber's firelight torches catch her diamond-encrusted bone bodice, nearly blinding me. Words as sharp as refter teeth, the Queen breathes across my face, "More than grandiose goals, then. Escape?" When I bite my lower lip, considering Elder Kanat, she glides the bar of soap across my throat, paying close attention to my fresh bite mark, and wonders, "What could be worse than the bride of Death? Hmm..."

I say nothing. The moment I'd fallen to my knees and proclaimed my proposal, I was prepared. Perhaps too desperate, filled with delusions of grandeur. But the Corpse King I'd met in the Skull Ruins or his macabre face in its resting state haunted me: the corners of his mouth were turned low in an expression of woe despite sleep. A deep woe of un-belonging I understand. If I may remove the mask again, if he surrenders it to me...

Gryzelda leans in and snarls, "You believe you will tempt my son with your ripe fruits?" I yelp, slamming my eyes shut as she yanks my hair further until my scalp burns. My Nether-mark licks ice along my back. What stuns her is when I crane my neck and grip her wrist, twisting until she releases my hair. Seething, I turn and stare her down, refusing to freeze. She blinks, wavering as if understanding I won't let her toy with me this time.

The Queen glowers. "You are a fool, Isla Adayra. I remember your conversation with my son. But know, you cannot tempt Death. You cannot cheat him."

"But Allysteir—"

"—has not carried Aryahn Kryach for the past five hundred years without sucking his poison. All Corpse Kings do. Banish your naivete of love. It is forsaken in this realm. Even if you survive Kryach's first kiss, you will never be the same."

Her words are pure venom. I hiss a warning as her hand roams to my throat, to my fresh bite-scar. I pant when she continues, "I'm going to tell you a secret, sweet bride. All believe I was strong enough for Aryahn Kryach to spare me, but I was not. I accepted him. To survive, you must permit him to rape your soul, to never fight, to allow him to pillage you again and again until not one shred of your heart remains."

He will eat your soul until you're all but dead...

"And I knew I had to try and stop you because you possess the strength to survive," sighs Gryzelda, her lips warm across my jaw, across my cheek. They are hot and hungering. Finally, she captures my chin and forces my eyes to hers. I knit my brows low. "That is why I did what I did in the garderobe, why I am doing this now. To prepare you. You thought you would be a martyr, sweet tribute. But the King will always do as Death desires. Kryach will ruin you as he did me...until there is nothing left but violence, fire, and blood. Nothing but your scarred soul."

87

I steel myself. Posture. Battle tears which long to flow along my cheeks because I do not hate her. I can't hate her dark scar of a soul. Instead, I pity her because she made the choice for one who has no choice. While the Queen scrapes her teeth along my neck, inhaling my scent because she is half-Feyal, my corpus roses bob to the surface out of the corner of my eye. They grow through the water. If the Queen is aware, she doesn't let on; she coasts her lips to the side of my head.

"I admire you, Isla. But please trust me when I say you will not conquer Death. You must survive by *accepting* Aryahn Kryach. He will take everything, little bride. My son will not thwart him. He is too weak, too indignant. Like his father. No, he will love every moment. Remember these moments, my child. You are already cursed."

I deny her words. I hold fast to the memory of Allysteir in the Skull Ruins, the Corpse King who fought for me, who shared his love of Scathyk, who soothed my skin while his mother did her test—who sensed the depths of my heart when he bit me and devoured my blood.

I did not fear when I removed his mask.

Perhaps I am naïve. But if I have a warrior's spirit, could I be the first to conquer the God of Death?

TWELVE

THE ROYAL SUPPER

ALLYSTEIR

"What the hell are you thinking, Aydon?" I confront my brother when I get him alone after the Feyal-maids have escorted our brides-to-be away.

"Your territory, not mine, Ally," he mocks me and sniggers before adjusting his tunic and collar.

"She's too young, and you know it." I stab my glove at him, understanding how dangerous it is to be in this smaller alcove alone with him. One wrong move, and I could lose an arm bone or more.

Aydon grins. "You believed you were the only one who could have a beautiful, young woman volunteer to be your bride? Oh, right, I suppose your little Isla offered herself to *me* as I was sitting on the throne. Don't forget, little brother, I bear the responsibility of all of Talahn-Feyal since you can't manage to fuck a bride for more than one damned night!"

I clench my phalanges, but by now, I've learned to check my temper when it comes to my blasted brother. More than anything, I wish we could return to my early days as Corpse King when his warfare would consist of shallow pranks with the nobles. A broken bone heals far quicker than our broken brotherhood. And despite how I accepted Kryach's Curse, I still can't blame the bloody bore. Not when the royal family bears their own curse of sharing immortality with me.

Aydon sighs and drops his hands to his sides. "Since Franzyna and Isla are friends, I vow I will treat her well as a bride, Allysteir. If you wish, I will inform Isla of my noble intentions. Nor will I consummate the marriage until she is of age. You could offer me a tip of two in the art of patience when it comes to wooing a woman—apart from pleasuring a fine pair of tits," he chuckles with the snide remark. When I glower and return to my wine flask, Aydon pauses and surveys me, brows lifting in perception. "Why, Ally, good gods! If your corpse could blush!"

I snort and stalk away, but Aydon isn't about to let this go. "You're considering it, aren't you, brother?" He stops me before I depart from the alcove, and I have no choice but to endure. With one snap of his fingers, Aydon could shatter my hand, and it would take all night to piece together. "Mmm, what did her blood and flesh taste like, Ally? How did Kryach find her?"

"None of your damned business," I snarl.

"Fuck! I knew her breasts were a bounty fit for the Isles, but for the God of Death to envy—"

"Careful, Aydon," I warn, injecting Kryach's spirit into my voice and flesh for the second time tonight. It requires less effort with Isla's blood and flesh swarming my being. From the blood-fire wreathing my corpse face and my voice pitching to a low depth, Aydon steps back, eyes widening from shock. "If you dare disrespect my bride again, I will bring the wrath of Aryahn Kryach so viciously upon your coxcomb head, the Isle gods united would not be able to save you."

I pat my brother's shoulder and return to the secondary hall to rejoin the other royals, leaving Aydon alone in the alcove with Kryach's shadow haunting him.

I'm already drunk when Isla arrives for the supper, but my damned cock responds at the sight of her. Damn it all to Kryach's hell, I love her body in her chosen gown. Caught between the world above and my Underworld, the shimmering, earthy gray silhouette of silk and tulle with cascading front panel embroidered in corpus roses flows past her feet in a tempting train. Accompanied by side slits, it showcases her luxurious, creamy thighs. Oh, gods save me!—the pleated fabric halters her bust but parts in a wide berth to display the inner valleys of her abundant breasts. The fabric is nigh-translucent, offering the barest hint of her rouged buds like the sweetest of pomegranate seeds.

All rise before my bride followed by Mathyr.

Kryach salivates in my mind, but I gulp wine to dull my lust and slump into the head throne, doing the bare minimum to acknowledge my bride.

Aydon greets her with a pretentious bow, his mouth rubbing too long on her knuckles. I avoid how his eyes ogle her beautiful breasts before he escorts her to her position. Equal in honor next to me as is the Feyal-Ithydeir way. All brides are granted their due. As far as I'm concerned, they will always be superior; for while Kryach curses me to house him and gifts me with immortality, he has shattered my brides' hearts and devoured their souls.

Mathyr remains the only survivor. Her and Aydon's father's seventeen years are still a mystery.

Isla lowers herself into the throne chair next to mine—one of bones and gold. My cadaverous fingers itch for her ardent palm. With her hair in radiant waves to shower her shoulders, no doubt from the Feyal-maids, she is a banquet for the eyes as the bated-breath of all other royals attests.

Despite my aloofness to my bride, I turn a deathly eye upon the other sovereigns, male and female alike, given my bride's magnanimous heart, and project Kryach's blood fire in a fervent warning: *she is mine!* Impossible to ignore their trespassing stares. But they bow their heads to her while I am an afterthought. They descend to their designated positions.

As if acknowledging my possessiveness, Isla touches my gloved hand. I flinch from her invasion but settle and allow her fingers to tarry. They dare to brush along my arm as if seeking my corpse through my robes and glove. Far too daring. Past brides kept their distance, granted me peace from striving too much. It takes all my resolve not to growl, not to damn near roar from her brazenness!

Kryach invests himself in my chest, his shadow coveting her, threatening to break my body's boundaries as he did during the Bite Offering. Our wedding night, I fear most. One way exists to prevent the Death God from reaping her soul. She must fear and hate me.

"Please, Lady Adayra, would you care to tell us of your family?" Aydon breaks the silence for the benefit of the sovereigns as the Court servants place the first course of bone-broth stew before us. By now, Aydon has informed Isla that messengers have been dispatched to send word to her family as well as her friend's. A minor matter to ease her concerns.

At first, Isla dips her spoon into the broth, no doubt enthusiastic at sampling the Citadel's menu until she lifts her eyes to my brother, flicks them to his Feyal-intended, to Franzy, and responds, "My family hails from Cock-Cross, Your Highness. As does Franzyna's," she includes her friend, who is obviously *half*-Feyal, but I admire Isla's loyalty. "We spent our childhood years together as she must have shared with you."

Aydon nods and reaches for his goblet while Isla spoons the broth. He barely acknowledges his bride-to-be, who shifts in her seat, eyes wandering to Isla. "I hope it will be a comfort to have a kindred friend in the Citadel during your nuptial period, however brief."

I wrinkle my nose.

Isla pauses from her spoonful and trains her eyes on Aydon, but it's another sovereign, the Eylfe King who wonders, "When can we expect the wedding, Lord Aydon?"

Aydon raises his goblet to me, winking because I relinquished all matters to him. For the first time, it's a loathsome regret, but I do not protest when my brother responds, "By the next full moon. It will be enough time to transport Lady Adayra's family to the Citadel."

Out of the corner of my eye, I monitor Isla's reaction. While I expect the color to drain from her face at the mention of such a brief engagement, the roses blush more instead. Kryach licks his lips, huffing, remembering her floral blood scent.

No, I growl internally. *I will not give you her soul!*

He chuckles and informs me, *All souls come to me, Allysteir. As yours will someday.*

Go to hell!

I'm already there, he repeats from the depths of the Void. *You merely carry hell for me, my beloved.*

Please...not her, I beseech him and reach for another flask of wine,

93

ignoring Isla while she traipses her fingers across my sleeve and answers the other royals' questions. Minor ones about her background—an orphan from birth until her given-parents adopted her, her farm—she is far too acquainted with slaying animals, including refters, her interests—dancing, games, growing flowers...I memorize her answers while arguing with Kryach. By now, I've mastered multitasking.

Why should she be any different? Kryach muses and clicks his teeth. *Perhaps this one is strong enough to survive me,* he baits me, tempting. *You could fuck her on the wedding night, spill your seed into her innermost depths, and grant me a portion of her soul. I'll let you keep most of her.*

Stop! I rage while my manhood twitches. Those damnable fingers of hers cross my arm, my wrist, my gloved hand. The warmth of her body. Her ample thighs. Her breasts.

You believed every bride was worthy. You simply believed in Finleigh most. Surrender this one to me, Allysteir. I adore her blood—enough to grant you another year. But you will spare yourself pain for another year if you gift me her flesh.

You know what they say, Kryach, I seethe and wrinkle my nose, driving him as far into the corner of my mind as I dare. *No gain without the pain.*

Isla will not become my mother.

Once I've buried the Death God's shadow, I jerk out of my internal conversation to hear Isla propose a question to the royals, "Could you please share with me the history of the Curse of your bloodlines?" Her eyes gravitate to mine before crossing to the other monarchs.

All pause in their supping, but it's the Wisp-Shee King with his lofty stag crown growing straight from his scalp, who initiates the conversation, "A rarity for a common cayleen to show interest in the history of the gods," he notes with some of his Shee language rising to the surface. A stroke of pride has me sitting upright, but I'm too wine-headed and slump soon.

"Unless you've found yourself as a living footnote in history," retorts Isla with her shrewd tongue, causing all monarchs to pause, surprised by her wit and gumption. All save for me, though I wonder how far her perceptiveness expands while she surveys the sovereigns.

"Yes, we were all quite stunned by your proposal, Lady Adayra," the Inker Queen commends her and picks aside the bones of the fowl appetizer, stowing them in her napkin. No doubt she will rune them later. I tolerate the Inker race more than the Sythe or the Shee.

"Isla, please," she requests, voice soft and respectful.

"And relieved," adds Drakos with a growl, never to be left out of the conversation, "considering Lord Allysteir's dalliance of testing the gods' patience."

"Bite me, Drakos," I quip to the Shifter lion, slurring my words, and raising my wine glass, ignoring his flamboyant mane of a neck ruff.

The Emperor stiffens, but before his alpha temper flares—though he knows I can best him in any battle—, Isla curls her fingers on the back of my hand and interjects, "It must be a relief. After all, my home is close to the Talahn-Feyal Void border, and refters attacked my family's farm and wounded my father two nights ago."

I freeze at her statement, turn slowly in her direction. Was the attack why she came to the Feast of Flesh? Guilt gnaws on me when I consider the Void, my responsibility to stem its tide, and how I tested Kryach by waiting too long. "Isla..." I lift my gloved fingers to her cheek, my chest's pangs growing to her faint smile.

"My father is well thanks to a mender, Your Majesty," she assures me.

"Don't let her cheapen her contributions, Lord Allysteir," Franzyna says, her voice squeaking compared to Isla's strong resolve. "Isla slew the refters who attacked her father, then carried him all the way back home. She will make a strong bride," she adds, lifting her wine goblet to her mouth, but her eyes sharpen against Isla's. I heave a deep sigh, registering the tension between the girls. The last thing I need.

"Hmm...I believe the Queen-to-be bears a spirit as strong as Skathyk herself," Narcyssa expresses from the opposite table's side.

A blush tethers my bride-to-be's lovely cheeks, and my ribs tighten in envy at how she and the Sythe Queen trade glances, their eyelashes fluttering.

My shoulders hunch, and I flare my nostrils because the other Kings and Queens fixate on my bride more than any other in the past. Given the ease with which she amuses them, how her bone-blade wit and beauty win them, I believe I will need Kryach more than ever with this dark, tempting flower...

THIRTEEN
"IS THERE ANY WAY TO BREAK THE CURSE?"

ISLA

I will know them by their crowns.

All unique and individualistic: the Shee King's stag-horned crown grows from his head of dark ash curls. The Inker Queen's of black silver thorns adorns her flaming copper hair. The Sythe Queen's bears blood ruby and black iron spikes. The Eylfe King, undoubtedly the most beautiful man I have beheld, needs nothing more than golden branches. The crystals, shells, and pearls of the Blue-Skin *they* Monarch as they've designated are as chaotic as the oceanic waves they rule.

And of course, the Corpse King's elaborate crown of bones and teeth.

They are too evasive regarding the Curse. The royals single me out, wearing me with their endless questions while Allysteir remains indifferent. And cold. But I can't deny my warmth from the Sythe Queen's declaration.

Long after the dessert course when most of the kingdom has departed, when Franzyna has passed out in her chair, when my human eyelids grow heavy with slumber compared to the immortal royals, who continue laughing and drinking wine, I finally pose the question I've longed to since supper's beginning. "Is there any way to break the Curse?"

All their eyes sharpen against mine. Their jaws turn rigid, postures tightening. Aydon stiffens from the opposite end of the table. Allysteir's hand grips mine in warning, but it's Narcyssa who reproaches me.

"We should all be grateful for the gods' sparing us by cursing monarchs as opposed to the ancient times when they toyed with the races," she implies, her eyes mirroring the blood rubies of her crown.

"But if there was a way—" I dare to continue, remembering Gryzelda's words. If there is a way to survive, to appease the gods, there must be a way to overthrow them.

The Eylfe King interjects, "Such matters should not preoccupy your weary mind, Lady Isla. Instead, you should consider your upcoming nuptials and how to please your soon-to-be mate as well as Aryahn Kryach should he choose to spare you."

I purse my lips and cast my eyes to each of them. I should shut my mouth. I should prioritize my gown, the wedding feast, my family, and a myriad of other bridal duties. But if Allysteir chooses to fuck me on our wedding night, I have less than a month until our union. Barely a month until the full moon to conjure a plan which does not involve the rape of my soul as Gryzelda had warned.

My Nether-mark turns icy at the memory of Kryach's presence on my body when Allysteir fed from me. Spine tensing and muscles tightening from my unchecked curiosity, I can't help but test the royals.

"My Lords and Ladies..." I stand to attention, posturing arrow-straight above their heads, and direct my steel violet eyes on them, ending with my intended husband. "I may not be royal-born, but I believe the gods would not have included an insurmountable challenge to end the Curse to taunt their pawns. So insurmountable, a way has not been discovered since the ancient times when the Curse originated."

The Inker Queen, her eyes as dark and mystical to contrast the whorls of silver magic swirling over her umber skin, declares in a fervent voice, "Do not tread where the gods have forbidden mortals to go, little bride. This is not your affair, nor your burden."

While Allysteir does not rise, his ascot flares, betraying how he must clench one side of his intact throat muscles.

Undaunted, I brace my hands into fists and narrow my eyes. "With all due respect, since I am risking the kiss of Death, I'd say it is my burden. The Void threatens my family and all these Talahn-Feyal lands I hold dear," I conclude, voice resounding. I raise my neck high while contracting my eyes upon Allysteir. Nothing in the world will stop me from loving this land from the highest clifftops of Nathyan Gyheal— these White Ladies—to the deepest pit within their depths.

"Enough, Isla!" Allysteir reprimands, rising to tower over me, his bone crown casting fractured shadows upon my face.

I match his gaze, pressing my lips, furrowing my brows, wishing I could detect his facial expressions behind this mask. "What are you hiding?" I demand, hissing, directing my words to all the royals while never taking my eyes off Allysteir. Imagine I am thwarting him through his mask. *What if I can save you?* I plead in my mind, on the verge of a beseeching whimper.

I shiver when he cups my face, when he sifts his gloved hand into my hair. But he reveals his true purpose when icy shadows lance my chest and drive me to my knees. I shriek from the power force. The other monarchs cackle—except for Narcyssa. Out of the corner of my eye, she regards me with an expectant gaze, as if waiting for me to rise. A lioness as she'd dubbed.

It's her resolve and the prickly chafing of the Nether-mark responding to Kryach's power bidding me to rise. To push my shoulders back, to challenge the Corpse King, the God of Death himself. Vines tickle the soles of my feet beneath my slippers, responding to my emotions. Corpus roses threatening to crack the Great Hall's foundation.

I wish I could make out Allysteir's expression when I stand face to face with him, when the other sovereigns fall silent and hold their breaths.

"As baleful as death as you are, my Lord Allysteir," I say, chin stabbing out, "perhaps this mere Cock-Cross girl has enough life to rise from the ashes. I assure you, Your Majesty, I will never be scared stiff..." I stare him down, matching those skeletal mask-eyes, no doubt an inferno behind the black veils. I don't blink.

Golden branches of his crown shimmering on his perfect face, the Eylfe King stands and ensues the slow-clap of a standing ovation. I detect a hint of patronization laced within the gesture. By the time he's finished, I'm ready to pass out.

Managing to lower onto my throne beside the Corpse King, I listen to the Eylfe King who alerts me, "You have tasted but a sample of Aryahn Kryach's power and bear it well, my Lady Isla. But I believe I may speak for all here when I say: do not test Kryach. He is the most powerful of all gods and is the reason we tolerate Allysteir and his procrastination... to the detriment of our own lands."

Despite my recognition of how the Eylfe King has masterfully insulted and paid homage to Allysteir, I slow-turn my eyes in the direction of my soon-to-be husband. My breath quickens at the notion of his power, but not once does his mask betray anything. Instead, he reaches for another wine goblet and downs it whole.

Narcyssa debates in her smoky, sultry voice from across the table, "One can argue love is as strong as death. After all, I love all my Sytherace and their human gyzdyas, and there are thousands within our land."

I bite my lower lip while her seductive lashes lower to me. I love her native Sythe tongue, how it adds a layer of beguiling spice to words like "gyzdya". One of few Sythe words I know: a host.

"Same as you love nothing," Allysteir grumbles, raising his wine glass to her in a direct mockery. "Death is final. That is the end of it, Narcyssa."

She may not challenge him, but I do, "Death may have the last laugh, my Lord, but it doesn't have the last emotion."

"What?" Allysteir lowers his shoulders, gifting me courage to continue.

I sigh, close my eyes and suck in a deep breath, meeting Narcyssa's eyes while continuing, "After family is gone, love remains. It's why so many mourn at passings. Its power defies death. Strong enough so a mere leaf blowing on the wind can trigger a memory. Or a rose's fragrance. Or the taste of a shortbread cake. Death may strip threads, but love keeps their memory alive." Following my proclamation, I lean against Allysteir's firm shoulder and close my eyes.

"Are you certain she is from Cock-Cross?" chuckles the Blue-Skin sovereign, spiny dorsal fin shuddering from their rolling laugh.

I twinkle a smile, admiring the monarch and their rolling chair decorated in pearls, goldened coral, jewels, and more. They pour a pitcher of water upon themself and sigh from their translucent scales flaring to the surface along with their keen barbs—a pattern they've had to perform throughout the night. The Blue-Skin they and Allysteir are the two sovereigns most respected...or feared. No one fucks with Death. Or the Seas.

When I yawn and nestle deeper into Allysteir's robe, he mumbles, "If you will forgive me, Lords and Ladies," he eases one strong hand beneath my waist, "I will carry my bride-to-be to her chambers. She is weary from the night's events."

How can he—oh, gods! I inhale sharply when he bears me, sweeping me into a bridal hold. All of him is cold as a frosted crypt, but the barest hint of a heartbeat thrums against the side of my body.

Beyond the hair-thin slit of my burdened eyelids, Aydon glances at Franzy and nods, waving to a few court servants, including Feyal-maids. "I have business to address with the royals. Please carry my betrothed to her chambers and try not to wake her. I'll check in on her later this morning after she is well-slept."

Yes, later because dawn has risen despite no sunlight piercing the under-realm of the White Ladies. I purse my lips, wishing Franzy and I could share chambers, but not tonight. In the morning, I'll find a way to get her alone, so we can get her out of the Citadel and beyond the White Ladies. Perhaps Franzy's father can get her passage on one of his ships and...my thoughts skitter through multiple rabbit holes. Each one ends with me never seeing her again.

It's too much for me to navigate. After all the recent events, it's a wonder I haven't passed out.

I peek one eye open to Allysteir thudding open my chamber doors with his boot. Astonishing how he carries me, but as shadows traipse around his robes, I understand it's not his strength alone. A pang of fear arrests my chest, and my adrenaline spikes. What if Kryach doesn't want to wait? Will the God of Death sample my soul now? While my thoughts stray to paranoia, the fear is real enough for me to tremble. But my Nether-mark is still as a sleeping grave. Why?

The King pauses, his corpse mask lowers to leer at me. Through gritted teeth, he snarls, "What the devil?"

He's not looking at me but at the floor where vines bud through the marble. Thorns from several blooming corpus roses harness the ends of the King's robes. He freezes.

"A bone powder machination." Allysteir shakes his head. "Fine joke, Aydon. I'll have a word with him later."

I purse my lips and swallow, squeezing my shoulders. Eventually, he will learn the truth about my floral followers. And my Nether-mark. But I'll delay as long as possible.

Once he lowers me into the bed, I long to pass out. But my guard is up, gripping the bed sheets until my knuckles whiten. The King must notice because his hand wanders to my cheek. I flinch, and he tilts his head to the side. How much does he perceive beyond his mask? I gasp when he leans closer.

"Calm the fuck down, Isla," he commands in an iron voice. "You are not my bride yet. We won't be fucking tonight."

I only halfway relax—enough to calm my breath and remove my slippers while he gathers the heavy blankets around my waist. Despite the burning hearth in the room, it does not chase away the Underworld's bone-deep chill. Will the sunlight ever stroke my face again? Will I ever scent the damp earth as I shift the soil for flowers to grow? I bury my face in my hands and rake my nails through my scalp before hugging my arms around my chest.

"Breathe, damn you!" Allysteir curses with a groan. "I said I wouldn't—"

"You said *we*," I interrupt and arch my neck to hurl daggered eyes at him. "You meant you and Kryach, didn't you?"

He pauses, his macabre mask's unseeing soulless eyes fixed on me.

When he doesn't respond, I press, testing, striving for any trace of the King I met in the Skull Ruins, "How far will it go, Allysteir? Does he share his plans with you? Will he devour my soul in one gulp or will he violate it slowly as you rape my flesh?"

"Kryach will do whatever Kryach will. As I stated at the supper, Death is final, my Lady."

"And you?"

Again, he pauses, but he doesn't answer. Instead, he touches his gloved fingers, featherlight, to my cheek. I suck in a deep breath, clench my hands into the sheets, then release as his glove descends to my throat, to his fresh scar. When his mask dips, I know he is studying beyond the scar, lower to my breasts through the translucent fabric of the gown. No, he won't bed me tonight, but it doesn't mean he won't sample and allow Kryach to feed on his debauchery. I armor myself.

After what feels like hours with his masked eyes frozen upon my flesh, the Corpse King eases the blankets around my neck, leans in to peck my forehead with his mask, and commands, "Sleep, Lady Isla. I will return later and join you in your midday meal."

"Does that mean you'll feed from me again?" I wonder, biting my lower lip, remembering the pain before his venom plunged a fiery need within me.

"Perhaps..." he rises from the bed and taps my nose. "It depends."

"On what?"

"On how hungry I am, how appetizing you smell, and how healthy you are. Don't want to drive myself into a feeding frenzy well before our wedding. I prefer to savor, Isla Adayra. Now, go to sleep. Dream of sweet heather and butterflies."

I part my lips, stunned by his words, an echo of a song Mathyr used to sing when I was a girl. Is it all true? The shadow lullaby? His death shade seeking souls to reap? Will he reap my soul along with Kryach?

Regardless, I have no doubts: the royals are hiding something. I have a month to learn the truth. If there is a way to end this Curse or hope I survive the wedding night.

On his way out, the King's black shroud of robes brushes my corpus roses. Once he's closed my chamber door, I whimper. Because every rose wilts. I fall asleep to their decayed scent.

FOURTEEN
SHE MUST HATE ME

ALLYSTEIR

Kryach is too silent.

Thoughts of Isla plague my head, summon heat to my core, and pain in my jaw from how I've clenched my teeth throughout the night. Never in all my years has a bride irritated me more. Almost as much as the monarchs with their passive-aggressive chastisements, their egotistical bragging, and incessant pestering of my bride. I suppose I should thank them. After all, Isla's curiosity is boundless and the gods will not tolerate a human learning the secret the Cursed do not know.

In the bed, she reminded me of how she'd pressed herself against the skulls with nowhere to run. Cornered prey on the verge of tears but with knuckles so pale because she was prepared to fight...with her teeth if necessary. Prey who turns predator in a heartbeat. Except she could never overpower Kryach. In the past five thousand years since the Curse origin, not one bride has.

He's right: why should she be any different?

Still, no bride has ever challenged the royals. Nor myself. Brides in the past were too fearful of the God of Death. Isla must fear, too.

I huff through my shadows cloaking my figure as I meander Citadel hallways, evading notice.

How I long for the taste of her flesh, her blood scent, her body's warmth, and I imagine the shape of her tears should she ever spill them. Lovely tears I would collect.

"Blood and bones, how she steals my waking thoughts and breath!" I growl into my mask, heaving warm puffs of air to flit away like white-dressed girls.

At least Kryach is far too preoccupied with harvesting souls, I have time before he returns to haunt me. The echoes of his power always remain.

Ignoring Aydon and his political prattling within the hall, I stray beyond the Citadel borders. I've done my part. Isla has done more. Let my brother deal with trade matters, the Nether-market, or any Void issues. My mind may be as sharp if not sharper than his, but I prefer to soothe those edges this way.

It's the one time I do not drink.

Throat thickening, I swallow hard, growling under my breath from the pain, but I hiss and push onward. I need my head clear as I sort out my new bride.

For the next hour or two, my footsteps carry me across innocuous, little corpus bird bones littering the mountain paths until I arrive at the crest of the Raven Skull Bluffs where I linger at the overlook. Here, I survey the Isle of Bones. Unsurprised by the presence of more families since last night was the Feast of Flesh, and the Isle is a popular locale for Ith parents and their children, I pause to observe. Then nod a silent commendation to the little ones who select their first bone. One they will never consume. Whichever they choose becomes a perma-seal and symbol upon their lives—incorporated into their bone rights. I still remember my first: a wishbone I have never shown a single bride.

Perhaps Isla will be my first.

No. I banish those foolish fantasies. Once Kryach learns of Isla's questions, of her unchecked curiosity, he will press me harder to take her on the wedding night. If she cannot be pacified...tempered, I must prepare myself for the pain. Because I won't surrender her.

Nor may I reveal it to her. As far as Isla is concerned, fear must be her default. But I have a feeling it won't be enough this time.

If I long to grant my dark rose another breath, she must do more than fear. She must hate me.

Traveling the mountain avenues into restricted territories, I adjust my shroud and weave the shadow power around myself as a shield. A few onyke scurry about here and there, their thick hands—a contrast to their long, wizened limbs—batting at my robes. An off-bred race of the flesh-eaters, onyke populate the mountains around the Citadel and the lowland hills to the south of Talahn-Feyal. The pesky, little spirits retreat once Kryach's power curls closer to them.

I press the whole side of my lips tight, jaw hardening. Kryach must be harvesting more souls than usual. The explanation for the God's silence, for his lack of torment, considering how much we love the taste of her blood—her flesh so virginal yet ripe as if she could taste new every time. Impossible for humans once bitten. Their human blood is not strong enough to dilute all our Ith venom.

I pause, wincing at the fork in the road. I take the left with its sinister warnings of old skeletal remains dangling from nooses roped to blackwood trees. Bereft of magic on account of the sacrilege of the human addicts, the bones rattle a familiar melody. They stalk me as I descend the winding paths deeper into the heart of the Abhayn Dhunh Mountain—named for a lady in ancient times who lost her lover to refters. I flex my fingers. While Skathyck may be my favorite, I have a soft spot for the tragedy of Abhayn Dhunh who wandered the mountains, seeking the spirit of her lost love until her tears formed a river inside this mountain, a river which curves all the way to the Bone Sea.

When I approach the final cavern hall leading to my secret glen, my thoughts stray to Isla. Perhaps I will bring her here. Snarling, I tense before heaving a sigh of defeat. It was simple to ignore many brides, to observe them sleeping in my bed after they'd cried themselves to sleep. None ever volunteered. None ever longed for me. Nor tempted me from the Bite Offering. Or Kryach. I bristle, banish the image of him devouring my bride.

I arrive at the door. One I constructed with my bone magic and Kryach's. If the refter skulls aren't warning enough, his shadow-essence is. Not to mention how I alone hold the key.

Twisting it inside the hole, I suck sharp wind through my teeth at a familiar wail beyond the skeletal door: they sense me. Pain explodes in my spine, wreathing to the back of my neck, invading my chest cavity, threatening my heart. Throat dryer than bone powder, I remove my mask and push open the door into the hidden valley.

The pain does not fade. I endure it when my lovelies stagger toward me in a wavering dance. My recent feeding from Isla makes me stronger.

"Hello, Aislyn," I greet my 116th bride who sways back and forth—her eyes vacant and unaware of anything, save for my familiar presence.

"Well met, Aoyfe," I add to my thirty-seventh bride.

Once, she was as radiant as her name with curls of splintered sunshine.

Now, a few tufts of white hair grace her pale skull riddled with scars fresh and old. My earlier brides are similar. After Kryach was done with them, their bodies' shell alone remains. These *refter* forms which desire flesh and blood. But Kryach's form of a sick offering Kryach is how their subconscious still acknowledges me, seeks me, craves me. He claims it's charity to let me keep them like this. But it's nothing but a joke—his morbid humor.

"Mayve." I nod to my 392nd bride. She must have got her hands on a fresh onyke, judging by the black blood splatter on her upper chest and the claw marks on her cheeks where strips of skin dangle.

Dozens of my brides shuffle through the bone trees toward me. This valley was my mother's secret before it became mine. An enormous glen inside the mountain of rolling hillsides of gray moss, bone trees grown from the magic of ancient elders, and the River Dhunh flowing to the Bone Sea.

I touch a glove to a nearby bone tree. It sheds powder, ever-growing bark dust. Along with random onykes and corpus birds as well as cronefish in the river, the powder is enough sustenance for my past brides.

My nostrils welcome the scent carries on a shadow on the wind. I smile, scanning the gray hillsides. "Ifrynna," I murmur her name.

To this day, my brides falter and scatter before the enormous spirit Guardian of the Underworld who crests the cliffside where the river disappears, shaking her three skulls in greeting. She snorts upon her advance, her long, skeletal tail scraping its keen bones against the trees and casting bone powder for my refter brides to lap.

"My King," her center mouth proclaims, drifting warm breath from the cracks between her toothy smile.

I reach to stroke her ghost white fur on her back and her massive, muscled hide—translucent to reveal her exoskeleton underneath. "Fairing well?"

"You know how much I love the Feast of Flesh, Your Highness," she acknowledges, her other two bone heads priming their expressions on either side of her, ever alert. "Especially when the little Prince invites other regions. Haunting or intimidating many races is a better treat than catching a Nether-cat, my Lord."

"Roaming back and forth as usual, Ifrynna?" I snigger, remarking on my Nether-tri-hound's ability to trespass into the Void. As a guardian, she is more than welcome, and since this Underworld of the White Ladies boasts of many entrances accessible to guardians or those with god-souls, Ifrynna comes and goes as she pleases.

Ifrynna follows as I wander to the Dhunh River where a few brides hunch over the water to catch a fish with their keen nails or jagged teeth. Wincing, I pause, plagued by memories of Orlayth, Saoyrse, Sinyead, and others—far worse than the pain infesting my corpse.

"You are stronger, Allysteir," comments my Nether-hound, observing me with all six eyes.

I sigh and clench my glove. "You already know."

Next to me, the upper lip of her far-right skull curls back to offer a toothy grin. "The first volunteer since your unfortunate mother raises quite a stir...even in the Nether-Void. Especially when Aryahn Kryach pays the dark realm a visit."

I freeze in my tracks and face Ifrynna. "Kryach?"

"In all his glorious, dark God-flesh." She deadpans.

Blinking a few times, I search the labyrinth of my mind, seeking an explanation, but Kryach's essence and power dwell within me, not his spirit. "Kryach never leaves his Isle-realm, save for the rare occasion when he wishes to torment me in person." Something he does every hundred years or so. Like a tether, he'll summon me through one of the infernal gateways so he may converse face to face. "So, why...?"

When Ifrynna slow-turns her three heads to me, luminescent pupils dilating, a muscle ticks in my one good cheek. All my nerves turn raw. Kryach disappeared the moment after I'd consumed Isla's flesh and blood. I was far too preoccupied with savoring her, confronting my brother, and enduring her questions at the supper to assume anything was different from his usual soul-reaping. Why would he leave his empyrean realm?

"He's been whispering her name within the Nether-Void, Allysteir," Ifrynna says, prompting a tingling in my chest. "Seeking any souls of her ancestors to learn more, my King."

Never in all the centuries has Kryach done such a thing. It means he's showing such interest in my bride for one reason alone. For the first time in history, Kryach wants more than my bride's soul. He wants everything.

Over. My. Rotting. Fucking. Body.

FIFTEEN
"IF ANYONE CAN SURVIVE THE GOD OF DEATH, IT'S YOU, ISLA."

ISLA

At first, I believe it's Allysteir's gloved fingers upon my throat rousing me...until they coil around my neck. They choke me, suffocating my air. My Nether-mark flares, barraging a violent heat along my spine. I thrash in the blankets and open my mouth to scream until a firm hand slams on my lips, forbidding more breath. Tears stream from my eyes which fly wide-open to Elder Kanat. The black capillaries in his skin writhe, pulsing through the surface—evidence of a recent feeding, of his strength.

"You foolish, insipid girl!" he hisses in my face, breath hot as flaming coals.

Whether it's some birth instinct, part of my childhood in an orphanage, or my history battling refters, I don't have a healthy sense of fear. My blooming thorny weapons grow from the floor while I bite Elder Kanat's hand. Hard!

Jerking back, Kanat snarls, baring his honed teeth. A flush of pride rears in my cheeks because blood trickles the backs of his knuckles. Before I can move, Kanat pins me to the bed, straddling me with his long braid thwacking my cheek with its small wishbones. My attack, my struggle spurs him on. I freeze when he mouths my neck above the King's mark. Disgusted, I swallow hard and thrust my face to the side while grappling for air from how he's mounted me. His scarlet robe is a blood moon against the dusky backdrop of the velvet bedspread.

"Did you tell him my lips were on yours?" he demands, purring low. I wrench my neck away. "And my chest vertebra in your hand? My prior claim?" When he thrusts his body harder, I whimper from the pressure. My skin crawls from his lips voyaging to my cheek, his claws digging into my wrists from where he secures them on each side of my head. "Your moan in my mouth?" he finishes, stabbing his hips and something *hard* between my clenched thighs. "I should spoil your virtue now, so you have no choice but to be my bride."

My Nether-mark turns to pure ice. Ignited, I hold back bile and hurl my spit at his face, glorying in his teeth gritting when I dare him, "Go ahead! With the King's venom and Aryahn Kryach's claim on me, the God of Death will never accept another sacrifice from you. Or maybe he'll strip you of all magic or simply strike you dead for interfering with his offering." I wag my brows, triumphant.

Elder Kanat and I match wits—a stalemate of stares. His eyes are darker than ever; the forest transforms to deep green smoke as he squints, eyeing my lips, though his jaw tightens in scorn. I heave breaths and wrinkle my nose, refusing to retreat.

Fear steeps my spine when he opens his mouth and scrapes his teeth along my neck. "Or perhaps I will pit my venom and every ounce of my magic against the King's." He leans in and nips my ear, stabbing his hips deeper. I squirm, slamming my eyes shut. "For what I have planned for you, little Isla," he finishes in a whisper, "I will sacrifice everything."

"Will you sacrifice your blood, Elder?" a familiar voice interjects.

Relieved, I sigh and open my eyes to the Queen herself standing on the side of the bed. A long bone dagger in hand, she presses the blade against Elder Kanat's throat. Behind Gryzelda stands Franzy, her arms squeezing tight to herself. Her amber eyes are heated in revulsion upon the elder.

Out of the corner of his eye, Kanat seethes at the Queen, then turns back to me. I purse my lips but lean back into the pillows as far as possible, putting as much distance between my inner thighs and his member as possible.

His eyes waver, he snorts, and pushes on my hands. The Queen relents, removing her dagger slow, retrieving it once he climbs off me and the bed. She sheathes her dagger at her scabbard fixed to a gold and iron belt around her gown.

I prop myself on my elbows and sneer at the Elder, then stick out my tongue. After tugging on his robes to right them, Kanat sniffs, narrows his eyes on me, and twists his mouth into a glower.

"This isn't over," he finalizes and shoves his way past Franzy and the Queen.

"Run away, you bony bastard!" I taunt, reveling in his low growl before he slams my chamber door.

Franzy rushes to throw her arms around me. "Isla!" I smile and welcome her warmth, her embrace, ignoring how my mouth brushes the Prince's bite mark on her neck. "I came to talk and saw the elder threaten you. I didn't want to risk the soldiers, but the Queen's chambers are next to yours, so I—"

I kiss her lightly on the lips and cup the side of her face in reassurance. "You did the right thing, Franzy. Thank you." I nod at Gryzelda in gratitude, eyes softening while hers do not.

"I didn't do it for you," she announces, her words clipped and predictable. "The last thing this kingdom needs is a Curse-bond broken. You offered yourself with your proposal, and my son accepted your offering. His venom and Kryach's essence circulates in your blood now. It's simple." She juts her chin out, then nods, dismissive while swaying toward the door, but I smirk to one side anyway. She might have a scar of a soul, but maybe it's warming to me. "My son will arrive soon with your midday meal. I suggest you tend your wounds and prepare yourself."

"Aren't you going to tell the King?" I wonder as she departs.

Gryzelda pauses and shakes her head. "No. And this is the last time I help you. If you can't handle a simple elder, how will you survive the God of Death?"

Chewing on my lower lip, I ponder her words and examine my wrists. Huh...I hadn't realized Kanat had drawn blood. When I glance back, the Queen's gown is disappearing around the corner of the closing door.

After I wince from the wounds, Franzy hurries to grab a rag and the basin of water resting on a table in the corner of the room. I beam as she spills some of the water on her way to me.

"Thank you, my bonnya sweet," I say, dabbing at my wrist wounds.

"You're always welcome...leyanyn," Franzy sighs her familiar term of "sweetheart" endearment from our childhood—names we adopted for each other. But melancholy tinges the name. She doesn't face me and applies more pressure to the claw marks, swallowing.

Regret knots in my stomach, and I squeeze my eyes shut. "Listen,

Franzy, I'm sorry. There was a reason I—"

"It should have been me," she interrupts, pressing harder, but I bear the pain because I deserve it. "I was going to volunteer, Isla."

"What?" I straighten from her revelation. My Nether-mark slaughters my back with its ice and heat, alternating so rapid, it leaves me breathless.

Franzy focuses on my wounds, on cleaning them while her auburn curls eclipse much of her face. "I was going to volunteer as Bride of the Corpse King." She pauses, swings her eyes to me. They're wet with tears. "Three of Fathyr's vessels sank, Isla. I didn't tell you because I knew you would try to stop me. And your family's situation was far worse with your father's injuries."

"But the bones—"

"They may have been enough to pay your debt, Isla. Not ours." She shakes her head, eyes glistening. "I never could have expected you to do what you did. I didn't think you were going to make it to the dance. I assumed you'd be spending the night in an Ithydeir prison."

"Elder Kanat was going to—"

"I know what he was going to do," she interrupts again, gritting her teeth and binding strips of cloth around my wrists. "I watched everything from beyond the bridge. I saw the bone he gave you. And I saw you run. I don't blame you, Isla," her voice softens. Heavier remorse weighs down my chest as she continues, "But I was going to help us. I planned to volunteer and wipe both our debts. Then, you plunged into the River!"

She huffs, finishes dressing the wounds, and presses her brow to mine. "They were the longest moments of my life. Waiting for you to surface. I was too late. So, I volunteered for the Prince instead. Once I told him about our friendship, he agreed. And he also said he would cover

Fathyr's debt and arrange for new vessels. And he won't bed me until I turn eighteen. Prince Aydon is...kind."

Pursing my lips, I nod but wonder if it's more than kindness. If he consented so he could learn about me, but I won't crush Franzy's hopes. Not with how she looks at him or how her fingers stray to the mark beneath the transparent gauzy strap of her new gown. The fabric is a perfect shade of deep crimson to accentuate her auburn hair and amber eyes along with the demurer neckline lingering at her satiny gold collarbones.

"At least," her voice cracks, her fingers fidget before they curl into mine so she may finish, "I'll be here. At least I'll get to say goodbye."

I smile softly to the side and roll my eyes. "Come on, Franzy, you know me better. Gryzelda lived, didn't she? I will, too." I posture, adopting the regality of a queen, but my voice is overconfident with the underlining of doubt.

"If anyone can survive the God of Death, it's you, Isla," Franzy offers a feeble response, but her hand weaves around my gown to thumb the small of my back. Her rubbing doesn't soothe the Nether-mark, doesn't pacify it as the Corpse King's presence does. But her words are a balm.

Now, I have the added problem of Elder Kanat. How long before he tries again? And what of the Queen? She's right. If I can't deal with one elder, whether or not he is the most powerful in the land, I won't be strong enough for Aryahn Kryach. I lick my lips, considering an alternative: the King. Surely, I may rely on Allysteir to help me thwart Elder Kanat.

So, I force a smile, clutch Franzy's hands, ignoring the fluttering in my stomach, the heat on my back, and announce, "Come, I need your help. I must look my absolute best!"

SIXTEEN
OH, THE GAMES SHE PLAYS!

ALLYSTEIR

I remain in the shadows and channel Death's power around my being until I am a silent specter. Whether or not I'd prefer to drive my power into Kanat's heart for his audacity of invading my bride-to-be's chambers, better to wait and observe. After his initial protests to her proposal and her revelation of how the Elder had claimed her as a Feyal-bride, more is at stake than my territorial pride...and rage.

Blood thunders in my ears, but I grind my teeth and cool my head which requires far more corpse ice than usual when Kanat rubs blood between his clawed fingers. A sinister smile creeps along his face.

I growl. Isla's blood. I can smell it from here.

If Elder Kanat wasn't so damned respected and renowned in Talahn-Feyal and if he didn't possess the skill to communicate with the Void spirits, I would bring him to his knees now. Suffocate him with Kryach's shadows and demand the truth while he chokes and begs for mercy.

I follow from a safe distance. However formidable Kryach's power,

Kanat is the highest elder. It would be foolish to launch a direct attack if he is communicating through Void portals, whispering to the spirits, seeking answers to Isla's heritage. I remember his reference of having knowledge of her background. Vengeance kindles my veins to pulse, my muscles to quiver. What could he want with my bride?

Whatever the case, I'll protect her. Aside from me, no one will ever hurt her.

A fresh wave of hunger ransacks my corpse. With my other brides, I was able to pace myself following the Bite Offering and endure longer periods between feedings. Now, I yearn to bury my teeth in her neck again.

I am yours, Corpse King.

Yes, every scrap of her sweet rose flesh belongs to me. Later, she will gift me her heart but only after I break it. My breath catches from the thought, my insides warming, but I banish all thoughts of Isla and channel fury instead.

Embracing bloodied rage, I direct it to hover around me, masking me in shadows while following Kanat to the lower recesses beneath the Citadel of Bones. To the various tunnels—some used for storage, others for sewers which lead to a mile-long drainage system and reservoir near the Bone Sea. Some halls are reserved for servant cemeteries. Thousands of Feyal and human servants lie buried in these catacombs: a position of due prominence for their service, though not honor. Sole gravesites like the Hall of Heroes or the Royal Tombs guarded by dragon bones hold such esteem.

My bones hum from the collective power force within these halls.

At least it doesn't take much to keep pace with Kanat. As Ifrynna had observed, I am stronger. Pain lessened. Not from drink since I haven't embarked to the kitchens. I'd planned to check if Isla was awake. A detour below the Citadel was not in the agenda. I bite back a curse at Kanat keeping me from her.

He progresses down another staircase, paying no heed to the onyke eyes glowing in the darkness like sharp points of swords. Bone powder showers the air, and the elder mumbles a common chant. A meager torch's light fills the descending hall.

I travel by shadow.

At the base of the staircase, Kanat pauses to glance over his shoulder. Squints as if he senses my presence. A smile curls my mouth because he would never dare ask, nor confront me.

Above all, Kanat is a cockroach. He's clawed his way from a common Feyal birthright. No noble lord birthed him. His half-bred status—a byproduct of an Ithydeir mother and a human father—caused upheaval among the elite elders when they had no choice but to induct him after he'd passed the annual Elder Rites. An enigma time has not revealed other than one explanation: Kanat was a prodigy. He's labored more than any elder to excel, challenged himself with the most powerful of the nation's bones—save for the ones Aydon and I carry.

It is no surprise to learn of this secret shrine in the deep pits beneath the Citadel. A shrine and an unmarked tomb where skeletons slumber in the body-sized gaps in the walls. No coffins. No crypts. These are not honored dead. Our Ithydeir race would never leave corpses unburied unless...

While Kanat fetches a skeleton and prepares his altar in the center of the chamber, I drift to the far side of the room where the other remains are housed. As if sensing my chill, the elder shoots his head, long braid swinging to the left. When his eyes flick in my direction, I hold my breath, strengthening my power. Annoyed, I stiffen my jaw. Eager for the challenge, part of me yearns for him to confirm my presence with bone powder. One simple chant. But I'd rather learn his plans for Isla's blood.

Elder Kanat returns to his preparation while I examine the skeletons. Tensing, I seethe, understanding why they are unmarked, but I do not break my shadow shield. Refter bones. He's not communicating with the spirits of the ancestors. He's using black Nether-magic to communicate with the gods!

Glaring and strengthening my shadow force, I face the altar when Kanat wipes Isla's blood upon a skull. Fire ignites the candle wicks protruding from the skull eyes and mouth. Black magic and enduring truth. One spark, and the altar will flame from the oil baptizing it. On the edge of the altar is a pouch Kanat fetches. I lift a brow, curious until he sheds his robe, his outer tunic, his underclothes until he is naked as a mole rat. Fitting. However, I didn't expect his limbs and torso to be lean. Not with all the consorts he feeds upon which should fatten him.

He tips the bone pouch into his hand, then smears his skin with the powder. Protection from the fire. Kanat retrieves something from his carmine robe and scatters it upon the skeleton: a few strands of silver and flame hair. No doubt confiscated when he'd invaded her chambers.

I'll kill the knave with my bare bony hand!

Kneeling before the altar, Kanat crosses his arms over his chest, closes his eyes, and opens his mouth to recite:

"Gods supreme beyond the world of Nether

Heed my prayers and offering unstained

Grant to me your power of aether

And the secrets of the isle-bride explained..."

He sets the altar on fire. It ignites into a towering inferno, harnessed by god power. At once, their spirits gush into the chamber, surrounding it. Their collective power shakes the cavern walls and upsets the skeletons.

Bones crash and topple to the floor, but they hardly matter compared to the gods' presence. My stomach churns. For while I may be able to hide from Kanat, I cannot hide from the gods.

Until another invades my being and eclipses me in his supremacy, which transcends all the lower gods. Yes, lower. The Highest angyl Goddess and the demon God are not present. Aryahn Kryach and one other are High Gods.

As much as it pains me, I bite any smart remarks, remind myself I'm here for my bride, and muster a wincing, *Thank you.*

Kryach sniggers in my mind. *It's been fifty years since you last spoke those words to me, Allysteir. Rest assured, you won't wait long before you speak them again.*

I don't respond. Not when Kanat arches his neck, braid spilling like corded ink along his spine. Reverent, with tears in his eyes and arms crossed over his chest, he gazes at the spirits of the lower gods and opens his mouth to beseech them, "Infinite spirits and prime forces, is she the one?"

My breath surges from my nostrils. The Mallyach-Ender.

Bathed in the omnipotent flames of the still-burning inferno, Morrygna, the Goddess of Doom,—responsible for sending her large-breasted Ban-Sythe ghosts to haunt laundry-washing mothers with their mournful dirges—drifts toward the elder. Other than Aryahn Kryach, the Feyal-Ithydeir and humans bring their gifts to her shrine most. Bless her with offerings of bird bones, owl eyes, raven wings, seeds, and cups of breast milk.

I roll my eyes at Kryach's internal lewdness, considering his annual mating with her upon the Night of Masks in the dead of winter. Her floor-length hair of fateful crow wings rivulets in mid-air as she hovers over the elder in nothing but a dark and tattered robe open to her luxurious dark flesh marked with runes—silver and luminescent as the moon.

"Kanat, son of Caoymhe," Morrygna cites his Feyal-mother's name, her eyes of burning starlight causing the elder to shrink. "You bring us the blood of ruin. Of doom."

When the goddess casts her dark and silver smoke of the contrasting faces of the moon into an unbreakable circle, my gut clenches. My throat turns dry as winter bones from the mirror she creates. It casts a vision of my bride. Naked and bound with ropes woven over her breasts and lower regions with her back on a cold, stone altar. Her hair splays all around her head like a halo of hellfire and Isle-light. Thunder pounds in my ears from the blood between her thighs staining the altar in a sacrifice.

Morrygna shifts the smoke in the mirror to the image of Kanat standing above my bride with a scyan in hand.

Steady, Allysteir, Kryach coos in my mind when I'm on the verge of snarling. Of roaring when Kanat leans in to kiss my bride while scrawling her sex blood over her flesh in black magic symbols as she trembles, as tears glisten upon her cheeks. Not once does she whimper, nor beg. Rage clouds my vision when he brings the scyan to slit her throat and spill her blood like she's nothing more than a ripe lamb.

The vision disappears.

The lower gods nod in assent as Morrygna permeates the room with her smoke and addresses Kanat, "If you wish to spare your world the downfall to come from our wrath and take your place amongst our Isles, then you will perform everything as you have seen. On the Nyche na Maysc, you must sacrifice the Nether-marked one to the lower gods when her mortal blood flows. You will then be worthy of a celestial seat."

The Night of Masks. Less than a year away.

What did she mean by Nether-marked one?

Aryahn Kryach says nothing. Does nothing. He observes his lover Goddess of Doom plot to rob him of my bride. Of his bride soul according to the Curse. *Why Isla?*

The God of Death remains silent in my mind as the lower gods evanesce.

Kanat raises his head to Morrygna and declares, "I will obey according to your will, great Goddess."

Before he can speak another word, Morrygna and the pillar of fire disappear, plunging the chamber into utter blackness. Without hesitation, I flee the pits and don't stop until I reach the secondary hall where I collect one of many masks I have stashed.

By Kryach's cursed soul, I will not allow such a vision to be fulfilled!

Yes, Isla undoubtedly knows I am the one from the Skull Ruins. But it doesn't mean I'm ready for her to view beyond the mask. Not when Kryach gifts me with the barest restoration for the bounty of her flesh and blood.

Is that why you whispered of her into the Nether-Void, Kryach? I demand in a snarl, my muscles quivering in the kitchens as a servant prepares a meager bounty of fruit, lean pork cuts, curds, barley loafs, sweet wheat scone, and honey milk for Isla. And one other singular treat. *Did you know, you damned devil?*

While I wait, the God of Death offers nothing but a deep chortle.

I'll kill Kanat before I let him lay a finger on her. And I'll kill myself before I let you take her. I'll fucking walk into the Void and rattle the bloody Isle gates until all the lower gods shatter my soul! Then, see how you play your damned God games without my flesh to stick to.

He growls a solemn warning in my mind, but I accept the tray from the servants.

My bride is waiting. It's time for our games to commence.

But the moment I kick her chamber door open with my boot, I nearly drop the tray.

Kryach laughs!

Never in all my centuries has a bride managed to prompt more than a smirk or a snigger from Kryach. Nothing like this.

"Hello, my King," Isla utters in a voice as sweet as a honey lotus but seductive and predatory as a wanton Sythe in heat.

Damn it all to hell!

"Bloody angyls and sacred demons!" I curse and kick the door closed as fast as possible before anyone can see. "What the devil are you doing?" I raise my voice and set the tray on the nearest surface. It teeters on the edge of the cushioned ottoman, but I could care less.

"Not the devil," she responds, silk-wrapping her wit as I stalk toward the bed where she lies. "At least not yet," Isla concludes with a wink but doesn't move a muscle. For good reason.

Kryach foams at the mouth at the sight of her angelic flesh. Fresh-charged blood rockets into my member. Roses, corpus roses, caress the surface of the bed, and upon them, she rests.

Utterly naked.

A few lingering blooms she's strategically positioned over her breasts and sex along with tresses of her fire-lined silvery hair. But with how much she's gasping, chest heaving, the blooms are precarious at best.

She is exquisite...ethereal. A banquet of tempting flesh I would love to sink my teeth into. Her blushing cheeks and ripe breasts were designed for my hands to cup. Her luscious lips and even the soft plumpness in her belly and thighs I adore. If a corpse could blush, all of me would turn red as currants at the sight of her body.

Slowly, she smooths a hand along her skin from her throat and downward, easing across dark crimson petals. Until her fingers traipse across her left breast, palm teasing and tantalizing by sliding the blooms away but covering the rouged buds without offering the slightest of peeks.

"I thought you might appreciate a sample before the wedding, Allysteir." She smiles and mimics her previous movement with her other palm, smile spreading because she's caught my barest muscle twinging in my cheek. The mask, my betrayer. "After all, forbidden pleasures are the sweetest, are they not, my future husband?" she challenges.

Void, take me! I suck a deep breath of resolve, then turn, gathering all my strength.

She knows how to play the game better than you, Allysteir, Kryach laughs again, mocking me.

We will see. I adjust my mask. Without turning back to her, I chuck the bedspread over her. Petals scatter and cast their fragrance to tickle my nostrils.

Next, I fetch the tray and carry it to the dining table. Out of the corner of my eye, Isla threads her brows low. Puzzled, she weaves the blanket around her frame and approaches. I may have been unprepared at first for this Scarlet Skathyk. But I will never underestimate Isla again.

And I will plunge a bone blade through my damn rib cage and into my heart if Kryach so much as breathes on her.

SEVENTEEN
FORBIDDEN FRUIT

ISLA

"Did you know pomegranates did not originate from Talahn-Feyal?"

Allysteir cuts off the crown's ripe fruit. I imagine he's simpering beyond his mask. Mouth twisted into a part grimace due to his mangled face. It was wishful thinking for him to take my bait. Not that I would have minded if he'd had.

"They came from the god Isles," I proudly define, back straightening. Warmth radiates throughout my body, and the blanket nudges lower to expose my cleavage. I beam at him. Flutter my lashes.

If the King notices my action, he doesn't betray himself unlike when he first stepped into the room. Oh, I didn't need his mask off to detect the telltale rise and fall of his chest beneath his robes. Or the way he'd tensed, the mask popping to betray his cheek muscle.

If the Corpse King is attracted to me, if he's tempted, perhaps the God of Death may be tempted, too. Or conquered.

Allysteir wags the knife before slitting the sides of the pomegranate, marked by their white walls. "Should have expected a farm girl to know. Yes, my grandmother, my father's mother—the eighth Corpse King bride—her soul pleased Kryach, he granted her one favor."

I lift my brows, awed. A favor from the God of Death is no small matter. Listening, I track his movements, marveling at how smoothly he slices the fruit, given how half of him is a corpse, but I imagine five hundred years of living like one has afforded him much practice.

I blush from how he coddles the fruit, massaging it to segment it until he exposes the fleshy innards of ripe pomegranate seeds—broken by the pale center pulp. My mouth waters. I'm panting. Pomegranates are reserved for the elite underneath these five mountains.

"She could have asked for anything. Kryach would have granted her a soul roused from the Nether-Void itself. But my grandmother requested a piece of the Isles. A celestial boon as it were. She believed he would gift her with a star. And in a way...he did," he confirms after digging out the ghostly center, opening the fruit to a burgundy star-like flower, gushing its rich, sweet perfume into the air.

Eager for the offering, I part my lips, lurching until Allysteir wags a gloved finger back and forth. "Patience is a fruit, too, Isla."

I nudge my lower lip out in a pronounced pout. He chuckles, turns the pomegranate upside down, and knocks his knife hilt against the skin for the seeds to scatter into a golden bowl. Like gleaming ruby drops, they tumble. I thread my fingers to resist the urge to pounce and bury my face in the bowl. Careless of whether the blanket would pool to the floor. Heat colors my neck and cheeks, but my Nether-mark is still.

"It's an ancient belief that this fruit can indeed cure a broken heart."

Pensive, I tilt my head to the side, wondering if the vital muscle's beat is visible through his ribcage. "Is your heart broken, Allysteir?" I wonder softly.

"Everything about me is broken, Isla," he states but offers no glimpse behind the robes or the skeletal eye mask.

More patting the fruit. More delectable seeds spill from its bosom. "My grandmother ate six seeds from the resplendent fruit, then planted the rest along the western banks of the Isle of Bones where the water is warmest. Perhaps I will take you there." He finishes tapping, though a sprinkling of rubied nubs still nudges the inner skin.

I lean forward, but Allysteir covers the bowl with his palm, delaying me again.

"My King!" I moan, my mouth watering from the tantalizing fruit echoing of Eyleanan, and squeeze my eyes shut, gushing breath.

"First, you must know, my bride-to-be." He taps one gloved index finger along the bowl's edge, tempting.

I open my eyes to the vacant corpse orbs, hungering for what lies beyond the mask. My fingers ache to strip it from his face as I did in the Skull Ruins, to share something real between us. But real must be earned. My Nether-mark is my mask. The irony. He will earn mine when I've already stolen his.

"Isla." Allysteir lifts the bowl, rises, circles the table to stand before me.

Cheeks burning, I hold my breath, clench the robe to my chest, raise my chin, and expose my neck in a subtle boon. "Corpse King?"

He sighs, chin lowering, but he doesn't move the bowl toward me. "Your word is true. Forbidden pleasures are indeed the sweetest. I cannot touch you, nor claim a kiss until we are wed.

"There has never been a bride tribute such as you. The only one who ever truly volunteered was groomed for the life, offered as a sacrifice by the nobility. Aryahn Kryach...is pleased with you, Isla. Your flesh, your blood."

I beam, convinced I'm about to burst into flames. Hellfire ones. I creep a hand toward the bowl, to the fleshy seeds shining like dragon scales. But Allysteir tugs the bowl out of my reach.

"Allysteir!" I loose an anguished breath.

"Isla..."

He strokes a glove across my cheek to my lips, but I nip the tip, my teeth discovering bone and not finger. I grin through clenched teeth.

The King sighs, retrieving his finger, then taps my nose as if scolding a child. I pout playfully, but he bends at the waist until his brow touches mine—his skull mask black eyes haunting. I lose all breath and freeze.

"Aryahn Kryach does not offer the bounties of the heaven freely. This is Kryach's fruit. If you eat of this, you must accept his shadow mark."

The smile I'd donned from Kryach's pleasure and mine and Allysteir's banter dissipates at the mention of the price. At first, I pause, about to ask dozens of questions, but I've lost the will to speak. The King brought this fruit. To our first meal before we are wed. Forbidden fruit. Like my forbidden flesh.

It leaves me with only three questions.

"What does it mean, Allysteir?" I whisper.

He places his gloved fingers underneath my chin as he had on our official meeting. Tender. Soothing. It reminds me of the time in the garderobe. "It means you may never leave the Underworld beneath Nathyan Gyeal. The White Ladies will be your new and last home. And as you know, if the God of Death does not reap your soul when we consummate the marriage, your life, your soul will be bound to mine. An immortal Feyal-bride. A Queen."

My lips part. A stunned breath flees my mouth.

A Queen under the mountains. Forever.

Did every bride who survived accept the shadow-mark, including Gryzelda? No. All the Feyal-Ithydeir royals, including their direct family, become immortal. But not their brides. They simply achieve a longer life-span as all Feyal-brides.

I seek more clarification, cautious. "The only way to end my life, our lives would be to surrender our souls to Aryahn Kryach."

"Yes. Provided Kryach is appeased after our wedding, you may never leave here. Your life will only end if and when mine does. And your soul is bound to mine. For all eternity," he solidifies without missing a beat.

Does he even possess a heart?

I flick my eyes to the bowl of celestial fruit. I lick my lips. Then gaze at Allysteir's mask. My lower lip trembles with the knowledge. It means Franzy will grow old. Her soul will be her own—free to join her ancestors in paradise. And she may leave the mountains, travel the world as she's always longed while I...I will never see sunlight, my family's farm, the tickling grass, the stars...

I will be a prisoner of the God of Death. Of the Corpse King.

I purse my lips and ask my second question. "Allysteir...why did you save me in the Skull Ruins?"

Does he blink behind the mask?

"Ahh, I wondered if you would raise the question. My power is not exactly inconspicuous. And if you caught my parietal skull bone, it left little doubt as to my identity."

I swallow any urges to tell him the truth. Not yet. Not now.

He breaks from me to pace, and I release the breath I've been holding. Relieved he doesn't suspect I peeked.

The King's robes cast a deep shadow upon each pass, the seeds swirling in the bowl to rouse their fragrance as he continues, "Nor do I fault you for running off after I passed out. I never could have conceived in my wildest dreams you would volunteer.

"Perhaps you may believe I am damned. A monster. Heartless, even." He turns his mask to me from the side where I'm bathed in his darkness. Kryach's shadows curl beyond my blanket, weaving around my flesh like cold, black feathers—tempting me, beckoning me, summoning me. Despite my swelling chest and my flesh prickling, I set my jaw and refuse to shiver. Refuse to give the God of Death a foothold. He will never earn me.

Allysteir unleashes a deep exhale. "Every song, poem, book, legend considers me a heartless demon as all Corpse Kings. Nor will I afford you any inkling for your suspicions. Nothing but the coldest, hardest truth, my Isla. I mean to keep you here with me. For all eternity. Or until we wish for Death to claim our bound souls so we may travel the afterlife together. The most I can offer you is a crown, every jewel in my kingdom, Kryach's protection to roam this Underworld, and above all..." he trails off, and I almost gasp when the shadows wrap my chest in a shade of a claim. A deathly omen. Kryach touching what is forbidden before the wedding.

"Above all?" I arch my neck, parting my lips, waiting with bated breath. Will he say his heart? Love? I don't think I'm quite ready.

"Truth," he concludes, advancing toward me.

My stomach flutters at the thought of his hand beneath my chin, but instead, he sinks to one knee. Oh, gods!

He takes my palm in his, rubs his cold-bone mask lips upon my knuckles, and proclaims, "Death cannot lie, my Lady. I have secrets to

133

fill the seas, and I will love the opportunity to spend our lives revealing them to you. You will tremble. You will fear. You will break, my dark rose. But you will know such truth as you have never known. And..." his breath cleaves and heaves through the mask, his robes shifting to betray the effort of his words. "Beauty, Isla. For only in the realms of death is there beauty to make the gods in their golden Isles envious."

My heart howls in my ears. Somehow, I contain my gasping gushes. I clench my fingers—the ones in his hand—so I don't rip off the mask here and now. I lower my eyes to the fleshy jewels in the bowl. My tongue screams for the fruit, for the burst of sweet, bold juice of my namesake.

Why do I long for it so much? Do I not have the strength to resist this forbidden territory? Resign myself to a lesser fate as a Feyal-bride and a longer lifespan as a human to own my soul—however haggard and ruined after Kryach is done. It will be mine. I will dance with Franzy's spirit in the afterlife.

Unless this is the only way I may survive Kryach. Lose my soul's freedom to save it.

I open and close my mouth, but my heart doesn't sink from this truth. My appetite is not lost. No, it's more ravenous than ever. Ravenous for heaven and hell. For the temptation of the Isles. Ravenous for the secrets Allysteir spoke of. The beauty. This truth.

If love is as strong as Death, I must believe it lives in this deep darkness. Perhaps this is not simply my undoing. Instead, it will be my glorious redoing.

I avoid squirming when the Corpse King cups my cheek, brushing one tear I hadn't realized was there. He raises the bowl till it's in line with my chest. "You have only one chance to accept this gift, Isla."

A gift, I breathe and purse my lips, lifting my fingers to hover. They tremble above the bowl. I meet his mask eyes. Could the Corpse King himself be a gift? Not once does the Nether-mark stir. It offers me no warning. It does not haunt my flesh.

In one last act of desperation, I grip his gloved hand, battle my bone-dry mouth, and plead, "Let me see your eyes. Please. Just your eyes."

He doesn't move a muscle, a bone, or a single thread of his dark robes. My heart bleeds, aches, begs for the siren seeds singing into my hovering palm. But first, I must know. His eyes were closed when I'd removed his mask. If I surrender this, surrender my soul to couple with his, he must grant me something: a truth shown and not spoken.

Finally—after infinite heartbeats—Allysteir edges his mask lower till it touches the bridge of his nose to confess his eyes. One is glassy, vacant—hollow, and white as a ghost with withered skin and darkest shadows surrounding it. Cracks and black veins skitter upon his skull. But the other...oh, I sample the beauty in the realms of death he referenced. That lone eye is an orb of pure gold encircling a twilight speck. Gold as sacred treasure, as sunlight. Whenever I desire the sun, I will find it again. In the Corpse King's eye.

"Forever," I utter and nod, biting my lower lip when he blinks, then slides the mask into place, molding it to his face.

My fingers no longer tremble. I sink them into the pomegranate seeds, clutching six scarlet stars, mirroring the King's grandmother. Before I raise them to my mouth, I press my lips into a mischievous smile and joke, "Unless I'm the Mallyach-Ender, of course."

I place the seeds on my tongue. Close my eyes. Burst them between my teeth. Once the sweet, tart flavor soaks my tastebuds, I seize the bowl from Allysteir's hands, and like the damned, greedy bitch I am, I bury my mouth inside and devour every last glorious ruby gem.

EIGHTEEN
DID YOU JUST GIVE THE GOD OF DEATH A NICKNAME?

ALLYSTEIR

I didn't believe she'd accept. And never this soon.

While she licks the bowl with the juice staining her luscious lips and the upper slopes of her breasts and chest, I strive to dismiss how she referenced what the High Gods whisper—the Mallyach-Ender... the Curse-Ender. I put my mouth to her neck, wait for her to nod and arch to welcome me, and sink my teeth inside her flesh for Kryach to mark her.

Isla throws her head back and slams her eyes shut but does not scream. She snaps her teeth. Hisses a tempest. Then licks her lips to savor the Isle-fruit feast while I embark upon my Isla-feast, luxuriating in her flesh juice, marveling at its rapture. As if *none* of my venom has ever touched her.

She is the first dream the stars ever blessed the world. And the deadly point of a blade thrust into the fire. An autumn rose biting through the ice of winter and surviving till the spring thaw. No other bride ever accepted the mark. Not even Finleigh.

Once her warmth engulfs my being, Aryahn Kryach roars his Death chant. His shadow power whorls all around us, his wind disturbing the blanket till he exposes the angyl-wing flesh of her legs to her thighs.

Inside my mind, I growl while lapping her sweet blood, ravaging a thread or two of flesh. His shadows coil around her legs, roaming, seeking, and hunting for the perfect location for the marking. She doesn't unloose herself. No, she stiffens, locking herself. I snigger and lash my tongue upon her shoulder wound.

Good girl. Make him work for it. I press my lips, stained in her blood, to her neck.

"Allysteir..." she whispers low and beauteous and drops the bowl. It clatters to the floor, droplets splattering. She arches her neck. For me. Thrusts out her chest. *So sweet.*

A godly snarl invades my head from her gesture. *Hmm...it's rare for Kryach to express jealousy. But I won't let him rob us of these moments.* While Isla's blood trickles down the curve of her shoulder in a tiny stream to disappear beneath the blanket, my mouth lingers upon her pulse. It flutters like a trapped bird.

When Kryach's vagabond shadows rove along her spine, she gasps and arches her back, but I steady her. Swallowing her flesh and blood remnants, I wonder what she's pondering behind her closed, deep-set eyes—those long lashes, comely and dark. Infinite thoughts and images swirl in my head. Her dancing amidst the pomegranate trees. She'd pick as many ripe fruits as she desires. *Oh, all the places I could bring her!*

Again, Kryach growls. I shudder because he echoes my statement. A taunt of the riches of the Isles he would show her. But it's impossible for anyone not god or god-spawn to enter the Isles. Or *touch* the gates.

For now, I trace my tongue along her exquisite shoulder curve. I lick the blood. She moans whether from pain or pleasure or both, I can't possibly tell. Her lips have parted slightly, but her eyes remain closed as if she's memorizing every moment. *Sweeter.* I brush my ruined mouth upon each of her eyelids, cherishing her whimper, how she trembles and pants.

By now, Kryach's shadows have worked their way into her wild waves, scattering them around her neck and shoulders. But I study those blood droplets along her arm, blanket swallowing them.

"Oh!" shrieks Isla when the God of Death's shadows invade her mouth, prompting her to tip her head back, granting me more access to her skin. As if Kryach longs to sample her early, to break his own boundaries, his law writ in the Isles.

Awed, I gaze at my bride-to-be. No bride in history has ever *tempted* the God of Death. Never before the wedding.

His shadows nuzzle her throat, her collarbone. They linger on my teeth mark before descending to her cleavage. Isla clenches tighter. *Yes, my dark rose. You know you are truly mine.*

A snap of God teeth in a direct threat—wrathful but empty. Once my gloved fingers touch the blanket's edge, she softens. Eyes not opening, she allows me to ease the velvet past the curve to the bloody line weeping down her arm. Scarlet fruit juice dampens her skin along her chest. It lingers in the crease of her cleavage, enticing.

She lowers her chin to me. In response, one lone shadow voyages to her pomegranate juice-stained lips, but she presses them. She forbids Kryach from entry. The God seethes. Cold and deathly, his shadow collars her throat. Another empty threat. Instead, she murmurs my name.

Blood and bones!

My hands ache to touch her long, fair legs where the blanket barely covers her lower regions. I can't possibly call them her nether-regions; nothing about her mirrors the cursed world.

Fully aroused, my cock barrages the boundary of my breaches—uncomfortable but nothing I haven't battled. A familiar war I've waged. And will wage again. Because Isla deserves to be worshipped like the Queen she will become. A beautiful irony how worship can exist in the same territory as torture. A territory, an *art* form I have mastered. I learned from the best.

The blanket sinks to expose her right breast: a full, white, floral offering with a single blood-rubied pomegranate seed resting atop her rouge, pebbled nipple. I fear I will defy Kryach. A threadbare crack in his law. An enmity of fire swirls in my stomach. Will I pay the price of his fury? In all my five hundred years, no bride has ever proven... irresistible. Obsessed with the image of the lone, piquant seed upon her ripened bud, I contemplate her forbidden fruit.

I don't deserve this.

Hesitating, I crane my neck to my bride-to-be. She sighs through her nose, tipping her head to the side, wincing from the pain in her shoulder. Of course, she knows the blanket has fallen. Desire exhibited, her fingers tiptoe across her throat. Death's wary shadows hover, his presence curling cold air across her breast to rouse the tantalizing tip. A silent, dark dare. Because my pain, my *punishment* is his pleasure.

For the third time, my name escapes her lips, covetous. I raise my eyes to Kryach's mark forming. Death encroaches in my mind. *We must go now or we will be late.*

I cage the howl to the recesses of my mind, not granting him any emotions. Death sniggers. He always gets the last laugh. After adjusting my mask, I retrieve the bone powder pouch stashed at my belt. Isla opens her eyes in time to find me opening it.

Intimate magic broken, she sighs and covers herself with the blanket.

Grunting, I blow the bone powder upon the fresh hurt in her neck, then chant a common Ithydeir healing rite. Isla grits her teeth. She gasps from the flesh and skin sealing until any trace of my teeth has vanished. Only the first mark.

And Kryach's. I glower.

Rising, I jab a gloved finger to the silver tray on the table, discarding the fallen bowl. "Eat and drink. You must recover your strength following my feedings."

"But the mark—"

From behind the mask, I wince, posture tightening. "See for yourself." I offer a gloved hand to her and draw her to the mirror. She will be too weak to stand on her own feet.

Isla accepts, but I furrow my brow, puzzled by the strength in her limbs. I'm baffled by her steadfastness when she abandons my hand and crosses the steps to the mirror.

Impossible.

After the Bite Offering, multiple menders had tended to her, replenished her blood force, but her knees were still weak. Now, she's stronger following a *second* bite. Bone powder only restores the skin and flesh—not the blood. With a single pomegranate as her only food today, Isla should not be standing. I expect her to pass out at any moment.

Straying to the mirror, I appear in the reflection, my chest at her back where her heat ravages me apart from the blanket shrouding her lower spine. My breath catches when she rubs one side of her neck and tosses her silvery hair from her flushed cheeks and neck to examine the shadow ink imprinted in the center of my first bite mark. Upon the side of her lovely throat. Inside the hollow eyes of the *skull*, blood-fire wreathes—ever-shifting with its power scarring her soul—now coupled to mine.

"I didn't even feel it!" she gushes.

"You wouldn't. Death is silent. He offers no warnings. Nor does he cause pain." *On the contrary, he ends it,* I don't add.

She traipses one finger across the mark, traces its outline, and flinches—startled when the skull opens its mouth as if to nip her finger, playful. "Now, now, *Ary*," she scolds and flicks the mark's caved-in indent where its nose should be.

"Did you just give the God of Death a nickname?" I ask, stupefied as she traces the live skull, too fascinated.

"A skull?"

"What?" I snort. "Did you expect a sickle?"

"No, it's..." she trails off, smirks, blushing more until I swear her cheeks house wineskins. "With your bite mark around it, it reminds me of a corpus rose. See?" She traces her lithe finger around the outline. "Your teeth prints are the petals."

Fuck!

Emotion—a chaotic whirlwind of raw torment and unchecked pride—clogs my throat. I swallow hard. It will take all my resolve, strength, and power to keep myself from her on our wedding night. To force her hatred until she learns to fear me, to fear him within me. Until then, I'll exult in every damned second!

Dumbfounded by this whole morning, I turn and walk away, unsurprised when she follows. Isla flits to my side as I embark toward her chamber door and inquires, "Where's your mark?"

I freeze in my tracks, turn my mask to her. Equal parts incredulous and amused by her adorable naivete. "Seriously?"

"Oh, right." She bites her lower lip, flustered. Then flutters those long lashes at me. "Where are you going?"

"Business."

"Death business?"

"Yes."

"Can I come?" She squeezes her shoulders together in a more adorable beseech.

I pause. Cock my head. Gape at her behind my mask. No brides were ever interested in my Death business. Isla bewilders me. In one morning, in one fucking hour, she's accepted Death's shadow mark, given him a nickname, and now she wants to accompany me to the Hollows. I remember how Aydon informed me of how she'd plunged into the Cryth River, struggled through the souls until they'd deposited her on the dais itself. I reflect. Conclude: Betha's doing.

Yes, Isla deserves a proper introduction to my Ban-Sythe guardian.

Shoulders slumping, I unclench my hands I hadn't realized turned to fists, then heave a sigh. "How soon can you ready yourself?"

Isla beams.

Outside her chambers, I wait, hoping I don't regret this. To my left is a mirror, and I curl my lip at Aryahn Kryach's reflection.

"You're a bloody eejyt," I insult him, biting my thumb from his malignant need to overshadow my mark with his.

Kryach shifts back and forth, his black hair like scrawls of dripping ink, his eyes of Nether vapors blinking. He cackles deep and responds in the brogue of our ancestors thickening, "Cannat mak a silk purse out o' yer sow's ear." An insult to my cadaver form no makeup could ever hide. Only one way to restore my corpse.

And she's opening the door.

"Be flattered, Allysteir," he whispers, blowing me a damn kiss. "I've never competed with any King. I've only ever used them."

I snarl, gnash my teeth. "You're a riddy. Bolt! Get to!"

Isla closes the door, collects her skirts, and rushes to me to peer in the mirror. "You were talking to him? Can I see?" she asks, words eager and breathy, lilting.

I—what? I'm shocked by her desperate search for the God in the reflection before her mouth puckers in a pout.

Kryach chortles.

Mine, you damned demon!

"Isla..." I whirl my head, surveying her through my mask. "What in Talahn-Feyal are you wearing?"

She glances down, does a twirl, so the tulle bridal skirts thwack against my robes. "Do you like it? I'm not settled. But I decided *against* white for a wedding gown. It's ghostly. And I might be a virgin, but I'm not exactly innocent if you know what I mean..."

She giggles and gestures to the exceedingly low-cut sweetheart neckline, her finger brushing the dark crimson corpus roses lining the bust cups. They wind to off-the-shoulder transparent sleeves haltering a small portion of her arms. My breath catches. She's bared much of her shoulder flesh, her lithe, tempting neck, and her upper chest. Her hair she's coiled into a mussed knot at the apex of her head, though recalcitrant strands dance upon her cheeks. Royal violet eyes gleam.

Smile radiant. As if...as if she's *proud* of Death's mark. And mine.

"I'm certain I will try on dozens of wedding gowns before I find the perfect one, Allysteir," she expresses—her voice silk and cream. "By the way..." she whispers. On her tiptoes, she leans in, her breath tickling the hairs on the back of my neck, "...I love how you call me your dark rose, my *Corpus* King."

One touch of my sleeve, one arm curling around mine, she welcomes my escort. Ugh! She could escort me into hell itself, and I'd follow. I'll never leave her side. My heart's bound to hers. And it's falling into her flawless embrace.

"Come, my Lady," I urge, offering her nothing else. There's no time. Because—"Souls are waiting."

NINETEEN
COULD THE GOD OF DEATH HIMSELF... LOVE...ME?

ISLA

"Why do you drink all the time?" I wonder, hoping my voice is casual and curious.

Once Allysteir pauses from his wine flask and cranes his neck to me, the corpse mask frown seeming to glower, I know he doesn't consider it casual or curious at all.

"Why do you think?" He tips the flask back, swallowing whole draughts.

"It's Sythe wine. I smell the venom from here. It's the strongest venom in the world. Other than Ith venom which doesn't work on other Ith of course," I ramble, not straying from the King's side.

He doesn't respond. Simply guides me through the halls of the Citadel, past iron and bone sculptures, tapestries conveying great moments in Corpse King history, and so many rooms, I lose count. Too consumed wondering if the Curse infects all his body.

I finger the shadow-mark. No, I didn't consider how it could affect my other mark. If the Corpse King quells the Nether-mark on my lower back, what will Aryahn Kryach's mark do? Will it protect me from Kanat? Chills assault my flesh from other questions preying on my mind. Can the God of Death contact me whenever he wants? Will he be able to *see* me whenever he wants?

I only hope accepting his mark, binding my soul to the Corpse King, is enough. Perhaps he won't reap my soul and leave nothing but my empty corpse shell.

While I obsess over my mark, Allysteir drains his flask.

After we descend the grand staircase and he ventures me to the river, to the same boat of bones, I pause before he helps me onto the vessel.

"My Corpus King..." I dare to curl my fingers onto the robe of his chest, seeking.

He captures my wrist, twists it to one side, then wags his finger back and forth.

Shadows curling around my body in a subtle warning, I tilt my neck and stand on my tiptoes until I'm a breath from his chin. I couldn't reach his mask with my lips if I wanted. "How much pain are you in?"

"Enough."

"Is it everywhere?"

He hisses through his teeth but doesn't grit them. "Enough," he repeats.

"Allysteir." I swallow soreness, certain my eyes are watery. "This is *new* to me. It's happened quickly. I've left my whole life behind. And I may lose my soul on our wedding night. Will you be patient with me please?"

Those hollow skull eyes gaze back at me. A moment later, he sighs, coils a hand around my neck, and taps the fresh marks with his thumb.

"I have been the Corpse King for five hundred years, Isla. You have been my bride-to-be for less than a day. I am the one who must beg for your patience. And we must depart because I cannot be late, my dark rose." He sweeps a hand to the boat.

I muster a smile, nod, and accept his hand—awed by his strength. While I sit in the boat center, he moves to the bow and circles his gloved hand around the skeletal prow with the bone daggers protruding through the skull's eyes.

"Come," is all the King states, diverting my attention.

Countless spirits herd themselves to the underside of the boat and thrust it through the water. The inertia causes me to lurch, but I catch myself and grip my seat. I peer over the side of the boat to behold the spirits. These gray ghosts with eyes of silver flames obey the Corpse King's whim. It's why they first attacked me, tried to pull me under when I'd plunged into the river...until they'd liberated me and hauled me to the surface. Now, I can't take my eyes off them. Crashing to my knees before the King's throne felt like coming up for air in more ways than one.

I kneel till my chest presses to the boat's edge. Glance back at Allysteir who lowers his chin to me but says nothing. Posture stoic. Hand not forsaking the prow.

Biting my lower lip, I take it as a sign and lower my fingers into the water. Oh! Icy claws don't bite my flesh. No, the spirits creep across my skin like cold feathers to tickle, to kiss. Carried by the souls, the boat descends through the river on its way out of the Citadel where it progresses around its western side, expanse widening.

"Allysteir!" I gasp, head lifting, hands flying to my mouth because I've never seen this side of the Citadel. The silvery ribbon waterfall cascades from the rocks upon which the highest tower rests. Beneath a series of connected arches, the river gushes—lit by countless standing lanterns which cast their flickering glow upon the water like drowning fireflies.

Spirits without number congregate in the dark water. Thousands. Hundreds of thousands. Sinking my hand until the water encases my whole arm, I laugh at the spirits drawn to my flesh, kisses tickling, growing goosebumps. For a while, I grant them both hands, both arms. Swirl my fingers as if I'm dancing with the spirits. More and more gather, drawn to my skin.

"They love your life," Allysteir murmurs. "These are the ones lost from history. Bones without rest, these souls have no ancestral home."

I beam at him, then coo to the souls, "Aww, is the King too deathly for you, pretty twinkles?" I coo to the souls. "Don't fret. I'll bring him to life for you."

When I glance again at Allysteir, he hasn't moved a muscle. Utterly frozen. No quivering muscle or shifting of his robes.

A lone scream like a death whistle pierces the night, chills me to the bone. A wail? Allysteir doesn't show concern, and I fear some joke is lost on me. Until *she* appears an inch from my face.

Breath knocked out of me, I fall back against the boat, remembering stories of these ghosts haunting the land, but I've never seen one. These ghosts bound to the Goddess of Doom, to Morrygna. The Ban-Sythe.

"Isla, this is Betha," he introduces the Ban-Sythe, who tilts her head to the side, studying me, lips pinched.

On my elbows now, I arch my neck and draw out her name, "Bay-thah." I mimic her movements, pretend I'm her mirror.

Water laps at the boat, and souls collect while Betha and I stare at one another. An eerie beauty to her, she reminds me of a burial shroud woven around a murdered bride. Long, faded hair—blue as woe—frames her heart-shaped face and calls attention to her gray mist eyes and her aged dress of flowing white tatters—ever moving as if caught by a swift wind. She opens her mouth, imparting another shriek, but this one echoes. When the blue streak of her hair passes me, I understand: the wails were hers.

"She is different, this one," Betha proclaims, her head still tilted. I beam.

"You say that about all my brides," snorts Allysteir, shaking his head, but his tone is casual and amused.

"They were. But she is. Her doom is deeper." She circles me. My brows knit low, puzzled by her words.

"Forgive Betha, my bride-to-be," Allysteir requests. "I claimed her from Morrygna a millennia ago when she owed me a debt. Betha is my best soul keeper. Skilled enough to come and go as she pleases. Some ties still bind her to the Goddess of Doom, but Betha's visions are not as transparent as they once were."

"She smells of roses. And death. And blood, Majesty," Betha mentions, sniffing my waves, her death whistle wails echoing faintly like a tint to her words. "The sweet, forbidden kind."

He stiffens. "Enough, Betha," he warns.

Hmm...why did Allysteir react the way he did? What does she mean by the forbidden kind? What else could Betha know? If I could find a way to evade the King, to return here, I'll find her again and ask.

For now, I nod to her. "Thank you, Betha. You were the one in the water. You stopped the souls from dragging me under."

The ban-Sythe tosses her sorrowful hair over her shoulder and confirms. "My welcome is for you. For you were homeless, nighyan. You did not deserve to be a lost soul."

Homeless, I ponder. An orphan babe discovered on the edge of the Nether-Void. Marked by it. My family: a given family. Franzy felt like the only one I chose.

Except for the Corpse King. Perhaps it was the truest choice I have ever made.

Too suffocated all these years, too full of life, my given-father always said. I never could have imagined what I've searched for would possibly be in the Corpse King's Underworld.

When I look up, Betha is gone. At first, I open my mouth to ask Allysteir for an explanation until I remember: she comes and goes as she pleases.

Hundreds of souls form a current. Their shimmering eyes remind me of the constellations. Sunlight in Allysteir's eyes, starlight in his river which spills to the Sea of Bones. But the spirits guide us into pitch black tunnels, apart from those silver eye clusters. I lean over and play with the souls, careless how a few splash at me, dampening my gown and scattering droplets upon my chest. Lightheaded from the tingling, I laugh.

Remembering an old Talahn-Feyal lullaby, I hum, but my flesh tingles when Allysteir's voice unites with mine in a deep hum. Smiling, I sing instead.

"Ghosts never sleep within his home
Roaming the courts and the catacombs
Come to the Corpse King's sole command
Fearing the shadows within his hands..."

I don't fear his shadows, I muse and smile at him.

My heart shifts. It shouldn't be possible with the spirits' ice, but warmth ignites my core. Out of the corner of my eye, blood fire from Kryach's skull-eyes inked upon my skin kindle—flames teasing beyond the hollow eyes. I purse my lips, then widen my eyes when my veins awaken with the blood fire to gleam.

A bond with Death! In my soul and in my blood.

"Ary..." I whisper my nickname, daring to summon him.

"Kryach!" Allysteir's voice pierces the darkness, causing me to flinch from the rigid protest.

The fire quickening in my veins ebbs, and I retrieve my arms. Bite my lower lip, skin still tingling, heat flushing my insides. I return to my seat without meeting Allysteir's eyes. I don't blame him for his possessiveness. After all, he's spent five hundred years seeking a bride to satisfy Aryahn Kryach. Could I be the first? Could the God of Death himself...love...me?

I gaze at my palms, trace a finger across the lines. Before Allysteir arrived this morning, my fear prompted me to the bed, to bait him. But ever since accepting Death's imprint, the need to foster growth, to flourish burns within me. First, I tempted Kryach. Now, I long to challenge him. To show the Corpse King, to offer him my beauty in these realms of Death. Beauty to make the gods envy. A desperate shudder erupts in my hands. My skin prickles.

"We're here," Allysteir says.

I glance in time when the tunnel welcomes me into a great domed cave crowned in ancient stalactites. Various bridges branch off from this cavern, spilling to a labyrinth of ruins through which river tributaries run. Cities of ruins. The Hollows. In the far distance, I squint to make out the upper territories where the Hall of Heroes slumbers—crypts glowing with their gold veins. With the carven scrollwork of the domed walls, I wager this room was a gathering place. Reserved for worship perhaps. Or city meetings.

A stalactite kisses me with a twinkle of a droplet. I don't brush it away. Blood gushes to quicken my heart until it pounds in my ears. The sound of numberless death rattles thickens the air. From hundreds of open coffins.

TWENTY
A WONDER, ALLYSTEIR. SHE'S A WONDER.

ALLYSTEIR

Decay perfumes the air. A too familiar scent. Death's shadows clot the cavern. Countless breath rattles echo off the walls, hinting of demise. Isla gapes, whirling her head. Now, she understands my prior words: souls are waiting.

The spirits berth the boat upon the rocky bank bordering the cavern. They become footsteps for my boots till I hit the ground. Turning, I extend my hand, welcoming Isla to join me. She shoots to her feet, and a smile tugs at the non-ruined corner of my mouth when she nearly loses her balance and falls into the shallows. Her feet are bare? So sweet. Such passion to receive my world.

And if I want to preserve her life, her soul, I must break her passion. My jaw tenses with the foreboding knowledge. *I must bring her to her knees.*

She stumbles, her chest brushing mine. I hiss. But my hiss fades at the blush tethering her cheeks—how she tucks a strand of her hair behind her ear as a petal sheds from her roses. Kryach chuckles. *Damn it all to hell.* I cage a groan and loop my arm through hers, turn, and escort her toward the coffins.

Dozens of Ith servants tend to the dying inside their beds whether offering blankets, pillows, prayers, hands to hold, common flowers, or support. Hundreds of candelabras bestow the walls with flickering shadows, but they can't compete with Kryach's.

Absentmindedly, Isla rubs the mark on her neck as I guide her to the coffins assembled in ordered rows. At least her fingers trace my teeth marks. The corpus rose petals as she'd likened them.

Her eyes swallow the fullness of the room. She smiles. She smiles at the dying?

My gut clenches. I pause and clutch her chin with one cool glove because I must know. While I love her jubilance, her passion, she cannot play here. This place deserves reverence. "Isla?"

She meets my corpse mask, smile growing. "It reminds me of the death ceremonies in Cock-Cross. They were more meager, of course."

"Tell me," I urge her, regardless of how I've memorized all Talahn-Feyhran death ceremonies. I need to know what it means to her.

She licks her lips, lower one trembling, and continues, "If a sick or an aged villager was close to passing, they would be brought to the town square. Family gathered, cast flowers onto their death bed. The dying would tell a final story while the townsfolk would hold burning candles. While they took their last breaths, we would sing them a lullaby. After Death came, we blew out the candles and returned home without speaking. Later, us children would create endings to their unfinished stories."

My hand strays from her chin to brush her cheek. "Thank you for sharing your ceremony, my dark rose."

She shivers and bites her lower lip but clenches her hands to deny herself any desire from these moments. More death rattles. Her throat constricts with emotion.

Good girl, I almost commend her.

"Not all the world believes in such ceremonies," I inform her, and her gaze rivets upon my skull eyes. "Too many struggle with Death, battle it. Or avoid it at all costs with healers and potions and rites without number. But here in Talahn-Feyal and especially in my Underworld, we honor Death. Recognize him as a friend and not a foe. As I have said: Death is final. Silent. But…" I conclude, raising a finger, "he causes no pain. Instead, he reaps pain and caresses the soul. I appreciate your respect, Isla."

Swallowing the thickness in her throat, Isla clutches my sleeve and answers, "You're welcome, my King. After all, Death deserves the ultimate respect, doesn't he?" The shadow mark thrums above her collarbone as if accepting her gratitude. I inhale when Kryach's appreciation deepens.

"Hmm," I muse. "These citizens believe the same. They come for the blessing of the Corpse King. Of Aryahn Kryach."

Isla nods, eyes straying to the coffins, pressing a hand to her airy tulle bodice.

I release her hand, approach a coffin where a thin, aged Ith man with sunken-in cheeks gasps for breath, his skin amassed with wrinkles like the beautiful lines of a tree trunk. Eyes of foggy gray.

"Donnyl," I speak. The man's haggard brows lift, his tired eyes widen, his fatigued hand rises. I know all their names. Their lives. Their memories. Their dying thoughts. In these final moments, I capture all. But I am a vessel. A stop upon their journey to Death's realms.

This is the boon of Death tangled into the Curse. It keeps me breathing through the rot and pain.

Isla's breath catches when I remove my glove with my teeth, assume the man's hand, and cradle it in my ruined bony one. My shadows extend, curl to Donnyl, stroke his face—dark and tender. I open my mouth to impart my shadow lullaby...

"You may weep for the life you have led
Tears will be gone once you are dead
Remember not your past nightmares
Enter Kryach's arms without a care
For your song will echo in the rain
And in the stars, your eyes remain
Close them now and end your breath
Rest in peace, thy spirit now to Death..."

I cradle the man's forehead. The Feyal-Ithydeir opens his mouth in one deep gust. Kryach's shadows reap his breath, stop his heart, and escort his spirit into my river. Strong spirits like his voyage through the river portal into the Void where he will embark to the spirit realm. To the forever Havens close to the Isles.

Without another word, I close the coffin, bone fingers lingering before I nod to the servants. His chosen bones will be bequeathed to his kinfolk. Meanwhile, I proceed to the next coffin and the next, imparting a similar blessing each time. Uncertain of what else to do, Isla stands behind me, threading her fingers. Most souls are too lost upon Death's edge to notice her.

Until...Glynna, an old woman with sagging gray skin and long, white hair like lace around her chest, points to my bride-to-be.

"Rose," she wheezes.

I turn where Isla peers at Glynna who isn't pointing to her but to the gown's flowers. Her smile as radiant as her violet eyes, Isla plucks one without care and offers it to her. Glynna's eyes brighten, but the aged woman longs for more. My pulse pounds in my ruinous throat with every rose Isla plucks, how careless she bares more skin, the neckline of her gown in threads around her cleavage. She gifts all roses to Glynna. What astounds me is how Isla braids the roses into her hair.

"There," she announces, "now, you look like a perfect dream for your final journey!"

"Lovely girl. Lovely bride," Glynna rasps before she closes her eyes to receive my blessing.

When we progress to the next coffin, a noble lady Ith searches Isla's person, and I smirk. Cyara is as envious at the end of her life as she was throughout it. Nor can I fault her. The irony: corpus roses do not grow beneath the White Ladies.

"Do you have more for my journey?" wonders Cyara to my bride-to-be, her eyes glassy and hopeful.

Isla chews on the inside of her cheek, her eyes flicking to mine. I prepare my hand to settle on Cyara, to offer my lullaby. Until I read no desperation in Isla's eyes, no plea for help. Instead, she sighs, drops her hands to her sides, palms open.

"Allysteir, my Corpus King, I am going to show you something...dear to me. A truth I've always known. And felt. More than ever."

I cock my head. My breath hitches. Kryach's blood fire dances upon her neck. My brows lift high as vines grow through her flesh, rupture from her naked arms and palms, and emerge beyond her finger lines. Cyara's bewilderment is no match for mine.

Thorns rise upon Isla's skin but do not draw blood. She arches her neck, eyes closed. If the act causes her pain, she doesn't show it. On the contrary, her lips part, her skin flushes. Rosebuds bloom along the vines. They germinate into full corpus roses with inner skull buds. My bride presses her eyes harder and bites her lower lip, concentrating, twisting the roses around Cyara's coffin, showering the air with the intoxicating fragrance.

By the time Isla finishes, Kryach's shadows billow along her body. She buckles, and I catch my bride-to-be before she falls. Her breath quickens as she steadies herself.

"Isla." I cup her face, studying her eyes. I say nothing, fearing I will stammer. And flick my eyes to her skin. "Your arms..." I growl. No, the thorns may not have pierced her flesh, per se, but they've littered scratches upon her hands and arms.

She shrugs, a sweet smile budding on her too-tempting lips. "It doesn't hurt. It feels...oh—it's rapturous, Allysteir! Utterly rapturous!"

She squeezes my arms before flitting to the next coffin, offering her blooms to the next Ith and the next. Mystified, I cannot deny her bliss, this exquisite radiance within her regal eyes. All I manage is to follow her, grant my shadow lullaby, my last serenity blessing to the people, but it doesn't compare to their jubilance when she bestows her rare blossoms. At one point, she creates enough roses to fill a coffin, granting a floral death bed.

What is she, Kryach? I ask the God while pacing with my bride.

A wonder, Allysteir. She's a wonder.

The God of Death provides nothing else. For now, I enjoy these moments, and delight in Isla uniting with me on my Death duties in the merriest of ways. Only one other bride accompanied me, showed any interest, but she gave me comfort and solace after my soul singing. She guarded her heart from these passing ones. On the contrary, Isla's heart swells with all she touches. As if she grows the unfathomable muscle while sharing her roses. No signs of wilting.

How can I hope to break her heart? To fracture such a spirit?

Give her to me, Allysteir. And you won't have to, hums Kryach.

You have her blood. You already want her soul. I'll be damned if I let you take her flesh, too, Kryach. She promised it to me. Not you. And I will only accept her flesh given, not taken.

He growls low in a subtle challenge. Always our point of contention. If there is one scrap of willpower, one iota of control I possess in this cursed affair, it's this: I must always love my bride, and she must love me. The reason why I break her, why I test her. My façade is good, but if Isla has taught me anything: love is stronger than death.

A handful of dying remain. A few death rattles. But my bride is winded, her skin flushed, infinite scratches on her moonlike skin. Still, she frolics to the next coffin. Her felicity shames me. Her cheeks shine with rosy starlight. Her chest thrusts out as she dances while she grows her flowers. As if she unleashes a deep burden.

The ground rumbles, and the wall shakes, too familiar. Distant heat curls from a nearby bridge. I turn, furrowing my brow because Ifrynna never disturbs my Death work. The tri-headed Guardian hound thunders her paws across the bridge, skeletal tail whipping like a rabid serpent.

Servants scatter upon her arrival. Not Isla. In the pause where Ifrynna huffs hot breath from her multiple nostrils, my bride-to-be skitters to the Guardian. Eyes wide and bright, they marvel at Ifrynna's form, awed tears glistening. She moves closer, pressing her fingers to her lips.

"Oh, gods! The Guardian of the Underworld." She bobs her head between the bone heads. I can't help but smirk. Of course, she would fall in love with Ifrynna.

Caught off guard by Isla's unexpected interest, Ifrynna sniffs the air around Isla's head, her breath tickling Isla's hair, prompting my bride to giggle. Dazed when Isla lifts her hand, fingers trembling but eager, Ifrynna and I blink when my dark rose strokes the hound's muscled hide.

"Oh, I wish I could grow hands like my roses!" gushes Isla, but Ifrynna shudders and leans away from the girl, directing her three bone heads to me.

"My King," the Guardian addresses me, "As much as I desire to learn about this brazen, little bride and vow to soon, your presence is needed. A refter attack. Upon the bridge to the Isle of Bones. Your soldiers have been dispatched, but they cannot stem the tide."

I growl. Grip Ifrynna's white scruff and haul myself onto her back. "Isla, Betha and the spirits will carry you home." I nod to the boat where they await.

What's going on, Kryach? I demand.

They are not mine, Allysteir. We both know I was beyond pleased with our sweet wonder's blood. And more with her acceptance of my shadow-mark.

What the devil is going on? I glance at my bride, nod to her. *Protect her, Kryach.*

I will. Now, go.

TWENTY-ONE
LUST IN THE LIBRARY

I S L A

Are refter attacks common beneath the White Ladies? Yes, sprinkled throughout this Underworld are refter pockets. I recall the one I killed with Franzy on our way to the Bone Games. But only one. My blood should have appeased the God of Death to stem the tide.

Whatever the case, I'll confront Allysteir later. For now, he didn't specify *when* the spirits will take me home.

My *new* home. An ache clots my throat with the knowledge of what I've done, what I've accepted. I rub the mark again. Do I possess the power to summon Kryach? Or does it all depend on the God's whim? Or Allysteir's?

Regardless, the roses help.

Thoughts of my family threaten to wrench tears from my eyes. Will I one day grow roses around my given-parents' coffins? Will I watch as Allysteir blesses them with his shadow lullaby? So much of my time in this Underworld has been survival, I've hardly given them a second thought while reaping a few joyful samples. And learning as much as possible about the Corpse King, his world, his Curse.

Somehow, I mustn't let myself feel the full weight of this day. It will come later. I'm certain my tears will rival the Cryth River.

For now, the simultaneous pain and pleasure of the thorns encroaching through my veins to slice the surface of my skin chase away emotions. Around the remaining coffins, I grow my floral banquet despite all the servants cajoling me to return to the Citadel.

I hope I will see the Guardian again soon.

Most death rattles quiet whether from sleep or stripped souls, I can't tell. From the telltale rise and fall of chests, Kryach has not reaped these ones yet. As I make my way to the boat where the spirits await, I bid a silent goodbye to the dying and hope my flowers offered them comfort.

On the way back, I play with the spirits a little. Roused, the Nethermark stalks my lower back, but nowhere near as strong. As if Kryach's mark has dulled it.

Would Betha know something about my mark? Her words echo in my mind: *her doom is deeper.* Eyes whirling in all directions, I seek Betha, call her, but she doesn't surface. Chewing on my lower lip, I sigh and return to playing with the spirits because I can't expect her to come whenever I desire. Still, I need to know what she meant regardless of what Allysteir believes about her distorted visions. Anything to help with the Curse, with Kryach, with this whole damned place.

Visions are rare among the Feyal-Ithydeir. The elders possess magic to receive them. Or speak with our ancestors. I grind my teeth, frustrated at the elders. Another reason why I knew I'd sooner become the damned and glorious Bride of the Corpse King instead of the Feyal-bride of an insufferable, self-righteous elder.

Most Ith use the simplest bone magic for more practical purposes: city construction or repair, purifying water sources, quickening harvest labor, healing disease, or offering their services in trade for marriages. Such services benefit all. Not like the elders who claim moral superiority for their ability to speak to the ancestors or their vain efforts to sacrifice to the gods, appealing to them for favor or personal blessings and power.

I crack my knuckles, remembering Elder Kanat's attack. And his promise to sacrifice it all, to pit his venom and magic against Allysteir's mark, to *spoil* me. Rage reddens my face. But since I possess Kryach's mark, the God of Death's protection, he is surely no threat, is he?

A shudder disturbs my body, and I do my best to banish all thoughts of the elder...until the boat carries me beneath a bridged arch where the river expands around the Citadel to the Bone Sea. From here, I make out the dim, gray shape of the Isle of Bones embedded in the center of the Sea. But the spirits do not cast the boat to the current but pause it before a set of stairs leading to a different entryway—not the Great Hall.

I blink, puzzled, brows knotting, but the answer is obvious. Court must be in session, and without Allysteir, I imagine the boat is forbidden to enter the Great Hall. Huh. How did he arrive at some other berthing location after our encounter in the Skull Ruins? After all, I left before he had and didn't officially meet him until an hour past my volunteering. Dismissing my wandering thoughts, I tentatively make my way out of the boat, placing my bare foot onto the lowest step not encased in water.

After blowing a kiss to the spirits, who carry the boat away, disappearing beyond my gaze, I gather my black tulle skirts and rush up the staircase to the arched blackwood door with its bone handle, eager to explore the Citadel. Perhaps, I'll run into Franzy and she and I may share an afternoon meal before the royal supper.

Beyond the door is a long vestibule complete with several stone pillars and arched ceilings. Torches from iron lanterns in the stone walls—ever-lit through bone magic means no doubt—are simple light sources. This appears to be a storeroom, but there's nothing here. Is this large and dank vestibule nudging the river built merely to withstand storms?

At the end of the vestibule is a staircase enclosed by side stone walls. No other openings. I pick up my skirts and take the steps two at a time, a spring in my feet. Upward it winds and winds, but sometimes, the walls break to windows lined in lantern luminaries to offer a river view. By now, I've climbed so high, the western Citadel arched bridge lies below me. How high does this stairway go?

Out of breath by the time I approach the boundless staircase crest, I put a hand to the wall, smiling when a sprig of thorn-clad vines stabs through my fingers to gird the stone walls in budding roses. *Hmm...*I wonder if I may grow other flowers. Maybe black death roses: the most common type of rose in Nathyan Ghyeal.

But not now.

Winded, I ascend the last few steps until the walls subside to a stone bridge curving a Citadel tower. An illusory fog swirls around the bridge, but beyond the gray shroud rolls the dark river. Wind disrupts my strands, and I breathe in the fresh, water-laced gusts, marveling at the weather elements of this City of the Dead. Could the sun shine anywhere inside the White Ladies?

I hurry across the bridge to the tower, to its blackwood door, hoping I don't end up in some bedroom. "Please not Allysteir's bedroom, please!" I whisper and clutch the bone handle, assuming a bedroom as significant as the King's would not be so accessible, nor unguarded.

Once I open the door, I gush at the beautiful library with its bounteous shelves swirling above and below me. Adrenaline lightens my chest, heart fluttering like moth wings. Did Allysteir direct the spirits to drop me off at the vestibule, knowing I would find my way here? Could this be his blessing so I may learn more about the Curse? No, he was far more agitated and adamant about silencing my questions than the other royals.

Forsaking my wonderings, I stray to the center of the library where a great ivory bone tree grows with wide branch-like steps to serve as a stairway. I beam because I've never seen such bone trees, grown through magic, and meant for the elite.

Slowly, I approach the tree to touch one macabre, spindly branch—whiter than spectral stags which haunt the mountains of Talahn-Feyal. Powder sheds onto my fingers. I gasp, rising onto the tips of my toes. It's a living thing! I've heard of these types of bone trees. Their artistry takes years to master, to perfect until the magic achieves *sentience*.

At once, the branches shift, startling me. Its center twists, branches pirouetting in a welcoming dance to present my feet with a bony step. Giggling, I don't hesitate to leap onto the platform, hands flying to clutch the branches. They are too naked...I smirk at the thought of decorating them. But I won't without permission.

When the tree lingers without transporting me, I stare at the levels. "Oh..." I debate, pursing my lips, then shrug. "You choose, lovely tree."

Something like a bow is the gesture the branches make before lowering me several levels until I arrive at the base tower level where multiple divans cozy up to the walls. Countless shelves burst with gold-lined leather volumes. Ribcage cases preserve the elite bone-encased books for protection, but their pages are open for display. I grin at the clever mechanism on the side of each case which allows users to turn pages without disturbing the volumes.

Spinning, I face one wall with its section titled: *Eychdryd*. History. Serendipity shines upon me, but once a familiar voice behind me utters, "Well, you found my hiding place, little lioness," I realize I'll need to wait before offering the tree my floral gratitude.

Turning, slow and cautious, I greet the Blood Queen with an informal curtsy after stepping off the bone tree platform.

"Please rise, Isla Adayra," Narcyssa commands, waving a hand and approaching. "After your glorious actions in the Great Hall and your brazenness at the Royal Supper, you should bow to no one. Not to mention our first unfortunate meeting."

Her fingers lower to my chin to reinforce her command, bidding me rise. I meet her eyes. Warmth engulfs my cheeks with a paradox of my knuckles whitening from fear of the mighty Sythe Queen. Of the keen diamonded fangs she does not disguise from beyond her blood-red lips.

I swallow hard to steady my breath which longs to burst but manage a weak, "Thank you for your help with the Shifter. Offering yourself to the wolf seems more of a misfortune."

When Narcyssa frowns and turns, I worry I've offended her. Forsaking the history section, I follow her to the autobiographies of former kings and queens. Her gown clings to her form like a deep, crimson mist coddling her rich bronze skin. A sweeping train. Long sleeves of ornamental lace. A high neck collar to arrest her throat which accentuates her pointed jaw and cheekbones sharper than scythes along with her blood ruby and obsidian crown. Ever a Queen.

"Would you have preferred I engaged in battle?" counters the Queen, her voice deepening to smoke and daggers. She closes the distance between us, lithe and claw-tipped fingers tiptoeing across my bare arm in a tempting challenge. Her hair engulfs me with the plum aroma of death roses, and I choke a whimper—chest heaving, gown slipping, cleavage deepening.

"Perhaps I could have clawed his muzzle and gored him with my fangs," she says. "Not only would a battle have guaranteed damage to your *exquisite* flesh,—" her eyes flick down ever so slightly, "—but it would have resulted in a declaration of war. And my Sythe can conquer his Shifter fool and great ego which mirrors his member dysfunction when matched against *my* lust in the bedroom."

She bares her teeth. I hold my breath, pulse thrumming from her claws traveling across the thrumming jugular until she closes her hand of silk and ice around my throat, undaunted by the Kryach's shadow ink, to solidify, "So, spare me your judgmental mockery. Unless perhaps you would care for a demonstration of precisely *how* I carry the most prayed-to goddess next to Morrygna of Doom?" She taps one claw to my mouth, traces my lower lip, leaning in to cast her tempting breath of wine and blood.

"I—" I croak, besieged by heat tangling in my core, my limbs shaking, nipples puckering with a craving assault. Not even the Nether-mark chases away the fire and ice of my emotions in the presence of the Blood Queen. Such emotions run deeper, weightier with Allysteir. With Narcyssa, everything is on the surface—wild and irresistible. Desire shimmers through me, flushing all my skin, roused by her deadly dance, awakened by the essence of her Goddess. But somehow, I clamp my parted lips, grit my teeth, and ball my hands into fists, waging war against my body. "No, no thank you," I nearly moan.

I almost follow with, *Some other time.* Because I hardly object at the thought of the Blood Queen's masterful and beguiling hands, lips, tongue, *stop, Isla!*—but beyond my infinite passion, I value a challenge.

For her and myself. No, the unconquerable lust of the Blood Queen will not conquer *me* overnight.

"Hmm..." Narcyssa chortles low from my meager refusal, from the evidence all over my skin, my heated blood. No doubt she scents my arousal and hears my pulse fluttering like a trapped bird. "Your heart is strong, little lioness."

She eases her hand from my throat, and I exhale, relieved in spite of my aching breasts. I internally chastise them and my whetted sex.

"Most humans would have already fallen to their knees, pledging their undying love to me or begging for the sweet relief my touch can bring." Simpering, the Queen gestures to my skull. "And it is not simply Death's mark which gives you strength. As I said, you should bow to no one. But neither will I bow to you." She seizes my hand and rubs her lips across my knuckles in a farewell. My skin tingles. And erupts with goosebumps the moment her lips flee. "Enjoy the library, little lioness."

As soon as she turns, I twirl to hide my burning cheeks and budding nipples, my chest heaving from the sultry encounter. Her smoky voice issues one fateful announcement, "And if Master Ibhry perchance bestows his favor upon you, he will welcome you into the *Unseen* Section."

A bolt of adrenaline strikes my spine. But when I spin to ask her about the section, the Blood Queen is gone. Nothing but curling shadows and the lanterns snuffed out to plunge the library in darkness. I sigh but turn to Master Ibhry. *Master Ivory,* I smirk, thankful to Narcyssa for the name.

I lift my fingers to grant the tree my gift until a hand seizes my wrist. A familiar but unwelcome body shoves me against the nearest shelf. I shriek. Pain lances into my back from a bookshelf's sharp edges.

When Kanat pins my hands above my head as he did on my bed, snarls low in my ear, "I am taking special accolades to spoil you now, sweet bride," and proceeds to raise the ends of my gown, all my instincts thunder.

One name, *one* singular name flees my lips in the wildest of screams, "*Ary!*"

TWENTY-TWO
THE GODDESS OF DOOM

ALLYSTEIR

I inspect the dead refters at my feet. Their ruined hearts weep blood over the bridge spanning the channel to the Isle of Bones. The scent of their decomposition and rotted blood permeates the air...no more than my chronic plague.

By now, bone warriors evacuate any visitors, most touring Feyal-Ithydeir families led to Nathyan Gyeal's center city. On the other side of the bridge, citizens bow to express their gratitude to their Corpse King for his protection. I indulge none. A hundred or so refters are no match for Death's vessel. Menders tend to the bitten while elders arrive to chant their sacred rites, to cast out any refter venom to preserve the bitten human citizens.

Vexed, I ball my good hand into a fist and slam it against the side of the blackwood bridge, snarling at this invasion. Behind me, Ifrynna snorts and nudges a refter corpse with her right head.

"Never before have so many gathered inside the Underworld," she muses.

"Not since the ancient wars," I confirm, press half my lips together, hissing through my exposed teeth.

The remnants of Kryach's shadow power twist and curl around the dozens of refter bodies. They were no match for such might. A mere annoyance more than anything. *A diversion*, I conclude.

I stiffen at the thought of how I'd left Isla alone, a tightness growing behind my ribcage until his voice quells my tension.

She is safe, the God of Death alerts me. *Fatigued from her day and resting now. But safe.*

Of course she is. I curl my upper lip back, dismissing Kryach's low chortle. He's never invested this much in a bride. It's why I could abandon her, knowing beyond any shadow of a doubt he would protect her. But he's hiding something.

Ignoring the bone warriors, I curl Kryach's essence, his shadows into the spilled Nether-blood of the refters, seeking a signature, some trace this was no ordinary attack. Ifrynna is too careful to eliminate refter threats before they ever grow to this substantial number. This many never could have slipped past my Guardian's notice. Which means one thing: someone opened a Nether-portal and released them. Only one goddess possesses the power.

Why?

*Go, Allysteir...*Kryach directs me, understanding my thoughts, my inclinations. He knows where I must seek answers.

Dismissing the refter blood splattered all over my robes, I heave myself onto Ifrynna's back and direct the twain Guardian, "Take us into the Void."

Ifrynna's eyes shimmer, eager and craving. I suck a deep breath as my Guardian charges across the bridge to the Isle of Bones, her mighty paws resounding thunder and shaking the framework of blackwood and bone.

Various portals to the cursed spirit world exist within the Underworld of the White Ladies who do their best to protect the spirit world. If Isla has never heard the legends of the mountains, I will tell her sometime.

For now, I strengthen my grip on Ifrynna's fur and direct her through the doorway located on the eastern shore of the Isle of Bones. No more than a slit between two great boulders facing the sea—only accessible to those permitted by a god. In my case, Kryach, but it's not him I seek today.

The portal energy thrums into our being. A mere tickle for Ifrynna, who ruffles her fur, snapping her teeth at the bits of spirit essence like dust bunnies. Darkness grows, swelling to welcome us. Crossing into the cursed Nether-Void means forsaking one's earthly flesh for a time. Unless you're an equally cursed being such as myself.

No mask here.

Stitched eternally into the essence of the Void and drawn to the torturous portal of a window, hundreds of spirits greet me. Thousands of wispy hands claw at me but pass harmlessly through my shroud of shadows. They wail, plead for reclamation, but I've learned to banish their voices. These souls committed grievances from torture to rape to murder and must seek the gods' favor before they may rest. Unlike the lost ones who frequent my river—cared for by Betha. Ifrynna snarls at a few, snaps her tri-jaws in a warning.

Forsaking the tortured souls, I drift through levels, past castles and cottages within the higher ancestral plane where the majority of races reside. Some lower gods wander among the temples, to tempt and toy with the newer elite spirits, to hear their stories glean their histories, eager to feed on the essence of their recent humanity. Never satisfied with their paradisiacal Isles. I flex my muscles and curl one side of my lip back, exposing all my teeth.

Fortunately, the lower gods are not permitted beyond the Void, and the royals satisfy the higher Gods with the Curse. Higher Gods such as Kryach and the Goddess of Love, and the *Highest* Goddess who never abandons the Isles' highest Pàrrysian fields where her angyls originate. Nor the Highest God of the deepest Nether-pits of the Void and his infinite demons.

Through more portals and beyond ancestral bridges, I ascend to the thinnest realm bordering the Isles where only the strongest of souls may travel. Or cursed sovereigns past and present. And the rarest seer with bone magic.

"It's been too long, Allysteir," my great grandfathyr announces from the familiar courtyard gardens where he often wanders.

"Not here for pleasantries," I seethe and pass by. He turns, understanding my necessity and does not tread near my shadows.

Through portal windows, my ancestors have limited glimmers into my world. They wish to know more about Isla. Intrigued by the first tribute in centuries and the first official common human. I bristle, smothered by their insufferable spirits.

It's been a couple decades since I visited. For too long, I held out hope I could comb through my ancestors' histories and learn something, some universal thread—one tug and the Curse tapestry would unravel. Or any knowledge of the Curse-Ender. But only the Higher Gods know such secrets, such power to rival all races of Talahn-Feyhran. None would ever surrender their favorite flesh playgrounds.

Without pausing despite my ancestors clamoring for my attention, I drive Ifrynna forward, thrilling in how my tri-hound navigates the higher planes, never tiring—her spirit form stronger, far more at home. Her essence thunders into me while Kryach's shadows harness me to the mighty Guardian.

Some lower gods fraternizing with the ancestors turn at my presence. One flick of Kryach's power, and they return to their frivolity.

I am not here for them.

Finally, I ascend to trespass upon the thin slit bordering the Isles, the territory where their infinite gates born of hellfire and heaven's starfire protect the higher gods' realms. She may be a fallen Goddess, but Kryach respects her enough to allow her to wander these realms beyond their gates.

Careful not to tread too close to the hellish flames and celestial inferno, I dismount, pace before the Gates, and speak one word. One name.

"Morrygna."

Nostrils flaring, my breath threatens to rage, but I steel my spine, controlling myself as the gates shimmer at the edges, bowing before the power of the Goddess of Doom escorted by her hellwylfs.

The dark, ragged robe she wears is closed, bound by silver ropes threaded with the kite tails of stars. Morrygna's black waterfall of hair is bound around her head in a spiraling, illustrious crown to bare the ruined side of her face, marred by brands until it's near beyond recognition. Her left eye, a spectral unseeing ghost, is a curse as goddess flesh cannot heal from the Isles' infinity fire. Doom's sight—forever dimmed.

Only the gods know the legend of Morrygna's scars.

"Corpse King," Morrygna addresses me, then gestures me to follow her through the pathways bordering the Gates. Ones marked by shadow trees.

Jaw set, fists tightened, I bid Ifrynna to roam, then embark into the spirit forests.

She lifts her left hand from beneath her robe, skin blotted to expose her Goddess essence. The dark side of the moon's teardrops flows through her veins, her arteries bearing the menstrual blood of sacrificial offerings. Doomed blood to grant her more sight to compensate for her blind eye. Her Ban-Sythe do the rest.

"I know why you've come, Allysteir. And no, you will not dissuade me. No boon you could offer. No favors you could grant."

"You risk angering Aryahn Kryach, Goddess," I alert Morrygna, lingering in her shadow, never raising my eyes to her blind one. Mine may also be ruinous, but it does not inhibit my sight. "My bride-to-be has found favor with him."

The shadow trees bow to the Goddess, others descend to their knees, whispering prayers the further we travel through the forest while her wylfs trail us. "Yes," her smoky voice echoes of war, of the embers of hell. "While the other gods are ignorant to Kryach's interest and his whispers among the ancestral plane, I am not."

"Is she the Ender?"

Morrygna snaps her teeth. She spews a deadly Doom shaft to force me to my knees. Death's shadows daunt her hellfire, numbing the pain to an echo. The hellwylfs surround me, teeth bared, threatening violence.

Rage colors Morrygna's eyes black as Nether-storms. "You dare to ask the Divine such a question?!"

Limbs heavy, I grit my teeth, breath halting. Rising slowly, I apologize, remembering my place and respecting how Morrygna has the power to crush my mere five-hundred years of existence; she was birthed from the darkness of the cosmos before time. "Forgive me, Goddess."

A withering sigh flees Morrygna's mouth, and she leans in to touch the side of my face, the whole one because Doom is not without respect. "I've always liked you, Allysteir. Do not disappoint me with your foolish pride. Not even a former High Goddess as I would release such a secret. And my fallen status renders it forbidden to me."

She drops her hand, sways to the side, wandering deeper, bidding me to follow and to listen. Breath heavy, I posture and furrow my brow, alert, prepared.

"Whether or not your future bride is the one all gods fear matters little to me," acknowledges Morrygna, her robe clothing the hazy ground, her war smoke mingling with the ancestral plane mist. "The mere possibility her blood may grant me another key for my sacred cause is my sole care. If I collect the favors of some petty lower gods and goddesses, more's the better."

"And you would offer an Isles seat to the likes of a vain elder? And my bride's flesh?"

"There are far worse things to lose than flesh. And yes, even goddesses may deal with pawns."

"Then, deal with me! The blood of every cycle. The first of our offspring," I add, desperation pulsing my adrenaline. "Dry up her breasts, take all her milk," I bargain further, careless of anything but saving her. Doom's desire for Isla's flesh and blood will vie with Kryach's for her soul.

The Goddess throws her head back and laughs. "So rich! The Corpse King, the one who wears the God of Death, who bargains with none, seeks to trade with the Goddess of Doom! Oh, Kryach and I will laugh about this on our annual mating."

"Damn it to hell, Morrygna, what must I do to save my bride?!" I roar, shadows penetrating every crouching wylf and driving them back, so I may close the distance between myself and the Goddess.

Slow and purposeful, Morrygna trains her eye upon me, before time's cosmos winking at me, hinting of demise and destruction, matching mine of death. "Do you know why they call me the Weeping Goddess when I have never shed a tear?"

When I blink, Morrygna raises her lofty chin and continues, "I bear the weight of the most ancient of woe. While Death offers a reprieve from suffering, from the scraps of mortality, I am the Goddess who gifts only harbingers.

"Oh, before such day, I cried such tears for all the doomed. I took their offerings and traded my tears to them so they could find escape or comfort."

She pauses, traces her ruined finger around my half-rotted mouth as if hinting of my shadow lullaby. My offering, my one gift in the damned business of Death—permission granted to me by Kryach. The trauma of Morrygna's lost moon-tears shames me. Defeated, I lower my head, lips parted to her scarred finger touching my exposed teeth, the blemished flesh.

"The most beauteous weeping...the highest Goddess of Angyls herself named the weeping trees for me. Until *they* came and burned away my beauty, including my tears. Ever since, I have vowed to weep a new river to bless Talahn-Feyhran on the day I reclaim what was taken from me. To trade the ashes of my suffering for Isle beauty. I have spent centuries seeking any child who bears the mark of doom in her soul or her flesh. Whether she is fated to receive it or deal it, I don't know and don't care. As long as her doomed blood grants me the power to reclaim what is rightfully mine."

"And Kryach?" I attempt one final plea.

A shadow of a smile graces Morrygna's face, her eyes soften, and she leans in to brush her lips to mine in a subtle Goddess kiss. In her kiss is the decay of a thousand ages, the cries of carrion, and the thunder roars of hundreds of infamous female warriors throughout our history who bow to their priestess, Morrygna.

Once her lips depart, I understand it is an oath of Isla's sealed fate. My shoulders lower in demise. Her seal pierces deep into my bones.

"I will incur the Kryach's wrath, for perhaps it is Death who owes Doom a favor."

Upon leaving the Nether-Void, my rage of powerlessness roils beneath the surface. Kryach's shadows wreathe around me—darker, deeper, wilder. My fists shake. Blood roars in my ears. Veins throb. Ifrynna says nothing, silent in the presence of my fury. On my way back to the Citadel, I cross paths with the Shifter Prince and clench my teeth hard. One breaks.

Carsten pauses. A wolf frozen in my shadows.

Maskless, I attack. I break my fist, bruise the other, dislocate my shoulder, fracture my rib cage. But I don't stop until all Carsten's bones break, till his heart slows to its barest beat, and his blood weeps into the Cryth River to feed the spirits. The truth brands itself into his deepest matter not to ever fuck with my bride-to-be again.

TWENTY-THREE
"HOW MUCH DO YOU DELIGHT IN PLAYING WITH THE GOD OF DEATH?"

ISLA

"*Isla...*"

Shades of ice curl across my naked form. The flowers lingering on the surface of the warm bath water wilt and shrivel into decay. From Death's touch. Still, I don't open my eyes. Lost halfway between the waking and dreaming world, not willing to surrender to reality.

"*Isla...*" the Death God coos, rousing me from my stupor, summoning me. A blissful right.

Other than my dreams, this is the seventy-sixth time he's exercised the right. Or perhaps the ninety-third, I lost track.

First, I swallow, shake my head, whimper my usual defiance, "No..."

My scalp prickles from Aryhan Kryach's nearing shade, and I shiver from his encroaching hands of smoke and silk. Memories replay from the first time I witnessed his power take this limited form. I clamp my eyes shut, soaking in the memory...

Kanat's hands on my naked hips when he'd bunched up my gown, his hot mouth on my neck, his organ prepared to stab into me all culminated in my scream. My scream for Ary.

Not Allysteir. Not the Corpse King.

Kryach's shade form leans in, growing frost within my veins. I tremble. Next, I descend beneath the water—another act of rebellion. After what has passed between us, these little tastes of spite, of refusing to acknowledge him, much less answer are my personal pomegranate seeds. A double-edged sword of tempting the God of Death and never yielding my soul's sovereignty to him who reaps all.

Beneath the water, I linger, lungs swelling, burning. Ever since the library, I've formed a thousand excuses for crying his name. Allysteir was gone. Narcyssa would not have helped a second time. I wasn't strong enough to handle Kanat alone, though I'd considered choking him with my thorny roses and shedding his blood.

But I'd screamed "Ary". From the moment his shade overpowered the elder and rendered him unconscious, I knew I would pay a price for such protection. Everything in my subconscious, in my soul had begged for his presence, wishing he was no mere ghost mark upon my flesh. After all, I deserved more, didn't I?

"Aye, my little wonder," he'd pronounced, leading me beyond the library and across the tower bridge, his vaporous hand weaving his shadow power around my body. "You deserve far more. But nothing comes without a cost."

Upon the bridge, I'd rubbed one apprehensive hand along my opposite arm and gazed at the specter hovering above me. "Name your price, Ary," I'd demanded and turned to face the Sea of Bones, welcoming the raw wind chilling my skin.

Ary's shade numbed me more as he coasted his fingers into my hair, sweeping it to one side of my neck to tumble upon my chest. A dark kiss of Death to roam my jawline. I'd shivered but refused to quake. I did nothing more than press my lips together and grip the blackwood of the bridge till my knuckles turned white as hawthorn.

"Access, sweet wonder," he'd whispered, murmuring kisses to the back of my neck until my scalp prickled. Thorns and thistles grew from my flesh while Kryach revealed more. "The key to you. I will come to you whenever I desire—your dreams, your most intimate private moments. You wish for more than a ghost mark upon your flesh? I will be the one who haunts you, body and mind. And it shall be our little *secret*."

It wasn't a bargain. It was his choice. Unlimited access to anything and everything. But he'd never specified I needed to reciprocate.

So, when I surface, I beam from sweet victory.

Now, he chuckles—a deep rolling wave of laughter to wash over me when I rise from the bath with the shriveled flowers clinging to my skin and hair. Speechless, I step out of the bath and offer a soft nod when the God shade drapes a black velvet bathrobe around my shoulders. My barest acknowledgments drive him madder. I stiffen when his hand strays into my hair to shift the soaked strands from trickling water down my flesh to the back of the robe. It's not an unwelcome sensation, but it's still strange and wild and...wondrous.

Like hushed wings. Snowdrifts and skeletons. Nether-silk and secrets. The secret binding us. A betrayal to Allysteir.

"How much do you delight in playing with the God of Death, little wonder?" Ary inquires, trailing my steps, stalking me as he'd vowed while I forsake the lower bathing room and ascend to my suite. Utter silence behind me when I ignore him.

Hmm...that won't do at all.

Smug, a smirk teases one corner of my lips, and I pause on the staircase, open my mouth as if to respond.

Out of the corner of my eye, the God shade freezes with a sharp intake of bated breath.

Oh, he gave himself away, and he knows it. Gloating and grinning from my bait, I tap my finger to my lips before curling a solitary vine from my finger to ripen a sweet bud of a corpus rose. Too tight to offer inner skull petals—as caged as my speech to him. Laughing, I fling the symbolic bud to the God and race up the stairs, reveling in his low growl.

My lips are sealed, Ary, I almost taunt but don't give him the benefit of my words.

Oh, how Ary has worked to catch me alone these two weeks! No simple feat when Allysteir and I spend so much time from sharing midday meals to his Death business to supper each night with the royals to tours of the vast Citadel and its grounds. The Corpse King hasn't offered me a reprieve. My family monopolizes the rest of my time, though I don't join them on tours. I have all eternity to tour.

Will Allysteir come for our mid-morning meal today? I wonder. After all, tonight is our wedding ceremony followed by a grand feast. And dancing! I'd lost track of how many gowns I'd donned. I've finally selected the perfect one. When Franzy's eyes lit up, I knew it was perfect.

One last gown to wear this morn. The runner-up and what I'd always imagined I'd wear for mine and Franzy's wedding.

Before the stand-up mirror, I drop my robe to the floor in an inky pool of crushed velvet. Kryach's shade form appears in the reflection behind me. I wink, hand gliding to my hip. All Ith cherish human flesh, our mortal fabric. But Ary treasures my body more than Allysteir. His tormented breath betrays him along with his shadows' chronic trespass upon my figure, curling frost buds onto my skin.

A fluttery feeling in my belly, I incline my chin to my shoulder to eye his shade hand hovering above my Nether-mark. Unlike Allysteir, who quiets it to hum beneath my flesh, Death nullifies it. But I'll never tell him how glorious it is. How soothing and peaceful.

"How long will you maintain this charade, Isla?" he demands, a dark snarl budding.

I can't help but face the mirror. Pride expands my chest.

Kryach has no true form, and yet, he may touch me and cast his deathly aroma onto my skin. He does every night as I drift off to sleep. The aroma is different every time. Sometimes, a winter twilight. Or lifeless leaves prepared to crumble. Or deadwood and gray rain.

At the moment, it's blood and decay. Shoulders back, I stand on my tiptoes and pull in a deep breath. His skull eyes blaze in anticipation. I'm on the verge of a riptide of laughter.

What a dangerous rush to test the God of Death!

I beam at how his eyes, black as hell pits, explore my exposed skin. When I not-so-subtly touch myself, his sharp intake of breath thrills me. Here in the Underworld, my muscles have softened from my lack of farm labor. A hint of additional plumpness enriches my thighs attributed to all the pomegranate seeds and shortbread I've eaten. And the hearty meats and wine at the royal suppers. Allysteir feasting on my blood and flesh has increased my appetite. Hopefully, after the wedding, I may persuade him to enjoy other *exerting* activities. If I last that long...

I balance on a tightrope of tempting and taunting the God of Death. One wrong move and my soul is doomed.

After a few more touches, I clothe myself in the white runner-up gown.

Ary finally snaps and touches my skin for the first time, collars my throat with his hand—cold and arresting as fog-shrouded iron. "Enough!"

Unease churns my stomach, but my lips part in an attempt to maintain this "charade" as he's dubbed it. Hopeful he doesn't notice my lower lip trembling. Swallowing a knot, I purse my lips, stare down those starless chasms, and respond flawlessly, "Surely the God of Death has far better things to preoccupy his time than to demand my attention, however a little wonder I may be."

"Finally, she speaks!" he professes and releases my throat. I nearly double over but catch myself, breath heaving while Ary circles me, shadows traipsing across my gown edges. "Perhaps the business of Death is slower today."

I roll my eyes and stray to the bed. "Hells balls, it is." Careless of my curse, I collapse against the bed, spreading my hands wide, stretching, and breathing in a fresh gasp.

Ary appears above me, hovering. "Or perhaps the Bride of the Corpse King is my business. After all, it is your wedding day."

Rising to my elbows so my chest thrusts forward along with half my cleavage to catch the God's wandering eye, I simper and confront him, "So eager, Ary? Will you devour my soul when he bites me tonight? When he fucks me?"

Ary offers a deep chortle. Not so much as a flinch when he leans in, shade arms hemming me, icy brow pressed to mine. I dig my nails into the bed covering, shift, but don't waver.

"What makes you believe he will touch you tonight, little wonder? You believe you may prepare yourself. You are strong enough merely because you wish to be? But Death cannot be cheated, sweet Isla. Not even by one as tempting and teasing as yourself."

"Oh!" I revel and arch my body, so Ary drifts back ever so little, a smooth grace, while I roll myself into a rocking position. I clutch my arms around my knees, bare feet easing beyond the gown ends. "So, you *admit* I'm a temptress?"

While I trace a lithe finger around my lips and grow black death roses between my toes, Ary snorts, responding, "You tempt fate, little wonder. Is your life of so little value to you?"

I shrug and pluck a flower, pick at the petals. "Or my soul is simply made of woe and storms, of hellfire and angyl light."

Scattering the bits of shredded rose, I position them on the bedspread, form them into something new, keenly aware of Ary's close presence, of how he stalks me. Madness swirls heat into my chest, flushes my skin as I create the outline of a black skull with the petal pieces, and continue, "Perhaps, if you suck my soul into the Nether-Void, it will simply spit me back out."

I tread on the boundaries of my birth. Of a babe discovered bordering the Nether-shadow world. Of the stories I'd created of my origin: as twisted as rose vines.

Glancing up, I smile at the God of Death and conclude, "Perhaps my soul will poison you, Aryahn Kryach. After all, Allysteir has already fallen under my spell. Desire, lust, even love...they are the greatest poisons not even Death has an antidote for."

It is my dare, my threat. The charade has ended. At the very least, he knows can't toy with me. I'd sooner break his favorite toy than let him fuck with my soul.

I'll be damned if I don't fuck with him first.

Ary sweeps his shade hand to disturb the petals before stroking my cheek, brushing his shivery fingers to my neck to settle at his shadow mark. Eyes closing, I harness my breath—heartbeat thundering when Ary puts his lips to my brow and murmurs in my ear, "Whatever else you are, little wonder, you are no mere girl from Cock Cross. But do not be fooled, sweet Isla. Perhaps you are under the Corpse King's spell." He turns.

I glower at his empty threat, his attempt to turn me against Allysteir. But I've overheard their quarrels when Allysteir believes I'm asleep. I've picked up on his body language in the middle of our conversations, body language he reserves for Aryahn Kryach. And his tone whenever the royals discuss the gods, praise them with false bravado and venomous smiles.

Balling my hands into fists, I slide off the bed to confront Kryach, "Well, now, I wonder what the lower gods would think if they knew the High God of Death is jealous of the royal he inhabits."

Ary growls, spins, and arrests my throat again. "Do *not* test me, Isla! I'll reap your soul if I damn well please. Allysteir will do nothing."

"Do it, then. Now," I dare, raising my chin, smile slow but building. We know what would happen. The Curse would break, the Void would disappear. No boundaries between us and our ancestors...or Eyleanan.

He huffs, icy breath of strong incense, of fire, of ash waft across my face. Finally, his breath slows, he cocks his head, and declares, "If you have such faith in your Corpse King, perhaps you should show him the mark upon your back," he baits me, fingers creeping cold as winter thorns to dig into the Nether-mark. When the familiar burst of ice injects into my nerves, I lurch into Ary's arms. Tears glisten in my eyes from the icy force, his power, his will.

"No," I whimper, thrash my head, struggling in his vaporous prison as he trails those fingers to my mark. And taps it like a war omen. Pain lances my chest.

Still, Kryach continues. Tapping, tapping, tapping. "You believe Allysteir is a perfect, tortured vessel for my evil Godhood. You believe you will save him, little wonder. But he will believe you are as damned as he is," he whispers shadows in my ear.

His lips descend to his skull brand in my skin, and I tremble with every invasive touch—a hint, a sample of what he will do. As the Queen warned: *Kryach will ruin you as he did me...until there's nothing left but violence, fire, and blood. Nothing but your scar of a soul.*

Vines birthing corpus roses curl and twist all around me, but they shrivel once they touch Kryach's shade form. Countless thorns tumble, harmless, at his nebulous feet.

The God kisses my tears, licks them from my cheeks, and thrills in my shudder. "Your woe is exquisite, my sweet wonder. When Allysteir learns you are marked by the same shadows he hates, and when he learns of your betrayal of giving me complete and utter access, what will stop him from fucking you and gratefully giving your soul to me?"

"No!" I cry, raise my fist, but Ary seizes it, his hand a powerful grip of a shade.

"Rest assured, little wonder, I vow to you I will take my sweet *time*. I will savor every precious moment, every bite of your tantalizing soul, poisonous or no. You will last longer than all other brides. So, even as you await an eternity with the Corpse King, all you will have to offer him is a beautiful but empty shell of flesh. And whatever is left of your soul will spend eternity hungering for *Death*."

Paralyzed, I do nothing when his mouth descends to mine, forges past my lips, and injects shadows which taste cold and lonely as abandoned graves and lost spirits. My knees buckle, but Ary forces me to remain upright. Wild and breathless, I gasp for air. Still, he does not release me. Decay in my mouth, ice as cold as the Cryth River. Waterfalls of tears spill down my cheeks, down my neck while the Nether-mark attacks me with fire and ice. Death's skull impregnates my veins with its shadow power. He seals his vow deep in my blood until the full weight of its truth rests upon my chest like a millstone. He's suffocating me. Now, I understand.

There is no tempting Death. There is no conquering him.

I have failed.

So, the moment Franzy knocks at my door, calling to me from beyond, the moment Kryach disappears into thin air, and she opens the door to my room, I don't hesitate. Tears flying from my eyes, I embrace her, kiss her madly, and savor her moan. Her lips and body are willing as I remove her gown and mine and drive her onto the bed.

For the next hour, we lose ourselves in one another. No, I can't forget Death's kiss, but the pain fades to her amber eyes and sweet mouth welcoming me.

What I love most: Franzy never asks questions. She simply gives and receives. And I've never loved her more.

TWENTY-FOUR
SECRETS, SCHEMES, AND SLAVES

ALLYSTEIR

When I hear the moans of pleasure from beyond the door, I smile and linger within the hall. Well aware of Isla's relationship with her sweetheart, I would never interfere. Quite common for royals to have consorts. My mother has taken several over the years. As long as such relations are never harmful…rich coming from me.

Kryach would undoubtedly enjoy conversing with me over the bedroom sounds if he were not consumed with Void business. With the wedding tonight, he will have everything in order. Considering all the lower gods and goddesses will be present, observing through the royals they inhabit, the High God of Death has many warning promises to carry out to ensure no disturbances.

Amused, I smirk at Isla's blissful cries and close my eyes, but after registering my dark rose's appetite for her lover is far greater and likely to last, I leave the meal tray beside the door and make my way down the hall. Simply because I am cursed doesn't mean I should or would restrict such companionship. I'll see to it Aydon does not either. I'd never trespass on the relationship Isla shares with her childhood friend, nor assume my bride-to-be's heart is somehow too small to accommodate others. Or her passion.

A familiar snigger from around the corner of the hall alerts me. I roll my eyes and withdraw my mask to face the Sythe Queen.

"Narcyssa," I address the sovereign who strolls near a balcony overlooking a sitting room.

The Queen slides a hand down her velvet black gown, its high collar and shoulders adorned in gold. Her neckline plunges deep to expose the alluring bronze flesh between her breasts. "Oh, come now, Allysteir. You can't possibly fault me for eavesdropping a little. After all, your future bride is quite *demonstrative*."

Her pupils awaken with a lustful rouge, and I curl my upper lip back when her High Goddess' essence of tempting wine and roses ripples and folds itself around my shadows. The color of deep scarlet roses, of dark secrets, of rubied lips. An open taunt. My bones themselves tense.

"Rest assured, I look forward to drinking her sweet honeysuckle," adds Narcyssa, licking her lips, too eager.

I growl. "Over my rotting, dead body."

Narcyssa flutters a hand, advances toward me. "I'm flexible. After all, the ones we wear have shared pleasure in centuries' past. And you do not possibly believe you will satisfy such a heart on your own, do you?"

"I'm warning you, Sythe..." I devour her provoking essence with my shadows and clench my fists.

"Poor Corpse King. So threatened. Whatever will happen when his bride discovers what I have to offer? When she discovers I may protect—"

Before she may continue, I harness her throat, squeezing the delicate collar. I savor the brief glint of fear and how her pupils falter before she adopts her familiar crooked smirk of lust, secrets, and calculating serenity.

"Never forget, Narcyssa," I threaten and jut out my chin, gazing at her with my ghostly eye, its dark cavity wreathed in Kryach's shadows. "I understand the specific secret of your Goddess' Curse. Such a secret may be revealed."

"Shall we trade in secrets?" Narcyssa scoffs and cups my rotted cheek, prompting me to seethe. More when she whispers in my ear. "After all, I have collected all Curse secrets and stored them in my bed. It is ever so large, so thick, so bulging..." she simpers.

I snarl when her lips brush my cheek, when her Goddess' fleshy scarlet essence wars with my cock. And so, I welcome her mouth when she dares to kiss me, when her tongue probes my lips' seam to trigger my lust. I sink my jagged teeth into her lower lip and devour her moan, the scrape of her fangs along my tongue, her hand lowering to grip my—

"Enough!" I roar and step back, masking myself in shadows, substituting lust for death, for rot, for decay.

Narcyssa tosses her scarlet curls over her shoulder and pats my cheek affectionately. "Sweet boy. We both know you won't fuck her tonight. But my bed will be open whenever she desires. And you are more than welcome to join us, so I may collect all those lovely secrets and gift them to my Goddess. You should know, Allysteir, my Goddess of Love is the most *envious*."

"Careful you don't turn green with it, Narcyssa. Especially when I penetrate my bride for the first time and she screams my name with such rapture to make the White Ladies themselves blush."

I leave the Blood Queen and her mocking laughter. Replace my mask. Seek my brother, unsurprised to find him and Mathyr attending to wedding details in the secondary hall.

"Well, such an honor for you to grace us with your presence," Aydon leers with his perfect grin, perfect eyes, perfect everything.

Dismissing his meager baiting attempts, I sway to the blackwood table and fetch the flagon of wine resting at its center. "My bride-to-be is otherwise occupied. And Death's business is delayed on account of the wedding. I trust you and Mathyr have everything in order?"

"Aye," Aydon answers, rolling up a number of parchments. "All elders and lower nobles throughout the kingdom will be present. And citizens from the surrounding cities will flood the Great Hall as well as ships to behold the procession of the Bride followed by the Bride and Groom.

Mathyr's eyes gleam enough to match the gems adorning the bone corset bodice she wears. "I have sent the flesh maids to prepare both brides and will join them soon to ensure they are...well-groomed."

"No more schemes, Mathyr," I command and rip into the cork with my teeth. "The day must be perfect for her."

Aydon snorts. "Because we all know how the night will go. Unlike you, brother, I shall see to it my bride is properly *pleasured* tonight."

I cage a low growl in my throat. "You stated you were planning to wait to consummate the marriage."

"I suppose we will have to see how the night goes, brother. The possibilities are endless for me, and I will take every opportunity unlike you."

Yes because I will sacrifice my heart on the altar of whatever is left of my soul. My honor is something Kryach can never steal. While Aydon will fuck as many consorts as he wants, the memory of love is what I may forever hold—even as the rest of me falls apart.

"Now, if you'll excuse me," Aydon mutters, donning his Prince crown of gold-lacquered bones to mirror his epaulets and tunic lining. "I have business with the elders before the wedding preparations."

I slug more wine. What business could Aydon possibly have with the elders? Probably some traditional ritual to incorporate into the ceremony. A ceremony he has promised will be the grandest in all of Talahn-Feyal history.

Mathyr excuses herself to Isla. I am far too tempted to follow, to ensure my dark rose is treated with respect. But I doubt even Mathyr would disturb this day's sacred rites. Above all, she will honor our traditions and my bride's flesh and bones, though I know she will be harsher than a Ban-Sythe when it comes to the grooming process. In any case, Isla can handle my mother.

So, I pursue Aydon. It takes more effort to mask myself because Aydon is familiar with my deception and Kryach's shadow power and blood-fire essence. I maintain my distance, following him onto the private train to the Elder Guild. His lack of escort is dumbfounding. While I have no need for any bone warriors, Aydon as Crown Prince and the true political foundation, never travels beyond the Citadel without them. Apprehension thickens in my throat, and I swallow. He's up to something.

Why the devil should I care? Not like I've shown any interest in Aydon and his schemes and secrets. He keeps the kingdom running because my pain is too great to bother with political matters. Talahn-Feyal is thriving. Our castles are well-stocked, our citizens' bellies are full, mothers are fat and happy, and throughout the kingdom, cities are known for their balls where the Feyal-Ithydeir may find their human matches. Menders are plenteous.

And tonight, the gods will be more appeased than ever.

But the refter attack on the bridge, Kanat's ruthful plans, the bane of Morrygna, and Kryach's obsession with Isla are my personal thorns. I grit my teeth. Because I'll be damned if Aydon's schemes drive another into my flesh.

On the way, an abundance of bone trains route to the Osdyel arenas—the lodging districts. Some will depart in the morning following the reception, but the kingdom nobles will remain longer along with the royals, of course. Aydon will busy himself with countless noble affairs over the next few weeks.

The Guild is a veritable grave of empty courts. Due to the wedding, all business has been postponed. Torches in iron holders are the only sources of light throughout the halls, making it simpler to track my brother. A couple of times, he pauses and sweeps back his cape to peer over his shoulder. But he shakes his head and progresses to the last court: Kanat's, the highest and largest.

It's worse than I could have predicted. I tighten my mantle of shadows to prevent the blood-fire tide from creeping beyond. The manacles. The shackles. The chains. Not since the ancient days of unchecked war has our race resorted to the vile stain of *slavery*. Now, its stain infects my eyes, penetrating me with its sick pestilence. A deeper rot than my refter. Heavier than the gods' Curse.

Under the glory of an ornate chandelier of fused stag antler bones sits an iron throne since only royals possess bone thrones. But the throne is empty as Aydon and Kanat stand in the court center facing the humans. *Shackled* humans.

Surrounded by Feyal-masters, the humans bow their heads, eyes trained on the ground. Not one is from Talahn-Feyal. Our humans understand their flesh-worth to the Feyal-Ithyderians, understand the protection of our laws. All these humans know is slavery—birthed in their blood, bred for this existence. The lack of children is hardly a comfort. This grievous wound will plague our sacred nation. A forever blemish.

My nostrils flare. Rage pounds blood to my ears. No pain could compare to this new disease birthed by my own brother. Seething, I somehow manage to control myself as he inspects the shackled humans, prodding their flesh beyond their meager fabric scraps, squeezing, testing them for strength. Chin high, he nods.

When Elder Kanat passes the young men and women, nodding his confirmation following my brother, my rage nearly erupts. Blood-fire quakes around my form. Almost shatters my shadow shield, threatening to strangle the life out of the elder.

Until my brother speaks to the flesh-masters, "Dispatch these to the nobles. See they are well-fed tonight. All expect a grand wedding feast after all," he snickers, and Kanat joins with the too-easy chuckle. "I trust the last haul was delivered promptly to the lower elders?"

The head Feyal-master bows his head and responds, "Just as you ordered, Your Highness. And your personal collection will be delivered shortly before dawn to your consort chambers as you directed."

"Good. I will dine on them after I leave my bride. Proceed," he dismisses them with a mere gesture.

The rattling of the chains echoes in my ears. Worse than any death rattle. I vow to Kryach Aydon will answer for this injustice! But I must tread carefully, cautiously. When he has the kingdom in his hand, the seal of elder approval, of the nobles, the respect from the royals *and* their gods...

Fuck it all, if I seek Kryach to right this wrong, I know what he will demand as a price.

"Thanks to your rule, the kingdom is more prosperous than ever," Kanat commends Aydon, interrupting my thoughts.

"Indeed," Aydon agrees, swaying to the other side of the room, to the court table with its documents and wine flasks. "The untapped wealth of the mines more than pays for foreign flesh to sate our elites' appetites. Necessary when demand is high for these significant events. Especially when our human population has dwindled due to much inbreeding."

My ears ring with the information. I harden my jaw. A double curse. An iron striking fire into my heart because I forsook this responsibility when I became Kryach's vessel. This is the price. I knew Aydon was on good terms with Kanat, close terms. But I never could have imagined this.

Once the next haul of humans is ushered in for Aydon and Kanat's inspection, I steal away from the Elder Guild, return to the Citadel, return to my inner chambers where I shatter every mirror to cover my roars.

Ultimately, I know what I must do. For the first time in history, the Corpse King must give up his bride. Body, mind, heart, and soul. I cannot sacrifice my kingdom and its honor for the sake of one bride...no matter how much I desire her.

Unless she is indeed the mallyach-ender. If so, I would sacrifice all honor. If she is the Curse Ender, no force in the world—not even the God of Death—will stop me from protecting her.

For I am as much a slave to my heart as to this Curse.

TWENTY-FIVE
"YOU ARE TRULY THE MOST GLORIOUS BRIDE…"

ISLA

"Isla?"

"Mmm…" I murmur to Franzy who curls her hips closer to my pelvis. I nudge my lips along her neck, brush her gilded shoulder.

She cranes her neck back, then scoots to face me. "Do you remember when you almost drowned in the Croys River rescuing a goat kid?"

My mouth dries from the sight of her beautiful body flushed from our lovemaking and the lantern light bathing her in a radiant glow and brightening her amber eyes. She doesn't hide her small mounds. I toy with her auburn curls, trace her lips, lower to circle her tipped buds—swollen from my mouth.

I beam. "Storm that night."

Franzy props herself on her elbow to gaze at me. I pause to give her my full attention. She presses her hand to my chest. "Your heart was so strong, Isla. Fathyr has taken me on his travels to countless kingdoms. But you have the strongest heart I've ever known. Stronger than the shifters or the Sythe or the Shee. When you almost drowned in the River Cryth, I couldn't help but remember the night with the goat."

I roll my eyes, flutters colliding in my belly. Then, I mount her, straddling, my silver-flame hair skirting her face. "You silly sweet fool! I'll always be here for you." I pause and kiss each of her blushing cheeks, love how she squeezes her shoulders.

When Franzy parts her lips, sighing a little, I pause and tilt my head to the side to listen. "You must vow to me to be the strongest ever tonight, Isla. Because I'm certain I won't be."

I furrow my brows. "What do you mean, leyanyn?"

"I-I'm not like you, Isla. You know how much I love you. But my love is *different*."

Body stiffer, I come off her, remain at her side. "Tell me, Franzy."

"I don't have the same feelings. About all this..." she gestures to the bed, to our bodies. "I love your passion, Isla. Always have. It's why I let you—every time, but I—"

I groan and rub my eyelids. "Why didn't you ever tell me?"

"Please..." She lowers my hands. "You know I love you. I've loved you since we were bayrnies. I simply don't share your *passion*. I love yours. I love to make you happy. What pleases you pleases me. It's simply more about loving your heart and not your body. Do you understand?"

I sigh, smile fondly. "What's on your mind, Franzy? You're telling me this for a reason."

"I don't know how—I've only ever been with you. What if I don't—"

Comprehension batters me, and I cut her off, "You don't have to do anything, sweet fool!"

"But Prince Aydon is so kind. And he's given me so much time with my family. He's already paid off *all* of Fathyr's debt and bought him a new ship, Isla. He said we could wait, but we will be married tonight, too. How can I possibly—"

"It's *your* body, Franzy," I insist, grimacing, clenching my jaw. "Feyal-Ithydeir respect our form. It's the laws of our land. Simply tell him—"

"I'm not like you, Isla!" she shrieks, rising so she's above me. Still, her tone isn't sharp. Only flustered. But I recognize her forced smile. My sweet, silly fool. "When he bit me, the pleasure in his eyes, how he licked my blood from his lips...no, it wasn't the same as the Corpse King with you. Yes, I was watching. We will never have your spirit, your storm..."

"Franzy—"

"You don't have to explain, Isla. Whatever it is you share, I am happy for you. And I believe you will be like the Queen."

I mimic the Queen's face and words, savoring her giggle radiating warm ardor into my skin. Clamping my lips, I let her continue.

"Whatever happens tonight, I want to make him happy. Because he has made me happy by accepting me. Because it means I'll always be close to *you*."

At first, I gaze at her, stunned. Too stunned for my sweet fool who I'd believed was hurt, angry with me for volunteering. Shame tightens my throat for how I've misjudged my bonnya darling. An ache in my heart festers for what we've lost because she won't be my wed-mate. But my heart leaps, trading shame for adoration because nothing will separate us. How I'll be damned if Aryahn Kryach dares to reap my soul. I'd claw my way from the Nether-Void to be close to *her*.

Tapping her nose, I lean in, gather her in my arms, and declare, "Most men need little, Franzy. To please them, simply remove your gown before they request. Then, lie there, close your eyes, relax, and he will do the rest."

"Will it hurt?"

I purse my lips, sigh. "It *shouldn't*. You know how delicately the Ith treat human flesh. How they honor it. Yes, I've seen my parents. And the animals in heat on our farm. Void-gods damn, I spied on this sweetheart couple near Cock Cross' Scarlet Quarters. She wasn't a scarlet walker girl, but they pretended she was." My voice sounds flat while her eyes center on mine, growing wide with curiosity. "She cried and moaned. But she had the same quivering, shuddering which comes when we reach pleasure. After, she had a little blood. But she also laughed. And they didn't stop kissing. So...maybe both?"

Franzy bites her lower lip but nods and snuggles closer. "Thank you, Isla. Are you scared?"

I throw her a look. "Why?"

She shrugs. "Because you've never dragged me to the bed so fast."

I laugh, hoping she buys my bluff. "Well, ye're a long time deyed," I pronounce in flawless Talan-Feyalian. *Enjoy life, for once you are dead, it's forever.*

Franzy cups my cheeks. Kneels up. Kisses me. Eyes darting between mine. As if she's read my lie and understands my body's trembling beneath my strong mask. How my muscles brace for the wedding night. The Nether-mark claws at my spine. Except it's not fear. It's hatred.

"Don't die, Isla, please," she whimpers.

Donning a proud smirk, neck high, I kneel up with her. Mimic her by cupping her cheeks. "Sweet fool. I'm the first tribute in centuries, I have the favor of the Corpse King, I've accepted Kryach's mark, and tasted the Isles' sweetness. And there is so much more I long to do!"

With that, I kiss her and grow vines bursting with purple bell-heather—Franzy's favorite. The symbol of admiration. Of solitude. It's who she will always be to me.

When Queen Gryzelda enters my suite a short time later, she doesn't balk at Franzy and me tangled together. She simply commands the Feyal-maids to escort Franzy to her suite for preparation while she oversees mine.

Now, I relax, tension abating in my shoulders as the Feyal-maids attend to washing and combing my hair while I settle into the heated spring water of the bath. Earlier, I'd applied a powdered seal over the base of my spine to conceal the Nether-mark. It won't dissolve in water and will keep through dawn.

At least Kryach doesn't appear for my preparation. Since our last encounter, I've stopped calling him *Ary*. Dread rolls in my stomach at the thought of what could happen. All will depend on Allysteir. No, I press my lips together, posture because tonight, I will no longer be Isla—the farm girl from Cock Cross, the forger of elder seals, the Bone Games victor, the wild girl who dove into the Cryth River, and the first tribute in centuries. Tonight, I will become Queen of Nathyan Ghyeal. My glorious redoing! Whatever happens tonight will be my own gods-damned choice.

I heave a sigh, remembering what Franzy said about Allysteir and me. How he's welcomed me on his Death business, cherished it. How he's joined me for every midday meal and brought pomegranates every time—careful and attentive to tap seeds into a goblet for me. He's already treated me like a queen, served me as one. Surely the same will apply to my...bride *flesh*.

After the Feyal-maids finish and depart, leaving me alone with the Queen, I brace myself and flex my fists beneath the water—prepared for her admonishments, her assaults. To my surprise, Gryzelda merely assumes a comb and gently rakes it through my soaked waves.

"I didn't have the heart to accept the shadow-mark," she confesses, fingering my strands.

At first, I want to dismiss her words. It was impulsivity, not heart. And maddening desire for the tempting Isle-fruit. But I still would devour them, would choose them.

To sample a piece of the gods, to tempt Kryach himself, to willingly accept immortality is worth never leaving this deep world.

To deny myself any freedom, any desire, any choice would have been a far worse prison than becoming a forever Queen of the Underworld.

"Is this where you remind me of how Kryach will leave nothing but darkness in my soul?" I tilt my neck ever so little, catching her gaze.

"No."

Silence thickens the air between us. On and on, she combs until I nearly sink deeper into the water, my shoulders relaxing, breaths easing. Until finally...

"This is where I tell you how to cheat him."

I stiffen, shiver from Gryzelda's voice because Kryach's mark hums within my blood, thrumming my pulse. Of course, he's still bound to me. Knit into the fabric of my being and emotions.

"Isla, how much do you know of the past Corpse King? My husband?" inquires Gryzelda, dragging the comb, fingers calculating.

"Only a little. He was young when he died. Allysteir was only—"

"Fifteen, yes. Very young to accept Kryach's Curse." She breathes deep, pausing in her pursuit of my hair. "The God of Death had devoured so much of my soul by then. My contempt for the King had grown because the more he fucked me, the more Kryach took from me. So, I sought reclamation, peace, *love* wherever I believed. It's why Allysteir was born of a different man than Aydon's father. But after the King executed him, the last seam of my soul cleaved. I knew I wouldn't last another night if Kryach sampled upon me through the King. So, I..." her words trail off, her hands frantic as she resumes her combing.

Tangled in countless knots, I embrace the heaviness in my chest. A heaviness for her and turn around, stopping her hand. Her storm-clad eyes of gray winter are lost in memories of the past. Of the former Corpse King who perished under suspicious circumstances following the break in the Curse. The urban legend of an assassination has plagued all of Talahn-Feyal.

Gryzelda's eyes darken with shadows. A contrast to her ostentatious gown. A gold-gilded bone bodice adorns it while fire and earth jewels decorate her magnificent skirts of pix-silk and lace. As if she enriches her body to the extreme because she may never reclaim her soul. At this moment, I don't begrudge her or any of her past transgressions. Instead, I pity her.

At the deep weight of her revelation, heavier than all the mines of Nathyan Ghyeal, I touch my fingertips to the back of her hand clutching the comb and shake my head. "I would never...Allysteir is—"

"No different," she refutes, shaking her head. "Loathing, indifference... they were the most I could grant him when Kryach took him. I knew I couldn't grieve or I'd grieve for all eternity! He's the son of my only true love. The one scrap of emotion Kryach could not reap from me even if the last Corpse King did. Allysteir will be no different. Kryach infects him too much."

Blinking rapidly, I shake my head in denial, my strands thwacking against my cheek. I consider all the events of the past few weeks. How Allysteir has honored me. How Kryach vowed to rape my soul whenever he desired. They are the most extreme opposites I've encountered.

No, tonight will not be my undoing. I will not be reduced to mere violence. A scar of a soul. It will be my choice, my desire my freedom, my *redoing*!

When we emerge from the bathing room into the inner suite, all the Feyal-maids have disappeared. Replaced with...

"Aynfean."

"Bainye."

"Dairyne."

One by one, they chant their names—aged names of our history, but it's their appearance which leaves little doubt as to *how* ancient they are. And *where* they've come from. And *who* sent them. Little wonder no Feyal-maids are here; these ones likely sent them scampering away, horrified.

Gryzelda's eyes sharpen upon them, but her throat constricts, tightening in apprehension.

My breath catches in my chest. Nerve endings tickle from their skeletons gleaming silver through translucent flesh...as if infused with ghost-light. Deep shadows congregate around their eyes, nigh reducing them to hollow depths. Skin as white as moonlit water but garlanded in threads black as the deepest sea trench. Threads bound to the God of Death—to Aryahn Kryach. I can't bring myself to return to the nickname I'd chosen. Not after what he did.

Now, I ridicule myself for my mouth drying, throat growing thick, chest warming. For appreciating this gesture because they are here for one reason.

"We are Death maidens," Aynfean declares, her voice eerie as claws scraping crypt stone.

Dairyne's voice is more of a death rattle when she adds, "We are here to prepare you for the ceremony. By the command of Lord Aryahn Kryach—High God of Death!"

I tilt my chin to the shadow-mark near my collarbone, sense its chill ghosting across my flesh. "Is that so?" I almost add *Ary* but catch myself before it leaves my lips. "Then, I suppose we shouldn't waste Death's time."

I battle my rising smirk but can't help it. Especially when the Death maidens advance and remove my robe. It tumbles to the floor in a pool of white silk. I shiver. More when their nightmary-ice hands settle upon me. Now, I'm grateful for Gryzelda who monitors my preparation, protectiveness in her eyes.

The Death maidens baptize my flesh in oil born within the god Isles! It must be starflower oil—as is only unearthed within the moonshine mines of the Isles. Because with every stroke of their hands, the liquid permeates my skin—my flesh—and honors it with the essence of the stars until all of me shimmers, ethereal. As jewels on fire.

Next, the Death-maidens rouge my lips, my cheeks, my nipples, my very sex with the nectar of heart-roses—the most infamous of Isle lust blooms. So rare, only one has ever been bestowed upon the mortal world. A legend of a maiden with the purest of souls who earned the favor of the Goddess of Lust and Love. The Sythe Queen's Goddess. My breath turns ragged because I recognize this honor, this *favor*. My sex moistens from the acclaim, but my quickening heartbeat registers it more.

They don't stop there.

The Death-maidens tangle their skeletal hands into my hair. I close my eyes to the ministrations, but all of me is aroused, whetted. Sensing my emotions binding to power, I open my eyes and beam, proud of my corpus roses growing around the room. The ivy bursting with buds climbs along the walls, upon the bedposts, and creeps among the furniture. Gryzelda parts her lips, awed. But she doesn't dare interrupt the Death maidens when they arrange my hair into a flawless waterfall of curls, a storm of silver flame down my back. I can't help my radiant smile when they pluck a few of my corpus roses and fix them into the crown at the halfway mark of the back of my head. A floral crown to a curling cascade.

Finally...the gown!

When at last they seal the gown to my frame, the Death-maidens and Gryzelda grant me a few moments alone.

I frame my hand around the bodice, inhale, and turn to face my reflection.

I fall.

Aryahn Kryach's shade catches me, bearing me, his vaporous touch triggering me. I reinforce myself, stand taller, warning him with heated eyes.

He drifts to stand behind me, pronouncing, "You are truly the most glorious bride to grace the Citadel of Bones. To grace my Underworld," he coos into my ear, his essence of cold but fresh Isle-dew to settle, tender, upon me.

My heart wavers between armoring itself to pounding a rapid assault against the God. And the beauty of my reflection, a mirrored Isle-Goddess. I gasp a multitude and try to steady myself, only for my hands to meet with his...with Ary's and not the mirror as I'd intended.

"You're. Not. Forgiven," I express when he raises my hand to kiss, to rub his vaporous black mouth across my flesh.

A deep, familiar chortle. "Did I seek forgiveness, little wonder? Would a God ever seek forgiveness from a mere mortal girl?"

My blood rushes. But I can't deny the fire awakening in my heart, *my* choice words I will never deny. So, I lean in. I whisper temptation into the God of Death's ear, "You will fall to your knees and beg my forgiveness, *Ary*."

A deathly hand cups my cheek. I flinch at the thought of him claiming my mouth again. But he lingers. Those hollow dusky cavities of eyes gaze into mine.

"You are the splendor of eternity," he whispers, and my breath stalls, adrenaline impales my blood, and I part my lips. Aryahn Kryach smiles.

"Why?" I somehow breathe, lower lip trembling.

"Little wonder, do you not know? For your love of the Corpse King."

I purse my lips, bite my lower one to punish its trembling. Somehow, I force myself to gaze into those deep cavities, into those starless and moonless trenches, and wonder: could the God of Death himself desire...love?

TWENTY-SIX
"SHE IS MY SAVING GRACE!"
THE WEDDING

ALLYSTEIR

"I feel like a peacock," I grumble.

"Wrong region, brother," Aydon scoffs, referencing the bird island of Isel-Sonne.

How I loathe all this pomp and circumstance.

Aydon insists on the finest of tunics—of gold-lacquered bone-lined armor and fire-gems to cover every inch of my cape. At least I have held my own on the Corpse Mask—one identity trait I will never forsake despite the desire of all the royals. Despite the Curse, my face is my own. My choice. My identity. No one else reserves the right to peel away my accursed mask. Not even my bride.

"You won't fuck her tonight, will you?" Aydon questions while donning my head with the refter-tooth crown of the Corpse King.

"No." But a part of me believes Isla will provide my greatest challenge—how I must ruin her to keep her at bay. Not that it's any of

Aydon's business.

"Of course not. You and your silly games, Ally."

"Only because I have far more *skin* in the game, Aydon," I sneer, tempted to confront him about what I'd witnessed earlier in the Elder Guild. But I know better than to disrupt this monumental evening. Aydon departs in short order from the secondary hall. I overhear his triumphant speech within the Great Hall crowded with more people than any other festival in our history.

Darkness, deeper than ever, shrouds the Underworld, signifying dusk has fallen upon Talahn-Feyal. By now, thousands will have gathered around the Citadel city along with countless ships and meager boats by water to bear witness to the future Bride of the Corpse King: the first tribute in centuries...and commoner. Ever since her illustrious plunge into the River Cryth, a sight I would have given my eye-teeth to behold, mass rumors have abounded among the people hailing her beauty, her spirit, her passion. By now, word has spread of her corpus roses offerings to the dying in the Hollows.

A deep breath of pride fills my lungs and rushes blood to my heart at the thought. How the people adore her.

Wait until they gaze upon her in her bridal garb, Kryach invades my musings, his tone amused, his pride dominating mine.

I curl my upper lip back behind my mask. *What the devil are you talking about?*

You will see soon, Allysteir. No need to thank me, but she certainly did.

I grind my teeth, incensed. All too soon, Isla will arrive, escorted by my mother into this secondary hall. From here, we will depart into an open coach to the main causeway bridge spanning the city to impart a glimpse of the bride to the people in all her majesty. Part of me wishes to delay it, to remain in the Great Hall with all the other waiting royals and witness Isla's grand entrance down the River Cryth. But Aydon insists on my joining the procession—on casting us as star-crossed lovers due to Isla's volunteering.

The moment he emerges into the secondary hall following his speech is when Feyal-maids issue inside from an adjoining hall, escorting Franzyna in her bridal wear. I smile at her traditional royal violet gown which accentuates her auburn curls gathered into a lustrous crown upon her head...and her amber eyes. A silver tiara adorns her brow, befitting her status as a Prince's bride.

As he passes, I arrest Aydon's elbow in a warning to tread carefully with Isla's sweetheart. A conversation we had during our preparation. A vow he made to me after my personal guarantee of using Kryach's power against him should he dishonor her in any way. Due to more *recent* events, such a guarantee was necessary.

Franzy offers a timid smile, chin tilted to her collarbone as Aydon greets her with a formal bow of his head and a brushing of his lips upon the back of her hand. "My deepest apologies our ceremony will not be so public or grand, my lady..."

Franzy shakes her head. "I prefer something smaller and quieter. Thank you, Prince Aydon."

"From now on, you will call me Aydon. Franzy," he lowers his voice to a deep lull and brushes his knuckles across her cheek. But I catch the gleam in his eye when he surveys her throat, his personal mark. Because while honor, desire to survive, and gratitude have me posturing whenever I view my bite mark upon Isla's flesh, my brother preens with entitlement. With flesh lust.

Nothing matters. Nothing whatsoever when the Death-maidens

embark into the secondary hall alongside Mathyr, who wears a knowing grin, her shoulders back, chest thrust so the pix-spun tulle and chiffon gown—studded with diamonds—catches the torch firelight.

Nothing whatsoever compared to Isla. She comes forth from the darkness like an angyl goddess descending from the Isles shining like a flaming sword!

Kryach, you damned devil! I roar inside my head, receiving a deep chortle.

She is the dawn rising upon a winter land to blind it into sparkling submission. She is the targeted point of a newly-forged lance in the moonlight. She is lightning at sunrise.

My breath stalls as Isla sways toward me. All these weeks, she has chosen a different gown, but this one is beyond my comprehension. While I'd theorized she'd ultimately choose traditional royal purple or a stunning white, she has adorned herself in the purest of gold!

Off-the-shoulders. A form-fitting floral bodice of nether-lace as black as midnight—broken by spun gold. And oh, gods! Spun gold forms the gown itself—skirts sweeping to an ethereal train disappearing beyond the hall. And sheer...so sheer and transparent to reveal her beauteous limbs of effervescent angyl frost skin made so by Isle-oil. I scent the tempting fragrance. And the attachments from the shoulders—sinuous golden, chiffon cascades—unite with the gown train.

Bound by corpus roses, her seductive curls bare her throat and flesh of her collarbone and spirit-fair upper breasts. My throat dries, tongue whetted from the barest erect edges of rosebud nipples peeking from beyond the bodice's floral lace. She steals my breath and also my blood, my flesh, my bones, my damned, cursed heart.

Isla advances to me and curtsies, lowering her chin. "My Lord Alysteir,

Corpse King."

I can do no more than place my fingers beneath her chin and lift her beguiling face to my eye. At first, I'd believed the vines on her arms were part of the gown, but no, these are her creations—corpus rose buds growing from their centers.

"Isla..." I somehow breathe and cup her cheek, leaning in, my desire unfathomable. Kryach's forbidden fruit, tempting me to take her tonight, to gift her soul to him.

Never! I seethe.

Will you deny her free will? Her choice, Allysteir? he coos in my head.

She won't get the chance.

Aydon sweeps in, interrupting mine and Isla's moment, reminding us, "The people are waiting, Allysteir. It is time for the procession."

Isla undoes me.

This is not my show. It's hers.

While I know what to expect and how to proceed with the Hollows and the dying, with refter attacks and Ifrynna, with Betha and the spirits, with my damned refter brides, Isla knows how to charm the people.

From our coach of varnished gold and diamonded bones, she waves to the adoring crowds from the leading bridge causeway. And goes so far as to grow heather and black death roses and cast them below to the peoples—careless whether anyone knows about her singular gift. As if she is coming into her own, embracing whatever power, heritage, or gifts her blood may hold.

My posture stiffens, and I lean closer to her, awed by her jubilation for everyone, including the wealthier citizens who have paid a higher coin to access a prominent bridge position. My adrenaline rolls in rippling waves when she halts the coach so she may approach individuals and families.

Rooted to my position, I observe as she bestows a kiss upon a child. Or tosses her curls and laughs at the exultation of her audience. They fawn over her. And I marvel, lips parted in wonderment.

Because she is my little wonder, Kryach echoes in my mind.

My *dark rose,* I snarl, territorial.

Whatever else she is, the gods have blessed her. Or *cursed* since she has endangered her soul by volunteering to be my bride. A soul I will protect at all costs.

The only time I disembark from the coach is when I must draw my bride from her cherishing audience. Otherwise, I'm certain she would spend all night with them. But the nobles are expecting us. And all those waiting in the ships and boats over the River Cryth. I can't resist lifting my mask to kiss her cheek as she waves farewell to the families on the bridge. She flinches. Not in repulsion, judging by the widening of her eyes and how she covers her mouth, stifling a giggle. Those blushing cheeks shame me. Her heart could receive all Talahn-Feyal. Perhaps all Talahn-Feyrahn.

Finally, we reach the end of the causeway which spills to a canal—a bridal barge receiving us. I offer Isla my hand so she may wander onto the bridge with its arched canopies of gold chiffon and torches. I find myself staring at the exquisite shape of her plump thighs through the transparent lacey fabric. Imagine worshipping between those thighs, tongue traveling upward to the flaming jewel of flesh. She must taste sweeter than the first dew that ever graced the world!

Her chin lifts, regal high, when the barge emerges into the Great

Hall where all nobles and elites and elders have gathered to witness the procession. Far different than her countenance with the lay-people, Isla shifts her body language, posturing to a queen. Queen of the Underworld.

When the barge docks before the dais, Aydon greets us along with his intended who kisses Isla's cheek and will stand as her maid-attendant. Nor am I surprised by Elder Kanat prepared to initiate the ceremony. In a way, it's a matter of pride and ironic amusement. Beneath my mask, I smirk, I wiggle my brows, my voice higher than anticipated when I take Isla's hand in my gloved one and pronounce my vows. After tonight, Kanat would be a fool to thwart me, to assault her.

Once Isla pronounces her traditional vows, once we share the ritualistic wine and hand-fasting bonds to unite us—when I know Isla will never sever the knotted cords tonight—once I slide the silver ring with hands clasped around a gold heart onto her left hand, I lift my corpse mask to accept her willing kiss.

And it is willing. To the applause of the nobles, of the royals, she kisses me. Her hand trespasses upon the ruined side of my mouth. A bare brush of her fingers against my exposed teeth. Her sweet fingertips trace them as if she considers them pearls.

Sweet, sweet, sweet! I exclaim, knowing Kryach can hear.

And yet, you will deny her tonight. You will hurt her. You will wound her, he challenges.,

No more than you, I snarl. *I will always choose the lesser of two evils.*

At least I do not make excuses for my behavior. I am a High God!

And I am a King. And she is my Queen.

Following our bridal kiss, Isla kneels. So lovely to see her kneel before me, her head lowered to accept the crown I bestow upon her fair brow. Heat radiates through me, beyond fond of my bride. A crown of pure

213

black crystal and bones spiked at their tips by diamonds—gold-lacquered twigs and vines woven between the bones and crystals. Perfect for her.

"I present...Isla Adayra now Isla Morganyach," I cite our monarchial surname she will embrace. Tenderly place the crown on her head.

As she rises to face the assembly, they respond in a standing ovation. At their blackwood table of honor upon the dais, the royals follow suit.

Not once does Isla wave. Pain assaults me at the thought of what will come later, what I must do when she rises higher, when she raises her magnified chin, accepting the role of Queen of the Underworld—a role she was prepared for once she accepted Kryach's shadow mark.

I escort her to the balcony where all those in the boats and ships along the River Cryth and the Isle of Bones beyond the waterfall-bridges may glimpse their new Bride of the Corpse King. Thousands of lanterns release. Cheers explode to shake the Five White Ladies themselves. The lanterns drift into the air, turning to a host of stars amidst the domed ceiling leagues above us.

I monitor Isla's reaction. How she parts her lips, touches her hand to her heart, undone by the laudation. But why? She is the one who has saved us all.

In my pain, in my misery, I'd gone so far as to challenge the gods themselves. Isla...she is my saving grace!

All too soon, we will sup with the royals. Then retire to our bedroom. And while many will expect us to consummate, where Isla may tempt me, I will never fall prey to such temptation.

Or Kryach will win.

And all will be lost.

"Will you tell me more about the rolling chair?" Isla requests of the Blue-Skin monarch, curious about the other races as usual.

Perhaps she has tiptoed around the invasive question, but tonight, my bride's exuberance cannot be contained. Full of pomegranate wine and sweets from the bridal feast and wearing a Queen's crown.

The Blue-Skin-they chuckles and gestures to their faulty legs concealed beneath their royal blue robes which nearly match their skin. "If you spent most of your life beneath the seas, you would find land-life most difficult to navigate."

She smiles. Fond and musing. Her sultry lashes tempt all the royals. The Sythe Queen most. Isla reserved a precious, few minutes for her family. For kissing them and hugging them before joining me at the royal table where she has thrust the most of her attention. Still, she undoes me, sweeping me into her passion.

This will be more difficult than anything I've conceived.

Her questions, like her appetite, are endless. Amused, the royals answer when she asks while she feasts on wild boar, honeyed pomegranates, haggys, raspberries and cream porridge, on pudding dumplings, and more. Her appetite unbridled as her curiosity.

Finally, in the wee morning hours, after Aydon has carried his worn bride to bed, I alert Isla how it's time to retire to our bridal chambers.

When she widens her eyes—her expression like spirits who cannot thwart Death, though her smirk contrasts her radiant eagerness—I know I will regret this. I will lament this. And later, I will magnify her and idolize her. I will enact such penance, she will forgive me.

Months later. Desire later. Everything...later.

TWENTY-SEVEN

"IT'S COMMON FOR MARRIED COUPLES TO SHARE EVERYTHING..."

ISLA

Breath heavier than an hourglass, heart throbbing enough to bruise my ribcage, skin tingling until corpus roses and thorns bud along my arms, I clench my clammy hands and strengthen my knees as Allysteir leads me to his chambers. The Corpse King's chambers.

Along the way, the elaborate skeletal sculptures and tapestries distract me from the blood thrashing in my ears. I remember the first time he'd carried me to my chambers with the aid of his shadows. How he'd commanded me to calm and vowed he would not do anything then but made no guarantees regarding our wedding...night.

I try to steady my quaking breath, peer at the vacant mask out of the corner of my eye. Blush and turn when he inclines his head to mine. His ascot veils any gestures. No guidance. I blink and close my eyes, reminding myself he's a Feyal-Ithydeir who must honor my flesh. During our time together, he has revered it, respected me. Yes, I trust

Allysteir. But not the God within him.

As if registering my emotions, my thoughts, the shadow-mark pulsates, the skull eyes erupting with blood fire as if warning. *Tread carefully, little wonder...*I imagine Kryach purring to me. I lick my lips, swallow. Surely he won't—not so soon. My vision swirls, legs weakening.

After we've ascended the tallest Citadel tower with my immense train glittering down the staircase like angyl's spun glass, we arrive before a great arched door of fused skulls. I shiver. They remind me of the Skull Ruins. I remember when I removed Allysteir's mask and stared at his contrast of a face with one side as soft, sculpted, and fair as an angyl seryph despite the threadwork of black veins upon his high cheekbones and the deep violet shadow beneath his eye.

But the other side was all the stuff of legend, of our songs, and little girls' nightmares. As if the Nether-Void scrawled itself on Allysteir with ruinous flesh, one ghostly eye, missing lip, and exposed jagged teeth. Macabre but beautiful in its contrast.

Will he show it to me tonight?

I wince when Allysteir forms a key of his shadows to unlock the skull door which parts. At first, he turns to me. As I open my mouth, the King places his hand upon my waist and sweeps me into his arms. I shudder and steady the crown on my head as he carries me inside, his muscles tight. When I slide my arms around his shoulders and neck, the tension beneath his tunic and ascot prompts his veins to pulsate through his flesh. His mask eyes do not retreat from my face.

My flowers follow us inside the chamber. I gush at the grandiose room with its ornate fireplace spanning one whole wall, the arched stained-glass windows overlooking the Sea of Bones, and the tapestry portrait of colorful bones and teeth. I don't reflect long when Allysteir lowers me to the floor an inch from the bed. As he does, those muscles tighten as if he's bracing himself.

Before I may open my mouth, the King cocks his head to me. Hands encircling my waist, he leans in—black hollow mask eyes marking mine—and commands in a deep, dark voice, "Strip."

I furrow my brows, but he turns his back following his order. Angry heat flushes my whole body. More when he tugs at my wrist, jerking me by the cord binding us. Glowering, I don't budge, but thankfully the rope is long enough for him to approach the corner table where he uncorks the wine flask. So, this is how he wants to play it, how he baits me. He desires my challenge, my fight to ruin tonight. For what reason, I can't comprehend.

I won't give him what he wants. Not when I have my own bait.

Still, my fingers tremble when I lower the off-the-shoulder sleeves, slide the gown down my body until it spills to the floor, weeping a golden river. While he pours two goblets of wine, back to me, I quickly release the crown of my hair so the corpus roses tumble off my body. Allysteir turns to face me the moment I shake out my curled waves.

I simper when he freezes. I don't need his mask off to recognize this was the *last* thing he expected. For me to call his bluff. For me to wear no shame as I stand with my hands on my hips and stare him down in all my glorious, bare flesh. The Isle oil bathes my skin as if I've swallowed moonbeams. Gratified by the King's breath increasing its tempo, I grin from a telltale bulge beneath his form-fitting breeches prodding his robe.

"Well?" I tap one finger to my hip in a subtle challenge. Wicked, I thrust out my generous bosom, nipples peaking from the room's chill. "The Death-maidens rouged them with pomegranate juice if you'd care to *taste*." Oh yes, two can play this game.

Allysteir growls. But I beam when the skull-mark hums, when shadows breed around my body as if Kryach wishes to stoke the King's jealousy. Or desire.

He grunts. Advances to offer me one goblet, the mask descending till his icy breath unravels upon my face. "Or perhaps I will simply bite a chunk from your *belly*..." His gloved fingers stroke my navel, pinching the tender flesh. I stiffen, narrowing my suspicious eyes as he finishes, "...since you obviously have more plump meat to spare."

Accepting the wine, I trace my tempting tongue around the goblet line and lower my lashes, seductive, and hum a taunt, "At least I have flesh to spare unlike your bag of bones."

"Oh, you naughty buxom bride," Allysteir chastises me, clicking his tongue behind the mask. I grin because I hint his amused tone, "Perhaps I shall turn you over my lap and give your ample bottom the rich spanking it deserves."

I thrill and tip the goblet, savoring the wine as it stings my throat with its heated spice before remarking, "You could try, but I'd hate for an extremity to fall off."

Spinning on a heel, I laugh at his stunned silence and wag my hips to jiggle my ample bottom in a double-downed insult. Despite my bare feet, I feel two heads taller. The shadows trail me, flirting with my corpus roses growing out of the stone floor cracks. This time, Allysteir has no choice but to follow when I tug on his tether.

"What are you doing?" wonders Allysteir, voice grim as I take full satisfying breaths.

I throw open his wardrobe wide. "Well, if *your* meat is too timid, I'll be seeking some proper nightwear. The gown was perfect but far too heavy for sleeping."

"Your belongings have not been transferred yet."

I wave a hand in dismissal and retrieve one of his many spider-silk robes, shrug into it, and slide my hair from beyond the fabric. The cord's magic allows for these menial purposes but snaps into place following.

"And now, she wears my Death robe," the King grumbles behind me.

I giggle and angle my neck to him, batting my eyes. "Something you wish to say, dear husband?" I sing-song, wondering how long he will put up with this game.

The robe swims on me, trailing to the floor. The barest slopes of my breasts peek from the center gaps but don't expose my buds. Finished with my wine, I swing to Allysteir where he's pouring himself his second goblet. Before he may lift it, I snatch it away, reveling in his clenched fist, laugh, and down the wine in one full draught. Careless of how it burns my throat.

"That was *mine*!" Allysteir protests as I lick my lips.

"There's a bit leftover right here if you want some," I mention, gesturing to the corner of my mouth where a droplet or two trickles down my chin.

"What are you doing?" he closes the distance between us, the shadows multiplying.

"Come now, Allysteir, it's common for married couples to share everything, isn't it?"

I tilt my neck to the side, exposing my throat to him. Rock back on my heels, perhaps a little too smug. The wine pulses more warmth through me and charges it into the spaces between my thighs. They grow hot with desire. Can the King, my husband, scent my arousal?

Before the urge may grow, Allysteir seizes me and thrusts me against the wall. My stomach grows heavy. A stab of icy breath arrests my ear from the King's voice, but it sinks into my core most, into my veins as if he is controlling the shadow-mark.

"You dare test the Corpse King in his chambers?" Allysteir warns deeply, and I shiver. I tremble when his tongue flicks beyond the mask to steal the wine droplet upon my chin. "You dare test the God of Death himself?"

"Allyste—" I struggle against him, but he presses me harder to the wall. Adrenaline pumps more blood to my heart. Responding to my emotions, thorny vines grow, bearing black death roses. But Allysteir thwarts my floral defenders with his shadows. The shades devour them, shred their petals. Tears brew behind my eyes.

"My sweet, dark rose...you believe you have wooed me, captivated me, tantalized me with your flesh, your blood, your beauty, your gifts?"

My eyes roll to their ceilings. Fingers lose feeling as I battle his shadow hold, this *Death* grip.

The only way to survive him is to permit him to rape your soul, to not ever fight back, to allow him to pillage you again and again until not one shred of your heart remains.

No! I can't believe this is the same Corpse King who saved me in the Skull Ruins. The one who remained at my side during the virginity test, shared Skathyck, and defended me to his mother. The King who sung his shadow lullaby over the dying in the Hollows. Allysteir who offered me Isle fruit and savored my flesh and blood. Who adored me with his kiss. And shared nearly every waking moment with me, shared secrets and history over pomegranates, laughed with me, loved...

I gasp when he grips my jaw, jerking my face to his. Tremors assault my body. I strain with his hands. The rope has become a prison chain.

Allysteir rips off his mask to bare the full weight of the withered side of his corpse face, this haggard ruin—deathly and macabre with teeth exposed in a perma-leering grin. I scream and scream until he wrenches my face closer and growls, "You long to play with Death? Now, I will show you what you will look forward to!"

A tempest of shadows bombards us. They surround my body in irresistible folds as if to snuff me out. Will they reap my very heart and soul?

"No!" I scream, thrashing with the dark, deathly embrace clawing into my blood. No flower, vine, or thorn may save me now.

Is this Death's true reaping? I thought it would be a current. I imagine becoming a current to fade into the undertow. To disappear with dark water. Until all you are is...cold.

The cold retreats. Fades like warm breath swallowed by winter air. When the shadows dissipate, when they part like billowing curtains, I almost scream. Shake my head in denial. Clutch at my aching throat, released from the King's grip. He stands behind me. But the strangulation marks upon my throat pale to the pain assaulting my chest, piercing my lungs.

No longer do we stand inside the King's bridal chambers. We stand amidst bone trees, a bone forest. The telltale hush of a dark river beyond my sobs and tears. But it's not the skeletal surroundings. It's *them*!

My legs grow weak, buckle. Allysteir jerks on the rope chain, hauling me up. "Rise, Your Majesty," he commands through gritted teeth and forces me to remain where I am. "Yes, now you understand, every legend is true. Every song. Every nightmare."

The refter brides stray toward me. Decayed mouths open. Eyes cadaverous—unseeing from the craze. And that silly, eerie rhyme echoes in my mind. My breath bursts. I hyperventilate.

Corpse King, Corpse King, he's coming for his bride
Corpse King, Corpse King, all you virgin nighyans hide

"I *am* the monster they teach children to fear," Allysteir continues. He holds me still as the brides moan and stagger toward me. Crazed! Wild! Hungry! For my flesh.

He'll steal your bones to make his brew
And your heart will taste so sweet in his stew

I whimper when Allysteir sweeps my waves to one side and trails his mouth along the side of my neck. "Yes, Isla. I am cursed. I am damned. And the moment you volunteered to be my bride, you damned yourself."

No, long before. Birth-damned. Birth-cursed.

My limbs quake. Memories of the Nether-Void. Of the refter bites of my childhood. The mark upon my back. A sign of my bond to it. Now, my greatest fear is paraded before my eyes. This is who...*what* I will become.

He'll carry you off to his cold and lonely bed
He'll eat your soul until you're all but dead!

I can't deny it. On our farm, I could face my fears with a pitchfork or in the depths of the Hollows with my scyan. I could defend Franzy. Turn off all emotion, pretend, make a sport of them, a cruel joke. Not tonight. Hundreds of brides, hundreds reduced to raped and reaped souls. Nothing left but scars.

"Why are you doing this?" I whimper. I claw for Allysteir, disturbing the chain, almost beg for his protection as the refter brides swing their hair like gray and frayed ribbons. Their mouths widen, teeth preparing.

"Careful, little bride. Some fates are worse than Death!" He shoves me forward with a cruel laugh. Allysteir forms a blade with his shadows. And severs the rope.

Paralyzed by the horror, I watch him fling the rope to the ground while he leers at me through his mask. I stumble but catch my balance at the last second. I swing my arms while the cut chain tumbles against my skin before it falls at my feet.

Too distracted, I don't notice the bride until her claws drag across the robe, shredding its back. She shreds my flesh with it. I scream! Not from the pain but because they close in. Terror-stricken eyes frozen wide, I seek an opening. Breath rasping, I find the sliver of space between their bodies and shove one out of the way. I duck under one diving for me. Countless teeth snap. Moans engulf my ears, drowning all other noises, including my screams.

But not Allysteir's voice, urging, urging, urging, "Run, my dark rose! Run, little Bride of the Corpse King!"

I squeeze between limbs. Shadows stalk me, preying. Nothing but claws and teeth tearing. They catch the remainder of the robe and rip it from my body. I squeeze my eyes shut, tears fly past my clenched lids as I run and cover my breasts. When I knock into a bone tree, I gasp for air, grip its body, shedding powder with my sharp nails. The moans follow, staggering closer.

Utterly naked, shame reddening my cheeks, I reach for the nearest bone branch and climb. Higher and higher. Nothing but will to escape as my breath turns shallow, pulse racing. No more star-flower oil. Now, bone powder coats my flesh, branch tips nicking my skin to draw blood.

I stop halfway up the tree. At its base, the refter brides congregate. Their arms strain, necks arched so they may wail. Tremors engulf my limbs. I curl my knees to cover myself as much as possible with my hair, with my arms. Peering through the strands, I behold Allysteir standing a hundred yards away. Tears streaming down my cheeks, with my heart sinking into my stomach, I cage a whimper, a moan when the King touches his hand to his brow in a gesture of departure.

He's leaving. My shoulders sag. It's not hurt. It's not ruin or woe. It's relief! The rotting flesh of hundreds of refter brides is far more preferable than the scrap of his Death face. I want to believe there's a reason he's doing this, some form of protection. But all I feel is hate. Ironic how I hate him more than...

Yes, little wonder...

I flinch from Kryach's voice. Of his skull wreathed in blood-fire as it whispers to me. *Now you see his true face. Will I see yours tonight?*

Yes, Aryahn Kryach is here to stay. All. Night. Long.

And he has given me my answer. My words. My thoughts. My strength!

Before Allysteir may turn, I press my lips into a tight seam, swipe at my tears, and burn my eyes against his. Gripping two branches on each side of me, I crouch in a gesture of a promise, my personal vow. He believes he may break me tonight. By morning, any tears I may have will be traded for wrath.

My glorious redoing.

Naked, huddled in the tree with hundreds of corpse brides surrounding me, I watch the Corpse King turn his back.

At last, I *grow*. My glorious redoing.

TWENTY-EIGHT
PROTECTING HER, PUNISHING MYSELF

ALLYSTEIR

She will believe the shadows I sent to heal the wounds on her back and neck are from Kryach. It doesn't matter. All that matters is she is safe.

Nausea hardens my stomach. Pain racks my throat. But tonight, I don't drink Sythe wine. I don't use shadows to afford myself any comfort. My lungs shrink. I struggle for breath. Wrestle against bile, but it comes anyway. I find a dark corner of the mountain to retch all the contents from our bridal supper.

Tonight, Kryach tortures me. Vindictive. Because she would have consented. Nothing less than Isla's hatred would have prevented her passion, her desire for our bridal bed. If I could have lied...but the Curse forbids it.

Adrenaline surges through my body. By the time I arrive in my chambers, the violence is uncontrollable. Flinging off the mask, chucking it to the ground, I stare at my miserable, damned face in the mirror. Clench my fists. Smash the glass to smithereens. Do the same with all the others until glittering shards cover the floor, until my fist is bloodied and bruised with glassy fragments lodged in my knuckles. My other is fractured phalanges which will require a full night of slow-healing. More than I deserve.

Her eyes were the worst torture. Whatever pain infects me tonight is nothing compared to her eyes. Or how she ran from me. I couldn't tell her how much I was holding my brides back, ensuring she could run. I didn't know Aislyn would strip her robe and flesh, how the others would leave her in nothing but her radiant flesh.

From the moment she emerged in her glorious bridal attire with her skin drenched in the dew of Eyleanan and the Death-maidens trailing her, I knew Kryach wouldn't wait. She'd enchanted the crowds with her roses. She'd accepted the crown to become Queen of the Underworld. Too envious, Death would never have permitted Isla to remain—to be bound to my soul, to be Queen forever. He would have devoured her soul. He would have stolen her from me to serve him in the Isles: a mistress in his Harem of Souls.

No, I don't allow myself pity. Nothing but self-loathing plagues my bones and weighs upon my head. Nothing but blood pounds my ears. My chest heaves from self-hatred.

Never before have I required such extremes. Most brides feared me, hated me. Still, I loved them all...fiercely, deeply, madly until they felt my love beyond my corpse. But Isla, she is the first who loved my corpse. The deepest, strongest heart I've encountered. My dark rose. His little wonder. And power enough to tempt the God of Death.

I'll be damned if I allow him to steal her.

Seething, I tear at my robe, tear it to funereal scraps until I'm as naked as she was. Naked, half-rotted, cursed—my reflection in the glass shards as shattered as my being. I grip a larger chunk. I drag it across my flesh. Hiss through my nostrils. Any pain is better than the torture in my heart. Jaw clenched, I scrawl the sharpened edge of glass across my arm and grind my teeth. I break them until blood clots my mouth and my muscles throb from agony.

The scarlet line doesn't take long to heal. My Feyal blood knits my flesh, restores it. I growl and cut three more lines upon my arm. "Why half?" I snarl to no one about my ruined self because the room is hollow. My mind is quiet because Kryach is with *her*. "Better for both sides to match, eh Aryahn?" I taunt the emptiness, the shadows of his essence in my mind. He will hear them later.

I'm delaying the inevitable. Kryach never changes. The hourglass of a year's worth of sand grains has tipped. If we do not consummate the marriage by the next Feast of Flesh which is held on the Night of Masks this year, the Nether-Void will consume all of Talahn-Feyal.

I have one year. One year to spend with my bride. One year to right the wrongs of this night. One year of days and nights to prove my heart, to love her fiercest, deepest, maddest. Fuck Kryach. Fuck Kanat and Morrygna and their dark vendetta. Fuck my brother and his political schemes and dishonor of our kingdom. Fuck whatever refters come over the next year.

I cut and cut. Carve through flesh, through veins, through muscle and sinew...to my fucking bones. If only I could carve out my heart until it unites with the carnal ribbons of blood pooling upon the ground. Nostrils flaring, veins bulging through my skin, rivers of tears upon my cheeks, I find the largest chunk of glass and discover my reflection.

The sides don't match. But they are close.

At dawn, I ride Ifrynna to my bride, climbing the cliffsides only my Guardian may conquer. By now, all my wounds have healed, but the blood-soaked rug was irredeemable.

As soon as Ifrynna's three heads crest the cliffs where the river cascades, the mystical sight is the last I expected. At first, I'm convinced the gods have transformed my refter bride hollow into an Isle paradise. Where once the bone trees were naked and eerie, flowers now clothe the cadaverous branches. Curtains and tapestries of flowers flutter in the wind like jubilant ribbons. No order. Utter chaos, a mosaic of heather, corpus roses, black death roses, scarlet heart named for Skathyk, white Inker, and various others I don't recognize from beyond the Underworld. Thousands of petals have shed from the trees to sprinkle the river.

Now, I remember how my bride's eyes burned as I departed, how they'd transformed to fiery amethysts as if vowing wrath and ruin.

Infuriated, I ball my hand into a fist as Ifrynna's paws skirt across mantles of blooms upon the ground. I am wrath and ruin. Rot and death. Isla is the opposite. This is her fire. Her baring her teeth and laughing in the face of death.

Not one bone tree is left unclad.

"A wonder indeed," muses my of-few-words Guardian, her toothy smiles growing as we embark past more flowering trees. Whole vines and roots bearing blossoms shoot from the ground.

Thus far, no sign of my refter brides. Or Isla. Until we make our way to the end of the great bone-tree hollow close to the river's berth where the trees thin. Cautious because hope is lost in the Underworld—

shredded as easily as diaphanous breath—, I swallow a knot in my throat as we approach two massive floral tapestries. They hang between two bone trees, concealing the clearing at the river. From beyond, the sparkly soprano of Isla's voice echoes. Far higher a lilt than I'd expected.

Ifrynna's breath grows heavier to puff against the tapestries, disturbing them. They flick to offer a glimpse. Of hundreds of my refter brides. Sucking in a deep breath, I hold it and will my shadows to part the blooming curtains.

My breath hitches. My shadows freeze. Tingling shock sprouts all over my body at the sight of my bride. Isla dances before my refter brides, hips swaying as she speaks to them from behind a barrier of shadows and thorny stakes. She's woven them full gowns of flowers. She's knit crowns of thistles and winterbells for their ragged streamers of hair.

In one impalement, Kryach's spirit penetrates me, filling every recess of my mind, my heart, my soul. Something feels...different. Death is always cold. Numb. Deadened. Never before have I sensed...warmth. An undercurrent—barely a ribbon, but I can't deny it. Even the tension in my body abates once it latches onto the undercurrent. But it's not long before his deep chortle resonates in my mind: a reminder of his ultimate power. Of why last night was a necessary evil.

I gaze at my bride. Awed with my heart braying so hard, it might crush my ribcage. Isla, herself, wears thorns. A crown of spiked thorns, a skin-tight gown of thorns to garb her. Protective armor. But her cheeks flush with the same passion, nor have her eyes lost their luster. No, they shine with incandescence as her flesh shimmered with Isle-oil the previous night.

Some refter brides crane their necks, hands grappling with the makeshift thorny shadow gate. Isla continues swaying, then tosses her hair back to reveal the shadow mark upon her neck.

"So, I ate the seeds. And then the fruit!" she imitates sucking invisible juice.

I shake my head, stunned. She's telling them...stories?

"The King bit me then and there. I thought he was going to touch me, but he didn't. Probably a good thing." She waves a hand, but her eyes flick to mine, violet and violent jewels pinning mine.

I make no moves, speak no words. Allow her to finish. "I joined him on his Death business. So grand to sail the River Cryth, past the Sea of Bones, and to the Hollows. The passing ones loved my corpus rose gifts. I hope you like my flowers, death pretties." She beams, exalting in how some brides moan, fingers straining for her. "Now, now, Aylsa, we will have no interruptions to my twisted tale."

"Davyna," I say.

Isla flicks her head up. Pinches her lips. Cocking her head to the side, she narrows her eyes upon me. "Did you have something to say, my King?"

Heaving a sigh, I dismount from Ifrynna, approach the refter brides from behind, and gesture to the one she'd pointed to. "That is Davyna. She always wore her hair twisted into heart-knots on her head." I trace a finger over the knots bound to her head, though they are now gray and frayed. And decorated with Isla's floral circlet. My bride stiffens but tracks my movements.

"That is Aylsa." I jerk a finger to my former bride four rows down on my right, pinpointing her from among the mass. "She has a scar beneath her right eye from the time she rode her horse and met an unfortunate encounter with a tree branch."

Isla postures, raises her chin, as sovereign as when I'd placed the crown upon her head last night. "I'll remember, thank you, my King. Perhaps you may introduce me to all of them *properly*...unlike last night's unfortunate and incidental introduction."

"You've made your point clearly, Isla." I extend a gloved hand.

She laughs. The sound—wind chimes from the Isles, soul sirens, icicles breaking due to a spring thaw—guts me. I knead my brow, understanding the depth of my transgression and how my penance will need to be tenfold to gain a foothold of her good graces.

Dismissing my hand, Isla faces the refter brides again and continues her story. I quirk a brow when Ifrynna curls onto the soft, gray meadow grass among the refters to listen, folding her massive paws one over the other. Isla grins at the Guardian's presence.

Closing my eyes, I listen to every word. Feast on them, including the bitter poisonous ones because this is her vengeance. Her thorns stake my heart. The new knowledge of the deal she made with Kryach when Kanat tracked her to the library, how he's accessed her all this time, haunted her every step. She knew and plied him and tempted him, and his shades enclosed her every night after I'd finished my lullaby. All this pierces me as deep as the mark upon her flesh.

Until the fateful wedding morning when Kryach assaulted her, forced her to her knees, and strangled his death-essence around her. Death gave her a sample. Last night, I gave her the full dose. Malice thickening in my throat, I growl under my breath. Sick of this endless cycle. At least Isla has joined with the games unlike my past brides who were on the receiving end.

Except for Finleigh who refused to engage. Who had the audacity to spit in Kryach's face every time. Finleigh rejected and ignored the God of Death but affirmed and respected and grew to love me. While Isla tempts and seduces us both.

My bride concludes her story, "It was such a pleasure to get to know all of you last night," her voice sparkles, and she blows them a kiss. "I wish it had been under better circumstances when the King was not acting like a malevolent and malicious *monster*."

Her words are a justified scythe carving my heart. I'm certain she would love to hold the vital muscle in her hand. And I would bow before her and allow her to squeeze it, to crush it like a pomegranate fit for her captivating mouth.

As Isla waves to the refter brides, Ifrynna rises, leaps over the thorny fence in a single bound to shake the ground beneath Isla's feet. My bride's smile is more radiant than all our kingdom's mines of jewels when Ifrynna lowers her great trio of bone heads to Isla. She snorts a laugh when Isla tickles beneath her ears one head at a time.

"Not to fret, my lovely Guardian. I have three flower crowns for you, too!" Isla squeals, then opens her hands, vines bursting with ease. Not one bead of sweat mars her delicate brow. I nearly shake my head in disbelief.

"Ifrynna..." my Guardian pronounces, triune-united.

Grinning and nodding her gratitude, Isla motions to Ifrynna's first head—the one whose expressions are the most subdued. "You seem more of a white Inker flower. As if you have depths beneath the shallow surface. But be careful, the inner black barbs are venomous," warns Isla with a side-smirk as Ifrynna's first head bows to accept the apt crown.

Marveling at my bride's perception, she moves to the center head, strokes her side only to have Ifrynna's hot center tongue lash her palm. Isla giggles. "You are scarlet heart. I can tell you are a fierce warrior who loves even fiercer." Ifrynna's middle eyes gleam, her smile toothier when Isla forms the heart-like flower the color of fruit wine with its golden center.

Incredulous, I shake my head but can't deny my rising smile, the warmth radiating through my body as Isla moves to my Guardian's third and final head. Stepping back, she taps her lips in contemplation. Ifrynna's third eyes, dark and labyrinthine, are unreadable—her expression as stoic and quiet as ever. Not even I have wrestled more than three words from Ifrynna's far-left head. My chest dulls with the knowledge. I wonder how upset my bride will be.

Finally, Isla nods, smiles, bows her head. "No pretty flowers for you, my beauty. You have roamed every inch of the Nether-Void, have looked into the eye of Eyleanan and Ifrynn for which you are named. But while hell may have staked its claim on you, dear one, you have conquered it. Just as I hope to one day."

Bewildered, I reach for a nearby branch to center myself, fingers crushing flower petals. Breath stalled, I stare at my bride as she removes the crown of thorns from her head, yanks a few long strands of her silver hair like spun star silk to entwine them around the thorns, then raises it to Ifrynna's third head.

Ifrynna doesn't move, as if she will reject the offering. But after blinking and tilting her head to the side to survey my dark rose, Ifrynna finally lowers her third head.

And once Isla beams and dons the crown upon Ifrynna's third brow, she opens her sacred mouth bearing few words and urges, "Climb upon me, wonder. Today, you will ride upon my back, and I will carry you wherever you desire within Nathyan Gyeal."

When Ifrynna lowers her body, Isla squeals louder and scrambles onto the Guardian's back. I thread my brows together, puzzled, because Ifrynna strides past me, then pauses. I approach, mere inches from Isla, close enough to touch her hand.

Ifrynna's center head lowers toward me and offers a toothy grin to declare, "The walk will be good for you, Allysteir."

"Oh, and my King?" Isla summons me. I lift my masked face to her. Curl my fingers toward her. She wags a finger, blows me a kiss, and finishes, "If you ever touch me again, I will rip out all your bones and feed them to the Cryth River spirits."

Ifrynna charges. Isla shrieks, thrilled.

Well, that's one idea I haven't tried.

TWENTY-NINE
I SURRENDER TO THE GOD OF DEATH

ISLA

All night long, he stayed.

I purse my lips, recalling Kryach's dark ghost shade lingering as I'd created a barrier of thorns to prevent the refter brides from pursuing me. Clothed in nothing but my naked flesh, I'd roamed the glen, touching every bone tree, memorizing the soft, gray moss tickling the soles of my feet. I'd bathed in the River Dhunh as Kryach informed me of the name.

He didn't say much. As if content to observe, to witness my regrowth.

I can't say it was rebirth yet. Whatever it was, I never slept. The power in my blood never weakened, never wearied.

Now at dawn, my body is beyond debilitated. Ifrynna rumbles low, a lulling purr, when I lower my head upon her snow-white scruff, nuzzling my cheek against the silken strands.

"Rest your head, sweet Bride of Death. Close your eyes, little wonder. Dream of Eyleanan," urges Ifrynna in a tri-command for each of her mouths. My eyes grow heavier from her deep yet soothing voice. "Even with my spirit speed, it will take a little time to reach our destination on the Isle of Bones."

I've never been to the Isle of Bones. But I love surprises. Confident she won't let me fall, I coil my arms around her center neck and surrender to my lids masking my eyes.

As I drift into dreams, a familiar shade voice murmurs in my ear...

"My love, my love, my wonder-lust,
Let me walk within your dreams
Upon pomegranates, you will feast
Now, give your mind to me..."

With no strength to challenge Aryahn Kryach when he stayed with me all night after Allysteir abused and abandoned me, and with the promise of pomegranates, I surrender to the God of Death and acknowledge: this is Kryach—this is Ary *asking* my permission.

When the motion of Ifrynna's body abates, I stir from my dreams, feeling the smile before I register it. Regret twists inside my belly because I am no longer bathing in golden starlight to tickle my flesh in effervescent dust. I am no longer being fed the ripe, jeweled seeds of pomegranates from the cupped palms of Death maidens. Or frolicking amidst endless paradisical gardens garbed in nothing but moonbeams while the God of Death pursues me with the promise to glorify my body all night long.

A heavy sigh pushes through my nose, and my shoulders lower in disappointment. Something prickles my skin at the collarbone. I peer down, noting the flickers of fire. No fuming flames but mere tickling flickers to lick my skin. Death's teasing.

I touch my throat, then cradle my flushing cheeks, aware of the telltale dampness between my thighs. Lips tight, I shake my head to banish the memory of the beguiling dream, wondering if Kryach will invade my mind every night. Or if I want him to.

Why would he taunt me? What does he have to gain when Allysteir and I are more divided than ever? Is this simple foreshadowing, and he still intends to reap my soul? Preparing me as a lamb to a slaughter??

Well—I blow an acrimonious breath from my nostrils, hiss through my teeth—I am no lamb.

If Ifrynna notices my change, she doesn't address me. My eyes adjust to our surroundings—to the three puffs of white spirit breath from Ifrynna's tri-nostrils and the potpourri perfume from mine.

I swoon. This is why the Isle of Bones is such a popular destination. On this southern section, which rises higher than the remaining Isle, shafts of pure sunlight spear the expanse from prestigious holes within the mountain dome far above my head. No wonder she brought me here. Spread before me are acres of magnificent gardens and pathways surrounded by trees. Bone trees *and* organic ones.

Elated, I gush. Adrenaline chases away my lethargy. I climb off Ifrynna's back and approach the main garden path flanked by Weeping trees—named after the Goddess of Doom. Beyond those trees spew fountains, trickle stream. Or a brook perhaps. Warm sunbeams radiate upon me, and I spin and spin with arms outstretched until I nearly lose my balance. Not good since I'm still wearing a dress of thorns!

Soft smile forming, I transform my armor. Here, I am safe. Here, no Corpse King battles me or strips me bare before my greatest fears. He can't turn away with no compassion or remorse. No longer can he leave

me in his bone glen with his refter brides and their hungering wails...
And the God of Death.

The Nether-mark lashes my spine with heat, and I sigh. Despite his quelling my mark, I'll keep him at arm's length. No, *full-body* length. I bristle. Allysteir will sleep on the floor, on a chair—or one level below in the bathing chambers if I have anything to do with it. And I will have *much* to do with it.

By the time I finish, I've cultivated a rudimentary gown of Weeping Tree leaves. Fitting because I can't bring myself to grow corpus roses. I flex my fingers, denying the urge to touch the mark, to trace my fingertips upon the indents of Allysteir's teeth. How can I let him bite me again, much less touch me? How will Kryach be appeased if I cannot grant him my blood, my *flesh*?

He won't. If I can't tempt the God of Death, I'll sure as hell make him suffer!

I turn to Ifrynna, but the Guardian no longer stands behind me. At first, I purse my lips, ribcage tight. No, the Guardian of the Underworld can't shadow me everywhere. Perhaps she knows these moments are mine. After a full night of growing my floral gifts to reclaim myself, to honor myself, I deserve to enjoy these beauties, to treasure them.

I embark into the gardens. Bare feet skimming upon the cobblestones, I travel the pathways past shrubs and trees flowering with musky white-Inker, rich and exotic scarlet heart, odorless black death, the citrusy sweet gayle, royal purple primus buds, milky thistles, and countless others. Suspicions confirmed, I discover the brook prattling upon mounds of stones to the right of the path. It descends beneath a little bridge, turning to a trickling cascade into a pond dotted with lily pads. Every now and then, I pass canopied but non-enclosed bone dwellings which serve as viewing stations.

I breathe aromatic scents, careless of the dirt collecting on my bare feet. To my left, a nightwing warbles its woeful call from bone branches. I smile at the Nether bird. More of a spirit fowl—a twain traveler. Throughout my years, their mourning melodies drew me to the Nether-Void, tempting me near, daring refters to attack me.

If the Nether-Void has beckoned me to enter its domain, if I am some mistress of Death, perhaps it's time to listen. Skeptical, I chew on my inner cheek. Does the answer to the Curse lie within the Nether-Void?

It's early, a little after dawn. The gardens are bereft of people.

The moment I turn to leave, icy claws prickle my spine. Gasping from the Nether-mark, I spin but find no one, nothing. No threat. No danger.

I clench my cold, clammy hands. Panting, legs wobbly, I squint through the trees, sensing the familiar undercurrent luring my blood. More melancholy calls from nightwings warble around me. Sharp pangs pierce my chest, my heart. but I move forward. By what power I can't comprehend, what lack of fear, I move forward.

At the barest edges of the garden, I sense it. As if thunderclouds have smothered the sunlight, the source of the undercurrent induces me. A long-forgotten memory beyond my birth stalks the boundless recesses of my imagination. Unless...it's not my imagination.

At the end of the gardens is the portal. Yes, countless portals to the Nether-Void, to the spirit realms, haunt the Underworld. Thousands of souls wail from this dark bosom, prompting me, wooing me, *summoning* me.

Approaching the great orb of swirling blackness, an ever-moving whirlpool of ink, I lift my hand, fingers trembling to the dark energy while my Nether-mark roars needles of fire and ice into my spine. Breath rupturing, I hesitate. Cold clots my veins.

Resisting the alluring embrace, I slowly turn. Too slow. Flapping wings echo behind me before a being, an ancient figure depicted in historical paintings, blocks my path. My vision spins. I almost topple to the ground. But the figure smiles and stretches his hand, captures my arm. Gold cuffs bind his wrists. With one brush, they burn my flesh with celestial energy. I never could have fathomed meeting an angyl!

Wings tattered and ragged, unable to fly, he grips my other arm. His eyes gleam when they study me. Mighty talons click upon the cobblestones beneath us. Everything in me shrinks before the creature in spite of his threadbare wings plumaged in smoke. His holy incense breath wafts upon my face. I can't bear to inhale.

When he opens his mouth with his resplendent gold tattoos humming beneath his dark flesh, I hold my breath. "Isla Morganyach, Bride of the Corpse King."

I freeze, swearing Nether-spiders skitter along my spine. The gold tattoos whirl upon his skin as if alive. As if they are bound to the gods.

"You will come with me. The lower gods summon you," his deep voice commands.

My mouth turns dry. Tremors invade my hands, but the angyl beams down at me. His eyes are mere black slits mirroring the Nether-Void. Pulse thundering in my ear, I close my eyes, caging a whimper. What could the gods want with me? It dawns on me the same time the angyl closes his hands around my arms, urging me forward by no more than an inch. He's testing. Of course, the lower gods want me. I am the first common girl who has ever volunteered for Bride of the Corpse King. I am the first who merited the God of Death's interest, his *lust*.

My eyes burn against the angyl's. The last thing I will ever be is a pawn.

Strengthening my dwindling legs, I drive myself back, refusing, "Over my dead bones!"

The angyl sniggers. That sinister snigger rattles my very core. Incense and smoke threaten my body. "I assure you, the gods do not have plans for your death...yet. But I am willing to snap your bones one by one if you try to run or scream for help, particularly from he who gave you his shadow-mark."

Dizzy black ghosts cloud my vision. I claw my throat for air as he advances. The incense grows stronger, plaguing my nostrils, weakening my legs. His smoke folds around me like a thick cloak, but its heat rivals my Nether-mark. It burns my eyes, yanking tears from them. Nothing compared to his tattered wings pulsing with Ifrynn dark energy.

The irony: I conquered one fear only for this angyl to drag me to another. Inches from the woeful souls. While I don't fear Death's shadows, I do fear this fallen servant bent to the lower gods' will and his promise of violence. Deep in my soul, I know he'd fulfill it.

I can't call for Ary. Nor Allysteir. Neither could arrive in time. Far too exhausted for fight and unwilling to freeze, I drag my feet when the angyl's hands bite into my underarms to haul me back.

Strength rivaling mine, the angyl draws me closer to the portal's violent wails. I rake my nails across his arms, his chest, struggling with his robes, but he regards me as no more than a nightwing fledgling. Paroxysms of gasps flee my mouth, swelling into a primal scream—one I bite to smother, remembering his promise. *The last thing I want is to pick a* bone *with this almighty being.* I shudder. Squeeze my eyes shut, whirl my savage head, reverting to my dark humor coping mechanism.

If Kryach senses my torment, he does not reveal himself. He must be reaping souls. Unless this angyl bears power to thwart Kryach—to mask his actions and my raging terror.

The portal thickens the air around me as if forming countless tethers to bind me, infinite hooks to embed in my flesh and swallow me whole. Bait for the God of Death is a lamentable fate.

As the portal magnifies, something cold assaults my collarbone. Lowering my head, I catch the skull-mark eyes turning blacker than midnight storms. Flames pulse in my dark veins. Adrenaline shoots into my blood, and power rockets into my body. My eyes whirl to their ceilings from the inertia. Thorns launch from my skin to stab the angyl's flesh.

He pauses, a low rumble of a growl. Humor multiplying, I snigger. Craning my neck, I bore my eyes into his and wrinkle my nose. "You said if I tried to run or scream, angyl. You mentioned nothing about *fighting*."

Gripping my arms, muscles bulging, wings tightening, he snarls at my worthy assailants of barbs lodged in his neck. When he deadpans, eyes turning the color of blood and gold, his jaw hardening, I understand he's done with my games. His fingers gore into my flesh. I whimper, open my mouth to unleash a primal scream.

"Aryuhdair!"

It's not *my* scream, nor *my* words. My shoulders sink at the familiar, deep voice behind me, at the parietal skull bone hanging from his neck.

The angyl pauses. His grip loosens, and he seethes. More smoke rushes from his nostrils, from his teeth.

Frozen, scream hacked off, I hold my breath. All my skin prickles when boots approach, when the protestor follows with a rigid command, "Release my sister-in-law or suffer my wrath, fallen one. We both know I, save for the King himself, have the power to strip you of those wings and any possibility of their restoration."

Waves of breath rasping, I angle my neck to Prince Aydon, who fingers his parietal skull bone in a warning promise—the most powerful bone in the kingdom next to Allysteir's. Muscles quivering, I press my lips into a solid seam and wrench my arms from the angyl. I'm relieved when he doesn't grip harder, though his claws rake my skin.

The Prince extends his hand to me. Grateful, I take it. My heartbeat slows, and I almost buckle.

Before the angyl responds, Aydon murmurs a chant under his breath while gripping the skull bone. A sudden force assaults the angyl, thrusting him closer to the portal.

"Fly away," I taunt before Aryuhdair roars, and the portal devours him. It closes, evanescing into thin air.

All my adrenaline dives. I crash to my knees, a raw pang in my chest and a sharp stinging along my arms.

Aydon catches me before my head meets the ground. "Lady Isla…" The Prince's concerned voice blurs in my ears, and I struggle to stay awake. Lids too heavy. But his chanting words and rubbing bone powder along my arms, the chalky sensation tickling my fine hairs, motivates my blood.

When I muster the strength to open my eyes, I meet Aydon's blue ones. Deep indigo, charismatic, and keen. And creased with worry. His warm fingers linger upon my arms, trace the flesh. I tilt my head to the marks, remnants of Aryuhdair's claws, fading to Aydon's healing power, his bone magic.

He touches his knuckles to my forehead to check for a fever. "Lady Isla, do you have any other wounds?"

I find my voice, but it cracks, a little hoarse. "N-no," I tremble and expel any remaining fear in a breath. "No, I'm not hurt. Thank you, Prince Aydon."

"Aydon will suffice."

His other hand encircles my arm, thumb rubbing my bare skin. Peering down, I note how many weeping leaves I lost in my struggle with the angyl. Heat spirals to my neck and reddens my cheeks from the gown strap dangling perilously low to expose half my left breast. Gaps at my waist reveal more skin from the angyl's claws and my thighs from where I'd kicked and dragged my feet.

"Oh, gods," I moan and bury my face in my hands.

Aydon chuckles, assumes my elbow, and raises me to my feet. I suck a sharp breath when his body nudges mine for a breath. He parts his lips before his features morph into the charismatic royal, smile too beguiling to be genuine, eyes narrowing with political cunning which betrays how he plays games. Long ones.

Lifting my hand to his lips, he kisses the back and declares, "Do not concern yourself, Isla. We both know you do not suffer the concern of modesty. And I am a Feyal-Ithydeir Prince," he offers the reminder, but I don't miss his eyes flicking over those gaps.

I swallow hard, an uncomfortable knot in my belly. Not desire but apprehension. Despite the Prince escorting me to a private coach stationed outside the gardens, I wonder if I have more to fear from Aryuhdair and the Nether-Void, from the lower gods.

Or from Aydon.

THIRTY

GET IN THE DAMN BED, MY KING

ALLYSTEIR

Three months pass with Isla never allowing me to enter the bed, nor so much as touch her.

We've passed into a quiet but comfortable routine. Morning meals together. She continues to accompany me on my Death business. Supper with Franzy, Mathyr, and Aydon. In her spare time, she prefers the tower library, though I find it amusing whenever she attempts to please Master Ivory...and fails. With an infinite number of floral species, Isla has spent long nights with her nose invested in books, researching the blooms of other regions such as Narcyssa's crypta strygoi or the native flowers of the Wisp-Shee. But whenever she attempts to present Master Ivory with an adornment, his branches shake every petal, leaving my bride to clench her white-knuckled fists to contrast her rage-reddened cheeks. She fumes and stalks off every time.

More than once, I've offered to provide her insight, but my bride, my *Queen* merely raises her hand to shush me and refuses. For Isla, everything is a challenge she must overcome on her own.

By the end of the first month, all the royals returned to their kingdoms and the nobles to their cities, affording Nathyan Ghyeal peace and normality. They will return for the Night of Masks: the last date for Isla and me to consummate our marriage.

Much to my gratitude, Isla and Franzy remain close. Out of respect, they share a bed in Isla's old suite. My conversation with Aydon was productive—potentially the most productive I've had with him in centuries. I know why. He suspects my knowledge of his recent transgressions against Talahn-Feyal. But he has respected Franzy by delaying their consummation until she requests. For now, he's on his best behavior.

At night, I simply observe Isla as I observed countless brides passing to sleep, always imagining their dreams, wishing I could grant them sweet ones. Patience unrivaled after a practice of more than centuries, I knit my fingers together, surveying my bride beyond the skull depths.

She has not stopped wearing my robes to bed. I don't know whether it's a good sign or a simple rationale on account of her desire for comfort. Regardless, it grants me a sliver of hope to expand my chest most nights.

Tonight, the jeweled coverlet of our bed has strayed from her body. From her side, she rolls in her sleep until she splays out on her back, arms wide, legs sprawled. The robe exposes her voluptuous hips and the alabaster basins of her ample thighs: a plentiful feast for my teeth. With her hair as abundant starlight and flame upon her pillow and robe parted to reveal her bare breasts—rouge nipples high and pleading for my mouth—Isla tempts me. In sleep, she combats me, bewitches me. Her dreams are a sword thrust into my rib cage until its tip nicks the barest heartstring to draw blood.

Her subconscious words are the masterful, piercing point.

"Ary..." Isla murmurs, one hand straying to cup her breast, the nipple swollen—the flesh around it wilted—and the rosebud knotted and puckered.

My jaw hardens. Whatever Kryach has infected her mind with, I have no access. He's formed a predominant barrier, so I may not influence her mind with his shadow power I merely shelter. I don't fault him after what I did to her.

Every now and then, she wakes. Shooting to sitting, she adjusts the robe, glances at me as if ensuring I am still in my place...resting in the deep chair opposite of the bed. Once she's satisfied, she rests her head upon the pillow again.

Except tonight, she rakes her fingers through her waves, blinking a few times, then narrows her eyes to slits, inspecting me. Cupping her forehead, inhaling deeply, Isla glances around the room before turning back to me. When her lips part, I work to not betray my accelerated breathing while my chest tightens, ribcage constricting.

Without her flesh, without her blood all these months, the torture is worse. The numbing poison of Sythe wine drenches my tongue, but it cannot hope to dull my thirst for her, my craving for her blood. How I've rotted more from lack of flesh. How bones protrude through my once whole side. I must rely on Kryach's shadow power to simply stand from this chair.

Flicking her eyes to my skull mask, Isla heaves a sigh and commands, "Come to bed, Allysteir." The resolute of a true Queen with the crown always prominent upon her head because she wears it even in slumber. Never forsaking it, it's as if she cherishes it, treasures it, and...fears its loss.

Wringing my hands, I slowly rise from the chair and make my way toward her until I am but a breath from her body. She stiffens upon my approach, cranes her neck, and hunts for the reality behind my mask.

"I do not wish you any discomfort," I alert her, dipping my head and finishing, "My Lady."

Isla huffs, folds her arms across her chest and calls my bluff. She sneers, "Get in the damn bed, my King. I may never allow you to fuck me, but it doesn't mean we cannot act as a civil *husband and wife*," she expresses, drawing the boundary.

Never is an impossibility. In time, she will accept me, desire me as every bride before her.

Shoulders sinking in surrender, in unchecked relief, I blink behind my mask...then gradually wander to the other side of the bed. Isla monitors me, hand flexed, studying me as I curve the coverlet back, and lower myself into the bed next to her. Her warmth infuses me. I suck a deep inhale. Her luxurious scent invades my nostrils.

"You've been drinking more," she comments, swinging her head to the numerous empty flagons upon every surface of the suite. Ones I've drained each given day for the past week. The Sythe wine and visiting my refter brides, visiting Finleigh are my only survival strategies since I've chosen to focus most of my attention on my bride.

After the first week, Isla asked to return. It takes time for her to learn their names, their faces. But she gifts them with distinctive flowers to identify them. Studying agriculture has become her second hobby along with riding Ifrynna and talking to Cryth River spirits, learning their histories, their passions.

Past brides never showed interest.

When I don't respond, merely fix my corpus mask upon her, Isla twitches, her fingers curling slightly, prompting more hope within me.

Until she clenches them. "How much pain are you in?"

After a long pause, I flare my nostrils, raise my chin, and declare, "Much."

Isla nods, chin dipping low before she snaps those bejeweled amethysts to me and hums, "Good. Go to sleep."

I refrain from sniggering mockery. No, she won't allow me to bite her tonight. Granting me the bed, the closeness is her first offering. Her olive branch. One I do not deserve. No, I must earn more and am well-prepared and equipped.

My dark rose, I admire her spirit. Her strength. Her passion. How she knows her worth. Isla was a Queen long before I placed a crown upon her head.

My little wonder, Kryach surfaces for the first time tonight, and I snarl deep in my throat. Low enough, Isla does not hear when she rolls onto her side.

Before I drift to sleep, I inhale, nostrils burning from her flesh scent of winter roses, star juice, and Isle fruit. Warding off the urge to snap my teeth, I address my bride's back, her lustrous waves bereft of their earlier adornment of corpus roses, gold thread, and pearls, "My Lady, if you will consent, I would like to take you somewhere tomorrow. A place beyond the Citadel. A secret haven."

"A secret like your refter bride glen?" she challenges without turning but a bite in her voice, her back muscles steeling themselves.

"If it would ease your discomfort, I will vow with my blood..." I pause, closing my eyes from the ramifications of what I've offered; it will weaken me, deteriorate me more. Regardless, I continue, "I will vow with my own blood: I intend no harm, and I challenge you: you will adore this place and beg me to return."

My bride perks her head and tilts her neck so her exquisite waves drape to one side. I recognize the luster in her eyes, how she cannot resist such a challenge. Despite how my heart has crept into my throat, I lower my shoulders, relieved when she pinches her lips and nods.

"Agreed, Allysteir. I will come with you tomorrow. But," she raises a finger and rolls over to face me, her brows screwing low, so shadows swarm her eyes when she cunningly defines, "I'll still have your blood vow."

Without another word, I bury my face in my robe, lift my mask, and drag my Feyal teeth across one of few avenues on my body bearing flesh and sinew and skin. Once I do, I replace my mask and offer her my naked wrist beyond the glove sheltering my phalange bones.

Isla touches the tips of her fingers to my blood. I hiss pained wind through my clenched teeth at the touch, but Isla stills, eyes softening and widening to gaze at me in awe. Her fingers linger, tracing the exposed flesh as my robe covers everything else. She discovers old scars...from our wedding night.

As soon as she unearths another scar, I withdraw, retrieve my arm, and grant her a wide berth. It doesn't take long before her soft, rolling snores fill the chamber. I chuckle, then close my eyes and breathe in torment from her body heat, from her scent tickling my nostrils. And I have to wonder if her acceptance is punishing torture more than a gift.

Because she's fast asleep when my remaining arm flesh turns to rot from lack of Feyal blood.

THIRTY-ONE
"I WILL ALLOW YOU TO TOUCH ME UNDER TWO CONDITIONS..."

ISLA

Rousing the next day, I acknowledge the lack of a chill. Dewy sweat lingers on my brow which means Allysteir is gone. My hand strays to his side of the bed. A slight indent along with some shed bone powder remains. I cup my forehead, panting. He must have left early on his Death business so he will have time for me later. I couldn't resist his challenge.

No, I haven't forgiven him, but nor am I a monster who desires his chronic suffering. Considering he drinks beyond his weight in Sythe wine every day, it's obvious he is more rot and bone and ruin.

Only one question: how much longer will he rot until I grant him my flesh and blood?

Squeezing my shoulders, I scramble out of the bed, throw a spider-silk robe over my shoulders, and rush from our room. I don't forget my crown. Grateful I don't bump into anyone, aside from servants, I hasten down halls and pause when I arrive at my old suite. But Franzy is not there.

That must mean…I purse my lips, then hurry to the Prince's suite one wing away. I arrive at the door where I bite my lip but muster my courage to knock. All these weeks, these months, I've gone to Franzy, who sleeps in a separate suite from Prince Aydon, but I should have known it wouldn't last. Not with how generous my bonnya sweetheart is.

Once Aydon opens the door and a faint smile crosses his face, eyes glinting and no tension in his shoulders, my suspicions are confirmed. Fully dressed in his Princely garb, he nods to me. I frown but nod back. As the Queen of the Talahn-Feyal, my status outranks him, however ironic. My crown is superior.

"Your Highness," he acknowledges and swings the door open to welcome me into his suite where Franzy sits at the corner breakfast table dressed in nothing but a silken purple robe. She smiles at me beyond the teacup rimming her lower mouth. Her cheeks are blanched, curls ragged, shoulders lower from *fatigue*.

Without another word, I bustle inside, ignoring the click of the door behind me. When Franzy blushes and smiles, leans in, and pecks my cheek, I deadpan with her, tilting my head to the side.

"Dynna fyash, Isla," she scolds me, pleading with me to not get emotional, then winks, returning to her teacup. "You said all it would take was me removing my gown, and he would do the rest. It didn't hurt much. He was very gentle. And no blood," she reveals and slides her hand to cover mine. "I am not so breakable as you may believe, my Scarlet Skathyk. Besides, you haven't shared a word about your nuptials."

I sigh, cross my arms over my chest, and slump in my seat, huffing while remembering mine and Allysteir's disastrous wedding night. And how un-orthodoxically quiet Kryach has been—apart from his frequent Death shades lulling me to sleep.

After tapping my finger upon my arm for a few moments, Franzy picks up on my body language, but her smile spreads. "I'm happy it hasn't happened yet, leyanyn," she expresses, squeezing my hand. "Though I'd never believed I would be the first following our marriage to men. Or royal men!"

"I was ready, Franzy. I truly was!" I gush, almost throwing my arms around her neck, masking the crack in my voice behind hardened resolve.

Franzy sets down her teacup, folds her hands on the table, blinks, and waits. More than grateful for her listening heart, I unleash everything I've held in since the wedding night. Why I've sought her more at our "Sweetheart Suite" and why I've avoided the King as much as possible. She's never pressed, nor asked. My mouth turns dry. My throat thickens from my adoration of her until a shameful knot invades my belly since I haven't given her the same respect. No, I've relied on her unconditional patience and forgiveness.

A few moments breathe before Franzy cups her cold teacup and screws her brows low. Finally... "How long do you think the Corpse King can remain alive while separated from his head?"

I blink. Then, the two of us double over, bursting with laughter until I throw myself at her feet, kneeling before my leyanyn. I bury my face in her lap while she strokes my hair. No tears shed, but I breathe heavily, emotion swelling in my belly and throat. After a time of Franzy allowing me to shiver with my face in her lap, she nudges her hand beneath my chin, urges my face to hers, and questions, "Nothing like it has happened since?"

I shake my head.

"He has respected your flesh?"

I nod. "He hasn't asked to bite me once!"

"Or tried to sleep in your bed?"

"Not until I practically forced him to." I recall last night's events.

With a heavy sigh, Franzy purses her lips, strokes my hair, and advises, "Forgiveness is a process, Isla. It cannot be achieved or earned overnight. But perhaps all it requires is a crack of acceptance, a first step. You alone must decide if you are prepared to take the first step. Regardless, I will always be here for you, my leyanyn."

It's one of few times Franzy claims my mouth in a poignant kiss of her own initiation. I bow before her, flutters engulfing my belly. Forgiveness will come later.

Penance first.

I can't fathom why Allysteir has blindfolded me when his Underworld is dark, but I don't protest. As he pointed out: I love a challenge. I also ignore how his bony arm weaves around my waist to secure me as we ride upon Ifrynna. And how I'd promised to rip apart all his bones and feed them to the Cryth River spirits. I suppose this is my crack.

With my crown resting on my hair, I maintain a regal chin, chest tauter than a new bowstring. My expectations are high. Ifrynna pounds her spirit paws upon the landscape for quite some time.

By now, we've passed the Isle of Bones and the reaches of the Bone Sea, forsaking the tide and the scent of salt and bone powder, until we embark into the deepest recesses of the White Ladies.

Allysteir closes his robe around me in a gesture of shelter. At first,

I part my lips, prepared to refuse, but I'd only donned a thin, silken gown. I cannot pretend icy bumps don't protrude from my skin thanks to the Underworld chill. Beyond the blindfold, darkness congregates deeper as eerie fantasies. Welcoming his robes, I stiffen when his tunic brushes my back, and the Nether-mark upon my spine pacifies from his touch. Kryach quells its heat far more.

As if sensing my thoughts, the skull rouses blood fire to kindle my skin. From the barest edge, the mark betrays the telltale burn of his skull eyes. Always watching. Why hasn't he come to me since? Why hasn't he attacked me as he had on the wedding morn? No Death-maidens either. My skin prickles with the suspicion of a false sense of security. Surely, he will strike soon.

None can hide from Death.

Ifrynna slows. Her body stills from a thunder to a trot and finally to a sliding standstill. Her body gives a resounding jerk; the inertial would have toppled me clear off her three bone heads if Allsyteir had not secured me. My throat constricts with the knowledge, but I blink behind the blindfold, relieved when he lifts his gloved hands to the sash at the back of my head.

Once my eyes adjust to the dim light of the dome-stalactites shimmering hundreds of yards above our head and the pockets of sky offering moonbeams to slant through the expanse, I see *them*. And gush! Allysteir stops me before I lurch and leap for the beauties.

"Allysteir," I whisper and gaze upon the wild horses, peering back because Ifrynna has misted away, her spirit trail evanescing in the distance.

"So as not to startle them," explains Allysteir, nodding at my gaze. "Only the Sleeping Stallion himself is a threat to the Underworld Guardian."

"The Sleeping Stallion?"

"The greatest bone horse of all time who wreaked havoc on Nathyan Ghyeal in the ancient days of the gods' war. The one who sired all ones like these. But he's slept for thousands of years, my bride. No need to be concerned. In fact, you should be more concerned over them."

I smile when he directs me to the herd where only a meager meadow separates us.

"Sometimes, I come here for solitude. I would often bring my brides here to offer them the same...tranquility." His hand settles upon the small of my back where I feel his energy.

I freeze but don't order him to remove his hand. Technically, he's not touching me yet, considering the glove. I remember what Franzy said.

The horses remind me so much of Ifrynna. They shake their ghostly white manes fine as white widow spider-silk. Their translucent hides confess their inner glowing skeletal armor. The opposite of the Corpse King. They never wear a mask—unafraid to exhibit their identities. I chew on my inner cheek, musing before craning my neck to eye his corpse mask. His bane. How I long to tear it off and stomp it into the ground, shatter it to pieces until he reveals everything. After what he did to me on our wedding night, he owes me nothing less.

"I am not the first bride," I assume, turning to the wild spirit horses.

"No, but I assure you this is only the beginning, Isla. As I promised, you will know such truth as you've never known. And beauty."

What of your beauty, Allysteir? I almost voice but restrain myself. Does he consider himself worthy of beauty? Or humanity? Does he *feel* anything?

Squaring my shoulders, I focus on the horses, so alluring and exquisite in the midst of their macabre spectrality. Some have muzzles with keen and hooked tips, reminding me of bone picks as if meant for boring deep into the darkest mountain caverns.

A few colts stray from the herd, trotting and butting their heads. Threading my eager fingers, chest expanding, I lurch, flinging forward as the colts approach.

"Isla, no!" warns Allysteir in a fierce whisper, but I'm too transfixed, too mesmerized by the ghostly, effervescent foals, I barely hear him.

My eyes practically glow as I collect my translucent gown skirts and canter toward them, arm stretched, fingers curled to touch. Stomach fluttering, heartbeat quickening as one foal flicks its head up, whinnies, and snorts before trotting toward me, I hold my breath. I wait. The foal creeps closer and closer to my fingers until they are an inch apart.

But once my fingers traipse upon the chilled muzzle, sinking past the spirit outer layer, two mighty stallions gleaming with spirit fire brighter than dragon scales thunder their hooves in my direction. Dagger-hooked muzzles and silvery pupils aim for me! All my eager elation turns into pure horror. I gasp, vision dimming. I freeze. Despite the horses charging at me, I can't possibly conceive of harming such ethereal beings, not when I am the trespasser.

Their icy breath barrages my face, inches from me. Countless shadows form a barricade between me and the defending stallions. And there is Allysteir. Striding to my side, eclipsed in Kryach's power, he stares down the spirit beings, addressing them through the whispering shades in an ancient, incomprehensible language. I tremble before the Corpse King and rub my arms for shelter. The horses that would have minced my flesh to meat snort, shake their manes, nudge their colts, and return to their herd.

Allysteir turns, his eternal corpse mask leering down upon me, darker than ever. He shakes his head, curling his shadows along the outline of my body while expressing, "Spirit horses are extremely territorial. Not even I dare to approach them."

Rattled, I loose a few breaths to regain my frazzled nerves but tense when Allysteir laughs. I screw my brows low with a deepening frown and cross my arms over my chest. "What?"

He shakes his head, blowing out a guffaw of a laugh. "You plunge into the Cryth River, you volunteer to be my bride, you withstand the Virginity Test, you tempt the God of Death and give him a *nickname*, you survive my refter brides and my assault, and yet, my wild dark rose is undone by a few bony ponies!"

I pinch my lips, ball my hands into fists, posture, and prepare to defend myself until I realize how right he is. The knowledge penetrates any layers of pride and pierces my rib cage, scratching at my heart. So, instead of countering, I sigh, then double over in laughter stitches, joining him. Together, we laugh. It blows through my nose and my cheeks. A blush overheats my neck and face while Allysteir's deep, rocking chuckle overlaps mine before his hands nestle my waist.

Triggered by the act, I stiffen. I tense, remembering our failed honeymoon night. But he surprises me when he pulls away. Those vacant corpse eyes register my body language. Our laughter fades like an ebbing tide, traded for awkward silence—a silence of tension knit from the night's horrific memories.

Still, I remember my leyanyn, how forgiveness is a process. Except mine must be earned.

So, I rise and adjust my crooked crown to embrace my role as Queen of the Underworld. No, I cannot embrace the role of a wife yet, but I am his equal. No, his superior. He needs *me*. All of Talahn-Feyal needs me. Aryahn Kryach needs—

"Allysteir, I will allow you to touch me under two conditions," I define, stepping toward him, lighting a hand upon his robe.

He inclines his full mask to my face. As much as I wish to demand he remove it, I will not. Because I will earn the right, too. Not steal it as before.

"I won't balk at the occasional brush of our hands at dinner...or our feet in our bed. But you must ask me before you engage in anything else."

The Corpse King bows his head in a gesture of assent. "I will do as you wish, my Lady Queen. And the second?"

Without missing a beat, I raise my chin and draw the hard boundary. "You remove your gloves when you do. Even if bones alone remain, I will have more than your gloves and shades, my Lord."

He pauses, weighing my second demand. My eyes flick to those gloved hands curling, the robes shifting because whatever underneath tightens, hardens from my commanding proclamation. Heart lodged in my throat, I hold my breath so long, I'm certain my lungs shudder.

Finally, Allysteir's shoulders sink. He flexes those gloves and raises one to his mouth beneath the mask. I exhale long and deep when he sinks his teeth into the glove to rip them off finger by finger to reveal skeletal, protruding phalange bones.

I gust breath as Allysteir approaches, bone fingers curling toward my body. But they do not settle upon my waist. Instead, they wander along my cheek, trace my face from chin to brow. My eyelashes tremble in a rapid flutter. My pulse thunders as goosebumps rise on my arms and the back of my neck. My first crack of surrender, threadbare and worn, but a crack all the same. Enough for his bone fingers to descend to my neck, to his rightful bite mark.

The Corpse King presses upon the mark. It aches from the memory of pain or the longing for the power I'd felt in those moments. He trembles, and I hear his rapid intake of breath, how much he struggles with the lone touch of my flesh, how much he suffers. I may be his Queen, but I am *not* a cruel mistress.

So, I sweep my hair from my chest, cast it to the other side of my neck, and bare my upper chest to him in a token of an offering. With a sigh, I widen the crack, rolling my neck, brow wrinkling because I'm still uncertain when his chilled breath drifts across my face.

Will he remember? His shadows traverse along my upper chest, predictive.

Allysteir curves those bone fingers to my chin to still its trembling. And when he tilts his head, when he asks—"Will you accept my bite tonight, my Lady Queen? May I feed from you?"—I nearly lurch in utter relief because he's passed my test. A seemingly small test but as significant as stepping onto this course of forgiveness.

I arch my neck, tip my head back, and whisper my acceptance, "You may."

Months since the last time he fed. When Allysteir sinks his teeth above my left breast, the sound of the galloping spirit horses almost swallows my screams.

THIRTY-TWO
FOR YOU, I MUST POSSESS

ALLYSTEIR

ONE MONTH LATER

I break free from Isla and surrender her to the healers because I'd needed to consume more blood and flesh. Thus, she requires healing beyond meager bone powder.

They lead her from the dining hall where I've fed from her and to the accompanying garderobe to heal her in private while I shake out my robes. I ignore the intrigued glimpses of Mathyr, Aiden, and Franzy, and retire to our suite. Starved of the passion we once shared, my feedings are a means to an end.

Kryach's essence cloys me thanks to the piquant aftertaste of my bride's blood lingering upon my tongue, the minute bits of flesh tucked between my teeth. Later, I will pick them out with my tongue and savor the tiny morsels. He. Says. Nothing. Far too silent for the God of Death. I tense, spine prickling with the suspicion gnawing upon my thoughts.

Most liken the High God to a grave, to a quiet corpse, but I know better. Death speaks volumes. It smothers everything else. Apart from love, Death defeats *everything*, including time. For infinite reasons, Aryahn Kryach is *never* quiet. For centuries, he has taunted me, mocked me, tormented me. My brides, most. Finleigh chose to ignore him, and he reaped her soul in rage.

I clench my teeth, cracking one, reflecting upon my former bride. Hissing wind through my teeth, I remember her fair hair of golden rippled curls, Finny's sweetheart-shaped lips. The depth of her blue eyes drew me to expose my face. Those pale hands had ripped the mask from my face on our wedding night because she couldn't bear any secrets between us. How she commanded me to her eyes. The tender authenticity in her fingers when they caressed my scarified mouth. And my cheekbone jutting through my shrunken flesh, the hollow of my eye. *Her* haunting lullabies sang me to sleep and suffocated Kryach's voice. She accepted me, received me, *loved* me before all others. Other than Isla, Finleigh lasted the longest. Yes, Isla would have received me, would have shared flesh with me, but she did not love me yet. Not the true me.

She loves the forbidden, the thrill of the strange and the challenge. Isla loves the Corpse. Finleigh loved the King. No, Finleigh loved the man.

Other than Isla and despite my affection and emotional attachment to all my brides, Finleigh was the bride I unconditionally and unequivocally loved. I wince from the memories. So bittersweet, her heaven I sampled. Perhaps because she united with me in ignoring Kryach, defied him in open rebellion. Oh, how he tortured me for it! I harden my jaw, remembering how he rotted my flesh more and afflicted me with so much pain. Finleigh's tears became my healing balm.

Perhaps Isla will redeem me, the one who will withstand Kryach: my eternal true love. And when our souls pass into the Forever Havens, I must believe she will welcome Finleigh's soul to unite with mine as her Franzy unites with her.

Ever since the wedding night, mine and Isla's hollow honeymoon, Death has *not* tormented me. Unless...chills spiderweb into my chest as I wonder if this is a new torture. The calm before the storm. Such a calm as has never been dealt before, but it occurs to me how much it makes sense.

Does it now, Allysteir? Kryach finally interjects into my musings. *Would you care to know how your precious Finleigh's soul is doing? Or how I may return her at any time if I thus desire?*

Stop, I growl in the alcove I've snuck into, but I can't control his shadows. They constrict my throat, penetrating its channels, restricting my air. *You've taken everything from me! You won't take Isla, too!*

Five hundred years, Allysteir. The God of Death growls. *I've inhabited you longer than any other because as much as your self-degradation cloys at times, at least you respect my work, my sacred soul work. Yes, I took my bridal pounds of soul flesh as it were, for they grant me the strength to continue reaping the souls of humankind as the laws of the Highest Gods have dictated. A far better solution than the gods' previous methods of bringing open war. Or do you disagree?*

When his shadows roar, when they hem me in, when they drive me to my knees to crack my meager kneecaps, I seethe, bow my head, undone by the omnipotent God's power. He is the darkest and deepest part of my psyche. I do respect his Death business. Moreover, I love it. I love nurturing the dying souls, singing to them, and granting them strength for their final journeys. It is an infinite blessing Isla shares in this love. With everything in my being, I believe she is strong enough to withstand

Kryach. He will reap a fraction of her soul's energy to sate him, so he may continue acting as the God of Death as time has dictated.

Yes, I may *hate* this fate with every bone in my damned body. But I understand it. Perhaps it is why I've lasted longer than any other Corpse King. I pray and hope Isla will last longer than any past Brides of the Corpse Kings.

Once I embark into our chamber suite where she has already donned one of my robes—her preferred sleep attire—, Isla smiles at me. Her smile summons my strength, my chest expands. Though I sense Kryach's essence darkening it with his ice, I approach my bride and gaze at the flesh of her upper chest and throat. The healers did well. Only my bite mark and Kryach's skull remain.

"Isla," I address her and clear my throat. She glances up after tugging the ends of the robe, more comfortable since she doesn't feel the need to tie the sashes. Closing the distance between us, I remember my place and ask, "May I touch your shoulder?"

"Yes, Allysteir. From now on, you may touch my shoulder, my waist, my hand, my cheek, and any other non-intimate locations on my body without asking. It's getting insufferable for you to ask every single time!" she huffs, and I can't help but adore her adorable exasperation.

"Hmm..." I test, sliding my hand along her waist to cup it and tap her spine. "Only non-intimate, my Lady Queen?"

She sniffs, rolling her eyes and spreading warmth through my chest. "Don't press your luck."

Raising myself, I simper beneath my corpse mask and declare, "Luck has nothing to do with it. I won't need luck whatsoever tomorrow."

"Oh?" She taps her mouth, those blushing berry lips I long to devour.

"Sleep, Lady Isla. You will need it for where I will take you following my Death business."

"*Our* Death business," she clarifies while folding the blankets back upon our bed and growing corpus roses to grace the bone-wood framed pillars.

I climb in next to her and test by sidling next to her. "Of course, my bride." I refrain from grinning even if my mask hides all my expressions. While her face is turned from me, I weave my gloveless bony hand around her waist. I will regret this. I should lock my lips, but I have never managed to control such urges. So, I continue, "I love you, Isla."

At first, she stiffens, curls into herself more, and breathes a deep sigh. I close my eyes, heart in my throat, awaiting her response. I don't move a muscle.

Finally, she responds, "No."

I close my eyes. Lower my head. Listen.

"You love the idea of me, Allysteir. You love a dream. That is all. But you respect me, and it's enough...for now."

I listen to her yawn, then settle my brow against her shoulder as her soft snores fill our room. Not once do I drift off, but her last words echo in my head all night long.

"Oh! Corpus King!"

Since she uses her affectionate term for the first time since our wedding night, I count it as a token as Isla twirls amidst the grove of pomegranate trees, her bridal gown smacking the bark as she hastens to pick as many Isle-fruits as possible.

I remain close to the shore of the little spit of island within the Sea of Bones. No one knows of it, save for Ifrynna. Isla rushes from tree to tree. Their canopies congregate to cast shadows upon her. She disturbs countless leaves as she plucks more and more fruit. A smirk teases my lips. She samples each one, wrinkles her nose, then tosses it behind her, oblivious to the juice dripping down her throat, and trickling down her upper chest. It stains her off-the-shoulders bridal gown the color of cassock. Of mourning.

She does not mourn here. I cannot contain my deepening breath, how I shift back and forth, hopeful as she capers about the abundant grove. Collecting the bounties, she is not satisfied until she has discovered the most flawless of fruits. The pomegranate aroma cloys the air with its sensual fragrance. She cannot rid the trees of them quick enough. Whichever ones her teeth do not gore, she crushes under her bare feet. The juice reminds me of blood flushing her fair skin.

Moonlight bathes her. I approach her. When I close the distance, so my shadow covers her where she has settled upon the meadow grass, Isla acknowledges how the pomegranates have drenched her flesh. The juice plumps and reddens her intoxicating lips. Countless seeds lay strewn around her—dozens of glistening gems bowing before her presence. Ripened seeds infuse her cheeks. Her nipples peak to mirror their rouge through the dark but translucent gown bodice.

"Isla." My throat thickens as I stare down at her, my eyes straying to where her gown has cascaded into a seductive crease between her ample thighs, confessing the shape of her sex. I clear my throat, chastising myself for my roaming eyes, for my throbbing cock, for my flesh-lust most of all.

It's the first time Kryach growls, his essence boring into my rotted flesh. *You don't deserve to so much as blink in her direction!*

And we finally have one thing in common.

I am a High God! He roars, and I wince beneath my mask, prepared to succumb to my knees from an attack. Instead, Kryach's shadows thin, they wane instead of thickening.

Except the blood-flame eyes wake inside the skull mark upon Isla's flesh. She arches her back as if roused by the Death God, When I make out the shades beneath her gown, I understand exactly what he's doing. My jaw hardens, instinctive while Isla clutches the meadow grass speckled with hundreds of fallen pomegranate seeds: those twinkling Isle buds like rubied star gems.

Before Kryach can continue his ministrations, despite how Isla welcomes them, I kneel before her. I hover my hand above her cheek, wondering if it's too intimate a region. But she licks her lips and nods, granting me permission over my silent pause. She taps my gloved finger, reminding me. Nodding, I remove the hand-mask. I brush my bony knuckles across her cheek. Lowering my voice to a similar tone as my shadow lullaby, I sing:

"May you leave the sunlight far behind
And accept my dark caress.
May you love the peace of shadow wind
For you, I must possess..."

Isla tightens her muscles, clamping her knees with a gasp; she's battling Kryach, her heart enthralled with my dark melody. My chest hardens from this war. An all-together new and unfamiliar one when the God of Death pierces my bones with his blood fire, igniting my deepest pain. As if he's burning my bones, inflicting a torture of deep-seated envy.

Despite the physical agony, pride kindles my heart's fire, granting me strength to continue, to roam my hand to my bride's juice-blemished lips, shedding bone powder in the process. Corpus roses knit along her arms as she closes her eyes, gasps long, and listens.

"May your tongue taste the sweetest wine
As day and night, I woo.
May your hands clutch my gems divine
Though none as bright as you.
May sweet and rich your blood e're flow.
Please moan with every bite.
May fairest flesh be all I know.
Your soul my true delight."

When I lower my spindly bone fingers to her throat, Isla moans, thrusts out her ravenous chest, and closes her eyes. Reveling, I rove those fingers to my bite mark and eclipse the skull eyes. Death thunders chronic growls to resound in every corner of my head. I grin. His burning shifts to gnawing as if a reminder he may devour all of me. He may spit out my masticated flesh and bones until they repair themselves in the slowest form of torture-regrowth. Because Aryahn Kryach owns all of me. Except my heart.

My heart, I present to my bride. The Bride of the Corpse King.

"May pomegranates rouse your love.
I'll tempt you, my dark rose.
May you lose all thoughts of worlds above
And sleep to my shadows..."

Upon my last deep and woeful notes, Isla's eyes open and deadpan with mine. Sultry lashes woo me as she rises on her elbows, tilts her neck to the side, and gazes at my mask eyes to express, "I don't want to sleep."

THIRTY-THREE
I WANT TO FEEL IT ALL...EVEN THE FEAR

ISLA

Perhaps it's these past few months where Allysteir has treated me with the utmost respect. Perhaps it's my appetite whetted thanks to all the Isle-fruit. Its succulent juice tarries on the tip of my tongue, and its beaded jewels shimmer all around me as if treasuring my figure. Perhaps it's the Corpse King's personal lullaby. Or all these combined.

But ultimately, I know the real reason I rise onto my elbows, arch my neck, and bare my eager throat with my lavish breasts straining with my gown. My erect buds crave the sweep of a hot tongue. Or cold in Allysteir's case as I assume.

Ultimately, it's those hungry shades and their audacity to prowl beneath my gown, the fire and smoke wreathing into my veins from the skull to quicken and heat my blood, flushing my bosom.

Aryahn Kryach has not breathed a word since the wedding night.

For thousands of moments throughout the months, I have felt him: his essence haunts my footsteps whenever Allysteir is not present. His icy presence stalks my flesh whenever I bathe, his damn shade appearing in the reflection of a mirror. But whenever I turn...he is gone.

Now, he believes he has the right to invade this moment, much less penetrate my flesh with those scavenging shades and deathly power lurking inside my blood? I internally seethe at the High God's trespass. This place Allysteir has shared with me—a secret unbeknownst to anyone else, save for the God of Death. And his grandmother who won favor from Kryach—the first bride to ever accept the Death mark, to sample heaven's fruits.

The Corpse King's mask eyes never depart from mine, chin refusing to stray. Oh, he knows what I'm doing, given his chest expanding, his robes shifting, and his member betraying itself beyond his breeches when he leans against my outer thigh.

The silence between us thickens. But Allysteir lowers his bone fingers to the straps of my gown, tracing the neckline. I shiver from their touch when they caress the upper swells of my breasts.

This moment of utter beauty—it's the same beauty in the realms of death to make the gods in the Isles envious as he'd vowed to show me. Just like the corpus horses. And Ifrynna. Like the dying souls in the Hollows. The Cryth River spirits. And his refter bride glen since I brought my beauty there. This tiny isle is made of such truth as I've never known.

And I want to tremble. I want to feel it all...even the fear.

So, I close my eyes, bosom heaving, ravenous as Allysteir drags at my gown sleeves, pausing when I suck a windstorm through my teeth. But not from him. Kryach nearly overthrows Allysteir's chilled touch with his icy claws. Goose flesh hunts my skin, except for the warmth between my thighs. Warmth grows when I part my lips, eyes still closed, and touch the curve of his finger bones, urging him.

"My dark rose," whispers the King, breath colder than the river spirits right before he tugs hard and frees my swollen breasts to his eye.

He wastes no time in cupping them. To forbid Kryach's shades from conquering my breasts first. I gasp.

The thought of a High God and the most powerful of kings vying for me stirs my innards to burn hotter than hellfire mines where only fire gems form.

"Oh!" I moan long and deep when he kneads my breasts. My fingers disturb the meadow grass, dig into the soil, and burst pomegranate gems. The fragrant juice stains my fingertips. As the Corpse King rubs his chilled-bone fingers across my ripe nipples, my whole body galvanizes to the touch. I lift my fingers to my tongue to sample the leftover juice, careless of the grass clippings and soil.

When Aryahn Kryach weaves his shadows and smoke around my breasts to compete with Allysteir, something flees my throat, caught halfway between a whimper and a scream. But my scream truly comes when Allysteir closes his lips upon my breast and sucks my nipple into the depths of his warm wet mouth. Not cold as I'd believed. Not cold at all!

I'd clamp my nails into his robes, but Allysteir binds them at my waist and warns me in a low voice, "Keep those eyes closed, my Queen. Half my mask is off," he hints, hovering above my mouth. I hold my breath as he continues, deepening his voice to a threat, infused with abundant Death-shadows, "If you so much as peep one eye open, I will stop everything. I will replace my mask and leave you drenched and utterly wanting. Am I clear?"

I shiver when he kisses my cheek, when his teeth scrape my rosy bud from his mutilated mouth, disfigured in the most delicate of ways. Upon leaning in, Allysteir launches shafts of Kryach's Death power to bind my throat in a dark collar. Snug, not tight. I return to our wedding night when he held me against the wall, but this is different. I sob. I crave more. Pangs in my belly, in my breasts, in my sex of a violent vestal chamber longing for fulfillment.

"Clearer than the stars I will *never* see again, my Corpus King," I snarl, trembling from his tongue snaking across my cheek. So warm and heady.

The shadows and smoke pause. And Allysteir chuckles. "For that comment, perhaps I'll make you wait longer, my dark rose..."

"Allysteir!" I whine and drive my aching breasts up, my nipples puckered and crazed, the emptiness inside my sex relentless and savage.

By now, his strength shouldn't surprise me when he wrenches my arms in a single thrust above my head before his mouth descends back to my breast. I shriek from his tongue sampling my bud. A flush suffuses my chest despite the needle-ice shadows and the contrast of heated smoke. A surge engulfs my inner cavity, and I buck my hips.

"Corpus King..." I breathe the title in a deep exhale as I clench from the irresistible urge.

"So sweet," Allysteir purrs a chuckle against my breast, nips at one swollen rosebud, rubs his teeth against it.

"Please...I can't—"

He pulls away to hover above my mouth. I moan from the raw air washing over my breasts. "Should I tell you of how you have tantalized and taunted me every night as you slept, my bride? Your dreams leave little to the imagination. And your moans. Or how you touch yourself as you dream."

I vault my demanding hips upward, begging him while battling Kryach who teases my thighs beneath my gown. "Allysteir, I need—"

"How you beguiled me among the royals on the night you danced at my Feast of Flesh? Or how I could remember nothing but the spirit in your eyes when your back was to the wall in the Skull Ruins? Or how I can hardly consider anything but the taste of your flesh and blood which is as soul, mind, and mouth-watering as ever?"

I gasp when he lifts the hem of my gown. Longing tears trespass along my cheeks when the spindly bone finger embarks on a delirious path to my distended lips where he parts them and chuckles. "Perhaps far more mouth-watering than even your insatiable yet virginal lips."

"Oh!" I shriek again, arching when he plunges one bone finger deep inside me. Hard as a thin iron rod and unlike anything I've ever felt—so unlike mine or Franzy's warm, supple fingers tickling and tempting one another.

"Or perhaps..." Allysteir adds another finger and twists both. I lurch, hips smacking the ground so more Isle-fruit juice bursts and stains my bridal gown. I clench my muscles around those hard-as-nether-stone fingers. "...perhaps I should tell you how I never expected, nor desired you more the night you bared yourself to me upon our wedding night. How I loathed myself for what I was *forced* to do."

All Aryahn Kryach's shades dissipate, disappear into a quietude—a still, un-moving skull, bereft of smoke, of blood fire eyes, of anything but Death.

I pinch my eyes, tempted to open them from how close the King is, from his words. But Allysteir breathes a vaporous warning against my mouth. Ever so slowly, he pumps those fingers in and out. I tighten all my leg muscles. Allysteir knits his power along my curves until my flesh is alive with hypersensitivity. When the King pauses his fingers, I strain against his other hand holding me down, circling my hips, demanding more friction.

"Allysteir!" I wail because I am close enough for those pleasure bolts of lightning to stoke my veins, the barest edge to light my spinal nerves. I lift my hips again, struggling against the erotic tension, but the King growls. He urges me down with his pelvis. I thrash my head from side to side, throat constricting with need, waves raging.

He rubs his ruinous mouth across my cheek, lower to my neck, to his mark. "I punished myself all night until blood drowned the floor of our room. I would have paid any price. I would have shed all my blood, all my rotted flesh, and broken my bones for you if you had merely *commanded*. You are and always will be my Queen. You have bound your soul to me. And he will never ever have you, my dark rose..."

When the King releases my wrists, so he may lower his mouth between my thighs, part the swollen lips, lower his tongue to my clitoral knot, and drive his fingers deep and hard into me, I howl to the highest peak of the Five Ladies! On the cusp of release, those lightning bolts hum throughout my body. I clamp all my muscles. Tempt fate when I lower my hand to cup his macabre cheek where he shudders, but he does not pull away. Because I've obeyed his command. Not once have I opened my eyes, but I trace the protruding bones, the flesh rotted and pulled back from his teeth, the exposed sinew, the sunken cheeks, the barren side of his scalp.

"Hmm," he murmurs against my wet sheathe, his voice rumbling into me. "You taste of pomegranates, Isla. The sweetest of the Underworld's forbidden fruit."

Oh!—his tongue's skill when he discovers the secret knot under the sheathed hood and trains all his attention on it, tonguing harder and deeper.

I thrust my hips up and gasp a storm of furious breaths to the climax—a crescendo pulsing up my spine to crash my hips down, down, down. I release all tension. My muscles wither from the aftermath of thousands of invisible feathers tickling my flesh.

Still, I do not open my eyes despite my quaking breath, despite how Allysteir withdraws his fingers, massages my labia, and chuckles, "You've turned the soil here to utter mud with your lovely flow, my bride."

At first, I clamp my lips together but then heave as he lowers my gown hem, sucks each of my nipples in a departing offering, then replaces the neckline before pressing his brow to mine. I know from the mask weight upon my cheek, I am free to look upon him again. Almost laughing at the sheer irony of how I touched but did not look. Then again, I did look. Once.

"Not uncommon for me," I admit, squeezing my shoulders, cupping my forehead, my skin flushed, my sex giving tiny bursting gasps.

"Not the best then?"

I offer him a soft smile, cup the side of his mask, thumb the skeletal side, and reply, "You know what they say about the first time. But perhaps with more...practice—"

He growls. "Oh, you naughty buxom bride."

"It was wholly unique."

"Unique..." he clicks his tongue. "Hundreds of brides and all I receive is...unique."

With an airy laugh, I prepare to tell him how wonderful it was. The first time when I'd pleasured myself was truly my best. The dead of midnight. On the edge of the Void. All my body alive with its dark energy as I'd tempted fate, tempted danger. And with nothing but the moon shedding her insipid light upon my naked skin, I'd bathed in a river bordering the Void, then lay on its shore where I'd first touched myself. My reclamation after the Void had done its best to destroy me as a child. That monumental night, I took back my power.

And when I'd first climaxed, it was as if all the gods and goddesses had unleashed their essence into me.

But I don't get the chance to share. My spine prickles at the sight out of the corner of my eye. My stomach caves in. And Allysteir flicks his head up and growls before hauling me to my feet, shielding me in a black, protective cocoon, and roaring for Ifrynna.

Because strewn upon the shores of this secret isle thanks to the tide are countless corpses of young women. All are clothed in a bridal gown... and marked with sacred runes of Doom.

THIRTY-FOUR
WHAT IS YOUR GAME, BROTHER?

ALLYSTEIR

After ensuring Kryach would escort them safely back to the Citadel, I sent Isla away upon Ifrynna, then summoned Elder Kanat to the little island where I wait, prepared to test him. Because this has his signature all over it. I roll my tongue against the bridge of my teeth, glowering behind my mask at the discarded corpses, runed with Doom and inked by refter blood symbols of black feathers and hellwylves: Morrygna's sigils.

I lean over to inspect them, wondering if it's time to enlist Kryach's aid. The stabbing sensation at the back of my mind ensures what his price would be. Yes, I am certain Isla is strong enough to survive the God of Death. But he would command me to revoke my blood mark upon her body, her freely granted offering to precede his. He will take far more than her soul or a portion. He will take *everything*, flesh and blood included. He'll leave me cursed with utterly *nothing*.

Once I sense the Sea shifting to betray an oncoming vessel, I turn to the opposite shore a few hundred yards in the distance. Snarl. I should have known the slithering snake of an elder wouldn't have had the courage to face me alone. Though I didn't expect my damned brother to accompany him; no other explanation considering the royal barge dropping anchor beyond the bone reef flanking the isle.

I curl my good lip back as Aydon, Kanat, and the elders climb onto the barge's attached skiff so they may embark onto the shore. Garbed in our traditional robes, Aydon, in his bone-armored boots, hits the shallows first, followed by Kanat lurking behind my brother as if the Prince is his mask.

But no mask in Talahn-Feyhran history could ever rival mine.

You won't ever hide from me, brother, I want to say to Aydon as he approaches, not a strand of polished hair out of place—his azure eyes sharp and keen to parade his political charisma. I hold my tongue despite permitting my shadows to creep all over, on the cusp of piercing any elder who would dare dishonor the bridal-imitation corpses. Most elders are too preoccupied covering their mouths with their kerchiefs to ward off the rigor mortis stench. It's the finest of perfumes to me. The same aroma permeating my refter bride glen. The fragrance haunting my accursed being.

Waves lap at the shore, knocking the bride-clad bodies against one another. A violent wind lashes the cavernous dome of this greatest territory in all the White Ladies. As if harmonizing with these ominous events. A hint of a storm on the air.

Thrusting my robe to molest the air, I coldly lance Kanat with my words, "Is there some affair you would care to share with your *King,* Elder Kanat?" It takes all I have to clench my teeth around his title and force the words beyond them. I want to strip him of it here and now, but while I could wield my parietal bone power to rival Kanat and the other elders, it would not rival Aydon's equal supremacy. Only with Aryahn Kryach's fullest power could I hope to overcome them.

Say the word, Allysteir, and I will bring them to their knees, carve the souls from their beings, and feast on them as mere delicacies.

Yes...right before he feasts upon my bride as his greatest banquet of all time.

Stay with Isla, I snarl, urging him back to the Citadel. Kryach hesitates as if hoping I will surrender to his whim. But he should know better. Only once in the past five hundred years have I ever done such a thing.

Once he departs, I harden my jaw, all my muscles taut as I face the elders and my brother. If I could, I'd give up all my bone power, my immortality, my soul itself to protect my bride, but the High God of Death considers my offerings as scraps.

No, ultimately, this is my brother's game. A game of minds and of wills. We are equal kings on the board, but he has more pieces than me. He has formed his alliances through political maneuverings while I chose to hide in my refter bride glen, to distract myself with Isle-fruit, with bony ponies, with punishment, and artistic exploits. Now, I will pay the price. All these lovelies pay the price.

I must not retreat today. Time for me to move even if I am my only piece. My king outranks his.

"Your Majesty," Kanat states, slipping into his venomous tongue more potent than a Sythe-sac. "Rest assured, the elders will unearth the identity of whatever being has thus dared to defile our sacred Underworld with such savagery. With our unified power, we will not rest until we bring the transgressor to their knees before your very throne, my King."

The other elders chant their agreement and their empty promises.

Meanwhile, I don't fixate on Kanat's eyes. Futile given how well-rehearsed he is. Instead, I use my mask as cover to appraise Aydon's physical and facial gestures. He does not flinch. Nor do his eyes wander to the bridal cadavers. Much to my chagrin, he regards me as I regard him—as if he knows I'm testing him behind my skull eyes, weighing his responses.

I want to bind his throat with all my shade power and challenge him. *What happened to my brother, Aydon? What happened to my bold older brother who roamed the tombs of the kings and climbed a dragyn ribcage housing our great grandfather's crypt? Where is my brother who spied on the elders and plotted endless pranks with me to disrupt their shrine practices?*

My gut tightens to the memories, to the knowledge of my past brother. Where is my brother who never desired power despite how much he was groomed for it? Who longed to travel throughout all of Talahn-Feyal and drive back any refters who dared to plague our lands? A goal we shared. We would be warrior princes for decades before your father passed, believing the Mallyach-Ender and the Mender of Worlds would arise in our time and conquer the gods themselves!

The brother who loved me and did not loathe me...

I clench my gloved fist, note how Aydon's eyes flick to my subtle gesture, then back to my corpse mask as if suspecting my thoughts. I seal my wretched lips over my huff. And long to roar what I have never mentioned since that cursed night five hundred years ago. *The brother I sacrificed everything for!*

I thread my brows low, eyes contracting, careless of whether Aydon may discern, careless of how he hardens his jaw while the elders debate amongst themselves. The words lodge in my throat, and I must swallow them. They are as rotted as my flesh. *What did I do to earn your revilement, brother? What did Talahn-Feyal do to deserve your dishonor?*

After longer moments of the elders prattling like the gaggle of useless geese they are, Aydon finally raises his voice, "After a sharp investigation, which *I* will oversee, I will order our finest corpse collectors to gather the dead, cleanse them of the accursed symbols, and to perform the ceremonial death rites as well as notify next of kin. As Elder Kanat assured you, Allysteir, this wrong will be righted. And there will be peace and prosperity once again in Talahn-Feyal."

All elders fall silent in the wake of Aydon's announcement, nodding in agreement, bowing to him. Not to me. Aydon postures, bearing beyond a princely regality because he knows he wields equal power. He knows my utter weakness. It's there in the slightly crooked smirk on one corner of his mouth, how his cobalt eyes pinch and shimmer.

So, as the elders depart to the shore to inspect the corpses for the beginnings of the investigation, I catch Aydon by his mirrored robe sleeve and seethe under my breath, "What is your game, brother?"

Breath heavy and on the verge of panting, I wait as Aydon glances at the elders, assuring they are distracted before he goes so far as to pat the mask where my cheek is in a direct mockery while he hums low, "My greatest desire, brother."

My breath hitches as he shifts his robes, righting them while simpering and striding away, vainer than a crowing cock. I release my shades until the isle trees violently quaver and shed hundreds of pomegranates to crack. Their fruit surges with juice and seeds like clotted blood to splash the bridal corpses.

Somehow, I wrestle my growl back into my throat. I long to summon Kryach and agree to any bargain because Aydon has added his marker to those who would dare claim my bride!

Except in Aydon's case, he wants her very much alive. And in his *bed*.

THIRTY-FIVE
WHAT LIES BEYOND HIS MASK?

ISLA

H ere I am again.

"It's been an ass' years, ye infernal tree!" I curse and grip one of Master Ivory's branches, hissing. All Ivory does is shake his branches as if crossing his arms in dismissal. I almost slam my hand against his immense base. "Ye're a bleedin' statya da! I'mma skelp yer beeg behind!" At best, my language isn't exactly polite and unbecoming of a Queen at worst.

Today, I am here for more than one reason. Ever since the pomegranate isle where the corpses marked with mysterious runes had floated onto the shore, Allysteir has given me nothing. Up till now, my motivation for getting into the Unseen Section was purely to learn how to conquer Kryach, but these days, he seems to want little to do with me.

Once again, Master Ivory does not relent. Every day possible, whenever Allysteir does not keep me busy, I return to the library to seek answers from Master Ivory, hoping he will welcome me to the Unseen

Section. So many times, I've been tempted to allow Allysteir to gift me the secret, but I am determined to earn this. Just as I earned Aryahn Kryach's respect the night I reclaimed the refter bride glen. Sometimes, I've asked Ifrynna to take me back there unbeknownst to Allysteir, though I'm certain he is aware of my presence later. At least he hasn't addressed it, nor forbidden me to enter. The glen inspires my floral craft.

Not that it's yielded results here, I consider, bristling when I attempt some of the rarest blooms I've researched in the annals of this library. Ice lilies cultivated upon the northernmost seas of the Deep North where dark blue-skins undulate ribbon-like fins. But for the umpteenth time, Ivory freezes as if locking himself tight...and all his treasures of knowledge.

"I don't know what you want, you damned tree!" If I can't learn any more secrets here, I must seek them beyond the Citadel. Somewhere deep in the Underworld.

"He has always been a damned tree," a voice slices through the gap, through my tension with Ivory. I flinch, turning to Aydon.

He bows to me, ever diplomatic and formal, holding the propriety of a Prince of Talahn-Feylan. Despite how he wields the most political power. I find it ironic, considering his parietal bone holds more power than my floral gift. Still, I straighten, squaring my shoulders while descending from one of Ivory's several platforms until I'm on solid flooring next to Aydon.

"I admire your persistence, my Queen." Aydon gestures to the tree. "I gave up long ago attempting to please Master Ivory, though I've spied my brother in the wee hours of the morn following his Death business entering the Unseen section. Always combing through the annals, hoping in vain to learn of the Mallyach-Ender."

I stiffen, purse my lips, and touch a nearby branch, dismissing the powder upon my fingers. "So, you do not believe the legends? That there is a Mallyach-Ender?" *An Ender of all Curses is a far stretch,* I remind myself. An impossibility. The threadbare fabric of legend.

Aydon steps toward me, his eyes bluer than blood-chilled veins. "I believe in Nathyan Ghyeal. I believe in Talahn-Feyal. I believe in faithfulness to my country." The heaviness of his words sinks onto my chest the nearer he approaches. When his eyes darken, he imprisons me in this position until my shoulders tighten. "I believe we, the strongest and most powerful of all regions, bear the highest responsibility of all nations. And the greatest burdens. We should be willing to do anything to maintain such responsibility."

Something in me shrinks to his words, but I can't fathom why. How could intense loyalty be wrong? When the tips of Aydon's fingers light upon the back of my hand to roam my knuckles, I draw a deep breath and hold the baited gust while pursing my lips.

"You understand such responsibility, Lady Isla," Aydon continues, fingers striding along the lacy sleeve. "How could you not? With absolute conviction, you vowed to doom yourself, to become my brother's damned bride, to become Kryach's very soul pawn—"

"I am nobody's pawn," I snarl from his words and not his hand when it pauses at the dual-mark upon my collarbone, the mark I never conceal.

Aydon leans in, close enough so his breath stirs heat across my mouth when he says, "You accepted the God of Death's mark. The soul tie to bind you to an utter stranger and the enemy of all virgin maidyans."

"Not my enemy." I shake my head and turn, but an inner voice gnaws on me, a voice reminding me of the songs and stories told to all children of Talahn-Feyal. Of how they all came true on our wedding night. Allysteir betrayed me. My body cannot stop tensing whenever I'm in his presence; my flesh will always remember as it remembers my childhood trauma. Sometimes, I wait for him to repeat that night in spite of everything.

Except Aydon causes me to flinch when he coils his hand around my neck, chaining me in place.

"You deserve more, Isla," he murmurs in my ear. I slam my eyes shut, biting hard on my tongue to ward off his advances. "You deserve to be a *true* Queen to unite with the real power of the throne behind the mask. You deserve to be worshipped forever and not used as my damned brother has used all brides. Kryach has reduced them to nothing more than rotted, walking corpses. Such a fate does not belong to you. Nor one of scarred bitterness as our mother who cannot remember what love is. Please consider Franzyna..."

When he invokes her name, my sweetheart, I gnash my teeth, but Aydon arrests my whole body by the waist while humming low, "Isla, do not mistake my intentions. I would *never* ever harm my bride. I cherish your love for her as I cherish her generous heart. Franzyina is more than either of us deserves."

Damn right! I almost thrust out the words but don't, freezing because Aydon's hands do not wander. They merely anchor me in place without the lasciviousness or possessiveness of Kryach's shades.

I listen as Aydon utters, "Imagine what could be, Isla. A King and Queen bearing a generation without the Curse. Such is the stuff of true legend to defeat the gods and earn immortality on our own merits! The first nation to bear a royal child beyond the gods' touch. And you would be free to love your sweetheart for a thrice-lifespan or more without the burden of a deathly soul mark. That is not your destiny, Isla. You know it is not your destiny to become a refter bride, nor to fade with nothing more than a scarred soul as my doomed mother."

No, it is not, I almost say but clamp my mouth shut because this is Aydon, the political Prince. His over-zealousness will be his downfall despite it birthed from the best intentions of which the paths of Netherhell are paved.

"And I give you my most solemn of vows," Aydon goes on, hand drifting to mine so he raises it to his eager lips to bestow a chaste kiss, "I would give you my parietal bone itself, Bride of the Corpse King, if you would revoke the marks and bind yourself to me. For I am convinced *you* are the true Mallyach-Ender who will break the Curse with the fruits of your soul!"

My jaw drops. Ice-wrapped millstones congregate in my stomach. I've jested about it. Reflected on it. Because Aydon is wrong about one thing: I may wear this crown, I am no true Queen of the Underworld. This crown is a mask...like Allysteir's. We do not sit in Court. At most, I am the glorified Mistress of Death. But the Ender of Curses!

"While Allysteir merely wishes to possess you for all eternity," Aydon adds, "I wish you for *all* of Talahn-Feyal. For all worlds. I will act as the humblest of vessels to fulfill such a destiny through our future child. After all...Lady Isla, it was *not* my brother who sat upon the throne in his skull mask guise that night. It was not Allysteir you vowed yourself to upon the Feast of Flesh..."

As his breath coasts across my cheek, nose skimming my skin, I do my best to deny the prediction I suspect, the confirmation when Aydon concludes, "It was *me*!"

I gasp the deepest breath in the same moment Aydon spins me and seals his mouth to mine. To my utter astonishment, my body yields. I open my lips to grant him entrance. Aydon presses me against the bone tree and kisses me fiercely until all my skin flushes to mirror my utter humiliation from surrendering to him. To so much as consider his offer.

Because there is one secret I have kept from Allysteir, from my parents, from the very gods. Something I never considered when I vowed myself to the Corpse King, something I'd never considered until Aydon's declaration.

I cannot bear a child.

Nor will I ever desire one!

Which means the Corpse King's line *must* end with me. If so, all nations will plunge into war. And Allysteir is bound to Kryach. As long as I am bound to him, I am doomed. But with Aydon...with this kind and charismatic Prince, who has born the entire nation and has treated my sweetheart with such care and affection, perhaps we may beat the gods...with or without a child. Allysteir will want me to bear his future child, but Aydon could be *persuaded*...

And as he'd declared: he was the one I'd truly vowed myself to.

No, I do not desire Aydon regardless of his shrewd offer. Still, I angle my neck to the side and welcome his mouth again because he could hold the secret to the murdered and marked imitation brides, a secret the Corpse King refuses to share. But I must tread as lightly as the Cryth River spirits. I cannot ask tonight.

Aydon is not the only one who can wear a political mask.

Frozen in this fatal limbo, I don't resist when he presses his body to mine, when he feasts on my mouth to scrape his Ith teeth along my bottom lip until he ruthlessly pulls away. A growl unleashes from his throat. Our gazes meet, suspended in the thick web of tension. I pant and manage a smile before Aydon nods and bows his head.

"My Lady Queen, I must return to my bride now. Thank you. I trust you will consider my offer..." He pays his final respect by kissing the back of my hand while I purse my swollen lips and say nothing. My flushed countenance betrays everything.

His offer is tempting. Too tempting. Because two choices present themselves: I accept Aydon and become the true Mallyach-Ender as we strive to conquer the gods with or without a child.

Or I remain the Bride of the Corpse King, the Mistress of the God of Death, doom or scar my soul, and leave the kingdom to darkness and destruction.

"I wish to take you somewhere else tomorrow following my Death business," Allysteir offers over our nightly meal. I, alone, eat while he contents himself with Sythe wine. Not as much as usual since he dined earlier on my flesh. He moved from my throat to my belly as he'd once indicated. No scars of course, but I remember the sharp pain of his teeth sinking into my plump flesh. It's been a week since my interlude with Aydon in the library.

The last time when Allysteir selected my inner thigh for his feast, I'd screamed loud enough to draw the attention of all his refter brides. I'd lain nude upon a bed of corpus roses with black death rose vines above my head. But I hadn't screamed from the pain so much as wailed from his fingers driving deep into my sex, thumb tickling my clitoral knot, and tongue twirling my knot while my thigh blood trickled upon the roses.

Sometimes, I chastise myself, chew my lower lip, ridiculing myself for caving so quickly. It's only been six months since our wedding night.

Then again, I half-caved to Aydon in far less.

But six months feels like six years in the Underworld of Nathyan Ghyeal. And Allysteir has proven trustworthy. Besides, why should I deny myself these pleasures? Not once has he asked me for any favors despite feeling his cock's desire every damned time!

I curl my fingers, reflecting on his vacant skull eyes, on the angles of his bone mask, so delicate, it reminds me of porcelain. Those hollow eyes do not shift, do not move, frozen upon my person.

What game is he playing? What lies beyond his mask?

Oh, confound it all! I clench my fingers. Because this Corpus King will drive me mad! Ever We never speak of Kryach, of the doom awaiting me.

"Another surprise? A *challenge*, my husband?" I smirk beyond the lip of my wine glass.

"You should know me by now, my beautiful bride," Allysteir casually adds and sips at his glass.

I raise my chin and subtly offer him a wink. "I will come with you tomorrow…if you tell me more about Aydon."

I register the shift in his countenance. Good. He hardens his muscles beneath those robes. His posture tightens like his clenched teeth. And I drum my fingers along the table absentmindedly because I know I've already won.

Finally, those robes heave, and Allysteir relents, "I am the younger brother, Isla. And a bastard!"

I close my eyes, understanding the meaning behind his words. "Tradition dictates the Corpse Curse goes to the elder brother. And one to follow in the line of Corpse Kings."

"The night my…Aydon's father passed, it was the longest night of my life…"

THIRTY-SIX

IT HAD SEEMED LIKE THE DECENT TRADE.

ALLYSTEIR

His blood drowned the floor.

A throbbing pang invaded my chest as I entered the royal bed chamber following the Corpse King's savage scream. Simply King since he was restored. The Curse would eventually mark Aydon as the successor once Thayne's spirit passed to the halls of his ancestors. Ever since Mathyr alerted me at the young age of eight that the King was not my true father, he was always Thayne. I suppose it was justification for myself and a burden relieved.

Whenever he'd regarded me with nothing but leers or sneers at our suppers, whenever we passed each other in halls and he'd bit his thumb after I'd turned my back when he believed I wasn't looking, whenever *Mathyson* took time to train me in court politics—a responsibility Thayne had neglected—and jested with me about how he'd steal a bone from Thayne's rotted corpse when they were younger and hide it for weeks before the King would find it, I knew long before Mathyr ever confirmed.

Nor did I care how Thayne considered me nothing more than bastard bone powder. Because I had Mathyr's protection. And Aydon's fraternity.

Thick as thieves, we would spend our childhood escaping our stuffy elder tutors, roam the wonders of Nathyan Ghyeal from the deepest pits aflame with jewels to the halls of the tombed kings to the Tolle Caverns—the secret exit out of the White Ladies. With our twin parietal bones, we would conquer bone stallions and ride to Talahn-Feyal's borders, straddle the kingdom lines, and taunt the Sythe patrols because all war was god-forbidden according to the Curse.

For over a decade, Aydon and I were inseparable. The wild Princes of Talahn-Feyal. The Underworld was ours. I remembered the night we slit our wrists down to the bone to drain as much blood as possible. How we mixed it and vowed a high-stakes gamble over who could find the Mallyach-Ender first.

We shared our deepest secrets. We swam naked in the Sea of Bones and dried ourselves upon the shore while eating Isle fruit from the tiny spot of land we only knew existed thanks to our grandmother's stories. Aydon shared his keen mind of countless historical records, how he would inherit the throne from Thayne and make Talahn-Feyal the envy of all nations in Talahn-Feyhran.

The years went by. We grew stronger. Aydon grew sharper. I grew... more *passionate*. Every girl I met I believed was destined to be my bride, be it milk maidyan, servant, or duchess. My passion for art and not politics grew—art I shared with every sweetheart, but all it took was one gnash of Mathyr's teeth for all those sweethearts to retreat. Except for Finleigh. A burning, never-dimming fuse. My first bride. My first true love.

Thayne confirmed his suspicions regarding the identity of my *true* father. And he threw Mathyson into the Void.

So many nights, I'd tempted fate and had wandered the borders of the Void, daring it to take me. My tears coated the ground to mingle with the black blood I'd shed from the countless refter bodies I'd felled those nights. I'd grieved because I could not conquer the Void, could not stop wondering what happened to Fathyr.

Mathyr was never the same. Then again, she was never the same prior either. Mathyson was simply a self-indulgence to soothe her soul scars because Thayne never could. Perhaps if Kryach had spared her out of pity, out of mercy, but he hadn't. He'd raped what he could.

I was the result of her addiction, of sharing her trauma with Mathyson who dared to love her for it.

One year later, I'd discovered Mathyr straddling Thayne as he'd coughed a fountain of blood. She'd whispered vengeful poison in his ear. And vowed to repay him for killing Mathyson.

Perhaps she'd never conceived the doom to follow. Regardless, she didn't regret her choice to assassinate the Corpse King. Not when she'd paid the ultimate price to appease Kryach and restore the King. To grant him a form beyond his pain and rot. Nothing in me could fault her; I'd also desired the truest form of revenge.

But a deep, throbbing pang invaded my chest from how Aydon, the brother of my youth, who'd always considered me his truest friend—despite his father and the court's mocking leers from my bastard status—shook the King while weeping. Aydon's screams and pleas for him to return would haunt me forever. The King's ghost had already evanesced, his spirit wandering the halls of our ancestors. I understood Aydon's grief. I'd felt it when Thayne had thrown Mathyson into the

Nether-Void.

What moved me most were Aydon's tears. Only three years my senior. The one who'd indulged all my childish games and escapes beyond Nathyan Ghyeal. Our dreams and goals and fraternity had never dimmed despite our differing personalities.

He knew his oncoming fate. Yes, Mathyr had survived the Curse, but it was never truly broken. He knew he would become a living refter corpse. It was a matter of time before Aryahn Kryach descended to inhabit the descendant of the former Corpse King. Aydon knew he would arrive here someday…but not so young and handsome with the entire Citadel enamored with him and singing the Prince's favor.

A millstone of grief, of regret, inundates my chest when I remember how the God of Death began to inhabit my older brother's form. Aydon would have slit his wrists before becoming the pawn of Aryahn Kryach. He was birthed for the politics of the throne.

I wanted *nothing* to do with it.

At the time, it seemed like the *decent* trade.

A deep knot encroaches into my stomach, tightening my rib cage when I remember how I dove into the River Cryth and begged the spirits to bring me to the God of Death. They took pity on me. I'd surrendered to their icy embrace and allowed them to drag me into their coldest source of an undertow until I'd found myself in the spirit planes of the gods. On the first level where Aryahn Kryach had somehow managed the will to lower himself to meet with me. *Me*! A bastard! A broken but illegitimate child of the true Corpse King. Not worthy of the honor or sacred Talahn-Feyal customs and traditions.

"Speak your words, Allysteir, son of Gryzelda," he dictated in a lowered voice bordering upon fatality like his river.

Son of Gryzelda. No, it was not the father. The Corpse *King's* lineage didn't matter. Mathyr's did. The fruit of *her* womb. He'd cited *her* name and not the Corpse King who was always loftiest among our regal ancestors' tombs. While my mother had scorned the God of Death for many years, he'd elevated her position to one of honor.

The King had forsaken so many brides after they'd turned refter, which I only knew since Mathyr had shown me the hidden glen she'd created for them—only *me* and not Aydon. The King had abandoned them to the depths of the White Ladies. But Mathyr had collected them, preserved them as best she could in the hidden glen.

Despite the high price, I approached Aryahn Kryach.

And begged him to give *me* the Curse, not Aydon. I fell to my knees, lowered my head, and respected the God of Death, the highest God in all the Isles, save for the long-distant angyl and demon Highest Goddess and God.

Aryahn Kryach paused. Soon, his shades engulfed me; they could nullify my soul within moments. But I kept my head bowed and leaned into those icy, fatal shades as they curled along my flesh as if curious. As if *intrigued*.

Finally, Kryach approached me until his deathly robe brushed its decay across my meager Feyal-flesh. The High God of Death tucked his fingers beneath my chin and uttered two words to change my fate for the next five hundred years.

"You'll do."

After his pronouncement, the shades stabbed into the fabric of my flesh, my blood, my heart, and the thinnest and darkest realms of my soul. Death was the ultimate, the finality to everything. It was the coldest and truest conquest. The undefeatable, irrefutable, untranscribable truth and beauty I could ever imagine. I hated him all the more for it. For how a Curse could be torture and punishment and yet beauty and understanding—of rot and ruin and yet temptation and tantalization. Perfect verity.

I returned to Mathyr. I returned to Aydon who still wailed over his father's body. They knew. In my *new* form, I faced them, standing only due to Kryach's power. The moment their eyes widened in unchecked horror while Mathyr's tears cascaded to the floor blotted in Thayne's blood, I knew my actions, my choice had broken her heart. I was her last scar to seal the coffin of her soul. Because the Curse fulfilled through Aydon would have been her final act of retribution. I'd stolen it from her...

"And I have paid the price every single day since. But my brides have paid the truest," I conclude, my past finished, my history revealed.

Isla sets down her wine cup. I drain mine and fill another bone goblet to grant me the emotional reserves to cope with sharing my past. For I could not hope to deny her this. Not when I've spent the past six months desperate to repair the bridge of trust between us in hopes she will forgive me for the wedding night, for everything.

Spine steeled, I tap the side of the goblet, knocking bone against bone because I rarely wear my gloves with Isla anymore. I slam the goblet on the table, causing her to flinch, but she recovers. With the grace of a true Queen of Nathyan Ghyeal, of Talahn-Feyal, of perhaps all nations, Isla rises, and strides around the table to me.

I hiss through snarled teeth when she dares to tiptoe her fingers to the lower edges of my mask. But while I wince, I clench my teeth—on the cusp of breaking one. Clench my phalanges when she ever so slowly lifts the mask. To my astonishment, she does not tear it from my face. She does not fling it to the floor to haunt me with its echo upon the stone. No, she merely berths it on the barest edge of my upper lip. All she does is expose my ruined mouth. Full lips on one side with masticated withered flesh stripped to expose my teeth on the other.

I slam my eyes shut when she tiptoes her fingertips along those jagged teeth. She's so fucking close, I smell her blood and flesh of the sweetest and richest Isle-wine. Her pulse thrums as it heightens to the risk she takes.

I gasp, I growl when Isla presses her luscious mouth to my broken one and kisses me long and deep and full.

THIRTY-SEVEN
WHO WAS YOUR FIRST BRIDE?

ISLA

What I love most is his history. Not his brokenness because I am not so invasive to desire his trauma. After all, I'd imparted a simple desire: tell me more about Aydon, and I will rise to your challenge. But his authenticity unraveled as a dark scroll dumbfounds me. He shared not only about his elder brother, but Allysteir revealed his Corpse King origin. No, I still do not love him. But I respect him.

Perhaps I never truly loved him. I love the novelty of everything, the emotion, the power of every life-changing moment. This same power I wield over him.

The fire in me cannot help but tempt him. Unless it's not him I am tempting...

So, I open one side of his mouth, prodding my tongue to plead for entrance. It's not long before his bony fingers light upon the waist of my gown, tracing the fading mark where he'd bitten me earlier as if his desire is roused again. I moan to his tongue flicking mine, tasting the pomegranate wine. He samples the roof of my mouth. A kaleidoscope of butterflies whirls in my stomach.

With the strength granted to him by the God of Death, Allysteir seizes my waist and draws me into his lap until I'm straddling his hips. His unchecked arousal beyond his robe nudges my belly. Heat engulfs my pores while my sex whets its appetite. My gown rises to expose much of my legs. All around us, the candlelight casts shadows, reminding me of Aryahn Kryach's. Prompted by my emotion, my desire, the skull branded in my flesh awakens.

I moan deeper into Allysteir's mouth when Ari's shades comb my nude legs and the inner curves of my thighs. Meanwhile, the Corpse King savors my mouth and lowers his phalanges to my breasts.

"Oh!" I cry when he rips, when he tears my gown.

I do not buck, nor lean away when I find myself a naked vessel of a woman in the Corpse King's lap. My hunger is too piqued. The candlelight ravages my body to glow as my desire heats and flushes all of me. My breasts grow heavy. Beyond his mask, I know Allysteir studies them as he traces a bony finger around one erect nipple—a deep coral pink, the rosy skin around it shriveling to his touch. For the first time, I grind my pelvis against him, grind my very sex against his length.

But shades without number, shades like constellations in reverse, fold around my body, plunging it into a cold quietude like an icy cocoon. I arch my back and stiffen, recognizing Ari's envious ploy. Instead, Allysteir dives his chilled bone fingers into my sex to nurture my heat. Thrusting my breasts against his robe, I grip his shoulders for dear... death. And ride his stiff finger bones.

When I creep my fingers to his length, Allysteir growls behind the mask, seizes my wrist, and wrenches it from his breeches.

"No," he states, voice firm and low.

Against him, I heave, burying my head in his shoulder. On the verge of delirious tears because he's injected another bone finger inside my inner chamber. He twists and drives them in deeper until I give a high, keening wail, my nigh-climactic pleas muffled by his robe. Through it all, I bite the fabric on the hard shoulder blade while thrusting my hips. I try again. Inch my hand to his member aroused beneath his robe.

Again, the King snarls, "*No*, Isla," and pushes my hand away while adding another tormenting finger. Thanks to his unbridled expertise, he knows how to leave me striving for more. I jerk my hips forward but can't seem to force those curved bones to strike my inner pleasure place: such a soft yet so-triggered spot. Other than the clitoral knot cresting my folds, of course. Allysteir rubs that outer nub with his knuckles to torment me.

Finally, I slam my frustrated fist against his chest. Panic hammers into me at the cruel snap. The crack. The undeniable fracture.

Mortified, I yank my sex from his fingers and scramble off his lap. I sweep the closest garment to cover myself, careless of how I upset the dinner plates. The leftover wine splatters the marble like blood. Tears stream down my cheeks as Allysteir rises. I don't know what astounds me more: how he moves toward me with utter ease and strength or how he betrays no sense of pain. Not so much as a wince.

"Isla—" His bone-hands stretch to me.

I shake my head. Violent gasps flee my mouth, and I gaze at his chest. "I was angry. I shouldn't have, Allysteir. I'm—"

The King chortles and moves towards me. Stunned, stupefied, I shake my waves to one side. How can he chuckle? His rib bone protrudes, budging against the fabric of his robe!

"I broke your bone, Allysteir! I punched, and I...how can you possibly—"

"You are utterly and consummately sweet, my bride!" exclaims Allysteir, closing the distance between us to gather my face in his hands, merging his bone powder with my tears.

"Not so consummately obviously," I add, my voice cracking.

Allysteir swipes at my tears, chuckling low. "At least you haven't lost your wit."

Undone by the raw emotion churning inside me, part loss from those fingers stoking my desire, part empathy from his sacrifice because I, too, understand what it's like to sacrifice myself—however my power and independence at the time I'd volunteered—I nearly buckle. Not like Allysteir. I never traded...

Until the marks below my collarbone catch my eye. No, I'd traded something far deeper than my flesh, my body. I'd traded my soul. Now, my hands long to claw at my flesh, to strip it clean of the Death mark, of Allysteir's. I want to accept Aydon's offer and revoke the marks...with the power of his twin parietal bone as he'd promised.

When I crumble, Allysteir collects me into his arms. I wince from his rib bone prodding me.

The King brushes his mask lips upon my cheek and proclaims, "Remind me, my bride, to tell you the stories sometime of how Aydon would impress his court noble friends by purposefully knocking into me to disturb my bones. By now, I find such upsets quite *amusing*...yours more than anyone's."

I nestle my head into his shoulder as he tucks me into the bed. At least my tears have dried, though my cheeks have turned to salty beds.

"It must be terrible...getting used to it," I muse as he folds the blankets around my body, now naked after dispensing with the tablecloth.

He shrugs. "Five hundred years of practice." Will practice be enough for me? If I find these marks difficult to bear, what will happen once Kryach leaves his scar upon my soul after fracturing it and stealing a piece?

If I last that long.

How long did Allysteir's *first* bride last?

"Corpus King?" I pause after calling for him once he's sidled next to me, mask facing me. Dismissing the cold, grieving hollow between my thighs, I snuggle closer, and with one hand beneath my pillow and the other brushing his mask-cheek's indent, I dare to ask, "Who was your first bride?"

I suppose I should not have been surprised he'd refused to open up to me. Instead, he'd wrapped me deeper into the sheets and wool throws of our bed and then sung me to sleep with his lullaby.

As so many times before, I've dressed in a new bridal gown. This time, it's a transparent scarlet red—a cascade of blood. My test, a reminder to Allysteir of what I desire from him. At this point, we've been married for over half a year. For weeks, we've shared a bed according to my boundaries. Boundaries he's honored while respecting my identity. A contrast to our wedding night.

Apart from his envy, Aryahn Kryach has been respectful but quiet. Too quiet. Nor have I minded his jealousy, his invasion, provided Allysteir is the last one standing. No...*I* am the last one standing.

Down the same barge, we depart. Propelled by the river spirits. This time, Betha emerges from their breadth, and I marvel at her revelation when she shares her ability to dream walk. Throughout centuries, she acted as the prime agent of the Goddess of Doom who haunted the nightscapes of the lands beyond Talahn-Feyal where the names of the gods are different from ours.

As so many times, I grow my power to bestow roses upon the sick and near-death. By early afternoon, Allysteir's Death business within the Hollows is finished.

Now, he directs the bone canoe through another watery tunnel branching off from the Hollows. It leads us deeper into the heart of Nathyan Ghyeal—away from the main hub of river traffic as found near the Citadel and its city and tourist locales. When ice rakes my spine to prickle my flesh from how the tunnel walls enclose us with no pinprick of candlelight from the Hollows' entrance behind us, I scoot closer to Allysteir. After all these months of marriage, my Nether-mark rears its magic. Allysteir's presence does not soothe it, and I excuse it as some immunity. After all, we've slept in the same bed, I've given him flesh, he's given me pleasure.

The mark numbs its unsettling ice, and I flatten my palms on each side of the platform seat while Allysteir's robe skirts the back of my gown. A black king to a red queen. For a moment, I angle my neck to peer up at him. As if he's always alert for my slightest gesture, the King shifts his mask, so his skull cavity eye meets my full ones. I turn away because it's pointless to ask where he's taking me.

It's strange. I huddle my arms around my chest, wishing I could stem the tide of uncomfortable emotion. Normally, I appreciate surprises. If only I could wave my hand in dismissal, chalk it up to typical human nerves as we embark into unknown parts of the White Ladies. But it makes no sense for two reasons.

One: While no sunlight dons its face in this Underworld, the wispy spirit lights roaming the waters provide more than enough glow.

Two: I leap at the chance for adventure...and a challenge. A little thing such as darkness or the unknown inspires my exhilaration and not fear.

So, why does apprehension gnaw on me when the King directs the boat around the curving waterways, past other outlets, and into the convoluted web of tunnels? I'd assumed he would take me to the refter bride glen. I'd believed one of the macabre but beauteous brides I'd floral-adorned must be his significant first bride. The one who owed his deepest emotions. His unbridled hatred was palpable from the mask nearly falling due to all his hardened muscles like iron-coated bones. I'd mourned at his lonely pain when his shoulders shuddered and posture stooped.

Whomever this bride was, she must haunt him far more than Kryach ever has.

THIRTY-EIGHT
A COMMON THIEF HAD STOLEN THE HEART OF THE CORPSE KING.

ALLYSTEIR

I dock the boat on the rocky shore of the enclosed cavern I alone know of. Save for the damned oppressor within my spirit. The height of irony he is privy to my greatest secrets, all my thoughts—how he lives vicariously through my flesh and bones and blood: an achievement the gods had always sought and desired for eons before the Curse. And yet, the God of Death never affords me a glimpse of his territory. Nor could I ever conceive of what has become of my former bride souls.

I clench my jaw, remembering how he has tormented me with their names, mocking me with hints regarding their psyche states, questioning me if I'd like to know more. Dangling his forbidden fruit always out of reach.

No name more than Finleigh.

Isla accepts my hand once I've offered to help her out of the boat. At first, she leans her head against my shoulder, sighing, breathing the scent of my robe. Why, I can't imagine. It must smell of nothing but bone powder. I register what she's doing when her fingers seek my chest, palm bedding on my rib cage.

So sweet, I muse and smirk behind my mask before laying my phalanges atop her silken skin. "The bone has reset, my bride. Do not concern yourself." I tuck my finger bones under her chin, raise her face, tempted to kiss her.

"Where are we?" wonders Isla, brimming with curiosity, so much, floral bud goosebumps bloom along her flesh as she scrutinizes the hollowed-out cavern with its three passages.

Leading her to the left passage, a dampness crystallizing the otherwise dull rocks to shimmer, I relay my history with Finleigh, a history I have never shared with any bride.

"It was my first Feast of Flesh as Corpse King..."

***

Somehow, I'd managed to escape Aydon and Mathyr's countless attempts at shoving maidyans my way. My dance card was bursting despite how they knew I'd never danced since the night I'd accepted Kryach. Court and commoners, the whole affair had grown insufferable.

After an hour of listening to Kryach's frequent snorts at maidyans or mild curiosity followed by a huff because he would never be satisfied—even if she were the most gracious and kindhearted soul who bore every bit of strength to match the Scarlet Skathyk—, I left the Great Hall.

Death was never satisfied. Death would never stop feasting.

Concealed behind the great tapestries sheltering my wrecked body, I gritted my teeth, observing more maidyans presenting themselves, stopping before the royal table. Nearby, the Cryth River and all its spirits guarded the dais leading to my throne. Some girls quivered in excitement, others in fear.

Perhaps if I could bond with one outside these political revelries or Kryach's omnipotent notice...

After all, the High God had invaded my body, my thoughts, my damned soul. I'd be more damned if he'd dictate my heart. It was the last night to take a bride before the Void released a war of refters upon the land Still, I believed love was the only force in the world that could defy death and fate.

Didn't Kryach owe me a love of my choosing? Not whichever soul bounty he preferred to gnaw upon. A love strong enough to conquer Death itself and save me from this choice I'd made? Or perhaps the Curse?

Kryach hissed inside my mind, *Give up your vain and foolish dreams, Allysteir. They bore me.*

Right, I retorted sarcastically. *Because the High Gods would never admit to the existence of the Curse-Ender. The World-Mender?*

You've managed to impress me far more in your first year than any other King in centuries, bastard Prince. Do not *make me regret my decision,* he growled. His deathly shades imprisoned me, lacing his dark fire into my being. Harsh and fatalistic, enough to drive me to my knees to fracture their caps. *You* will *appease my hunger tonight.*

I grit my teeth but managed to retort, *As you wish, Kryach.*

Several feet from my person, Aydon's ceremonious voice rose an octave to make an announcement from the throne. Oh, how he savored the opportunity to assume my position. Not that I'd cared. In Kryach's words, politics bored me.

Unlike the spry young woman wearing black to blend in with the shadows on the far side of the dais—close to the Citadel halls leading to the servants' quarters. No, she did *not* bore me. Especially when she diverted the guards standing sentry before the royal table by tossing smoke sticks—no doubt purchased from a Wisp-Shee—down the servant quarter stairs and hiding in the shadows. No shadows could conceal her, much less anyone, from me.

Kryach's shrug contrasted my piqued curiosity. *She is far too petite and slight, Allysteir. A King can do better. Narrow hips would never do well for bearing a child. Much less could her small breasts appease a wee newborn, much less a King.*

I snorted. *I thought I was a bastard Prince.* When Kryach snarled, I taunted him, *What do you care? All you desire is their soul.*

Kryach didn't bother responding. Yes, he would reap the profits of a bride's blood and flesh when I did, but one should never judge outward appearances. Kryach knew such a scruple better than me.

A strange firefly flutter expanded my chest when the maidyan vaulted from the long royal table. I held my breath as she seemed to soar through the air like a graceful bird until she rolled expertly, masterfully, and landed in a flawless crouch upon the corner of the dais. All the royals and the party-goers were oblivious to the acrobatic girl who'd somehow cheated the River Cryth.

Not me where I stood beyond the curtains of the secondary hall. A lock of golden hair escaped the dark cap upon her head. True she did not possess the breed of heartier hips preferred by the Court Ithydeir, but I appreciated her slender figure girded in the form-fitting black suit. The closer she approached, stealing behind the curtain, the fragrance of hawthorn and heather from her body and blood greeted me. A maid from the country. It was as if I could detect another scent thanks to the

God of Death's recent inhabitance: the scent of Doom. As if a host of ban-Sythe ghosts haunted her steps. A scent meant as an omen to steer me from such a girl. But I cocked my head to the side, more intrigued. After all, no one had ever managed to vault clear over the River Cryth. Whatever could this young maidyan desire within the Citadel of Bones?

The God of Death sighed, clearly bored of my keen interest as the maidyan paused the moment we came face to face. Or rather face to mask. I smirked behind my outer face because the girl tensed. Her hand strayed to her belt where an iron-studded dagger hilt reared its head. She reminded me of a wild, skeletal mare in Nathyan Ghyeal's depths. Untameable, demanding respect and privacy.

Or at least I'd assumed privacy...until she closed the distance between us, gripped my glove, and tugged me toward the closest hall. "Hurry," she urged, her voice rich yet delicate, much like the chocolate cakes our finest chef loved to offer. "There's not much time." Her face was just as pleasing. Her skin was silken and pale but dusted with freckles too numerous to count as if speckled by brown sugar crystals.

Regardless of the host of questions preying on my tongue, I caged them. And played along.

"What's your name?" the girl asked, but before I could answer, she prattled on, "I'm Finleigh, but friends *and* enemies call me Finn."

"And what enemies could such an exquisite maidyan possibly have?"

She paused at the end of the hall, blinked at me. "Well, you are quite the charmer of a steward, aren't you?"

Kryach chuckled inside me. I battled my rolling laughter. This lovely lady believed I was a steward. A charming one.

Trust me, Allysteir. She is no lady, I assure you.

Shut ye're mouth, Kryach. Over my cock, I added for good measure.

He roared laughter. *Give her a good coin, and she'll be more than willing to do such for you. And much more.*

"Call me Ally," I encouraged her, closing my gloved hand over hers, ignoring Kryach which had become a personal art form over the past year. By no means was I an expert. Yet.

She nodded. Smiled. Not a sweet smile. No, her smirk was mischievous, breeding with secrets.

Yes, she's collected many in her time. Most of them fruitless. Until recently, echoed Kryach, and I held back the urge to huff frustration through my nostrils. Kryach could merely glimpse beyond this young woman's deep blue eyes to unearth the tapestry of her soul. A power he'd never shared with me. No, all I'd received were his damned shades with the ability to soothe the dying to eternal slumber. And the rotted corpse, of course.

It wasn't long before I discovered the nature of the secret she'd learned. I hoped she didn't pick up on my jaw turning rigid or the subtle grinding of my teeth when she wooed Master Ivory and unlocked the Unseen Section. The first time I required Aryahn Kryach's shades.

"Ahh! Perfect!" Finleigh squealed and selected a trophy among the multitude in the room: the second-best prized trophy. Most would believe it was the ultimate.

I eyed her from the side as she curled her fingers around my ancestor's parietal skull bone: the original, the first Corpse King who had chosen to pass into the spirit realm with his bride rather than spend eternity watching his loved ones grow older and die.

"Well," she called to me while tucking the parietal skull bone into her accompanied sack, then placed her hands on her illustrious hips. "Not bad for a night's work. Two nights. But this one was far easier than last night. Company's much better, too."

I couldn't fight the smile behind my mask. I turned my full body toward her and kept my responses brief. "Oh?"

"Far more clothed, too," she hinted with a conniving smile. It was the first time the blood rushed to my cheeks. My knees weakened since I didn't have much blood anyway. Her scent overwhelming the room didn't help. "But I wouldn't mind a little peek under all that if you know what I mean. After all, I'm leaving Talahn-Feyal far behind by dawn. And if tonight is all we have..." she eluded.

Now, my chuckle was unrestrained to overlap Kryach's deep and annoyed groan in my mind. His shades curved from my body, but I managed to harness them until my thick robes concealed them.

Go on, Allysteir. Show her what she longs to see, taunted Kryach.

*Hmm...*I paused, musing because this little Finn the Thief was right about one thing: tonight was all we had.

I removed my mask. Slowly.

Each muscle around her eyes widened those orbs. Her brows tethered to my creeping gesture. When I dropped it on the bony ground, she did not flinch. I studied the scarlet walker girl. At first, she parted her lips, blowing wind through her nose until she wildly shook her head.

It's no trick, I almost said but didn't bother. She was keen. A raw cunning bred within her on account of her...controversial trade.

It wasn't long before Finleigh leaned away, her eyes never straying. They marked me as much as mine marked her. She bit her lower lip, chewed on the inside of her cheek, processing the brief time we'd shared.

When she peered at the parietal skull bone edging from her sack, I recognized the expression in her eyes when she snapped them back to me. Cornered prey prepared to do battle, perhaps prepared to conjure some magic with the skull bone. Magic I knew was too strong, too powerful, it would destroy her.

As she tensed, I raised my hand. Glanced at the glove, I huffed before ripping it away with my teeth to betray my exposed phalanges. "Please... take it. It will be a treat to watch the elders' reactions once they learn it's missing. And pilfered by a scarlet walker girl! After dawn, of course... when you've left Talahn-Feyal far behind," I added and swept my hand to the exit.

First, Finleigh didn't hesitate. I winced from the rush of warm hair, laced with heavy masculine odors but with an undercurrent of fresh herbs, mint the most prominent. I smiled, shoulders heaving, relieved she didn't use the skull bone's magic. But as I cringed while bending to pick up my mask, her fingers collided with my bones. Stunned, I flinched, nearly jerked away. But she beat me to it. Except when I peered up at her face, her eyes held no great fear. Nor did they narrow in disgust.

Instead, she glanced at the mask in her hand before creeping her arm to me to return it. I nodded and replaced it.

Once I'd firmly fixed it to my face, Finleigh's lips parted. Those knowing wintry blue eyes, cold and cunning, yet capable of cracking and thawing within instants, greeted mine. "Why?"

I could fill in a thousand follow-up questions. Why didn't I stop her the moment she landed on the dais? I could have propelled Kryach's shades to knock her into the River Cryth. Why didn't I alert her to my identity when we met behind the curtain? Or call the guards? Why did I allow her to drag me throughout the citadel as if we were mischievous children hiding from servants and guards? Why didn't I stop her from entering the Unseen section? Why did I allow her to take the skull bone instead of commanding a host of guards to cart her off to the prison? Or summon Kryach to reap her soul for her audacity?

If it's your desire, Allysteir, I would be more than happy to reap this pesky harpy's soul, Kryach opted, but I responded with stony silence.

For Finleigh, however..."If you so choose, my lady, I will not bat an eye. You may take my ancestor's parietal skull bone of the primary Corpse King. Pay off your debt to your Scarlet District. Or..."

"Or?" Finleigh did narrow her eyes. Her fingers curved, poised upon her sack.

I sighed and dropped my hands to my sides. "Or you could have more than a skull bone tonight. You could have a...a King."

I slammed my eyes shut because her expression would be far worse than her words. Those words didn't come. So, I dared to open one eye to glimpse her beyond my mask cavities, those soulless depths, to witness her pause and purse her lips until hope swelled my chest. An emotion predating Kryach. A tidal wave launched my heart into my throat. I nearly choked, awaiting her response.

"All the Corpse Kings' brides die." A natural response. A shrewd one. Inoffensive. She didn't echo any dreadful ditties conjured by minstrels of old, ones sealed into the ears of every Talahn-Feyal infant at birth. No, her words were factual. Well, almost factual.

I shook my head. "Not my mother." I hoped my cringe would not betray me. After all, Mathyr's soul was scarred. But if Kryach believed Finleigh's was already scarred, if he viewed her as only damaged goods—

I do—

—then, perhaps he would let her go. *Please let her go. Please let it be her...my first bride.* Oh, could I ever hope for such a boon from the God of Death when this was never meant to be my burden, when I volunteered for this, when I sacrificed myself for my brother?

Finleigh sighed, chewing on her lower lip before she reached into the sack and clutched the parietal skull bone. "I never believed all those silly songs the madams would sing to us when we were wee bayrnies in the District. Well, I did until your reign was announced, my Corpse King."

"Ally please," I offered, preferring the nickname Aydon called me when we were little. It would sound lovelier upon Finn's lips.

"You were never supposed to be King. Everyone knew it was meant for Prince Aydon. It could mean only one thing: you sacrificed yourself. And well, I-I've never heard of such sacrifice. Not even my mother... well, she—" her voice cracked, her eyes misted, but it wasn't long before her ice returned, where the thaw hardened again, "—she pushed me out, paid off her debt, and left me to the District. So, imagine my shock when I learned the one who holds the God of Death, the Corpse King himself, who steals bones to make his brew and prefers hearts to taste in stew, would sacrifice so much...for a *scarlet* girl he'd met an hour prior. A scarlet girl who dared to steal from Death."

I closed the distance between us but kept my mask on as her fresh mist of tears returned, as she lowered her chin. My whole being softened, chest threatening to cave in until I was nothing more than a bag of bones and rotted flesh at her feet. Instead, I dared to stroke my fingers across her cheek and breathed slowly and steadily to fill my chest. I marveled at her smoothness, at the angular cheekbones marked by brown sugar crystal constellations and her strong jaw betraying the sign of far too many nights clenching from...pain. Pain I would spare her if I could because ever since I'd accepted Kryach, my being was nothing but pain.

"It's Ally, not Death. And if it is your wish, you will be a scarlet girl no longer tonight. You will be a bride-to-be of the Corpse King. My lady consort until the day of our wedding. And on our wedding night—"

When she stiffened, I paused, brows knotting. I wanted to punch the nearest wall and shatter my bones for testing her good graces. I did my best to tread carefully, but she needed the truth. Moreover, she could handle it. "On our wedding night or on any night following as it will be your choice, Kryach may steal your soul, my lady. But rest assured, if he does, he will take my heart, too. For it is already yours."

And when Finleigh ripped the mask from my loathsome face, when she crushed her mouth to my dried and desiccated one, I knew everything about my previous statement was true. A scarlet walker girl, a common thief had stolen the heart of the Corpse King.

At the end of sharing my past with Isla, of marking the severity of her expression—one of ivy green envy and woeful adoration to blush her cheeks—I squeeze her pale hand, and gesture to the little cavern opening where we stand. A cavern guarded by a wall of bones that moves by my hand alone. Isla tenses when I sweep aside those bones by the power of Kryach's shades.

Her hand muscles tighten around mine as I lead her inside.

"Allysteir!" she gushes from my art. The bone sculptures I've fused with gold and gems from our mines. All sculptures of my past brides... to keep *her* company when I am gone.

A shrill screech reverberates off the walls. Lustrous golden strands blossom in the darkness. And there are her vacant eyes. A fine ghostly mist ever-disturbs those once midwinter orbs shimmer beyond her gold hair. Isla wraps two hands around my phalange bones in the presence of my first refter bride, of…

"Finleigh," I say, my voice no less adoring.

The moment I remove my mask and fling it to the ground to face my first bride, Isla squeezes so hard, she doesn't fracture my phalanges.

She shatters them.

THIRTY-NINE
THE UNSEEN SECTION

ISLA

was jealous. Until he flung his mask to the ground.

All my envy depletes to sheer awe. Because one truth I unequivocally understand: I do not love the Corpse King. I do not love Allysteir. Because his heart was never mine to conquer. Finleigh stole it centuries before me. And Aryahn Kryach took it to the kingdom of souls...

If only such a kingdom could be conquered by one such as I.

I should apologize for shattering Allysteir's hand. Some of my floral power burst into my veins in the moment. Prompted by my emotions, vines had slithered from my pores. Small but armored with thorns, they'd somehow coiled around Allysteir's phalanges as he'd shared the end of his story. They'd cratered his bones when he'd removed his mask. I should apologize, but I don't.

All this time...

Finleigh, or what was once Finleigh, seems to have more consciousness than his other refter brides. While her eyes hold hollow ghosts, and whatever flesh she possessed withered from her skeletal frame centuries ago, she opens her mandible jaw and whips her head, shaking her long curls as gold as Isle gates, but she doesn't attack. Upon narrowing my eyes, I discover the wig sealed to her scalp. After so many refter brides, I don't shudder, but I do squeeze my shoulders and rub my arm as he closes the distance between them.

I cringe and turn my eyes when the Corpse King cups the sunken cheekbones of his first refter bride and presses one-half of his lips to her teeth. An icy crypt traps my blood channels, deadening them when I dare to spy on the private moment.

From the side, I witness his deformities ranging to his neck, but I am trespassing on their significant moment. I swear my intestines shrink and wither as he murmurs her name. I release my breath, and it floats away like a delicate, cleaving ghost.

"Allysteir..." I say softly after he turns from Finleigh. She snaps her head toward me, those spectral eyes honing in on me. "Is she...?"

Righting his mask, molding it to his features, he nods and explains, "Kryach took most of her soul, but he left me with a piece. Because she was my first bride and first love."

First, I tread on the word. Yes, the Corpse King's heart may be as immeasurable as mine...well perhaps not quite immeasurable, but there is a reason Finleigh is here while all his other corpse brides linger in the refter glen. No, she may not be his one love, but she is his *greatest* love.

"A scarlet-walker girl..." I add, my pulse steady and tranquil because I am not jealous. But I am...curious.

Allysteir mistakes my words, slow-turning his head, half-lips grimacing. It's another reason I respect him, for his passion, his ardor of defending this piece of a refter bride's soul. He glowers, cording all his neck muscles. "You disapprove with your far more *virginal* sensibilities?"

Donning one hand upon my too-generous mound of a hip, careless of how my plump and less than graceful belly responds, I snort. "You know me better, Allysteir. But I do want to know why the elders insisted on my virginity test." I prickle, remembering how we'd bonded in the garderobe while I'd endured his mother's poisoned barbed fingers to prove myself to my King. Could he ever truly be my *husband* with this recent knowledge?

A visceral growl echoes from his throat. He turns to Finleigh, cups her cheeks, and bows his head to her brow. "None of that mattered before. Not until her. Fuck, he was jealous. He *is* jealous! Jealous of me. Jealous of how a prostitute could love a mere corpse of a man but not Death!" Allysteir raises his voice, his shades thickening to a whirling nightmare to chill my blood. "How he'd reviled and hated her because she refused to bow to his shade and had the audacity to ignore him day after day and night after night."

Not like how I ignored Ary, my brand of tempting him. Without realizing it till it's too late, a hint of a smirk creases one corner of my mouth. A suspicious heat preys between my thighs. Yes, I'd reviled him since the wedding morn when he'd shown his true colors of fatalism and nightmares. A brutal stab of pain engulfs my heart from the precursor to the wedding night when Allysteir followed with his abuse.

But I knew. I knew in full equivocation what I was doing when I called Ary's name and not Allysteir's when Kanat attacked me in the library. An instinct bred from a desire for connection. My chest tingles. I loved the chase. I loved wooing him, driving him mad prior.

And on the night of my rebirth, Ary stayed! He watched, respected, honored, adored, and even worshiped in my dream at dawn while riding Ifrynna.

Was Allysteir simply a steppingstone?

"Death's balls, it was *never* about purity. It was about him not wanting the reminder of Finleigh for any following bride," Allysteir proclaims, curling those phalanges, grating powder between them. "It became a convenient way to involve the elders to hold me accountable. Kanat most since *he* was the elder who slept with Finleigh. And one reason I hate him to this day." He sneers, grunting while sifting his fingers through his bride's hair.

All of me feels like a cold pawn in this silly game of gods and kings. I'll be damned if I let Allysteir keep playing me, leaving me in the dark beyond our amusing exploits in the bedroom or within pomegranate groves. Wherever he longs to take me next, I will agree. But it's about damn time I learn the truth behind the imitation brides washed up on the shore of the grove island.

And if Finleigh could woo Master Ivory to reach the Unseen Section, I know I can, too.

I scream at the top of my rutty fucking lungs!

I am exhausted from combing through countless pages of the rarest flowers rumored to grace the god Isles. Master Ivory is still *not* satisfied!

By now, it is the wee hours of the morning. At midnight, Allysteir came for me and offered his aid. When I'd refused, he'd encouraged me to come to bed, offered his *ministrations*. Of course, I was tempted, but I'd somehow refused and holed up in the library. Determined to please this infuriating tree, so it will welcome me into the Unseen Section.

Regardless if he can help me, a persistent furor kindles my chest kindles. If he revealed the secret, it wouldn't be *real*.

A significant scarlet walker girl wooed Master Ivory with...what? "What did she have that I don't?" I groan. "I'm the Queen of the Underworld and the Mistress of the God of Death."

A deathly chill envelopes my form, encases it, presses upon my chest. I inhale a fury of gasps to regain my breath.

"Little wonder..." the God shade whispers in my ear.

A violent urge—born of trauma from the wedding morn—overwhelms me, but I defy the adrenaline surge. I bite my lip in hope. And will it down because he is quiet but woos me with *honor*. "Ary?" I whisper his name, *my* nickname.

When the God of Death presses again, when those shade arms fold around me in a dark quietude, I buckle, understanding. Tears glisten behind my eyes. All this time, it was so simple!

Aryahn Kryach raises my worn body so I may finish the task. So I may, with a full heart and thoughts bursting with compassion and love, wrap and fold my arms around Master Ibhry in a *pressing* hold of a tree *hug*! An embrace of understanding. Master Ivory needs no flowers, no adornments, no embellishments. He's already beautiful. He desires my arms, my touch: the simplest and truest of gifts.

Because even trees want touch, want kindness, want *love*.

After a few moments with my eyes closed and Aryahn Kryach's shade retreating, Master Ivory opens his trunk. I fall through desolate darkness. My screams fade into an echo the library will conceal.

My body dives through a coiling serpent of a grandiose slide until I am several levels underneath the Citadel, plunging into the belly of a grand and enormous dragon skeleton!

Throat crusty dry, I heave gasps on my hands and knees, curling my fingernails into bone powder shed from the skeleton. I wait for my body to still. My breath bursts, my muscles twitch, sweat cleaves to my brow.

At last, I look up. All the treasures, the jewels of this Unseen Section are like flames in this trove of Corpse Kings' past.

I touch my throat, gulping lumps as I gaze at my surroundings. Here are jewels as large as Isle-fruits burgeoning on bone-grown vines and thousands of bone-enameled scrolls in a tapestry of colors. A golden mist like god vapors decorates this sacred place. The parietal bone skull of the original Corpse King, the one Allysteir shared from his past, slumbers upon a pedestal in the center of the Unseen Section.

After rising from the dragon skeleton and forsaking its enamel embrace, I brush my naked feet upon bone powder blankets, scanning the treasure. I am not interested in the parietal skull bone but the significant scrolls housing knowledge.

An hour passes of me rummaging them because nothing is accomplished in seconds, though Ari remains with me in his shade form the whole time, I read the transcription writ within a rebelling god's blood. Not Ary's. Not Ary's blood. I purse my lips and bite my lower lip when I consider this generous god and how I long to meet him.

And perhaps I will someday. But for now…

"The truth of the Mallyach-Ender and the *World-Mender*—"

I freeze because nothing else matters. Goosebumps pebble my skin. The secrets of the god-rebels themselves, the rebels the higher gods slaughtered in the early days of the Curse for their transgressions of whispering the secrets to the races. Even the High Gods themselves have limitations.

And they *love* to play with us humans!

Before I may explore further, a distant cry penetrates the Unseen Section. An echo of a scream. And while Aryahn Kryach's shade power transforms to a haunting wraith to eclipse my movements, I press on until I arrive in the vast underbelly of Nathyan Ghyeal. These White Ladies who must weep rivers of tears when I behold thousands of slaves working these mines to forge for gems, for riches to prosper Talahn-Feyal.

Thousands of slaves who hold the same eyes and skin and bodies as my...Franzy.

FORTY
SHE IS NO PAWN.

ALLYSTEIR

How quiet she was after I'd shared Finleigh. How I'd longed for the thoughts clustered in her mind. She rushed to the library immediately after we'd returned to the Citadel. Nor did I stop her because I grasped how she needed time to sort through the chaotic mosaic of her thoughts.

Instead, I wait for her. Wait with my Sythe wine in hand because it's been too long since I last fed from her. With my whole being rotting and withering by the hour as we draw closer to the Night of Masks, which falls on the Feast of Flesh this year as a once in five-hundred years' event, I require more blood and flesh.

Grimacing, harnessing what little air I may into my lungs, I lower my head in shame. How could I have possibly shared the truth to Finleigh on our wedding night itself but not to Isla. For all these months, I've maintained this ruse, fallen back to old patterns as I did with all my brides, building them up, breaking them, baiting them, playing the victim to Kryach's monster until they love me. And while Isla has accepted my respect, my favors, from the moment she shattered my bones when I introduced her to Finleigh—my darkest and greatest secret—, I knew she'd seen right through all my games.

Growling, guttural and low, I chuck the goblet to the floor, wishing the bones would break to oblige me with a painful distraction, but they don't. All I'm left with are my thoughts and Kryach's shades, his essence curling into my being.

Where the devil have you been? I demand and right my robe, trace an aimless circle on the table because it's all I am: an aimless circle. A dog chasing its tail.

She is no devil, I guarantee you, Kryach responds. *Well, she is half.*

What are you blathering about, Death?

Secrets, Allysteir. Secrets you will never fathom. Ones she will know when her time comes. And I will stand at her side that day. And bow to her.

I snort, stand, and kick the goblet with my boot, my jaw pained. *Aryahn Kryach, Zeyl Mortyy, Helyon, Thanades, Dagdya Crow, the God of Death...he bows to none, apart from the Highest God and Goddess.*

You will *bow to her tonight, Allysteir. You will give her the truth tonight, Corpse King. You will give her your crown, your mask, your robes, your wine, your blood, your flesh. She will take everything.*

My chest heaves in the wake of his words. His shades penetrate me with a quietude of truth. No arrogant rumblings or driving me to my knees. What little blood I possess roars in my ears. Dark and insidious. And still, I tempt his patience, the Deathly temper. *And what will you take?*

Silence.

Even if Isla had not interrupted our conversation with her vines and roots throwing open the doors to our suite, thorns protruding from her pores and spiraling from her crown, Kryach would have given me nothing.

Her wide eyes smolder with glorious amethyst flames.

I open my mouth but don't get the slimmest chance to speak. Isla coils her thorny vines all around my body. She launches me halfway across the room so my back crashes onto the bed frame, snapping my spinal cord. I gasp a whirlwind of sharp breaths through my nose. I seethe from the pain as she closes in on me. Her bridal gown sheaths snap behind her while her serpentine vines slither around my broken form. They fracture countless bones. I wheeze when one pierces my sorry excuse for shriveled lungs.

Isla straddles me. She rips the mask from my face and glares her amethyst daggers into my eyes unseated by flesh or skin—suspended within my skull cavities.

"Why are there *slaves* working the mines of Nathyan Ghyeal?" she demands in a snarling yell and punches the bed frame next to my skull.

A surge of air overtakes my lungs. Jubilation swells in my chest. "You reached the Unseen Section! You discovered the secret—"

The wrong words, the wrong words, the wrong words.

Isla slams her fist one inch near my body, sending a near vibration into my ulna bone. I count it a blessing she did not punch my chest since she would have undoubtedly shattered my rib cage. Her eyes narrow, and she tightens those vines. Her army of miniature blades digs into my flesh, shedding blood, defiling our bed.

I wheeze and respond with one word, "Aydon." When she grits her teeth, eyes widening with white shock, with alarm, I know exactly where her thoughts are. Because I shamefully have watched those slaves, memorized their eyes, their broken bodies, their...flesh. "No,

Isla. No harm will come to Franzyna," I assure her. "She is a Princess of Talahn-Feyal."

"And what of them?" She grits her teeth, digging those dagger thorns in deeper. "And how would *she* react if she saw them? Half her race? If she knew her husband was their harsh taskmaster?" The skin around her eyes creases, pained. But she steels herself, hissing. "Shut down the mines."

I shake my head.

Her eyes burn against mine. Her nails rake my cheek, stripping flesh to threadbare ribbons. I wince. I bear the pain and listen when she confronts me, her knees squeezing on each side of my hips. *Oh, fuck... not now*, I chastise my rising member. "Talahn-Feyal claims to respect human flesh the most."

"*Our* flesh." As soon as the words flee my lips, I register the transgression. This is not who I am. No, it *is* who I am because I have sacrificed everything to Aydon. For too long, I have used my suffering, my trauma as a weapon, So much of me wants to blame Kryach, but I accepted this Curse. I damn-well begged for it. Other Corpse Kings past have navigated the politics to care for their kingdoms, to take responsibility.

I abdicated.

Tonight, I pay the deepest price.

"You. Will. Shut. Down. The. Mines," demands Isla, either ignorant or dismissive of my cock pointing to her heaven center due to her nearness. "At the very least, you will go to Aydon. You will speak to him. You will be the fucking Corpse King!"

At the mention of my title, I somehow regain my strength, my fortitude. I use those Death shades to break all her vines and shatter her thorns to smithereens. Spine healed thanks to Kryach, I thrust her to the side and reverse our positions until my black robes fold around her like a dark cocoon. Fuming, I stare at her through my baleful eyes in my unmasked, fatalistic face. "I am a rotting corpse, Isla. And I am nothing, nothing, *nothing* more. Nothing without *you*, my dark rose." I hem her in, anchor her to the bed with my shades, forbidding her to do anything but thrash her pelvis, heave her chest, claw my robe, and arch her lovely throat.

"What does that have to do with—"

"Bloody boots and baybags, Isla! Don't you get it, my Queen?!" I yell, exposing my fractured, stained teeth. She huffs beneath me, her breasts prodding loose from their fabric cage of a bodice. "This is the Curse, my Curse, *our* Curse. Aydon wields the fullest power of the throne. I am merely the rotting corpse mask. And he desires you for *his* Queen, his bed."

"Oh, I can handle that pompous, silver-spooned, spoiled brat—"

I roll my eyes and interrupt, "I cannot contend with the full power of Aydon *and* the elders, Isla. He would expect a fair trade for his political efforts. *You* would be the trade."

"Allysteir..." her voice lulls to an appeal, her hand bedding on the robe upon my chest. "Then, go to the God of Death. Ary will help—"

"You would be *his* price!" I scream, I roar. My turn to slam my fist, shattering my phalanges.

Isla rises. So slowly, I don't notice her vines coiling around me until it's too late. Until she reverses our positions once again and stabs her voice into my ear. "I am *no* price. And *no* prize. I am Isla Adayra Morganyach. I am the first volunteer tribute in a thousand years." She narrows her eyes and pinches her lips as if staring right through me to the God-spirit I house. "And you, Allysteir, are not my husband. You are *not* my King.

And you will *never* be my husband after what you have done. You used me as your excuse, your pawn of leverage over Kryach. You used me as a convenience so you would not act as a true King. Worst, you did not *tell* me. You played me. You manipulated me. You built me up. You welcomed me into your world and made me your Queen. And then... you *hurt* me."

Her words shame me. They bore into my inner depths because I felt shame on our wedding night. While she rose, I sank. And bled. My stomach knots, and I fall. I sink my skull into the pillows behind me because she speaks the truth.

"But I am no pawn, Allysteir," she announces, and I lift my eyes to hers, to her smoldering royal inferno. "I am the eater of Isle fruit. I am the bearer of Aryahn Kryach's mark. I am the Queen of the Underworld. And the fucking Mistress of the God of Death."

I shake my head, violent, thrashing, my belly hot with hatred for the God. "It won't matter. None of it will matter." Tears glisten in my eyes when I consider my five hundred refter brides, their screams, their eyes turning to ghosts, to hollows without spirits. And I'd never sung them to eternal sleep. I'd only fucked them. Finleigh...

"Then, let's put it to the test," she demands.

A lightning bolt of terror assaults my heart, prickling me with goose flesh. "What?"

"The stakes are highest. But I am ready, my Corpus King." She grows those corpus roses all over our bed to don the blankets, the fractured bed frame, the posts, and canopy. She burgeons them into the floor to disturb the stone. She multiples them upon all surfaces until their dark aroma engulfs the room.

Finally, Isla turns her eyes back to mine, clutches my collar, and rips.

"Tonight, I am taking back the power you took from me, Allysteir. Because you will not fuck me, Corpus King. I *will* fuck you. I will touch you. I will touch *all* of you. Am I clear?"

I lick my half-lip. I shiver. I shudder in the wake of her agency. Ridicule myself for crossing her, for keeping her in the dark, for not sharing what I should have all along. For playing this ruse for too many months. No, she is no pawn.

With my shoulders sinking, pain inundating my body, but my cock fully aroused and swollen from her proclamation, I bow my head to her, the first bows of this night, and declare, "As clear as the spirits of the River Cryth that brought you to me, my Lady Queen."

FORTY-ONE
"YOU WANT ME, ARY! COME AND CLAIM ME!"

ISLA

BEFORE...

I lean over the ledge of the great precipice, which offers me a sobering view of the mines where hundreds of workers toil for the treasures of Talahn-Feyal's Underworld. The chronic crack of the whips from the overseers wrenches tears from my eyes. Those droplets tumble over the edge into the cold canyon air, disappearing leagues below me into the darkness. Could I hope for one to fall on a slave to grant them a hopeful kiss? I thread my clammy fingers before clutching my throat, voice shriveled and dry as granite.

And then, *his* familiar shade presence encircles me, binds me to offer me the irony of a numbing comfort.

"Flesh is the most precious to Talahn-Feyal. How could he—"

"Not him, little wonder," Ary reassures me, a deep, pacifying voice in my ear. It soothes me more than a thousand of Allysteir's lullabies.

I purse my lips and sigh, shoulders heavy. "Aydon."

"Mmm." Those shades form a circlet around my head to vie with my crown. "And the elders."

"You knew of this..." I trail off when a slave falls to the ground, expiring.

Ary's shade form shudders around my body, but his essence multiples over the caverns. "I am the God of Death, little wonder. I reap their souls when they are ready for eternal slumber so they do not suffer any longer. Yes, I knew. But it was not my place to tell you, sweet Isla. By the ruling of the Highest God and Goddess, I may not meddle in the affairs of the living."

He doesn't make excuses, and I lean back into his fatalistic shade, scenting a hint of Isle-fruit laced with blood, of smoke and flame, and the base of ancient incense. Intoxicating. Alluring. Bewitching.

"Allysteir should have—"

"Yes, he should have," agrees Ary.

"All this time, you've been waiting...for what?" I purse my lips, bow my head when another shrill cry invades my ears.

"For him to tell you everything, little wonder. For you to agree to what should have happened on your wedding night had I not interfered on its morn. Before, you were a mere conquest."

"And what am I to you now, Ary?" I press the base of my palm to my forehead, ridiculing myself for dwelling on this when all these lives suffer within the mines of the Corpse King's Underworld.

"The Unseen Section welcomed you, sweet wonder. Would you have me spill secrets only heaven and hell know, too?" he challenges, those shades nigh strangling my chest.

I seal my lips into a frown but curl my fingers into those shades, understanding. Besides, some things are better left to mystery for growth and amusement. Regardless...," "Allysteir could have done something."

"Not without a price."

Instantly, I read between the lines. *I* would have been the price. After Ary reveals the secret, the reason behind all of Allysteir's games, I coil my vines around those shades and tear them one by one in dark strips from my body before flinging him over the edge. His shade form hovers in midair. He faces me, wreathed in blood fire, hollow eyes simmering with smoke.

Balling my hands into fists, my nails cutting bloody crescent moons into my flesh, I stand and proclaim with my crown higher than ever, "I. Am. No. *Price*, Aryahn Kryach. And you can go fuck yourself!"

"I'd give my Harem of Souls itself to spend *one* night with you, little wonder!"

I thrust all my vines in a deliberate blockade. Yes, I know it's futile. He will pursue me because I gave him my consent on my first visit to the library. I loved his pursuit. And his quiet steadfastness on the night in the refter bride glen. But now, I run. Tears smoldering my flushed cheeks, I run back to the Unseen Section, ascend to the library, out of the tower, and beyond the bridge.

Through countless halls of the Citadel, I run until I arrive at our suite where I crash the doors wide open...

PRESENT

Atop Allysteir on the bed, I work to remove his outer robe layer, wondering how many linger beneath.

"My Lady, my Queen, please, we still have over two months..." when he trails off, and I pause from my pursuit to narrow my eyes upon his detached ones, to study any expression he may offer with half a mouth and sunken in cheekbones.

"Another secret, Allysteir? Another revelation?" I challenge, brows threading low while I continue to remove the outer robe.

"The Curse," he heaves, eyes diving low as if he longs to close them but can't due to his withered lids. "It grants us one full year from the date of our wedding night to *consummate* the marriage."

At least he does not hinder me when I unclad the inner robe. My fingers are aggressive, violent to mirror my pain. Blood wars, bludgeoning my ears. "And that is the reason for all these games. Because you were too much of a coward to grant me your trust, your respect with the truth. Nothing is left but necessity, my Corpus King. I understand. But you were wrong. You. Were. Wrong."

"I will go to my brother, Isla. I will use my parietal bone and all of Kryach's power if necessary," he baits me, voice pleading with desperation as I tear at the inner robe to nothing but scraps. Only his tunic, his breeches left. Already, the bones of his rib cage make subtle indents through the tunic while a bulge protrudes from between his thighs.

I roll my eyes. "You will do it anyway after tonight, Allysteir. Whether or not Ary takes me or if the cycle renews, you will fulfill your vow. And I will fulfill mine."

I unbutton his tunic.

"Isla...please," his voice cracks, and I pause when his phalanges light upon my wrist. I lean my head to one side, detecting the avenue of his eyes and the tears trickling down his cheeks when he continues, "I cannot lose another bride."

I purse my lips in understanding because at heart, Allysteir is a lovesick fool. No, he was never meant for the throne, for messy politics. After five hundred years, he is still a swooning boy chasing after his true heart only Finleigh holds. It's why tonight is necessary, why I cannot wait. It is a fool's errand to imagine anything but this vain respect between us—and a burning flicker of pleasure. If it doesn't happen tonight, it never will.

In full resolution, chest swelling with confirmation, with power, with utter belief, I reveal, "I was never your bride, Allysteir."

I rip the tunic from his body. He does not stop me. He does not stop me when I pursue his breeches, keenly aware of his bulge.

I free him to a true naked corpse to mirror his cadaverous face. A skeleton bearing remnants of rotted flesh, of shriveled organs, of threadbare blood to pump the essential muscle somehow beating within his chest cavity. So unfathomable. So otherworldly!

The blood flows most to his lower region, to his...

"The gods truly do have a sense of humor." I reflect on the single *whole* part of Allysteir. Not only whole, his cock is a high tower: a hard quivering column twitching the moment my fingers inch closer.

"Kryach's humor," grunts Allysteir, baring his teeth. "Each god has their own style. This is the morbid humor of the God of Death."

I glimpse at the aching member. My mouth waters. I bite my lower lip, bind my hands around it, and blush when its warmth throbs beneath my palms. I almost flinch but then revel because Allysteir throws his head back and gasps. The first time someone has touched him in a long time. "I'll enjoy his humor tonight, my Corpus King. But first..."

I forsake his cock. I move up, scooting gently so I don't disrupt any bones. Up and up until I hover upon his chest to instruct, "Tear my gown, Allysteir."

Expecting resistance, it stuns me when Allysteir obeys. He uses his bony hands' strength to rip the bridal sheathes until I am a pale and plump naked woman sitting atop the Corpse King. I sink onto his cadaver face, part my distended and eager pubic lips to his heated mouth. So determined to observe his unmasked face when he pleasures me.

I inhale a deep gust when Allysteir traces my plump belly, then drags his phalanges in a direct arrow for my sex where he rubs my rosy nub. When he plunges three rigid phalanges inside my slippery chamber, I buck and gasp. Allysteir feasts on my vulva. His masterful tongue works my pubic lips, sweeping to my burning clitoris. I shudder. Color scorches my cheeks, suffusing my heavy breasts, and I moan when the King's other bony hand voyages to brush my nipple. More, I need more! I roll my demanding hips forward onto his face, thrilling when he sucks and nips my swollen nub. It near surges over his hard fingers. He kneads my breast flesh, pinches and twists my nipples. Inside me, the dam prepares to burst.

Before it can, I jerk out of those rigid finger bones and move lower. Without preparation, because I *need* none, without reservation because I *have* none, without any thought because I *want* none, I slam my sex onto the full length of the Corpse King's amassed member. And shriek from the pain and pressure—this stinging, hard pressure. But my scream is louder when Allysteir nudges my clitoris with his hard knuckle while his aching finger bones dote on my breasts.

Caging a whimper, I ride him. Desperate, demanding, daring, careless of how my corpus rose thorns penetrate his meager flesh and draw more blood, I ride him. My drenched sex slides up and down while the King's turgid member throbs inside me. His eyes glaze over. I imagine he would shut them if he could. Allysteir's hands roam to my pelvis and sink into the rounded flesh of my hips. He grunts and thrusts inside me, his momentum mirroring mine. I lean over so my breasts become low-hanging fruit over his face. Prompted, he suckles my nipples as if they are succulent pomegranate seeds.

The dam inside me cracks to release a predictive burst. Naked, face flushed, my nipples contracted to ruby rouge pebbles, I ride out my jubilee. Accepting the adrenaline-fused pain, I throw my hair back, thrust out my chest, and cry my climax in a feral voice, "You want me, Ary! Come and claim me!" I dare the God of Death.

The King climaxes to my words, penetrating me, stabbing deep to the hilt. He braces. His eyes widen, pupils dilating. Neither of us could ever hope to hold our breaths. But we don't have to.

I don't fade to evanescence.

I don't slip into the fabric between worlds.

Death's icy fingers don't close over my body to reap my lost spirit into the River Cryth.

I am naked blood and flesh and bone and heart.

And most of all...I am here.

The next moment I gaze at Allysteir, I lurch, I gasp, I almost scream. No corpse gazes back at me. Now, an Ithydeir man, handsome and young and virile, stares at me. His flesh and blood hand roams to my cheek to brush away strands of my silver flame hair.

A bone-deep chill shivers through me when he proclaims, "Isla, it's me. And I knew you were the one."

Swept into the moment, in the lingering endorphins flooding my flushed body, I sink my shoulders in utter relief, welcome Allysteir who

337

gathers me into his arms, kisses me with his full mouth, and makes love to me all night long.

For the first time, no shades haunt our bed.

FORTY-TWO
THIS IS KRYACH'S SCAR

ALLYSTEIR

"Isla, Isla, my dark rose..." I breathe again and again in the aftermath of our latest shared climax as she rakes her nails into my back from her desired position. All night long, we have remained in bed. Our true honeymoon.

Gasping, heaving, my breath hot against her face, suffused with a blush to mirror her breasts. Thanks to my renewed and hungering mouth, those tiny stones of buds are puckered and swollen. I brush my knuckles across her cheek where her holocaust of waves cleaves to her sweat-ridden skin. "Dawn is coming, and I must leave for Death business soon. Please tell me you are spent," I beg her, my cock twitching inside her velveteen walls. A wonder it hasn't fallen off by now.

Isla cups her forehead and blows a sigh of pomegranate and wine-fragrance—her only sustenance this long night—while closing her eyes. She offers a feeble nod. "My sex is sore, my breasts are sore, my muscles are sore, and you've left little love marks all over my thighs and belly."

She points out while plumping her lower lip into a fervent pout.

Chortling low, I rub my nose to hers, thrilling in how my restored locks cascade onto her burning cheeks. Not dark like Aydon's inherited from the former Corpse King but a rich cinnamon hue which led the King to suspect Mathyr's affair.

"Don't fault me. I wished to sleep hours ago," I remind her and eject myself from her inner chamber.

She gives a little whimper. "Sleep is overrated. We have eternity to sleep. And...you are beautiful, my Corpus King." Isla sighs, head sinking into the pillows as she studies me, fingers roaming the ridged muscles of my chest and lower. I was never overly packed but prided myself on my leanness thanks to climbing the White Ladies' hidden depths to unearth their recesses and endless caverns. With my being restored, I have returned to the strength of my youth. And I could not appreciate my bride more—for her flattery and her fortitude.

"Thank you, my Lady Queen," I express from my heart with a gratified smile.

Isla whimpers into my mouth when I kiss her lips—a mere brush before rubbing my mouth along the center of her body until I arrive at the marks she referenced. How often lust coincides with the need for blood and flesh. Maintaining stamina through the night to match my bride's required more sustenance. Isla did not give me beyond a second or two to brush bone powder over the marks.

I love how her plump, little belly pulses from her frazzled breath. A few corpus rose petals have strayed across her pale flesh, and her thighs part when I open my mouth to bestow a warm kiss upon each mark, summoning the power of Death's shades. Sweat mars my brow as it requires more effort. No longer a prisoner to Kryach, I do not bear his essence despite housing a fraction of his power. After five hundred years with the accursed God of Death haunting my mind and soul, I'd say I'm damn well entitled.

Finished with her belly, I pause before descending to her thighs and trace my fingers across her soft flesh, heat in my chest as if a thousand fireflies have raided it. "I imagine what your birthing marks will look like, my bride. Rest assured, I will never heal them."

All Isla's muscles tense. Brows knitting in confusion, I tighten my chest and glimpse at her as she nudges me away and curls her legs into her chest. I do not care for the glower pillaging her otherwise sensual lips, swollen from my mouth's ministrations.

"What do you mean *birthing* marks", Allysteir?" Her tone is contemptuous.

Tilting my neck, I reach for her, puzzled when she flinches. I hover my palm above her knee before settling my fingers there, too aware of my dark rose's heated temper. "Isla, I am the Corpse King. The Curse is not yet ended. You merely survived as my mother survived. Kryach has found favor with you. But the cycle must begin anew."

"Why?" Her brow furrows and she binds her arms around the underside of her thighs, lowers herself so her legs press to her breasts as if she could conceal their magnitude. "We are immortal."

I sigh, rubbing my eyes, attempting to explain. "If Mathyr had not killed the last Corpse King—what I mean is...yes, we are immortal." My hand strays to the right one nestled on her thigh, grateful she does not flinch. Grateful her hold relents, and she allows me to pursue her, to gather her nude form onto mine. Our chests and brows touch in a bonding moment between husband and wife. "But our greatest immortality will be reserved for the spirit dwelling beyond the Nether-

Void. For the halls of my ancestors."

She crinkles her nose, lips parting. Before she may respond, I cover them with my fingers, delaying her despite her brow furrowing, so I may continue, "Please fret not, my bride. We will live long lives. Beyond my grandparents' happiness. They lived for two hundred years beneath the White Ladies, Isla. I aim to surpass them. I aim for five hundred to restore what was lost to me. We will live to watch our wee bayrnies grow to their fifth generation."

Again, Isla tenses. Spiny thorned roots grow from her skin. Her eyes turn icy, those amethysts hardening to royal diamonds. Hoping to placate her, to restore the peace and joy we have shared this night, I open her mouth beneath mine, roam shade power along her spine. I remember how she appreciated such a touch to calm her. Mouth dry from eagerness and gratitude, from my love for her, for her strength, and how she'd survived Death, I pray my next words calm her. They will offer her hope as they do me. "By then, whichever son or grandson or great-grandson chooses the Curse mantle will be fully prepared...unlike me."

The moment I draw my lips to her quickening pulse, Isla pushes my chest, forbidding me from kissing her. "Allysteir..." Puzzled, I meet her eyes. She closes hers, sighs through her nostrils, then deeply inhales. Her breasts nudge me from her expanding chest. Finally, her eyes open. Resolved, they are deeper and darker and more adamant than our Underworld mines. "I. Do. Not. Want. Children."

I blink. My throat constricts. Not once but multiple times. My heart plummets into the barest recesses of my being. "Isla..." I cup her cheek, striving for rationality, but she flinches. She stares me down with those adamantine amethysts.

"No, Allysteir. You have played into the gods' hands too long. This is why the Curse continues. You grant him too much power."

I sneer. "He does have power."

She shakes her head, grasps my arms, kneading the full flesh, the muscles. "Not over me. Please, Ally, I—"

"Don't," I interrupt, warning her, tensing. Finleigh's name. My first. My truest.

If Kryach were with me now, he would have a smart remark about my first love, my first bride. He would goad me about how he has forced her into eternal servitude in his Harem of Souls. Disgust creeps my spine, breeding bile in my stomach. This is not how I envisioned the night going. No, Kryach did not reap all of Isla's soul, but this *resistance* must be his trespass, his scar. I must thwart it.

Or he will come again, he will demand more. If the gods do not have the blood and flesh of our descendants, they will unleash refter war upon our lands.

"You will feel differently once our babe is in your arms for the first time," I tell her without meeting her eyes. But all her muscles stiffen while she strokes the base of her throat for comfort. "Or when you carry our child."

"When?" Isla whispers in shock, her hand lowering to her belly.

I lean away, eyeing the fleshy pouch. "*When.*"

"You didn't follow in the line, Allysteir. Another can—"

I growl from her disbelief, from how soon she has forgotten my trauma. "My *mother*, Isla! Not my father!"

She screws her brows lower. To my astonishment, Isla beats her fist against my chest. But this time, she disrupts no rib cage, cracks no bones. Frowning, I catch her wrist with my strong hand, phalanges buried beneath the strength of muscle, sinew, and flesh. I twist her wrist to the side, lower it to the bed to settle into a valley of corpus rose petals as she gasps. My chest twinges with emotion from how I conquer her. Too simple to pin her body. She freezes, petrified. Remorse twinges in my chest when I recognize the same expression as our wedding night.

Still, I battle this soul scar. How could she possibly conceive of reigning as Queen but not bear a child? For the first time in centuries, I am the King of Talahn-Feyal. I must make her understand.

But when I open my mouth, she lashes out, "You ignorant fool," Isla spits in my face, trembling as I hover over her. "Aydon is in your mother's line, too."

I snarl and crush my pelvis to hers, grinding for one split second. "Aydon. Cannot. Produce. An. Heir."

Her eyes widen in white shock. "What?"

"Why do you believe he has haunted your steps? And pursued you? If you can survive Kryach, Death itself, he believes you will be the one to restore his seed, his child."

"Fuck it all, Allysteir! I don't *want* a child! I don't even know if I *can* have a child!" she screams, straining against my hands.

I huff, blowing frustrated wind in her face, and release her. "We will know soon."

"What?" She rises onto her elbows, thrusting her bared, incensed chest out.

I roll my eyes and slide off the bed to clad myself in a fresh robe. "Kryach's track record. All Queens who have survived him have born a child within the first nine months. Upon first consummation."

Isla balls her hands and folds her knees under her. Eyes burning with acidic tears, impaling mine like hot, iron spears, she crouches on all fours and hisses, feral, "How could you not tell me this, Allysteir?"

"I assumed you knew." I bind the robe sashes, face myself in the mirror, and nod proudly at the reflection. I hold the gaze, lingering, hand pursuing my cheeks to roam my jawline peppered in fine bearded hairs while I address my bride's riotous reflection. "Surely, you did not believe volunteering as Bride of the Corpse King would hold no expectations."

"Expectations..." she treads on the words before her vines attack. They drag me back onto the bed, so she may straddle me and dominate me as she did last night. "I'll end it, Allysteir." She gestures to her belly in a direct warning, her cheeks blanched, drained of all color. Utter disgust. "Before it can form. The Inker Queen...she has power and crystals. The Wisp-Shee King, he has herbs. Hell, I'll go to Narcyssa, and she can bite—"

Triggered by the monarchical name, I reverse our positions with my limited shade power. I ignore her thorns lacerating my flesh. It will heal. I have flesh to spare now. "Do you truly have a death wish, Isla? Do you understand such a transgression? Withholding an heir? The consequence that could befall our entire realm?"

"More than binding slaves to your mines?" she challenges in a flagellating snarl while her thorns coil my neck to draw blood.

"This..." I bow low to her ear and hiss, continuing, "is Kryach's scar. You said you were the Mistress of Death, Isla. Now, you have proven it."

She overcomes me. Damn it to the Nether-Void, she overcomes me and strikes me again and again, bruising my chest, my arms, my shoulders, my cheeks in a tirade. Before I do something unthinkable, unspeakable, I flee the bed, our bed. I turn my back to her, delaying the onslaught of her vines with my shade power.

"I am off to the Hollows, my Lady Queen," I inform her while approaching the door, forsaking her as my heart burrows lower. "When I return, I hope you will be in a better state."

I open the door. Isla throws a pomegranate at me, but it slams against the door. I hear the fruit split open. The seeds tumble to the floor. Sighing deep, I press my forehead to the nearby wall. And mourn. Tears stream from my eyes; the fruit is not the only brokenness this night. Nor can I ever hope to repair.

Because all I do is fuck everything, destroy everything and everyone I love. Finleigh only forgave me because we fucked everything together.

FORTY-THREE

"YOU ARE NOT THE ONLY ONE WITH A CROWN."

ISLA

There now, my leyanyn," Franzy soothes me while I shiver in her arms. I sniff, rubbing my face into her shoulder, marveling at how ridiculous this is. I am the strong one. I am supposed to be. That's how...

Huh. Franzy hasn't ever run to me. She's always there to receive me. She confides in me about her problems, but she doesn't run to me.

Franzy strokes the back of my hair, and I press my lips to her neck, wincing when I cross paths with her latest mark from the Prince. And then, I remember all those in the mines. The faces from her homeland. Regardless of how she grew up here, she deserves to know. She's always spoken about her time visiting Zynnia. If anyone can get through to Aydon, if Allysteir can't or won't, maybe his Feyal-bride, his wife, my Franzy can.

"I wish I could take this burden from you, Isla." Her words stop me before I may share anything. I crane my neck to peer at her through watery eyes, red-rimmed no doubt.

"What?"

Franzy offers me a sheepish smile. "I was happy, leyanyn. I would have married you regardless because I love you. And the bond of love is stronger than any desire, including the desire for a child." She touches her silk robe, one hand lighting on her stomach. A fleeting second. "I would have asked you once if we could...adopt. But if you had said no, I would never have pressed you," she explains.

Gushing more tears, I throw my arms around her neck, almost toppling us to the bed's headboard. "Oh, Franzy, I don't deserve you."

"Leyanyn, you deserve every good and sweet thing. We both do," she speaks in a hushing tone, stroking my hair again.

"The people in the mines do, too."

Franzy stiffens beneath me. I pull back to eye her. Her nose scrunches, brow furrowing, lips pressing together before she asks, "What do you mean? Aydon has shared little of the mines, but from what I've learned at Court—"

"You do Court?" I interject, my brows lifting in shock.

Donning a silly smirk, Franzy rolls her eyes and pinches my cheek. "I don't spend all my time trying on bridal gowns, eating Isle-fruit, growing flowers, and chasing after Death, Isla."

"Franzy, I didn't mean—"

"I didn't either," she reassures me, scooping my hand into hers and rubbing my knuckles. "We relate to this Underworld in different ways, leyanyn. I love how you have found your place accompanying the King to the Hollows. You could never sit in a stuffy court all day, Isla. You would snap and split the Great Hall with your thorns."

We giggle, but I lick my lips and fix my eyes on Franzy, waiting and listening. She squeezes my hand, and a sweet heat nurtures my belly and flushes my neck as she expresses, "I love the Court, Isla. Even if I don't speak much, I love listening to the problems of the nobles, the people, and even the elders."

I make a face, and Franzy smiles to one side, squeezing my hand in a hint before continuing, "Aydon is exceptional at political intervention. He has a keen mind. But he gets overwhelmed at times. I see it. And relieve his tension now and then with my flesh and blood. He cares deeply for Talahn-Feyhlan, truly Isla. He is so loyal to our country and puts our people first."

Our people. But not *her* people.

Oh, Ary, how can I break her heart? I scream in my mind even if he can't hear. Tiny curlicues of smoke drift from the skull mark, but I don't get the opportunity to do more than narrow my eyes, perplexed.

"Aydon has shared with me how he has never produced an heir despite his five hundred years, Isla. He wishes he could spare Allysteir of the responsibility to carry on the Cursed line."

I turn rigid, squaring my shoulders straight back. "You mean spare *me* the responsibility," I add, curling my upper lip in disgust.

Franzy takes my other hand, traces soft circles, and nods. "Yes, *you*, Isla. As all our hopes have rested on you. And I knew you would conquer Death, leyanyn. You will conquer this burden, too," she encourages me and pauses to touch my belly.

I wince. "What do you mean, my bonnya?"

Franzy reaches out to caress my cheek. "It means I believe in you. It means I will be here for you. Whatever you choose. If you seek an Inker for a potion or a wisp-she for herbs or the Sythe-Queen, Narcyssa herself, I will be with you, leyanyn. Or..."

"Or...?" I brace myself.

"Or if you choose to carry the child to their fullness and never again bear another, I will be there." She wipes away my tears. "You will have wet nurses, but I will take the majority of the burden, leyanyn. You need not do anything you do not wish. I will raise the child with Allysteir. This was never your choice. So, you may choose to be a vessel for a brief few months, but you need not be a mother."

I drop my face into my hands, overwhelmed by Franzy, by her too-willing heart, and sigh my shame from a childhood song sung over pregnant mothers in Cock Cross.

"*Blood and flesh to heart and bone.*

Your body becomes his growing home.

Pain and sorrow to joy when born.

Your canal to grant him his first morn..." I trail off from the maternal song. My voice cracks halfway through.

Franzy heaves a sigh. The gauzy, salt-ridden film coating my eyes blurs my vision, but she takes my hands in hers and kisses the backs of each one. "Remember the *end* of the song, my leyanyn.

"*Breasts and milk to shoulder to bear*

A voice to soothe his lone nightmares

Eyes to lips to feet to hands

Help us to raise him on this land.

"Do you understand, Isla? The first part is "your". Not the rest. If you choose, only your body bears the burden. In the past, menders were rare. Remember the women who died in birth? Our ancestors wrote this song to encourage the whole village to share the responsibility. And we don't have a village, my leyanyn. We have the Citadel of Bones. We have all Nathyan Ghyeal!"

"And most of all, I have...you," I conclude and touch my lips to hers, a brush of my mouth.

Franzy smiles and straightens my crown. "You'll always have me."

When I lower my head, thoughts retreating to the mines, I chew on my inner cheek, knowing she will sense my resistance. The revelation stalks the back of my throat, pounding on its doorway.

It doesn't take long. "Now, what is it?" Franzy simpers and pats the back of my hand.

"I shouldn't. You've already done so much, I—"

"Isla Bandya Adayra Morganyach!"

Uh oh. Franzy only ever uses such a tone when she's angry. I can't help but avoid her eyes. Her body language turns rigid as a bow before she snatches my chin and tugs my face back to hers. I cow beneath her burning emeralds, biting my lower lip from her chastisement, "You may battle the Corpse King and the God of Death, but you never battle *me*, leyanyn. You are not the only one in this room with a crown." She sweeps a hand to her princess circlet resting on her bedside table. "Tell. Me. Now."

I spill my guts. I reveal everything from the previous night about discovering the Unseen Section, the secret path to the mines, the slaves with her face, confronting Allysteir, and finally testing the God of Death.

Franzy remains silent the whole time. By the end, salt from my tears bathes my cheeks in a crusty layer. I collapse into my sweetheart's lap, grow blue heather around her, and tell her, "Allysteir will go to Aydon, I swear he will. I won't let—"

"Thank you for telling me, leyanyn. But Aydon is *my* husband. If a conversation must be had, I will speak to him. You handle your husband, but you will not confront mine."

"But Franzy—"

At first, she pinches her eyes, brows knotting low in a warning. I gulp. "Promise me you will not confront Aydon." She raises her hand to the air, palm to me, fingers straight, awaiting. "You have done more than enough this long night, Isla. You have not slept. You are weary. You must take time to consider the next steps for your body. It will take time to summon an Inker or a Wisp-Shee, and I may help you. But for now… promise me."

Shoulders sinking low in understanding, my heart too fatigued for debate, I acquiesce and press my palm and fingers to hers on a hand-bond.

Franzy nods. "Now, my leyanyn, remove your robes and lie down."

I draw my brows together, my body growing heavier from the suspicion. "What, why?"

"I am going to help you sleep." She smiles and touches the fastenings of Allysteir's robe.

My hands fly to hers. "Oh, Franzy, you don't have to—"

She shoves my hands away and undoes the feeble robe tie. "I *want* to, leyanyn. It is almost dawn, and you need rest. I've already had mine. Along with a fresh healing from menders last night."

"But—"

Franzy blows frustrated breath through her nose, huffs, then tugs me closer by those robe bindings until her nose prods mine. "If you truly love me, then respect my will *and* my gifts. The bed is warm and soft and sweet from the purple bell-heather I love so much and adore you for growing. Now, let *me* adore your body and quell its tension. The King may have his lullabies. But my hands have treasured your body for far longer."

I tremble, self-conscious for the first time with her. Franzy slides the outer heavier robe off my shoulders and casts it to the floor. I shudder as she pauses to trace a finger around my lips, her words choking mine and stealing my breath.

"My lips have kissed your lips and tasted your essence. My eyes have watched you grow as your flowers. And my heart knows you as it knows myself. That is something no Corpse King or Death God or future child can ever take from us, my Lady Queen, Isla Bandya Adayra Morganyach."

Teary-eyed, I touch my brow to hers, thoughts too scattered to think straight. My heart thrums warmth in an arrow to my thighs. Adoration clumps my throat when she releases my skin from the robes and gazes at my flesh, her eyes coasting across Allysteir's little bite marks.

Sighing, Franzy rubs her thumb across one mark and expresses, "I will kiss all of these tonight." She cups my shoulders, smiles, and urges me to lie back.

My spine collapses onto the bed of bell-heather.

I shudder when Franzy rubs her lips to mine in a flutter of a kiss before she voyages to my left breast and circles the rosebud with her tongue. I moan and cup my forehead, my throat, reveling to her knowing tongue expertly teasing the nipple, licking and lapping at the flesh to urge it to rise and swell.

"Oh, leyanyn!" I moan again when she closes her lips around the rosebud nipple and sucks it deep into her mouth.

After suckling for a few moments, she repeats the pattern with the right breast, then hovers to eye the full flesh, how the nipples have turned to flushed pebbled diamonds.

"I learned what you love first," Franzy kisses me, and I gush, arching my back to her hands kneading my breasts, squeezing my erect nipples. She urges my blushing breasts together, and I clench my fingers into the flowers. I rip at petals when she blows on each nipple, a hair's breadth from kissing. "I learned how you love when I tease you with my tongue, suckle you, then tease you with my fingers, then suckle you again."

Tears glisten in my eyes as I gaze at her, heart pausing to her poised above my ruby gems, her breath warming them,

"Please, Franz!"

Without warning, Franzy pinches and tugs my nipples, then finds my mouth. Opening it, she trails her tongue around the inside. "You will call me Princess during our remaining time in bed. Am I clear, leyanyn?" She twists my peaked buds.

Sweat riddles my brow. My sex aches for more, but I know her unrivaled tongue won't migrate lower without my acceptance. Remembering her words, "you are not the only one with a crown," I surrender mine to the pillows next to me and bow to her.

Franzy smiles, my sweetheart, my dearest one, my...princess. After my gesture, she plunges three fingers deep into my sex and swallows my scream with her mouth. Finally, she rubs my distended lips with her tongue. Heat eddies through my body, flushing my skin as if a firefly host glows inside my blood.

"Oh, Fra—"

She snaps her gaze to mine, withdrawing her fingers. I shriek from the loss of them and her tongue.

"Princess! Princess! Princess!" I correct three times, hoping they are enough.

"Better," commends Franzy, and I can't deny how I love the praise from her lips.

But I love her lapping at my swollen labia more, swirling her tongue around my clitoral nub. Miniature waves of pleasure engulf me from her pinching my left nipple as she sinks her curving fingers deep into my sex. She sucks my clit so hard, I climax. The soft wet sounds of her mouth rise and fall in pleasurable splashes. My breath, quick and rhythmic to the orgasm, mirrors my heated pleasure. My breath climbs to the peak of a great mountain.

Finally, I exhale, the tension relieved, my shoulders and back sinking against the pillows. Franzy withdraws her fingers and scoots to lay on her side. Lids heavier than anvils, I snuggle against her, curling into the royal bell-heather as my Princess sings melodies of our childhood to lull me to a much-needed sleep.

But I dream of my future child...and Death.

FORTY-FOUR
"THE WAR, BROTHER. I WILL WIN THE WAR."

ALLYSTEIR

Before I depart for my Death business in the Hollows, I make my way to the Great Hall where Aydon will be skulking, ensuring everything is prepared for Court. Thanks to a servant, I've learned Isla has found solace in the Crown Princess' arms. Perhaps Franzy will encourage her when it comes to bearing a child.

I pause in a stone alcove on my way to the secondary hall where I slam my fist against the stone, gratified by the pain and deep vibration humming into my bones without rattling or shattering them.

I rub my stiff jaw and neck, contempt for the gods and their games searing my belly. If it was solely up to me, I'd steal my bride from Nathyan Ghyeal, from all of Talahn-Feyal, and we would travel the world free of any burden, including children. But it's not up to me or her. Isla may have wooed Kryach, may have survived him, but he and the other gods will not spare her child, *our* child.

Chest rigid, I put my trust in the Crown Princess to soothe and temper

Isla while I go hunting for the Crown Prince.

Thankfully, none of the servants have suspected my restoration beyond my heavy robes, gloves, and mask. The irony. Once I'd achieved full form, once I'd met her eyes, those royal diamonds undimmed by the Curse, I was ready to march straight into Court, chuck Aydon off my throne, and issue an official proclamation to all of Talahn-Feyran.

In the past, while I allowed a few privileged staff of the Citadel of Bones to look upon my features during the precious year following Kryach reaping my past brides, I vowed never to show my restoration before the Court. Not until it was full thanks to my bride's survival.

Now, I am hesitating.

Regardless, I look forward to the moment he discovers my transformation. Above all, he needs to know first. Nor will I make it easy. Stronger than ever, I take rapid but full breaths as I stride into the secondary hall where, true to form, Aydon hunches over the table, combing through bone scrolls of Nathyan Ghyeal's center city and its zoning bylaws. Beyond the curtains of the Secondary Hall is the chattering sound of stewards, court envoys, nobles, elders, and more gathering to commence the day's business.

Caping the room in shadows to mask our conversation as well as myself, I approach Aydon from behind. More mischievous than usual, I vault the shades to upset the scrolls and cause my brother to startle.

He stiffens without turning, mutters under his breath, "Allysteir..."

"Oh, come on. One good thousand turns deserve another," I casually reference his endless pranks on me throughout the decades.

"I must commence Court soon. What do you want?" He bends to one knee to collect the fallen scrolls.

"Shut down the mines."

Aydon pauses. His brow furrows as he stands, posture sharp as a bone hook. After straightening the scrolls and placing them on the center of the table, my brother finally turns.

"After five hundred years of wanting nothing to do with Court or politics, spitting out the very notion as poison, now you choose to gnaw on the bone of the one political arena which reaps more revenue than all Nathyan Ghyeal's tourist cites combined."

"I won't command again," I snarl behind my mask, my shades traveling close to Aydon's robes, spiraling to the crown upon his head. *My* crown.

Aydon straightens his robes as he'd done with the scrolls. "Command. Hmm, interesting choice of words, considering who wields the true power of the throne."

"That would ultimately be my bride. it seems she wandered onto the edges of your mines last night as I learned of you transporting slaves into the center city. Who the devil do you think you are?"

Aydon shrugs and sways to the other end of the table to fetch a decanter of Sythe wine. After pouring himself a goblet, he offers it to me, but I shake my head, dropping *another* hint. Aydon's apple bobs in his throat, conveying a hint of distress. Good, he suspects.

"The devil's poor Prince brother, it would seem." He sips from his goblet, swirling the liquid, eyeing me from the side. "Except the devil has never taken an interest in my business in the past."

"When you bring the hell of slavery into the Underworld to grieve the White Ladies, it becomes my business.

Aydon slams his goblet onto the table, sloshing the liquid onto the blackwood. Knots of apprehension form in my stomach as he turns his whole body to me and sneers. "You took the choice from me, brother.

All those centuries ago. And you wanted nothing, *nothing* to do with the throne. That was our bargain. Do not believe you are the only one who can get your hands dirty for the sake of Talahn-Feyal."

"You forget, Aydon." I lean in, unraveling those knots one by one and chilling them to pure ice serpents poised to attack.

"Oh?" My charming blue-eyed brother taps his finger on the table, eyes narrowing in a dare.

"I accepted a Curse. For *my* body. I did not use others."

Aydon snorts. "Tell that to all your brides, Ally."

I growl. "Not slaves, brother! Never slaves."

"However they dressed up and played bride while you played the tortured, romantic king, you know as well as I: they were the greatest slaves to the gods."

Raking my nails on the table, shedding blood and splinters while all my skin crawls, I seethe, "*You* are no god, Aydon."

Aydon winks, his tapping finger infuriating me, increasing the bitter taste in my mouth. "No, brother, don't you see? If the gods require our flesh and blood and bones, perhaps we are *more*."

Fed up with his elitism, I direct, "Shut down the fucking mines already. You will choose other workers from Talahn-Feyal. And pay them a worthy wage."

Aydon throws his head back and laughs. "As if you could find the amount necessary to appease our economy and the nobles! Who do you think is responsible for prospering our country all these years? For satisfying the elders enough to keep them in line? For ensuring the Mender Guilds throughout the land are enriched so they may perform their duties? For maintaining an abundant reserve of resources during times of famine or refter upheaval whenever you tested Kryach's patience? A reserve of trade thanks to the *mines*," he concludes, gritting his teeth, cocking his head, and deepening his eyes on me.

For the final nail in the coffin, I raise my gloved hand to his cheek, pat it mockingly as I did in our youth, and acknowledge, "Such an accomplished Crown Prince should have no problem conjuring a solution. But do it quickly...or I may alert Kryach."

Before I turn, Aydon seizes my glove, my robe sleeve, rips them from my person, and tears the mask from my face to reveal my restored smolder. Aydon leaps back, elbows sliding against the table, disturbing the scrolls to tumble onto the floor.

"Surprise!" I taunt him, threading my brows, enjoying myself at Aydon's expense for once in centuries.

Aydon rights himself and rises from his elbows. Chest surging, Aydon snarls and demands, "Where is she?"

I wave a hand. "With Franzy, I imagine. We had a bit of a row, you see. The irony. What you *want* most, what I *need* most, and the last thing Isla wants and needs is a child."

"So, she...?"

I roll my eyes. "Of course, she survived. We should never have doubted her. *I* should never have doubted her. I won't make such a mistake again. As you should not either. Especially when it comes to her loyalty to her leyanyn, your Feyal-wife, brother."

As if dawn is breaking, Aydon registers my words, kneads his brow, and drops his hand to his side. "I will shut down the mines. *Temporarily,*" he adds the disclaimer. Naturally. He would never dare piss Isla off now. "But rest assured, if the elders and nobles do not agree to another solution before the Night of Masks, I will have no choice but to institute the original source of workers."

I straighten, pride lifting me higher, higher than *my* crown Aydon wears. "By the Night of Masks, Isla will swell with our child, and the gods will be appeased in the future renewal of the Curse. Hmm, how fitting since today marks the beginning of harvest in Talahn-Feyal. Quite fitting."

Aydon glowers, his features screwing low in an unsightly manner for the Crown Prince.

"Aww, how does it feel to be too late, Aydon?" I mock him, pat his cheek for good measure.

Calm and collected as usual, Aydon merely winces and lowers himself to snatch the scrolls in the wake of my shadows corkscrewing along his back. He mutters something incomprehensible under his breath.

"What was that now?"

Scrolls in hand, Aydon deadpans, flaring his nostrils to proclaim, "You won this battle, Allysteir. But perhaps...you will *not* win the war."

Smirking to one side, triumphant, I pat my brother's shoulder, drawing out my contemptuous derision to conclude, "Oh, come now, Aydon, Talahn-Feyran has not seen war since before the Curse. I'm simply one of the lucky royals to have survived...thanks to my bride."

I turn to depart, but at the last second, I barrage my shades to constrict his throat, knock the crown from his rutting head, and wrench him an inch from my eyes in a lethal assault of a warning. "By the way, Aydon, this is for you daring to kiss my bride."

I shoot him through the air, beyond my shade barrier, past the curtain until my brother's body barrels against the throne. It crashes to the floor, alerting the court audience. As predicted, the inertia is too much. Aydon tumbles down the dais and falls right into the Shivering River.

As the court erupts with bone warriors rushing to rescue the Crown

Prince, I make a sucking noise with my teeth, bend to fetch the crown, then issue into the Great Hall. The sight almost comical from Aydon's struggle with our warriors vying with the spirits dragging him lower while the elders chant meaningless rituals. As the Court erupts from the event, I march past the fallen throne, down the dais, and to the edge of the River Cryth.

Soldiers turn their swords on me from the invasion of a foreign presence. I merely grin and wave my hand across the water to quiet the spirits who release my brother. With all audiences' eyes on me, I direct my shades to fetch my brother from the waters and deposit him soaked and dripping at my side. By the time I finish, not one Court member is left standing. Comprehension on account of my power.

No hesitation anymore.

With the crown in one hand, I clap Aydon on the shoulder with my other, and proudly declare, "Yes, my people: proud citizens of Talahn-Feyal, both Feyal-Ithydeir and human. Let cider and wine gush throughout the land. May the harvest be more bountiful than e're before. And let feasts be held in every castle and city and small village as we host a grand banquet tonight to celebrate and honor the autumnal equinox... and my bride. Isla Bandya Morganyach is the Tenth-Bride of Talahn-Feyal to survive Aryahn Kryach, God of Death. She has saved us all!"

Aydon's dip in the Cryth River utterly forgotten, the court envoys scramble to transcribe the message which will catch like wildfire by the day's end. The other court members explode in applause. Aydon wears a proud but faux smile, leans in, and whispers, "The war, brother. I will win the war."

FORTY-FIVE
THE QUEEN'S FALLEN CROWN

ISLA

When I wake, it's to a servant knocking on the sweetheart suite Franzy and I share, but my leyanyn is gone. Snatching a robe from a nearby hook, I bind it around my figure, hustle to the door, and open it to a stewardess.

She nods to me, holding a tray of shortbread, pomegranates, and a cut of lean pork. "The Crown Princess sends her regards and trusts you slept well, Your Majesty. She went to Court to join her husband and sends you a midday meal and hopes to see you at supper in the secondary hall."

I press my lips together and nod, accept the tray, and bid the stewardess farewell. But despite the food's temptation, I set it aside and issue into the hallway. Energy renewed from my long rest, from the love of my leyanyn, I consider someone else I have underestimated. Someone I should have sought more than the scarce times I'd had over the last nine months. If anyone can give me answers, *true* answers to my future, it's none other than the ghost of Doom.

Flustered, I bustle down the next hall and the next until I arrive at the bridge overseeing the Sea of Bones outside the library tower. The same bridge where Kryach chose his price of *access*. I remember how exhilarating it was to tempt and taunt the God of Death. Now, he feels more distant. All I bear is his mark which seems as delicate as a frost flower on a dark windy night. One touch, and I fear I'll crumble it to black, crystalline dust.

Here, I linger, purse my lips. Some invisible force squeezes my lungs despite how the salt-laced bone powder wind plunders my nostrils and rifles through my chaotic waves. Though I have survived him, though my future rolls out like a twilight tapestry before my eyes, I am blinder than ever.

Allysteir and I will never have the relationship we once shared. Before this morning, perhaps. Yes, I understand his motivation, but he does not understand mine, much less respect it.

And Ary...

"Ary," I whisper his name. "Where are you?"

When nothing but a cold burst of wind carried from the Sea of Bones greets me, I sigh, rocking back and forth before rushing down the long, twisting staircase. I run past the vestibule and to the alcove of descending stairs.

By now, I've discovered how to summon the River spirits, except for Betha. They usher the boat to me, to my bare feet. Chest lurching, I waste no time climbing in. It becomes more difficult to swallow as the spirits carry me past the Citadel arches and to the deepest parts of the Sea of Bones, past the tourist areas and into darker waterways housed by cavern walls. I curl my shoulders forward and close my eyes, trusting the spirits: these smeared constellations inside the water.

I survived Aryahn Kryach. So, what Doom could Betha have referenced? I call her name until my throat cracks, dry and brittle. I sing countless melodies I learned growing up and new ones from the Citadel, including Ary's personal lullaby. Rolling with the current wherever they wish to bid me, I follow the whim of the spirits, but nothing works. No trace of Betha.

One last desperate attempt. A selfish one, but Betha is not the only one I wish to see.

"Stop!" I whisper to the spirits once we near the barest crag of black rocks. Nudging the side of an enormous dark mountain face, this small clump of great rocks shines like obsidian thanks to the souls glowing around me. It will be perfect.

If Aryahn Kryach won't respond to anything else, I have to imagine he will to this. Other than the souls, who have no eyes, I couldn't be more alone.

So, I instruct the spirits to berth the boat against those rocks. Awkwardly climb out. But it doesn't feel awkward to remove the bridal gown and cast it upon the rocks. Not my crown. I breathe relief, shoulders sinking. It reminds me of another desolate night...near the Void.

Here, in the solitude of darkness, I am the moon clad in frost and starlight waiting for Death's shadows.

I lower myself onto the rocks and drape my body in a flawless arch across a large, jagged one. A nude opal cameo against a velvet black backdrop.

A moment later, I cup both my breasts, close my eyes, and circle, fondling my flesh. I inhale, nearly coughing from the brittleness of my mouth. I trace little spirals until I arrive at the withered areola and finally, the rose-tipped nipples. I impart a sweet pinch to each one, whimper in pleasure, then gravitate my hand lower to my mound. Just as I poke the skull eyes, I beam and peel back my pubic lips. I hiss through the tightening pangs in my chest.

The shade form appears. Parallel to my body, he hovers above me so I may breathe his essence of pomegranates, of dark smoke, of Isle-incense.

"Ary...?" I whisper, seeking his eyes through the mysterious shade veil.

"What are you doing, Isla?"

"If it's the only way to get your attention..." I elude and slide my finger deep inside myself, resisting the urge to giggle.

"And you believed *this* was the best environment?"

I shrug with a tender laugh, excusing, "I didn't want Allysteir walking in like last time."

Kryach blows icy breath across my face. The fragrance of the Isles laced with the sound of death rattles, of decay. "What could you possibly want to discuss now, Tenth Bride of Talahn-Feyal?"

I rise onto my elbows, toss my waves onto my shoulder, and demand, "Am I pregnant?"

Ary's shade drifts back and forth, smoke expelling as if infinite sighs curl from his being. "That question is not your most desired. Ask again."

"Am I the Mallyach-Ender?"

At first, he gives no response until his shades transport my bridal gown to cover my body. "Dress yourself, Tenth Bride. To answer such a question, you'll need more than your skin clothing you."

I waste no time in scrambling back into the sheathe so Ary may navigate the boat into the deepest and darkest cavern of Nathyan Ghyeal where the spirits themselves don't dare to traverse.

This is why.

"Ary," I whimper as the boat nudges another dead refter bride floating along the surface of the water. The corpses are so preserved, it's impossible to tell which ones have been here the longest.

Utter silence from the God of Death out of the corner of my eye. When I turn, he disappears, veiled into thin air. But he doesn't leave me alone.

"*Lovely blood under faces of white.*
Ash and runes but not one bite. Not one bite. Not one bite..."

I stare at Betha. At her sorrowful hair mirroring the fallen brides, though hers is far longer and the eerie blue of a funereal shroud. Weighed down by woeful tears, her gray mist eyes barely regard me—too lost in her mission of collecting the corpses. I gasp when she plucks a bride from the mass and props them on a rocky ledge upon the cavern wall on my left.

Smothered somewhere on its exit, my gasp perishes, and I spin my head at what is no ordinary cavern. These are ancient ruins partly submerged.

"*Light a candle, a thousand or two*
A lonely grave for the lovers of Doom. Of Doom. Of Doom."

I whip my head from one side to the other while Betha's shrieks echo off the cavern walls, fading before they reach the other tunnels. Thousands of alcoves, little ledges, house the delicate corpses. Propped to sit, the brides seem ready to do some sort of court. These ruins were once an ancient assembly. Has Betha been here this whole time placing each bride in her designated place? These unfinished burial graves?

Fatigue numbs me to my core, heavier than nightmares. Now, the Nether-mark flares its fire in the wake of all the bodies, summoning me to action.

Betha wails and flits about the corpses, corpses I soon comprehend are not refters at all. Leaning over the boat so I may weave strong vines around one, I peer closer to find kohl ink upon lashes and lids smearing their fruitful cheeks. Not sunken like true refters. Someone has packed their mouths with pomegranate seeds.

"No," I moan, on the verge of wailing like Betha, thankful I did not eat before I came. They've been dressed this way as a mockery.

"*After sun has fallen and dusk is nigh*
Listen to his stolen lullaby...Stolen. Stolen," repeats Betha, and I pinch my eyes as she snatches another imitation bride, kisses her brow, and lays her inside another burial alcove.

It's the same lullaby, but not the same words.

"Allysteir would never do this." I shake my head, denying Betha.

For the first time, Betha turns her heart-shaped face to me, her eyes glassy and gray as an unseeing mirror. "Not Corpus King. Too busy. Too lost in love. He cannot see." She hovers in mid-air above me, her long gown more shredded than usual. Of course not Allysteir. This and the refter brides on the pomegranate isle can only be the work of Kanat. Or the lower gods. Or they're in league with one another.

I sigh and offer her the body I convey within my vines, black death roses sprouting, but Betha lifts her hand. "*Vines are welcome but not the rose.*
Pretties may awake, only Doom she knows
Doom they speak on Death's hallowed ground
Awaiting the night of the Queen's fallen crown. Fallen crown. Fallen crown..."

Silent, I chew on my inner cheek and help Betha with her task. My heart thuds slower and duller with every corpse. They do not bear the runes of the slaughtered refters on the pomegranate isle. No, these slaughtered girls...the work is cruel, slow, and vindictive from the premeditated makeup and costumes adorning them to their mouths stuffed full of seeds.

What did she mean by fallen crown? I touch a trembling finger to the jewels resting on my head. "Betha," I finally address her after an hour or so passes of us thinning the corpse collection. "Am I the Mallyach-Ender?"

Betha charges through the air, carrying the scent of corpus roses, of blood, and breast milk, and deep water. *"While an Ender you may be, Your blood spells doom, we will never see Unless you flee the Underworld, my Queen, Tenth Bride The Night of Masks when Kryach is most spirit-blind..."*

Yes, the night where the veil between the spirit world is thinnest, where the Void is strongest. Bone warriors throughout Nathyan Ghyeal will be dispatched to protect the Citadel and the tombs of the royals. And Kryach will be the busiest working to stop armies of spirits from fleeing the River Cryth who long to dance with the people and drag them to the depths.

On my first night here, I considered how I could help Franzy escape. Not myself. Perhaps now is *our* chance. If I am the Mallyach-Ender, I cannot allow the lower gods to steal me into the Void or permit this Doom to be fulfilled.

And there's only one person I may trust.

FORTY-SIX
THE MORNING OF MASKS

ALLYSTEIR

"What do you think of my mask for tonight, my Queen?" I tease Isla.

She clamps her teeth on a shriek when I thrust her hips against the wall of the shaded alcove, shackle one wrist above her head, and sink my teeth into her radiant flesh. Hunger too piqued as I've starved myself between feedings which she damn well knows. And enjoys, given her willful smirk whenever she catches me drinking more Sythe wine than usual.

"I thought it quite fitting. In memoriam of our wedding night," I goad her, drag my tongue against her flesh.

Isla hisses. "I'll forgive your mask, my King...only because mine is far superior. But unlike you. I won't spoil my tricks for this night."

I chuckle. Ever since our true honeymoon night, much has changed between us. Isla still accepts my attention, downright demands it. But she is colder. More aloof. Pleasure her sole focus. She was as regal of a

Queen of the Underworld on the night of our grand revelation when I wore my crown but no mask. It was the first time she played the role. As if her crown was a costume piece.

Over the past couple months, I've tested her, tugging on her boundary line to determine if she snaps it back. Sometimes, she does. Most times, she loosens it. But not penetration. How my bride loves the mastery of touch.

"Corpus King," she whispers during my feeding. I cant my head to discover her watery eyes, her florid cheeks. She licks her lips, parts them. I expect her to hiss and demand me to let her go. All it would take is her raising her voice for my family to hear in the adjoining hall.

I've urged her into this position—the same as our wedding night: against the wall. But when she cocks her head without her crown shifting, Isla opens her mouth and slams her teeth shut in a direct snap. A taunt.

I grin. My bride loves her games! I stem her pain with more Ith venom but not much because she loves the pain. Her eyes roll to the backs of her head, lost in our wedding night's memory. She overlaps it with this one, to reclaim the emotions. Unlike then, her fingers do not clench.

Yes, my bride. You are safe. You are here. And I love you, my dark rose. I speak nothing. She knows.

I sink deeper to consume another sample, grieved when I discover blood has trickled onto her gown. "My apologies, My Lady Queen," I whisper, tracing the low gauzy neckline.

Isla's lavish breasts expand from her breath with every passing second. Nipples aroused and enthused with rouge to prod her gown, crimson to mirror her buds.

I lick another trickle of blood from her fresh shoulder and chest wounds, avoiding the urge to tear at the blotted fabric.

"Your apology is not accepted."

I glimpse upward to smirk at her. "So, you wish to play, my Queen? What apology will be enough?"

Isla presses the back of her head to the wall, licks her lips, and groans lightly, thrusting her bust and hips forward. "Actions speak louder than words, Corpus King."

"Then, allow me to show you how ardently apologetic I am..."

I waste no time in freeing her breasts of their bodice cage. One solitary line of blood trickles to her right nipple, tantalizing along with her erect flesh. Hungry enough to match my appetite. I suck the bloody rosebud deep into my warm, wet mouth.

When Isla moans, I cover her lips with my hand, nip her nipple in warning, and whisper, "Shh, my bride. Nothing but a thin wall between us and the secondary hall. I am all too aware of your great appetite, my bride, but I highly doubt you want all the stewards and my brother and mother to join us."

Thanks to my interference with Aydon to shut down the mines, Isla has been satisfied, though I've mentioned nothing of his warning to re-open them. I've spent too much time combing through economic proposals, hunting for employees who aren't catering to the Citadel, haggling over worker pay. As exhaustive and boring as ever...unlike my bride.

Beneath my palm, she huffs. Her queenly eyes, hot with tears, burn as they narrow with a warning. A sharp stinging pain engulfs my hand, but I don't flinch or recoil. "Did you just bite me?" I challenge her in a low Ith growl.

Isla feigns innocence with an adorable shrug, but her cheekbones plumping from an unabashed grin betray her.

Simpering, I collar her throat, snug but not tight. A master of my newfound strength by now. Isla gasps through my hand collar, but she cannot whimper or moan when I fondle her left breast and twist the nipple sharply. Her knees shudder, a captivating flush warming her. Again, I suckle her right nipple, hard and dark as a dried pomegranate seed, flesh around it like shriveled pink cherries. I squeeze her breast and remark, "I wonder how large they will grow when filled with the milky sustenance for our child. Hmm..." I close my teeth around her bud and tug.

Isla gasps, throwing her hair forward. I loosen my hand enough to permit her to seethe, "Perhaps I'll drown you in the milk, Corpus King. Oh!" She moans again when I pinch her nipples, then shift her gown to her hips. Kneeling before her, I drag her underthings to her ankles, pry her willing thighs, and inhale her essence.

"Or perhaps you'll drown me with your fluids now, my dark rose," I quip and drag a finger across her damp sex, enjoying her licking her lips and clinging to the alcove walls while I part those hearty, pink lips like perfectly-cut fruit. Soaked fruit. Utterly soaked.

She looks so beautiful with her gown gathered at her waist, her alluring breasts heavy and heaving. I lean my cheek against her belly, delirious from its soft roundness. A result of more than a few extra helpings of shortbread and pomegranates. Tonight, I will announce our pregnancy to the Court, to the peoples of Nathyan Ghyeal, of Talahn-Feyal, and all the visiting royals.

Isla's lacy underthings imprison her lovely ankles, exhibiting her sinuous calves to her exquisite round thighs to her fleshy flaming jewel of a center exposed and ready for the plundering. That plump dangling nub, swollen and needy.

"Allysteir," she whispers, eyes closed.

My chest warms, tingles with the image of her body growing to prepare for life. "I will love and cherish your body after the birth, Isla. More so." I brush her aching bud with the tip of my finger.

"No," she whimpers, thrusting her pelvis out, her sex seeking my finger.

I chain her back to the wall with one hand, hover my fingers a couple of inches from her feminine pleasure. Grinning in victory, I trail my finger along her slit, teasing. "Invite me in, my Queen."

She snaps her eyes down to me, screws her brows low, shakes her head, and mouths the word, "No".

"It changes nothing, Isla. My love for you has not dimmed." I rub her clit again, tormenting her.

She tips her head back, presses her lips together, and slams her palm onto my shoulder, nails raking up the side of my neck to demand, "Now..."

"Invite." I trail my finger lower. "Me." Circle her drippy opening. "In." I dip my fingertip inside and collar her waist with shades to prevent her from bucking. I force my digit in deeper.

I withdraw my fingers, my hand from her mound, and rise, only to discover her hands curved, prepared to strangle. Her eyes burn with frustrated lust. I slam those hands to the wall above her head. "It doesn't have to be the same," I promise against her mouth.

She shakes her head, eyes violent. "It can't. It won't. Never the bed. Never again."

"I'll work with that. We have eternity." I kiss her, savor her moan, trail my lips down her throat, to her full breasts. "What could be more different than fucking you against a wall in forbidden shadows?" I cup her mound, smirk at how she licks her fruitful lips, debating.

"You don't deserve—"

"Of course, I don't," I agree, rolling my eyes. "I'll never be a worthy husband, my bride. I am simply your Corpus King whom you fucked first," I default to self-deprecation. "Allow me to return the favor."

Isla opens those amethysts and lurches, snapping her teeth an inch from my throat. I smirk to one side. "Naughty bride. Are you saying yes?"

"You're a real piece of work," mocks Isla.

"Hmm...perhaps the greatest truth is how I am one whole piece now, my bride."

"Oh!" She gasps when I unleash my cock and nudge her eager center while growing shadows around us. I lean in and hum in her ear while pressing her fingers to my chest, hinting, "But my strongest and fullest muscle has desired you since the beginning. And will long after our children are born."

She rolls her eyes, grits her teeth from my member prodding her. She knows I'm *not* referring to my lower muscle and instead the one in my chest.

"Or perhaps I'll go to Aydon after I push the little monster out."

"Shall I fetch him and alert him of your desire?" I call her bluff and lean away, but Isla grips my collar at the last second.

Our eyes deadpan in a stalemate, and I snigger, victorious. Vehement, she bites my mouth, chews my lower lip while our tongues devour one another.

Before another moment passes, Isla grips my cock and pushes it to her drenched sex. "Fuck me against this wall now, Corpus King."

No hesitation. I suck her neck, grip her breasts, and lunge my cock inside her sex. Not simply warm but hotter than Nether-hell flames. I forge my way inside, her tight center welcoming me like a celestial pool. I pound her against the wall, propelling her up with the momentum, swallowing her groans with the shades. I feast on her ripe breasts and tantalize her dilated clitoral nub until her inner muscles clamp hard around my member.

But I don't get to revel in conquering her climax. Not when her hand scrambles lower, and she grips my member's edge and milks me. I come hard and fast to unite with her.

"Isla..." I growl at her breast and suck on each one to leave retaliatory marks. Her eyes glaze over with ecstasy and raw triumph.

After a few moments of our piqued breath united, Isla squeezes the edge of my organ and simpers. "That's what you get for playing with fire, my King. But thank you for the ride."

She rights her bodice while I cage my still-pulsing cock. Before she can tug on her undergarments, I rip them from her ankles, inhale their scent close to my nostrils, and smirk when she tries to retrieve them.

I wave them above her head, deny her, and touch two fingers to her lips. "I'll be keeping these, my swollen bride. After Court, I'll tell you all about how the Ith lords and elders tugged at their collars and paled from its overwhelming and alluring aroma."

Isla pouts and jumps to snatch the soaked lace, but the moment she falls against me, I catch her and murmur against her mouth, "Did you know Ith can scent a human woman's pregnancy pheromones?"

"Allysteir!" she protests while I drag the lace across my face. "Not to worry your pretty little head." I capture her chin and rub her lower lip with my thumb, narrowly missing her snapping teeth. "*You* are still the savior of Talahn-Feyal. All pride and credit to you, including for the babe growing in your womb. I am your humble king."

She narrows her eyes before tapping my wrist where I imprison her under-lace above my head. "Your game, Allysteir?"

I wink and touch my lips to hers. "It is the Day of Masks. My treat. My trick. Ultimately, a...*warning* to my brother not to fuck with my bride. And anyone else. Forgive me for my over-protectiveness?" She chews on her lower lip and rolls her eyes, stamping one foot, but I read between the lines.

"Just remember where the line is, Corpus King."

"If ever I were to forget, I am certain you will have no trouble drawing a new one for me, my dark rose." I pocket the aromatic lace, then kiss the backs of her knuckles.

"Sweet talk will not get you through immortality with me." She sticks her tongue out.

"Considering the enormity of your sweet tooth..." I chuckle when she smacks my chest at the shoulder but quickly follow her out of the alcove and into the secondary hall where Aydon, Mathyr, and Franzy are midway through their first course.

Aydon rocks his fist against his chest, coughing as I breeze past him to the end of the table. From ear to ear, I grin a taunt, knowing he can scent her lace. Isla slides into her rightful place at the *head* of the table diagonal to her sweetheart. As usual, they greet each other with a tender kiss.

"You're looking well, Mathyr," I compliment my mother and her ornate garb, appreciating how she's woven Aydon's father's malleus, incus, and stapes—the smallest bones in the body—into her hair to form an organic and proud broach.

Since my restoration, Mathyr has warmed to me more. What

dumbfounds me is her newfound kinship with Isla, but I chalk it up to their shared survivorhood.

"You're looking better, Allysteir." Mathyr smiles, sipping her pomegranate juice.

"No doubt *feeling* better," Aydon grumbles under his breath. "Should I alert Isla how often you and Finleigh were late for meals?"

Isla ignores Aydon and whispers something sweet in Franzy's ear, causing her leyanyn to giggle.

I adjust my crown, reach for my goblet of pomegranate juice, and click my teeth. "Poor Aydon: we both know I may be late for breakfast, but you'll be late for your own funeral."

"Enough," Mathyr's steely voice chills the heated tension in the room, so even Franzy and Isla sit to attention. "Let us discuss more positive topics. Like the impending Night of Masks, the arrival of the royals following our breakfast, and how the mines have opened again to afford more productivity for tonight."

Isla drops her fork speared with blood sausage. It splatters carnal juice across the tablecloth. I fix my eyes on my Queen, on her cheeks reddening from anger, eyes narrowing in a dark, royal rage.

Before she or I may act, Aydon dabs his mouth and suggests to Isla, "Perhaps you should thank the Crown Princess, Your Highness. After all, Franzy insisted on reopening the mines."

All the color drains from my Queen's cheeks.

For the first time in all our months of togetherness, Isla does not touch her food.

FORTY-SEVEN
THE NIGHT OF MASKS

ISLA

"Run, Isla," he whispers, disrupting my bath. "Run."

I snap my head up from the steamy water and spin my head everywhere, searching, calling out, "Ary?"

After a few moments of the wind lashing the stones of the bathhouse and the bath steam curling in the air, I sigh, resigning myself he won't show himself. Over these past few months, he never has. Not since the one time with Betha...when he called me Tenth Bride or Isla. Not little wonder.

Except for the faint phantom voice of deep twilight in my dreams. Of the scent of gray dew and dead leaves. Of woe and everlasting loneliness. Because despite how many souls Ari collects, however many he may keep for a time, I know how little his spirit feels. It's why the gods pine for mortal flesh to stick to.

Ary longed for mine most.

Despite my flushed cheeks and my heated skin, I shiver and chew on my index fingernail, wondering why.

Run, Isla...

I knead my brow, struggling for breath. He knows I'm planning to run. For months, I've made such plans with Alysteir's mother, leaving all others in the dark. At first, I included Franzy. But after sharing my first few unsuccessful attempts with the herb, she grew resigned to my keeping the cursed child. When her brows would lift in anticipation every time she saw me, when her eyes would immediately drop to my belly, I pulled away from her and confided in the Queen. It's knotted my stomach every time I've faced my leyanyn...until this morning when I learned of her choice to re-open the mines.

Something is different about her, whether it's all those weeks in the Court or how she's seemed to form an alliance with Aydon—nor can I fault her. After all, he is her husband. I couldn't expect everything about our relationship to stay the same. My stomach hardens with nausea as I swipe at tears. No time to confront her. The Night of Masks commences soon.

I sigh, press my determined lips together, and clench my fists in the water, considering Allysteir's forthcoming announcement. Here in the bath, I frame two hands around my swelling stomach and touch my heavy, too-tender breasts. I frown. Another secret he'd kept from me, another part of this Curse business. Because the gods must have their games, their blood, their shells. Yes, Allysteir might credit his past brides' sacrifice, but he treats me like a savior. I glower, heaving breath. Because I'm not a savior. I'm simply the gods' shiny new pawn, their shell, the new Queen of Corpses to birth the next cycle. Trapped under the White Ladies forever or until Allysteir and I choose to retire to the Forever Havens.

The last thing I want is to become part of the Curse.

I am not here to breed the next Corpse King.

So, for the hundredth time, I grow the Wisp-Shee herb, banned by bone magic in Talahn-Feyal. For the hundredth time, I chew the leaves, slam my eyes shut, brace myself, and wait.

And like all the times before, nothing happens.

"No..." I whimper and rake my nails through my hair and into my scalp. "I am not the Mallyach-Ender," I murmur, swallowing the pain in my throat, the urge to sob. "Now, I am the Curse," I finish in a whisper, battle the dizzying wave of nausea, and choose to float along the surface of the water.

When my hair branches in the water to become a silver flaming halo, the skull mark out of the corner of my eye haunts me. Adrenaline charges into me, and my skin crawls. I'll never be able to run with this mark. Six seeds, six delirious seeds were the beginning. No, the real beginning was when I listened to weasel-faced Ganyx and forged an elder's summons to participate in the fythdel games.

"Is this why nothing will work?" I demand of Ary, stabbing a finger at the mark. "If I have to, I'll take my freedom." With blood. With violence. It doesn't matter. Whatever it takes.

First, I scratch until the skin around the mark inflames. Next, I grow a thorn right from my palm and drag it across the flesh. Tears brawl with my eyes. I gasp windstorms through my nostrils while I spill blood and death's ink until they mingle in the water. My Nether-mark burns. For the first time, I don't curse it, I don't will it down. I lean into the power, *my* power—whatever dark force exists inside me. I pit my will against the God of Death until my blood soaks the fatal mark and my knuckles turn whiter than white Inker blossoms.

The thorn snaps from the pressure. I slam my palm on my collarbone, on the bloodied Death mark, and scream through gritted teeth. The pain is acid carving through my flesh. I unleash a last shrill shriek. Everything quiets. The blood beneath my palm slows. Through my soaked strands of hair coating my face, I gaze around, almost expecting his shade prepared to stop me.

Nothing but my piqued breath.

Before I get the chance to remove my palm, something splits deep inside my core. Arching hard and sharp, I throw my hair back and grip the stone ledge around the sunken bath so hard, my nails leave permanent indents. At first, I start to shriek, but it's cut off, suffocated by the soothing current rippling through me. Deathly shades serenade my body, enveloping me in a tranquilizing tide to combat the pressure between my thighs. A dark, slow current.

When the water warms, I slowly turn, clawing desperate hands at my throat, already suspecting. Gasping, I somehow keep my scream at bay. I almost fall. I almost sink into the bloodied water. Instead, I grow from relief, from joy, from hope. I grow hundreds of scarlet heart blooms to drink the bloody water. I grow floral dragon's breath to purify the liquid, to eliminate any trace of evidence.

I let the tears fall because even if I didn't want it, even if I never wanted it, it still deserves my tears, the salt of wounds, the memory of emotion.

My freedom won through fire and blood and violence.

When all that remains is the sac floating amidst the shades—a final offering of the undeveloped, tiny form inside—I nod to the essence of his power and whisper, "Take it, Ary." I breathe, only to understand what all this meant when his shades retreat from my body and vanish into thin air along with the sac.

Because the skull mark has disappeared. The mark condemned me to life eternal in the Underworld. Everything Allysteir needed. And Talahn-Feyal.

I knot my brows because not all the ink was gone. I couldn't finish. So, why would he do this? Why would he give up his greatest chain binding me to him, to Allysteir?

"Run, Isla..." are the words to greet me from somewhere beyond the veil of worlds.

Sighing, I ease my body out of the bath, knowing under ordinary circumstances, without the God of Death's magic, without potentially Allysteir's Ithydeir venom in my body, none of this could be accomplished without pain. The pain would have lasted for days. Emotions would have mirrored it and lasted far longer.

At the scarlet droplets tumbling from my sex, I understand I may bleed for a short time. Instead, I smile and frame my hands again around my stomach which will eventually shrink back to normal. I can only hope the trace amounts of blood and whatever aftermath of pheromones will linger long enough for my escape.

I swallow the thickening wave of guilt in my throat, considering the millions of women who have had those experiences and bow my head in respect for their sufferings.

But I can't afford the emotion. Because tonight is the Night of Masks. I must look my best.

I set my jaw and fetch my robe. Tonight, I will run, I will leave Talahn-Feyal and never return. A sorry excuse for a Queen perhaps, but I was never meant to be Queen. Just as Aydon said, I volunteered, I promised myself to *him*, not to Allysteir.

As I wrap myself in a robe and make my way up the staircase to my room, Ary's shade curls across the back of my neck, his voice dipping to the deepest, ominous low to warn me, "*They're coming.*"

"Well, now, I wholeheartedly confess, you have upstaged me," Allysteir comments when I appear before him, embarking into the Secondary Hall, fully clothed in my ensemble for the evening. "Of course..." he assumes my hand and rubs his mouth upon my knuckles while I smile from his mask. "You did the first time I saw you in the Skull Ruins. Our first meeting, you have perfectly captured, my Lady Queen," he finishes.

I trace one finger around the tiny skull, one of hundreds strategically positioned to create a mask echoing the Skull Ruins.

"And you have embraced my namesake for you and how we first bonded in the Hollows," I remark on Allysteir's mask, though it's more of a non-mask. After centuries of wearing the corpse mask, Allysteir's painted one becomes him. I curl my fingers to his cheek, marveling at his youthful beauty, how he carried the weight of the mask, the Curse for so many years. A spark of anger heats my blood. No one should.

Allysteir grips my wrist and kisses my palm before it can settle. I smile softly at the elaborate corpus roses with their skull centers. A pang invades my chest. Chewing on the inside of my cheek, I refrain from touching the space on my collarbone absent of the skull mark. Veiled beneath my black, lacy neckline so Allysteir cannot see.

Tonight, I'll leave all this behind. I'll leave the Underworld with its spirit lights, the refter bride glen, the Citadel of Bones with its wonders, the Sea of Bones, and pomegranate isle. I'll leave all this truth and beauty behind in pursuit of my own beyond Talahn-Feyal.

I'll leave Franzy.

When she enters the secondary hall alongside Aydon, garbed in a flowing, dark green gown reminiscent of our last Feast of Flesh a year ago, the knife twists deep into my heart. Shame curls heat to tingle my cheeks.

"My Lady Queen," Franzy greets me with an official curtsy. I nod, smiling at her mask of woven white and purple heather. It compliments her darker gold skin. She imparts the same curtsy to Allysteir. "Your Majesty..."

The King is quick to take Franzy's hand and raise her while shaking his head. "None of that nonsense. I know you're married to my flouncy brother," he jerks his head to Aydon, who's already proven his point by offering me a customary bow and kissing the back of my hand—specifically the wedding ring—, "but I insist: no standing on ceremony here."

"I have a feeling this will be a night no one will forget," Franzy mentions with a smile.

"Ahh, an echo of the past," Allysteir responds and leans in to kiss her cheek. "I believe you are right again, dear Franzyna. As Aydon knows, I am looking forward to sharing with the entire kingdom the news of our future child."

Aydon shifts his gaze to me. I don't balk or squirm despite how his blue eyes seem darker, more predatory concealed within the eye holes of his mask of black death roses and skulls. At first, he cocks his head, pinches his eyes. A bolt of terror shoots up my spine.

Does he know?

I sigh heavily and touch Allysteir's arm, playing into the ruse since everyone in this room knows it's my unwanted fate, "No need to spoil our evening so soon, Allysteir. Let us enter the court so we may dance and eat and enjoy the festivities first."

"I agree," the matriarchal voice behind Aydon and Franzy dictates as she sweeps into the room wearing an illustrious velvet gown of deep umber, adorned in gold-shimmered bones and jewels.

"Mother," Aydon and Allysteir both state, bowing to her.

She captures each of their cheeks, but a new pattern has formed ever since Allysteir's restoration. A deeper fondness in her palm for him. Her gaze lingers upon his face as if she wishes to memorize every part of him as if fearful he could return at any moment to the rotting corpse he once was.

"Slantya, Franzyna," she greets the Crown Princess. "Well met on the Night of Masks. You are lovely and glowing."

"Thank you, Your Highness," replies Franzy, curtsying in spite of Allysteir's statement.

"Our Isla is right," Gryzelda confirms and crosses the few steps to my side to gather my hands. "It is a night of celebration and glorious frights. The spirits are restless for their King and Queen. As the Princess rightfully proclaimed: let us give them a night they will not soon forget."

The Queen's grace and poise in such a heavy gown shame me. My greatest adornment is my crown, but I've selected something closer to a bridal gown. Scarlet for this night, empire-waisted, and flowing from the bust to maintain the pregnancy illusion. The sheer, light fabric at the thighs and downward frees me to dance. Allysteir knows nothing will keep me from dancing.

Tonight, I will dance with Franzy. When we are alone, I'll explain. I'll say...goodbye. No, the worst thing I could do is say goodbye. Because if her heart breaks before my very eyes and I'm forced to watch, I'll lose my nerve. How can I tell her it's the only way? How can I explain the gods must have their blood, their Curse? The very thought of entering into the Curse turns my stomach to rot.

For now, I remain at Allysteir's side as the trumpets and Court criers announce our arrival. The crowd hushes, their conversations perishing. Once the curtains sweep aside to reveal the Court, I swallow hard, eyes widening from the glittering sight.

Masks. Hundreds of masks in all varieties and ensembles greet me from corpus rose ones, made popular by my Hollows-gifts, to Corpse King imitation ones to pumpkin heads with twisted, carven smiles to ghostly fabric tresses stitched together.

While the hundreds of attendees lower to their knees, apart from the other royals at the reserved table closer to the throne, I marvel at the thousands of pumpkins hollowed out for this singular evening. Candles in each one reveal carved corpse skull patterns glowing to memorialize the past Corpse King. Along with the rich harvest of gourds floating upon the River Cryth, they symbolize an age of prosperity to come thanks to the God of Death sated by...me.

Floating high within the Court's domed ceiling, the brightest fire gems in all the mines dance by bone magic, casting flaming prisms upon the River, the crowds, and even the tables laden with the finest Talahn-Feyal foods.

When Allysteir seats me on the throne, then extends a hand to the kneeling crowds from all over Talahn Feyal, my heart drops into my stomach upon his proclamation.

"People of Talahn-Feyal and royal visitors from Talahn-Feyhran: we welcome you to our most joyous of all nights. Two festivities in one: the Night of Masks and the Feast of Flesh. And in our greatest time of fertility and fruitfulness, we invite you to celebrate with us. And know your King is restored and the gods are sated due to the Tenth Bride of the Citadel of Bones of Nathyan Ghyeal, of all Talahn-Feyal: Isla Adayra Morganyach." He turns to me as applause booms to shake the walls of the Court and cause the spirits to quiver the River Cryth.

I shift my weight on my throne, uncomfortable at the pageantry on my account. Helpless against the urge, I find myself itching at my collarbone, at the mark I've rejected.

Can I possibly run from the gods?

Lining the dais are the elders, including Kanat in their center. Eyes rooted on the King, though I could swear one of his irises manages to move aside from the other and prey on my figure. Paranoia has me fidgeting until I turn my eyes in the other direction. To the royals. All sovereigns fix their eyes upon Allysteir, save for one: Narcyssa. Instead, she studies my every move, assessing. I clamp my hands in my lap, forcing myself to posture. I remain unmoved under her scrutiny. She offers a leering smile, but I lift my chin and turn my eyes to Allysteir who concludes his first speech of the night.

"Once the Feast of Flesh commences, I will make another significant announcement, but for now, my people, I bid you enjoy the revelries, to feast, to dance, and to celebrate with us!"

The music plays as soon as he sits upon the throne. I heave a sigh, grateful the speech is over for now until I flinch when the King assumes my hand. He cocks his head to the side, curious at my prickling. Forcing a smile, I maintain the ruse and swallow when he kisses my hand.

Thousands of spirits flutter through the crowd to join with the revelries. These are the harmless ones. Ancestral spirits of gaiety and grace to join their descendants. Tonight, Aryahn Kryach must be expending all his power to stem the tide of all the other spirits from entering the Underworld.

Whatever diversion the Queen has plotted to help me escape must be good. It must happen before Allysteir announces my "pregnancy". Because while he may be a blind fool, Kanat is not. And Aydon most certainly is not. They will call my bluff, and I'll truly have no hope of fleeing the Underworld.

The gods will rip right through the veil of worlds to take their flesh and blood. Kryach won't stop them. Not even my Nether-mark will help me then.

FORTY-EIGHT
THE NIGHT OF MASKS – PART II

ISLA

"Your rib cage bodice is quite becoming, my Corpus Queen," compliments Allysteir, spinning me outward, so my tattered gown ends crack the air.

I do my best not to press my body against his, always deviating into a teasing twirl or pivoting so my back sidles his chest. With any luck, he won't scent me too much to discover my treasonous act. Treason against him, against the gods. *Not* against myself.

"I thought it a worthy tribute to the past," I note as his hands come down on my hips to tug me back.

"Or the future," the King hums in my ear, lighting his lips on my neck.

When I wince, he sighs and loops his arms around my waist, settling them higher beneath my breasts where the rib cage bodice interferes. I blow soft relief but tense to his next words.

"We all have a part to play in the Curse, my dark rose. The Curse is the very breadth and being of Talahn-Feyal, of this whole world, knit into its fabric for centuries. We all may loathe it, but open war with the gods was no longer an option. And now..." His hands rove downward, but I twirl at the last second to face his mask, to capture his cheek in an able ruse while my breath hitches from the end of his statement, "...all I am is thankful. After five hundred years and a thousand brides, you have survived, you have saved me. No, I will never be worthy of you, my bride, but I hope you may accept your role in the Curse so we may live and not simply survive."

His words pierce my heart, and I am thankful...for the mask which hides the remorseful heat tingling my face. Whether or not he's right about how we all have a role to play in the Curse, I refuse to play it. Whether or not I can run from the gods, I must try. I respect Allysteir's desire for peace, for the existence beyond the ruinous corpse he carried for centuries—and all the deathly brides haunting him. He deserves more, more than I can give.

When he presses his lips to mine, warm and hungry, I shudder and almost tell him, almost ask him to come with me, to escape. But I'll never forget his words: *I mean to keep you with me here for all eternity.*

Allysteir's heart already followed Finleigh's beyond the ends of the earth. He won't follow me beyond the Underworld.

"If I may have the honor of dancing with her Royal Highness, Queen Isla Morganyach."

At first, the King wrinkles his nose in disgust at the Sythe Queen. But I light a hand on his arm and remind him, "It's a night of celebration and union, Allysteir."

He eyes Narcyssa, fingers digging into my waist through the rib cage bodice, but after I stare him down for a few seconds, Allysteir finally relents. His hand retreats from my waist. Narcyssa and I share a grin while Allysteir issues an Ith growl as a warning when she closes the distance between us.

"Be nice," I scold him and welcome Narcyssa's hand.

The Sythe Queen's alluring aroma from her High Goddess permeates my nostrils the moment she swings me closer to the Royal table as if to goad the other sovereigns.

The heat in my belly twirls when Narcyssa leans in, her breath of honeysuckle wine contrasting her rich and seductive gown of blood rubies. True blood since these gems were mined from the ichor valley of blood falls. I recognize them from some research in Master Ivory's library.

"From what I've learned, the former Corpse King is celebrating much tonight," mentions Narcyssa while tugging me closer, two fingers tapping in succession down my spine. "But from what I scent, you have far more to celebrate, don't you, lioness?"

I part my lips, wincing from her fingers journeying lower to cross my Nether-mark, which blazes with a lustful heat. When the Queen tips me back and pauses with her lips hovering above mine, I lean into the heat on my lower spine. I use it as a touchstone to thwart her, "It depends on what you are implying...Narcyssa."

She raises a brow as if stunned by my informal address, but considering her lioness title, however affectionate, one good turn deserves another. I shouldn't keep my answers so vague, but Narcyssa has aided me before, and her Goddess is the highest next to Kryach. Outside Talahn-Feyal, Narcyssa could prove to be an ally and not simply a curious party flirting with me from time to time.

"You are the Tenth Bride to survive the God of Death, but you have come out wholly unscathed, have you not? No claws clipped. No fangs ripped from their roots. I would state my compliments are in order, but we both know it was not solely your doing," she adds as if baiting me.

I screw my brows low. "Oh?" I call her bluff, wincing when she snaps me upward, brushing her lips across my cheek, lighter than an eyelash.

"Why, love of course. As we discussed at the Royal supper. Love as strong as Death." She gestures to Allysteir who lingers at the head of the sovereign table, drumming his fingers impatiently.

Grateful for the mask to veil my cheeks which pale when I know they should blush, I somehow lift my chin. "Of course. Love."

After one more twirl, Narcyssa cups my shoulder, her thumb nudging my neckline as if seeking. When her pupils expand, blacker than Nethertrenches, I don't shrink. I lean away. Her hold grows stronger.

"Why? Is there something else for which I should offer my compliments, little lioness?" She digs in her thumb. I swallow the lump in my throat. How could she know of the mark, much less how I carved it off?

Before Narcyssa may latch onto my vulnerability, and before Allysteir may charge from the Royal table, Franzy proves to be my rescuer. Except she doesn't ask for permission. I breathe a deep sigh when she harnesses my waist and drags me from the Sythe Queen, pressing her lips to my cheek and whispering in my ear, "My turn to save you for a chance, leyanyn. You were pale as a spirit."

I bind my arms around her neck and dip my forehead onto her shoulder. More shameful knots gather in my chest. Emotion wells in my throat.

"Why, Franzy?" I moan into her neck, end with a whisper, "Why?"

She stiffens, understanding I'm referring to the mines. But a Cryth River spirit billows around us, interrupting, laughing cold and airy, trying to join our dance. Franzy rolls her eyes and sweeps me away from the spirit, further from the Royal Table, further from the River, closer to the center of the Court. Most give us a wider berth, recognizing the Crown Princess and the Queen of the Underworld. A Queen for a short time longer.

"When did you lose faith in me, Isla?" murmurs Franzy, brow furrowing in confusion.

I open my mouth, but no words come out. Especially when she cups my cheek, fingers traipsing across several tiny skulls while she leans in to match her emerald eyes against my amethyst ones. Except hers seem far more royal. It's the first time I balk. Only Franzy has the power to bring me to my knees.

"Please, Isla. I know you wouldn't have stopped trying. The herb. But you stopped sharing with me. You stopped coming to our suite. And now..." her fingers are steady as she lifts my mask so she may behold my whole face. My blanched cheeks, the tears streaming from my eyes, my lower lip trembling. "You avoid me, but when I saw you earlier in the secondary hall, you looked like you were ready to spread wings and fly right out of the Underworld."

I bite my lower lip over a shameful huff, then wrench my eyes to hers because she deserves no less. "Franzy, you were right. We relate to the Underworld in different ways. But after tonight, I won't relate to it anymore."

As the minstrels lull their instruments into a slower tune and the spirits collect in pairs to mirror the romantic music, Franzy purses her lips and nods before tipping her brow to mine. "I am sorry, leyanyn. I understand why you stopped coming. I swear I never meant to drive you away. I had a very good reason for my reactions. But what I said to you on your wedding night is every bit as true tonight as it was then."

When Franzy cups my shoulders, her palms nudging the raw wound, I cringe, unable to help myself. Knitting her brows together, she tilts her head to the side before folding back the neckline. I suck a gasp through my nose, but it's smothered by Franzy's shriek. She hurries to right my neckline before pulling me close.

"Isla, leyanyn, please don't tell me you're..." she trails off, glances around at the dancers as if waiting for a lower god to pop up at any minute before seeking my eyes beyond my mask. I lick my lips, not answering because I don't need to. Franzy knows me enough to determine my plans.

"I could get you onto one of Fathyr's ships," she bargains, connecting the pieces. "He does frequent trade in the Bone Sea. We can still write to each other. We can—"

I touch my lips to hers, stopping her mouth. A common occurrence. Then, I embrace my bonnya sweet and assure her, "All the plans have been made, my Princess."

Franzy's eyes widen so much at something behind me, the whites free themselves of her irises. Amidst countless other shrieks, gasps, and similar gestures of stunned silence from the crowds, she gasps and motions, "Is *that* a part of your plans, Isla?"

When I turn to face the edge of the Court a few hundred yards away where the River Cryth winds outside the Citadel, I nearly scream with everyone else. Deja vu returns to me from the night Allysteir brought me to visit the herd, the bone horses, and how Ifrynna misted away. How the only creature who could threaten the Guardian of the Underworld is:

"The Sleeping Stallion," I murmur at the sight of the enormous black bone horse pawing the court floor, fracturing the tiles, the momentum shaking the River and sending dozens of spirits plunging through the waters to escape. Terror scourges my blood until my pulse hammers through my skin.

"Obviously, he's not sleeping anymore," whispers Franzy, humor unusual for her. She leans in, nails digging crescent moon indents into my flesh.

Head as high as the Court ceiling, the Stallion trains its predatory dark eyes on all the white-shocked partygoers, marking everyone for an early grave, just punishment for disturbing its territory. For in ancient times, the Underworld belonged to all spirits and twain travelers; the Stallion, a machination of the Highest God of Ifrynn, of hell, ruled. No doubt, it's why Kryach created Ifrynna and named her so to mock the Highest God.

When the Stallion jerks its head, shaking its mane as long as three tapestries stitched together, and snorts puffs of breath like a drove of ghosts, the Court erupts into chaos. Dozens of bodies knock into me in their attempt to escape the fatal threat. I squeeze Franzy's hand for dear life. And stumble when a new body barrels into me. But she raises me to my feet.

This can't be the diversion the Queen spoke of, can it? She would never harm Nathyan Ghyeal, would she? How could she awaken the Sleeping Stallion after centuries of rest?

Out of the corner of my eye, the Stallion rears up. Its massive body shudders before the creature crashes down, hooves smashing multiple revelers, shattering bones to powder. Pain racks my chest. I've only lived here for a year, a simple year, but if this loss of lives is on my account...

Just as the Stallion whips its muzzle, preparing to attack with the monstrous extension of a jagged claw, my heart jolts when Ifrynna appears. She strikes the Stallion from the side. The powerful momentum of her trinity jaws drives the Stallion toward the River. But the roused creature is strong, stronger than her. He recovers without falling and takes an offensive stance.

More bodies batter into me. More screams. More people scattering for any exits.

Franzy tugs me along, dragging me closer to the dais, but I can't help but gaze back at the tri-hound, terrified for my friend who has carried me so many times safely through the Underworld and back to the Citadel—my friend whom I gifted with three floral crowns, my friend who listened to my stories.

Once Allysteir arrives, his hand settling on my arm, I claw for his robes and plead, "Allysteir, please, help her!"

By now, Aydon has arrived at Franzy's side. Both Ith men lead us toward the dais while Ifrynna and the Stallion circle one another, assessing for weaknesses. More people make for the tunnels.

"No!" I scream, lurching when the Stallion smashes into Ifrynna, knocking her to the ground to split the Citadel floor. Allysteir propels me back, my protection first and foremost in his mind. No, our future child's. The *nonexistent* one.

Then, Gryzelda's hand lands on my shoulder, her other on Allysteir's arm. "I'll take her, son. Go. You and Aydon alone can protect the White Ladies."

At first, Allysteir hesitates, lips parting, eyes darting between me and Ifrynna. Aydon mimics him, but he steps forward while fingering the parietal skull bone at his chest, prepared to defend Nathyan Ghyeal with everything.

The Stallion rams Ifrynna into a pillar. It topples to the ground. Some of the ceiling fractures, tumbling with it. I squeeze my eyes shut from

Ifrynna yelping, then growling while the Stallion pursues her, unrelenting.

Understanding this is my one chance, I lean in, kiss Allysteir long and full on the mouth, and assure him, eyes wide and panicked, "If you go now with Aydon, I'll leave with your mother. I'll go where it's safe. But you have to be there for her, Allysteir. Or I swear I'll use whatever I have so *I* can help her." I deadpan, stabbing the nail in the coffin because it is my coffin in a way: our last farewell. Except no lullabies await me. "For our child, Ally," I lie right through my teeth and touch my stomach to drive my point home.

Allysteir pinches his eyes, pained, swallowing, his throat apple bobbing before he turns to Aydon, nods firmly, and urges me to Gryzelda. In the background, the Stallion rears up, fatal hooves charging. Ifrynna dodges out of the way at the last second and snaps her jaws, biting the Stallion's neck, drawing blood.

Confident when Allysteir and Aydon charge with their twin parietal skull bone magic, I fling off my mask and tear down one of the branched-off halls with Gryzelda and Franzy as fast as our feet can carry us. But halfway down one court hall, Franzy slows, her breaths rasping.

"Leyanyn?" I glance back and extend my hand to close over hers.

"Isla, there is no time," urges Gryzelda, her eyes fervent in the dim cavern torchlight which reflects her gems to cast prisms across her face. She lowers her voice, murmuring so only I may hear, "Nothing has gone according to plan. If you wish to leave, if you wish to escape your fate, escape the gods, we must leave now."

Winded, Franzy waves me onward. "Go, Isla, I'll be fine. I just need to catch my breath. I'll be right behind you."

I whimper, clutching onto her fingers tighter as if it's the last time I'll touch her. Dread rises to pierce my heart. If she doesn't come with me,

I fear I will never see her again.

Franzy smiles at me, squeezes my shoulder, thumbing the fresh wound from Kryach's former scar. "Everything is as it should be, Isla. I promise. We may not dance the night away and drink Sythe wine, but we did dance. And now, it's time for me to send you away." Tears shimmer in my eyes, veiling my vision. Raw agony preys on my throat, restricting my breath, anything to a mere whimper when she finishes, "Time for you to run. Run, Isla. Run!"

She pushes me. And I obey her. I run. For the first time, I run while Franzy stays. Convinced my heart is crumbling, I follow Gryzelda, racing down passageway after passageway until she leads me to a place I have not entered in a year. One year. A fateful night with my back pressed to the dead-end wall of the Skull Ruins.

This time, when Gryzelda leads me through the Ruins, past pillars and walls, and passages of fused skulls, with her never releasing my wrist, a cold apprehension lances my nerves. My Nether-mark awakes with icy claws.

We reach the familiar dead end within the hollow room. Gaps confess where skulls once were housed before the King's magic unleashed them. Like whole teeth knocked out of the wall of a mouth. Gryzelda feels along the wall, fingers grappling for something unknown to me.

I chew on my lower lip, wondering what is happening in the main Court, if Allysteir and Aydon have overcome the Stallion. Where is Franzy?

"Maybe we should—"

"I found it!" Gryzelda announces, injecting two fingers deep into the eye sockets of one skull.

I jerk from the wall shuddering, from the skulls rumbling, and the wall caving in to reveal a dark passage. As I near the passage with Gryzelda hurrying me along, I narrow my eyes. More ice. Hoarfrost. A maddening winter storm of a chill.

I take one step inside to discover a staircase *descending* not ascending.

Two deep green irises emerge from the darkness. My Nether-mark howls a firestorm at the base of my spine.

But I'm too late. Elder Kanat blows fresh bone powder into my eyes and chants a ritual. My knees weaken, my vision blurs, and my mind dizzies. I crumble into his arms.

FORTY-NINE
"WE WILL TAKE YOUR BLOOD, YOUR ESSENCE, YOUR SOUL."

ISLA

I wake to a stone table under my back.

When my eyes adjust to the torches around the underground room, I understand it's not simply a room. These are catacombs, and it's not a stone table: it's an altar.

I take a deep gust. Incense overpowers my nostrils, stinging their insides. But the ropes binding me sting more. Ropes woven over my nude form, barely covering my breasts and lower regions. A layer of bone powder coats my skin. Its musty scent invades the air. I scrunch my brow because my thorns could snap them within moments. I prepare to unleash my power until the low voice hums a trilling tune behind me.

Out of the corner of my eye, Kanat's robe sways from side to side as he sets about the task of placing different types of bones, all runed in Doom symbols, around my body. Symbols mirroring the ones on my flesh.

Roused, my Nether-mark scalds my spine's base, but it's not the mark concerning me most. It's the ones Kanat has painted on my skin. It's the scar where I clawed away Kryach's mark. Because I believed I could win my freedom. But Allysteir was right: I cannot run from the gods.

When I move to summon my corpus roses, my body strikes an invisible wall. My heart spasms in my chest. I can't so much as lift a finger. Dread massacres my stomach. Some invisible weight presses on my chest with a dark, infecting magic due to those symbols upon my skin along with the bone powder sealing them. Only a little movement granted from my eyes to my neck and face. Everything else is paralyzed.

My eyes bulge from the realization—from the trauma of my past of when the refters held me down as a child. All I want is to release the most primal of screams. Instead, I imagine water closing over my head, shrouding my body. I return to the River Cryth when the spirits dragged me deeper, so I may drown the scream. The water finds another outlet through my eyes.

Gryzelda's figure blocks my blurry vision, her proud crown adorning her head while mine has been placed between my thighs. I wince, understanding why: it's constructed of black crystal bearing the energy and essence of the past nine Queens who survived before me along with their bones spiked by diamonds. The rags I'd soaked with an Ith repellent and camouflaged perfume to catch the aftermath of blood are gone. Now, the slight crimson stream trickles to the crown.

While Kanat hums idly, progressing with his bones on the other side of my body, I swallow the burning in my throat, blink back tears, and face Gryzelda, voice cracking, "Why?"

The Queen leans in. Her fire gems remind me of carnal blood drops as if foreshadowing what will be spilled tonight. I flinch when she cups the side of my head and fingers my hair which fans out all around my head.

"I warned you, little bride. But you refused to listen. You cannot run from Kryach. You cannot run from the gods. All you can do is survive while they rape your soul. But you denied the gods the blood and flesh from your body. Now, they will take the blood they desire. You could have had your vengeance later."

I shake my head, wishing I could thrash, but the most I do is seethe, "He's your son, Gryzelda! Your *son*!"

The Queen lifts her chin, her eyes turning cold and hard as iron dagger hilts. "My son died the moment he accepted the Curse, and the God of Death invaded his body."

I clamp my mouth because it's useless to argue with Gryzelda. Her trauma scars define her far more than her survival. Perhaps she never truly survived. Those scars lodge in my chest. Somewhere, a part of her is lost—the strong woman who is missing and traveling within the veil between worlds; she's traded it for allying herself with the likes of Kanat. She traded it for her bones and jewels. Her well-meaning warnings became her poison along with her greatest default: vengeance. A poor aim at me when she could direct it at Kanat and exchange her revenge for justice.

My lower lip trembles as the elder stands behind my head and removes his cloak, his grin malevolent as he leers at me. "As inviting as your flesh may be..." he draws one finger across my cheek to the corner of my mouth. I cringe and snap my teeth at the elder as he finishes, "it only produced one interest for me. A sacrifice. Perhaps that will console you if you happen to survive. But I doubt it," he sniggers, leaning in to whisper his conclusion.

I launch a well-timed spittle, grinning when it finds its target in his left eye.

A low growl invades Kanat's throat, but it doesn't take him long to blink and recover. Or to dig his fingers into my jaw and each side of my mouth. Plugging my nose, he wrenches my mouth open and lowers a bottle for me to drink. My first instinct is to savor the familiar taste of the pomegranates until I realize they've been laced with black death roses: a subtle poison. Before I can retch the ritualistic liquid, Kanat slams his hand onto my mouth, preventing me, forcing me to swallow. Wiggling my head is the most battle I can manage while the silky, sweet tang warms my throat. I cringe, not missing the bitter aftertaste.

With one cast of bone powder and a few words, he snuffs all the catacomb torches until everything is black as a Bone Sea storm. The incense wreaks its wrath upon the room, encroaching onto my skin.

At first, I hear nothing, see nothing, smell nothing, feel nothing. Naked in the dark.

Until...the goddess appears in my vision. My mouth parts, but her gaze suffocates all my words—of her one whole eye like the dark side of the moon and her other: a blind, white phantom. Her black hair falls around me, casting the scent of smoke and blood and bone and the sweat of the hardest birthing labor as she leans in and cradles my head. Beneath her hand, I shudder and stare at the defiled part of her which reminds me of Allysteir in a rueful, ironic way.

"Your doom spoke to me," Morrygna utters in a smoky, dark voice. "How you would deny the gods the fruit of your flesh. Now, we will take your blood, your essence, your *soul*."

No tears come. Fear is a pointless emotion. Better to become a sword, even a sheathed one.

In the barest of gestures, Morrygna touches one finger to the blood between my thighs. She smears it across my forehead and seals her lips to mine. Whatever pain I felt when Allysteir bit me is infinitesimal compared to this. This isn't flesh and blood. This is goddess teeth gnawing on my soul strings, on the threads of my essence as she'd vowed. No armor, no thorns, no flowers, nothing can act as a shield. Before Morrigyna, my soul lies naked upon an invisible altar birthed from the runes upon my skin. There is no shame in my screams, or my tears. I writhe from the neck up and launch countless thorns from my pores all for Morrygna to destroy them with her smoke without ever parting from my lips.

For a fleeting moment, I wonder if this is what it would have felt like for Kryach to rape my soul.

Except Morrygna ends the kiss, smiles upon me, and concludes, "I took my fair share. Now, it's their turn."

One by one, the lower gods appear, claiming their soul threads. If I could arch my back, I would. Paralysis makes everything worse. To know I am powerless to respond naturally to the pain. Except for my thorns like feeble toothpick arrows against the gods.

All. Except. One.

By the time they are finished, thunderclouds riptide through my mind, dizzying my vision. I'm drowning in masses of shorn thorns. My adrenaline has plunged. All the gods depart with my soul strings. How much is left? One thread? The irony. I'd waited for Kryach to reap part of my soul, to leave a scar. He set me free only for all the gods beneath him to reap my soul.

So, why don't I feel scarred? Or damaged? Yes, I am weak from the ritual, from the aftermath of pain, but like the night Allysteir left me, I'm ready to grow. No, I'm ready to *feed*.

The paralysis fades because I can curl my toes again while the feeling returns to my fingers, tingling.

But the fertile green eyes hovering over me are unmistakable. "My kiss for last," Elder Kanat boasts, leaning in. His scheme all along. Now, I recognize his handiwork, how all the refters were practice for this moment. Dressing them as brides was his brand of mockery. "And when I kiss you, little bride, the gods will welcome my soul into Eyleanyn where I will reign alongside them for eternity."

"You're no god," I hiss, feeling my Nether-mark rousing an ember heat up my spine. "You're a spineless, little coward."

Elder Kanat chuckles, ignoring my taunt. I brace myself, tensing for the kiss, remembering the first time his lips met mine. But before Kanat's mouth lands, he chokes. I stare wide-eyed, curving my fingers more as blood spews from his mouth. Not as wide-eyed as him.

Until he drops, revealing the familiar figure gripping a dagger bloodied from Kanat's back. The parietal skull bone hangs at his chest.

"Aydon," I gasp, breathless, eyes casting low to the fallen elder. "The gods, they're gone. They..."

Instead of the brusque posture, pressed lips, and honed indigo eyes I expect, Aydon steps over Kanat's corpse, roams his gaze over me, and smiles. "There is one way to reclaim yourself, Bride of the Corpse King." When his hand brushes my belly, I cringe, leaning away as much as I can.

"Where is Allysteir?" I whip my head around, expecting the King to show at any time.

"Unconscious along with Ifrynna. Not to worry your pretty head, Isla. Our parietal skull bones united were more than able to defeat the Sleeping Stallion. I avenged Nathyan Ghyeal of Elder Kanat's treachery in awakening such a beast. As I told you, we bear the most responsibility of all nations, the greatest burdens. And I have surrendered everything to protect my country, my people. Allysteir always played the woeful victim as if he made the greatest sacrifice—"

"A rotting corpse for five hundred years!" I shriek, advocating for Allysteir's price, but Aydon growls low and chains my throat. I heave, lurching. My body hasn't broken free of the paralysis.

"Oh, how he rubbed it in my face every day, reminding me how he took the Curse for me, but he didn't have the guts to take the throne, to take the curse of carrying the kingdom every damn day. And yet, he still called himself King while I suffered as Crown Prince."

I let Aydon monologue because it's useless to debate him, to convince him of anything but his sick and twisted victimhood. Biding my time, I drown out him railing about *his* curse, how he was subjected to immortality alongside Allysteir, but every woman he fucked could never produce an heir. A fate solely for the Corpse King.

"You killed them," I whisper, my gut clenching as I remember the girls, the corpses Betha showed me, discarded like dolls in the Sea of Bones. I clench my eyes, remembering their bodies.

Aydon adjusts his robe and leers, waving his hand. "Oh, you must have stumbled upon my burial hole. Failures, every one. Blame Kryach if you wish. And help me take the war to the gods. You will get your revenge. Imagine an heir of the Underworld free of the Curse, free of the gods and their games. The first in all our world's history."

"And what? Be bound to you forever?"

Smirking, Aydon rubs his knuckles across my cheek, sweeping aside my hair. I wrinkle my nose while he concludes, "I was on the throne, Isla. You promised yourself to me. And now, you will fulfill your promise."

He thumbs the mark beneath my collarbone...Allysteir's mark while fingering the powerful bone at his chest. I inhale sharply, understanding he will overlap his brother's mark. And with his parietal skull bone, he may annihilate it.

No more words. Monologue over. I try to jerk, but my limbs are still too heavy. As Aydon opens his mouth to unleash his Ith teeth, my heart convulses. I convulse the moment his teeth approach.

"*May the one who loves me not*
Never have another thought," the new voice invades the catacombs with the cursing chant, echoing off the walls. She speaks in flawless, ancient Ithydeiran, but I recognize the words, understand their meaning—in more ways than one.

Tears flow down my cheeks.

Aydon turns, snarls, and raises his parietal skull bone to thwart her, but my rescuer lifts her bones, bones I know all too well, and continues, "*If his heart be ever dark,*
May hell claim with eternal mark."

Aydon shudders. He falters, hands shaking his parietal skull bone in the wake of the bone magic engulfing him. Jaw low, lips parted, I gaze at the Crown Prince as he falls to his knees. As he struggles for breath from the next incantation.

"*May the flesh rot from your bones*
As you surrender to your eternal home
May the blood boil in your veins
As you fade to nothing."

With a gurgle, Aydon crumbles to the ground. His body ruins to less than the refter corpses in the catacombs, becoming nothing more than ash, bone powder, and black blood.

Breathless, I turn to my liberator as she advances to me. I speak her name, "Franzy."

FIFTY
MY GLORIOUS REDOING

ISLA

"Franzy!" I gasp as she unbinds me after placing the skull and scapulae bones on the altar. "How did you find me?"

Franzy smiles, helps me to my feet, steadies me when I stumble, and hands me my fallen gown. "Well, I had a little help." She inclines her head to the passage behind us, the one leading to an ascending staircase where a familiar, spectral figure of eerie beauty appears. I can't help but smile at Betha, nod in gratitude.

As Betha drifts toward us, with her dress tatters flowing like white currents, I tug my gown onto my frame, then cup Franzy's shoulders, my limbs shaky. I hold back a whimper. "Leyanyn, you used bone magic. You—"

For the first time in our entire relationship, Franzy kisses me, stopping my mouth instead of the other way around. Too stunned to do anything except gulp breaths, I listen as her amber eyes sparkle, and she reveals, "I'm protected, Isla. In more ways than one." She tugs at her neckline to expose the flesh.

My hands fly to my mouth to stifle the shriek from the mark. Aryahn Kryach's skull wreathing with shades and blood fire.

Franzy grasps my hands and grins. "Yes, I ate the Isle fruit. Death has found...favor with me, Isla. I am *twice* protected." Her hands lower to her stomach, to the swell I never noticed was there until now.

My eyes shoot open wider than the Citadel doors. "Franzy!"

She smiles and cups my cheek. "Aydon was a bastard. It didn't take long for me to learn, but I played along and kept the truth from you because it was the only way, Isla."

I thread my brows low, wondering, "What do you mean?"

"I've been smuggling mine workers onto my father's ships. For the ones who want to say, I've taken small quantities of treasures from all over Nathyan Ghyeal, whether the Citadel, the mines, or the Unseen Section to pay them a fair wage."

"Franzy..." I cradle her face in my hands with a remorseful sob.

She kisses me again. "The morning you came to me after your honeymoon after I helped you fall asleep was the day I ate the fruit and took the mark. I pleaded with the God of Death to take the burden from you, leyanyn." My breath catches to her words. "Your pregnancy was your only protection against the gods. And when you stopped coming to me, I believed you'd resigned yourself. Perhaps it was wishful thinking. I should have known better. I should have known you would never stop until you'd taken your freedom, even if it meant challenging the gods themselves. I'm simply sorry I didn't come sooner."

When she lights her fingers on the skull and scapulae upon the altar, I ask with a fluttery feeling in my belly, "Whose bones were more powerful than the Crown Prince?"

Franzy smirks. "Why, the ones you won in the Bone Games, of course. The Scarlet Skathyk's!"

Brows soaring high, breath stalling, I embrace Franzy so tightly, my lungs feel ready to burst. "I was so wrong to underestimate you. Please, please forgive me, leyanyn."

"Always, Isla Bandye Adayra Morganyach."

"You have her forgiveness," interrupts Betha. "But not the gods, Bride of the Corpse King." Franzy and I turn to the ban-Sythe who roots her gray-mist eyes to inform me, "Doom's mark is upon you now. The gods will return until they strip your soul to nothingness. You have denied them the flesh and blood of a renewed Curse cycle."

I rub a rune on my flesh. They compete with the Nether-mark for fire and ice. Ironically, after nineteen years with the cursed brand on my spine, I can bear with these others.

"Can I run?" is my first question to Betha.

She shakes her head, her blue hair of faded woe falling over her face like deep shadows. "Before, you had a chance, little bride. But with those marks, they have taken a sliver of your soul. Now, they may find you at any time. And you have no protection."

I meet Franzy's eyes as concerned as mine, purse my lips, and turn to Betha. "How can I get rid of them? How can I reclaim my soul?"

Her eyes darken, gray and gravid as storm clouds promising doom. Betha raises two fingers. "One of two ways, Isla Morganyach. Give your body to the Curse to become its next vessel for the Corpse King..."

"Never," I seethe.

"The only other way is impossible for a mortal."

I huff, dropping my arms to the sides. "I cheated the Nether-Void as a child, can grow any type of plant, volunteered for Bride of the Corpse

King, have tasted the Isles, wooed the God of Death, carved his mark from my flesh, and survived Doom and the lower gods. I may be mortal, but by now, I have to believe in the impossible."

"Remember, little bride, I did warn you."

Without another word, Betha gathers me in her ghostly arms, colder than deep winter, and carries me through dark tunnels and endless passageways until she dives with me into the River Cryth.

I gasp too many bubbles from the initial shock. Deja vu rears inside me from this icy crypt closing all around me. Unlike last time, I don't battle the spirits. By now, they know me. I trust Betha. Ironic. Born of Morrygna of Doom, the ban-Sythe who became the agent of Death. But I trust the weeping wailing one.

As the spirits enclose my body, their forms like bitter ribbons wrapping me, I imagine what it would be like to be a current. To fade into the undertow. To disappear with dark water until all I become is...death.

The moment my spirit surrenders, the moment my body falls into the undertow is when the spirits haul me through the dark water. They carry me through the shadows of the fabric of the world. What I thought was cold in the River Cryth is nothing compared to passing through the veil into the spirit world. Infinitesimal. A tempest of frost and ice howls over me, numbing my body. My breath seizes, spasms in endless ghost puffs until I crash to my knees.

I catch myself, hands splaying on what feels like black marble, but it shifts like shadows to mix with the water droplets tumbling off my flesh. An undercurrent of power reverberates into my body, latching onto all the runes upon my skin.

At my back, countless spirits gather, whisper, chilling my flesh with their gasps and words. But once I lift my eyes, all the spirits' voices fade to nothingness.

The golden Gates of Eyleanyn.

The entrance to the Isles. To the home of the gods.

Already, the heat from the infinity fire of the Gates kindles my chest in a dire warning, contrasting the deathly cold at my back. And my side. To my right, Betha floats and hovers with a soft smile as if reminding me of my former words. Of the impossible. If I want to earn my freedom, it's on the other side of these Gates.

I don't look back.

With every fiber of my being quaking, my heart heavier than an anvil, and my teeth chattering, I stand, approach the Gates, and close my palm around them.

First, I cringe, recoiling from the pain searing my flesh from those Gates. I stare at my palm, at the infinity brand I know is eternal. Because I am mortal, I am forever marked by god-fire. The truth is sealed into my flesh, my blood, my heart. But tonight, I must be more.

Tonight, I will no longer be Isla—the farm girl from Cock Cross, the Bone Games victor, the wild girl who dove into the Cryth River, and the first tribute in centuries. Tonight, I will no longer be the Queen of the Underworld.

This will not be my undoing. I will not be reduced to mere violence. A scar of a soul. Nor will I become a vessel of the gods and their maddening games. Perhaps this is the truest choice I have ever made, my own gods-damned choice. My desire, my freedom, my glorious *redoing*!

I grow.

I grow corpus roses, black death roses, white Inker, scarlet heart, and a host of others. I grow vines to bind the gates so I may climb. In moments, the infinity fire eats my vines, splitting them. My right foot stumbles, my body colliding with the gates so the flames scorch a part of my gown but not my skin. All the runes on my flesh awaken, some with fire, some with ice. But I lean into my Nether-mark until it becomes my touchstone. My swirling, unbroken eternity knot: the *triskeyle* has shadowed me all my life.

Behind me, thousands of spirit voices ripple into my ears. My breathing is louder. My heartbeat thunders in my skull to suffocate all sounds. Nerves charged and crackling like lightning, I grow more and more vines to scale the Gates. This pain, this toil is nothing compared to the nightmare of becoming the Curse, of carrying a damned child. I press onward, growing and rebirthing. More vines for the infinity fire to split. More flowers for the flames to wither to fragrant embers. More thorns for the inferno to shatter.

The Gates smolder more of my gown until it hangs in loose tattered ribbons on my flesh with only the rib cage bodice shielding me. By the time I reached the pointed bars of the crest of the Gates, it feels like it's been hours. My muscles scream in agony, my throat aches from the windstorms I've inhaled. My hands and fingers throb and bleed. Enough sweat has dripped from me to form a well at the base of the Gates.

When I lift my head over the edge, dozens of eyes of vengeful conflagration greet me. The eyes of the lower gods. Still, I do the impossible, careless of anything save for the vines I bind around my hands three times. Once I get over these final bars, I will fly in a final taunt to the gods waiting for me. Spirit screams echo behind me as I raise one leg over the pointed bars, snagging a gown tatter. It catches fire and rips.

Tears like rivers blur my vision from the Gates' heat. My breath cleaves and heaves while my hair clings to my sweat-soaked skin to constrict my vision. But I haul my second leg over and dangle, holding on to the crest for dear...death. Eyes and mouth agape. The last of the vine-bindings on my hands wither and sever.

I let go.

I fall.

I soar through incense-laced wind and wait for my body to shatter upon the hard ground. Instead, I land on a raiment of shades, soft like a bed. All that remains to clothe me are a few dark gown shreds, the rib cage bodice, and these...shades whispering blood fire across my flesh.

Dazed, I thrust my head back to stare directly at the gods—breathless and quaking in the wake of their heated eyes, of their mouths open and hungering. They wear the skin of the stars. They drink the dew of constellations. And pure liquid sunshine. As if a dam bursts from their individual runes, a wave of ice unleashes in my being. Compared to them, I am a mortal husk, bleeding and shriveling in their god shadows.

But I have climbed their Gates.

I curl my bloodied fingers into the Isle soil. And smile. It feels like crumbs of dreams tingling my fingers. As the gods close in, I dig my fingers deeper into the soil, close my eyes, part my lips and sigh softly, waiting for them to reap more of my soul. What did I expect would happen? They will not be tricked or cheated. Betha was wrong. Only doom awaits me.

A multitude of claws descends toward my hair, my face, my skin, my body. They prepare to strip it clean.

Before they land, the shades surround me in a bone-chilling embrace, ever-swirling with the deepest and most powerful of blood-fire.

A phantom voice of deep twilight, a voice from my dreams, with the scent of gray dew and dead leaves, thunders into the god circle like a final, crashing storm, "Nobody touch her! No one fucking touch her!"

The gods hiss, seethe, and snarl, breaths like poisonous vapors drifting across my face. But they relent. Reluctantly, they inch away, though their eyes do not flee from my being. They part like ethereal waves before the familiar shade voice.

When he advances to me, every boot step like an ominous drumbeat, I understand he is no mere shade here. All the lower gods bow their heads before this High God. All except for Morrygna who stands proud and tall behind them.

Too slowly, as if he is turning time itself to lull, his being appears before me.

On my knees, I slowly lift my eyes. First, it's his black robe as long as a bridal train falling like deep dusk upon the ground. Next, it's his armor of infinity iron to mark him as the final authority none may war. Then, it's his skin, so dark and lustrous—a midwinter twilight sky bereft of stars. His eyes hold the stars, white as the dreams of the first stars upon the earth, the first spirits ever reaped.

"Ary..." I whisper. A great infraction when the lower gods sink into crouches, fuming and growling.

Kryach's eyes narrow upon mine for a fraction of a second before they turn to the Goddess of Doom. "Your signature in all this, Morrygna?" he challenges.

She smiles, her features far more macabre from the twisted leer. "It appears all our signatures are writ upon her, Aryahn. Except for yours."

He curls his upper lip, baring a sharpened canine in a menacing glower, but Death does not growl. He maintains a cool head and faces all the lower gods. As he does, the shades from his hand bind me closer, acting as a sheath for which I'm grateful.

"She has conquered the Gates of Eyleanyn," he dictates, voice of deep, authoritarian shadows. "Isla Bandye Morganyach has earned the right to a *request*. So..." he turns to me, stretches his arms to the sides, exaggerative and mocking, and inquires, "...what is your request?"

Gulping the knots in my throat, I dare to survey the gods, to look Aryahn Kryach in the eye, and respond, "I want my freedom and all these marks *gone*."

Aryahn Kryach sweeps back his cape. Shades curl against my body as he pronounces, "Morrygna?"

Stardust shimmering on her dark robe, the Goddess of Doom strides through the divided sea of lower gods, inclining the marred side of her face to me and her blind spirit eye. She raises one blotted hand from beneath her robe and proclaims, "The Trial."

FIFTY-ONE
THE SPIRIT ROSE

I S L A

Morrygna clothes me in a raiment of doom. Out of eyesight of the other gods, she'd guided me to a house nearest to the Gates reserved for god servants. Only her presence was necessary for the servants to flee. Isle magic shimmers at the edges of the lowly estate, but the shimmers bow to Morrygna's shadows. In a limbo-like waiting room, Morrygna helps me dress.

Despite how light the dark material is, it is heavier than ashes and mourning. Still, it's far better than my gown strips and mere rib cage bone bodice. Nor could I resist the offer from the Goddess of Doom. Her hands, though tender, feel like despair as they tie the gown strings at my back. The dress itself seems like strings as if she wove it from the strands of her very hair. Her breath drifts across my neck—deep and dark and cold as a winter storm.

"Thank you..." I say once she's finished.

Morrrygna's fingers pause, lighting on my hair. My breath hitches as they linger to stray into the strands. "I hadn't expected gratitude so soon."

I lift a brow and curve my neck to bend my eyes to hers, studying her phantom one. "But you expected it regardless?"

"After the Trial," the Goddess replies with another tangled smirk and trails a solitary finger across my cheek.

I shiver, pinching my eyes, scrutinizing Morrygna. Knowing better than to ask questions, I phrase them as statements, "You have seen my path."

"Mmm." the Goddess does not relinquish her finger as if memorizing my soft, whole skin and flesh as if she will trade places with me when the trial is over.

"You set it in motion..."

Morrygna curls her palm around my throat and grins: a malevolent labyrinth in a single gesture. "With a little help," she hints.

I bite down on my lower lip, discerning where the help came from, hoping I will get the opportunity to confirm should I pass this Trial. But for now, Morrygna has finished. Her last act is feathering her lips across mine. Nothing like the catacombs whatsoever. This kiss is a promise from the dark side of the moon as if she is gifting me with a silver tear for hope. As if the one who understands all fates and all demises may grant me such a thing as *hope*.

"Come, little bride. You have performed to the last pulchritudinous detail. And I am quite eager to watch you continue."

As Morrygna leads me out of the servant dwelling and to the location of this trial with Aryahn Kryach as the forerunner before all the gods, I can't help but wonder if the Goddess of Doom has acted as my true champion in all of this.

"It is called an oubliette," Aryahn Kryach explains the vast, fathomless, and hollow chasm before my eyes. "A place of forgetting."

The God of Death's indomitable force and shades are an eternal comfort compared to the monstrous cavity awaiting me. Ten thousand chills skitter up my spine. It seems as if ice needles probe the runes. A deep gray fog sheathes the ground, so I cannot even perceive its bottom. From the fog echo the screams and wails of hopeless lament. Of souls with no passion, no purpose, no…identity. I slam my eyes shut, wishing I could prevent my tears, but they tremble across my cheeks all the same. How can such a place exist in the realm of the gods?

"Yes, Isla…" Kryach whispers in my ear from behind. "The place of forgetting. While all lost souls may still have hope to find their way, the forgotten ones end up here."

Stomach so heavy, I imagine it must sink six feet into the ground, I turn my eyes to the moonlit snowdrifts of Kryach's eyes and plead, "And my trial?"

All the lower gods hiss and puff behind me. I wince from their damp salivating, of those poisonous fumes singing my back while the God of Death explains, "You must make it to the other side. To the domain of the Aether: the essence and birthplace of all the gods where only the Highest God and Goddess can tread. You must collect a spirit rose no god may pluck and return with it as proof of your presence where no mortal has ever nor can ever tread."

I turn to Kryach, meet his eyes, black as Nether-moths prophesying my destruction, my eradication, my *suicide*. His shades curl around the gown tresses, an echo of the past, but they do not seduce my skin as before. I dare to wander closer to the God of Death until our breaths mingle, until the lower gods snarl behind us, and even Morrygna tenses.

Defiant hands on my hips, I list the instructions in an outright mock, "Cross a boundless oubliette of a canyon, walk where no mortal can, and fetch a rose no god may pluck."

"If you fail, the lower gods will claim all your soul."

Turning to the lower gods, I embrace the roiling heat of their marks on my flesh and the one in my belly, thrust out my contemptuous chest, and proclaim, "Challenge accepted!"

Their grins are what I see last before Aryahn Kryach's shades pitch my body straight over the edge of the canyon. Their jeering laughter fades to my scream as I plunge miles in seconds. Through those layers of fog, I slam my eyes shut.

And wait for my bones to shatter on the black rocks below.

Thousands of shades cushion me inches from the ground. My breath rasps, quakes as they settle me until soil greets my fingers. Cold soil and black crystals humming with Nether-energy. My spinal mark hearkens to such energy. Fog spirals around me, fingering my gown edges, longing for my skin, my flesh, my blood, my bones, my...heart.

When I rise to nothing but an endless curtain of fog and hear the whispering voices inside it, I understand in the deepest fabric of my being, the forgotten souls *are* this fog. A squall of screams, wails, cries, and howls plunges into my ears. They plead for me to join them, to unite with them. Instead, I bullet into a run, my feet pounding across the black sands with crystal smithereens slicing my skin. My blood scent permeates the air which only drives the spirits to knit around me, to create more fog, and restrict my vision. Tears blister my eyes. I keep running.

"We are the *Nothing*, little bride. We are the *Forgotten*," their collective voices chant inside my ears, deafening them. "Forget with us. Forget everything until you are Nothing. In Nothing, there is peace."

I keep running, huffing deliberate and desperate gasps, wincing with every step. More blood sheds from my slashed feet. The fog clears too late for me to see the jagged rock about half my body's size. Crashing against it at running speed, it knocks the wind out of me. I shriek from the bruising my ribs have taken. I struggle for breath. Nearby, I hear a bubbling, peer over the edge of the rock, and clench my teeth around a shrill scream. The rock broke my fall but saved me from something worse. On the other side is a deep hole. No bigger than my body, but what is *inside* the hole causes my knees to give out. Tremors rack my body. I lean into the fog.

Liquid hellfire gurgles from the pit, prepared to swallow anything so unfortunate to cross its path. It singes my gown. Its heat cloys my face. Fathoms below the heat echo the voices of the damned, of the worst of humanity writhing and screaming from an infinity of punishment.

This isn't any canyon. It's the entrance to hell itself!

All I want is to turn around and climb out of this Void canyon. I'll beg and plead for Kryach's shades to return me to the land of the living. But with the fog shrouding me, with the god runes humming ice and flames all across my skin, with this endless chasm of Nothingness—dark and strange and somber and starless—I can't conjure an image or a thought of the living. Only the dead.

Windblown tatters of fog whirl into my mouth. They rush down my airway. They impregnate my lungs to transform my very breath.

I *breathe* Nothing.

I cannot run Not with the hellfire pits ready to swallow me. So, I haul myself to my feet and walk, grateful for the splintering pain, for the blood dripping from them. Am I even going in the right direction? How long have I been here? Minutes, seconds, and hours purl in an infinity cycle until I am certain time is meaningless.

The Nether-fog disrupts my ears with their aged chants. The cold dives into my canals, infecting my eardrums. "Listen to the Nothing. Hear the Nothing. No pain. No pleasure. No purpose. Be Nothing."

I *hear* Nothing.

Sight and touch and smell. Blood and heartbeat and mind and soul. With waterfalls of tears upon my cheeks and blood sluicing from my feet, I preach those truths to myself and claw at the fog. But the more I breathe the Nothing into my lungs, the more it suffocates everything until I am alone with my thoughts. I want to stumble and fall, curl myself into the lonely Void ground, and simply...*be*. My breath is strained, weak.

But I remember climbing the Isle Gates. Glance down at the puckered flesh of my palm. Pressing my determined lips into a tight grimace, I fortify all my muscles and break into a run, careless of the hellfire pits. I must get out of this canyon. Hellfire heat curls toward me. My bare foot strikes the edge of a hole, but I leap over it. Hellfire tickles my soles, burns the blood, but I land on the other side. More crystals split my skin. I wail, certain the bottoms of my feet are mere strips of flesh.

Like gauzy curtains, like bridal veils, the Nether-fog eclipses my vision until nothing exists but white blindness. White because darkness would be a gift. Darkness is velvet night, filled with secrets and lust and whispers. White is absent and hollow.

I *see* Nothing.

Smell and touch. Blood and bone. Heart and mind.

Don't stop. Never stop. The fog will use my weakness as a sword to draw my blood and pierce my heart. Wear my skin as armor. Kindle fire in my veins. Forge a rib cage of iron to protect my weakest and ficklest of muscles.

The Nether-fog caresses my back, hunting my spinal cord, injecting into my nerves, numbing them.

"No," I whimper when the pain of my feet dims, when it vanishes, when I touch myself but stroke, caress, thumb, pinch, squeeze, grip, perceive...nothing.

Because I *feel* Nothing.

My legs give out. I cannot walk. So, I crawl—or what I only conceive is crawling, knowing the black crystals must be shredding my palms, my knees.

Still, the Nether-fog doesn't stop hunting. It leaches into my skin to feed on my blood, on my veins, on my essence.

I *bleed* Nothing.

Waves of raw horror cause me to roll onto my back. I seize, I convulse from the knowledge of the Nether-fog invading the very recesses of my mind to rob me of all thought, of all memory.

I *remember* Nothing.

A parasite searching for what is truest and deepest, the fog Nether-fog tucks itself into the chambers of my heart, squeezing through them to feast upon the muscle. Upon my spirit. Splitting threads. Severing the cords one by one. Frazzled threads. Ragged threads. *Dead* threads.

I. Am. Nothin—

Isla...Bandye.

The whisper is feminine. Somehow, she has found a way through my mind unbeknownst to the Nothing.

Bandye.

She gifts me with the promise of something...familiar. She tickles my thoughts, the neural ties between them, the synapses. She nudges the name into my *memory*.

And I remember.

The Nether-fog retreats from my mind. It frees my thoughts. The chains of forgotten power break.

Bandye.

Something tingles, feather-light, upon my skin.

The Nether-fog abandons my nerves and flesh until I may stand again. And walk—through pain, through the lacerations on the soles of my feet. Blind, I walk, feeling along my way.

"*Bandye*," another feminine voice joins the first, but the name is blurry at first. Like hearing underwater. "**Bandye**!" A thousand feminine voices. I smile as the Nether-fog drifts from my ears, liberating my hearing.

When I choke and cough, spewing cold fog from my throat, I take a deep gust of air, inhaling air unburdened by the Nether-fog.

Finally, it gushes from my pores, disappears from my blood, from my essence, and from my sight. But the white does not retreat from my vision. Instead, it shifts until the source of the feminine voices greets me. Surrounding me by the hundreds, young women—garbed in bridal wear echoing the centuries of Talahn-Feyal—hover, chanting my middle name in unison. I know who they are!

"**Bandye!**"

A name from the Void itself.

But it's the one directly before me with her golden hair radiating upon her shoulders, her cunning midwinter eyes, and mischievous smile who captures my attention most. I smile back.

"Finleigh," I assume.

She kisses my cheek, lifts her chin in a subtle nod, and urges me, "Go, Bandye. We have the Nothing."

Strong as magic and mayhem and mania, I run again, beaming. This time, my footsteps barely brush the ground—my limbs light as dreams and airy wings. Behind me, the bridal host tidal wave dams the Forgotten spirits until the Nether-fog is but an afterthought. Free of sin, of nightmares, of death, with the promise of a crown and the radiance of the first dawn in my spirit, I run headlong until I arrive at the very end of this gorging chasm where a deep drop-off awaits me.

Before I may allow any uncertainty to creep into my heart, I lean into the lurch of my chest, relax all my muscles, close my eyes, and smile as I free-fall into Aether oblivion!

Inside the Aether, this essence of the gods where no mortal has trod, I float. Engulfed by the cosmic energy, I laugh because it feels like water, like existing inside a womb. This womb does not drown me but cradles my form in its heated embrace. I giggle effervescent bubbles to ripple like a symphony of spherical stars. I catch them as if they are fireflies. I hold their luminous warmth to glow between the cracks of my fingers before releasing them only to create more.

In no time, currents like prismatic butterflies drift across me, pulsating into my skin. I waste no time plunging into one of those currents to ride it. I whirl to dance with the rippling tide until I've forsaken my body and become heart and spirit and flames and fantasy. And the fabric of prayers and hope and dreams.

In and out of what seems like hours, I swim and play and blow more starry bubbles, content to merely exist in this birthplace with its energy currents.

He comes to me first.

And then *her*.

I could never conceive their names because they are timeless. But I know their identities in the deepest part of my soul. Their skin shines like diamonds dipped in hellfire and angel light. Eyes birthed from this womb of time no *mortal* can tread. And they are why.

Draped in the folds of the first darkness and blood fire, he sifts his hand into my hair, stroking the hellfire I inherited from him: the *Highest God of Hell*. Clothed in the raiment of angel wings and moonlight, she brushes my cheek, shedding the glitter of stars onto my skin: the *Highest Goddess of Heaven*.

The strongest and Highest hearts to mend the bridge between heaven and hell with the purity of unconditional love.

I am the fulfillment of their promise. *I* am their dream come true.

The Nether-mark, my eternity of a triskeyle, is their sign and seal.

Tears cascade down my cheeks. This feels like coming home. I reach for them with the feeble mortal arms they formed for me. They kiss my tears, and I memorize their fragrance. I linger between heaven and hell, sharing triune quintessence and the lifeblood of my true makers who carried me through the Nether-Void, created my mortal fabric and left me in Talahn-Feyal to grow—to protect me from all other gods.

I have grown. My glorious redoing. My rebirth.

"Where is the spirit rose?" I wonder in a whisper of starry bubbles when their arms loosen.

They smile at me. Their confession in a single gesture.

I am the spirit rose. I can never lose my essence. My greatest power is growth of spirit.

So, I grow again. A rose of pure, glowing silver as frost and silk in moonlight. Veins of pure flame networking through it. A center of black ebony. And golden filaments shooting from the bud. The scent of death and blood of hell but the after-aroma of celestial, honeyed nectar.

When I lift my head to show my creation to my true parents, they are gone. All of the Aether is gone.

Instead, poisonous vapors prey on my back. I've returned.

With a shimmering grin, I rise on an invisible and eternal throne, turn, and face all the lower gods, Morrygna, and Aryahn Kryach.

I present my spirit rose and proclaim in a voice like the first sunrise, "Trial complete!"

FIFTY-TWO

"REMOVE THE MASK, ARY. I WILL HAVE YOU WITHOUT ANY SECRET."

ISLA

"Thank you for the gown," I express to Morrygna after all the gods have departed. Including Aryahn Kryach. Pride expands my chest. By now, much of the gown ends have turned to dark scraps, but everything else is intact.

She smiles, and I swear her one whole eye glints with a flicker of starlight. Or perhaps silvery moonlight. Either way, I grin back at her.

"The gods won't stop hunting you," the Goddess of Doom warns me, smoky voice deepening as she pats the head of one of her hellwylves.

I shrug. "I look forward to it." But at the moment, I looked forward to something more. Heat clawed up my neck and dampened the space between my thighs at the sheer thought of what I wanted.

"You may return to your world now. To Nathyan Ghyeal."

I lick my lips, musing, and shake my head. "It's not my world. Not truly." Perhaps for a time.

Morrygna strides toward me. Incense-laced smoke curls around her, her hair like a dusky river draping both sides of her body to her waist. I meet her eyes as she circles me, follow them as she taps her chin, studying, assessing...judging. When she stands before me again and drops her arms while tilting her head, she inquires, "What do you want, Bandye?"

In my hands is my spirit flower. At first, I study it, finger a petal. Thorns sharp enough to spear. Without hesitation, I drag one thorn across my hand and hiss an inhale. Steadying myself through the pain, I clench my fist and wring out a trickle of blood drops into the center cup.

When I raise the flower to her, glancing at Morrygna, she blinks, swallows, then accepts my parting token, gripping the thorns. She deadpans. "Do you know why I am called the Weeping Goddess?"

I gift her a knowing grin. "Name the river Feyr Ayn-Asgaydh."

"Free One," approves Morrygna with a nod. "The irony. When you will leave and she will stay."

I shake my head, a heaviness settling in my limbs at her last statement, but I don't linger on it. "She is the true Queen. She has her freedom. And now, you will have yours."

Morrygna inhales the scent of my blood inside the spirit rose, nodding. "Gods are forbidden to shed human blood. Thank you, little bride. Where is your freedom tonight, Isla?"

"No bride." I bob my brows with an eager smile, the delicious heat spreading "A mistress."

"Then, allow me to escort you, little mistress."

Upon wings of smoke, Morrygna carries me over the great river of liquid fire. I thrill at the energy humming into my spirit. At the edge of the river is a monstrous staircase as high and steep as a cliff with a crest I can't detect. Endless shades drape it like ever-moving netting. But the Goddess of Doom sets me at the base of the staircase and reveals, "This is as far as I may go."

I take a deep breath and gaze up at the mountainous staircase, my mouth drying as if the river embers have coated my tongue.

"How much do you want him, spirit rose?"

I turn, angling my neck with a wry grin, and proclaim, "Enough."

Morrygna nods, twisted smirk creasing one side of her face, phantom eye glowing. Her last farewell. Her blessing and encouragement.

Without another word, I pick up my gown skirts and start climbing the staircase. At first, I take the steps two at a time, jumping, my limbs light as petals on air. The river's heat consumes the air. Ash kisses my strands. I don't get to the halfway mark before I slow, heaving for breath, my throat sore. Sweat pools down my back and the sides of my face. I rip at Doom's gown, tearing to my knees.

On each side of me, the shades approach, curling toward me, lascivious and wanting. He must know I'm here. That I'm coming...for him. For answers. For his promise.

Still, I press onward. One aching, painstaking step at a time. A kaleidoscope of butterflies flutters with burning wings in my chest as my breath heaves and cleaves. I set my jaw, steel my eyes, and climb. Stumble to my knees when I make it to the halfway mark, forcing myself to keep the end goal in sight. By now, hours have passed. My gown sticks to my sweat-ridden skin.

Not once does he show his face. Out of sheer spite, I crawl up the staircase, pushing and pulling myself up the steeper it gets. My mocking humor gets the better of me. "Look at me, big bad God of Death. I need a grand staircase the size of a damned cliff. Mwahahaha," I cackle in a deep, deprecatory tone. I swear a dark snigger ripples from the shades.

Seething, I gaze at the crest where an enormous skull gapes at me from beyond the shaded shroud. "Fine, you want to play games. I have my own." I stick out my tongue.

All my muscles harden like bone. More than ever, I grow. Black death roses and spirit roses unite to gift me a moving aisle on top of the staircase. An aisle of royalty. Of my divine right to enter his godly realm. I don't stop growing. Not even when I've arrived at the summit and pass through the towering mouth of the skull, smirking at the thought of it devouring me.

The shades follow.

I roll my eyes when the skull mouth opens to a rocky black pathway coiling over lava pits. On each side are jagged rocks and statues as tall as towers—all in the likeness of the God of Death.

"No way is your cock that large," I taunt one of the statues, crossing my arms.

The shades billow around me, nudging my back. My Nether-mark rears for the first time with a harsh slash of ice. Shaking my head in disbelief, I groan and break into a run. "I'm coming for you, Ary!"

The pathway rounds to a solid mass of obsidian-like stone with grandiose double doors of solid gold embedded inside the mass. My first thought is to use my vines, but when the shades bind my body in a chilled blanket, Déjà vu prompts the memory of my time in the library. I sigh because I've already done the hardest work to get here. All I must do now is...knock.

I rap a couple times, beaming when the doors thunder wide, opening to—

"More lava?" I shriek, lurching back. "Are you serious?"

I spin my head back and forth, marveling at the familiarity, recognizing this court: an eerie reflection of the Citadel of Bones Court. Except Aryahn Kryach's subjects are all spirits drifting by the hundreds toward me. Thousands of bride spirits collected through the ages ever since the birth of the Curse. Death maidens. And stewards. All existing to serve the God of Death.

Before any can so much as whisper across my figure, all drop and bow to me. Kneeling low to the floor. Incredulous, I knead my brow, battling a headache. "Enough games, Ary," I plead in a whisper.

At once, the shades hook me. I suck wind through my teeth as they launch me across the court within seconds, pillaging my air until my knees crash upon the dais.

The God of Death's robe brushes my cheek. Hands fanned out before me, I take a few deep breaths, steadying myself before I rise to face him, to gaze up at him since he's two heads taller.

I furrow my brows, lips pressed to a scowling seam because he wears a skull mask. So similar to Allysteir's, but I understand the Corpse King, all Corpse Kings have ultimately modeled their mask after Aryahn Kryach's…as well as the Underworld beneath Nathyan Ghyeal. Perhaps it was the God of Death all along who had formed such a place.

"Ary," I speak his name like a prayer. My name.

No armor here. This is his domain. His court. The City of Death. My fingers strain to touch his lustrous skin of starless night. To unleash his robe while he frees me of this ruined dress. His starry eyes gleam as they survey me, their spirit fullness mirroring mine.

"Why have you come, Bandye?"

I sigh, dropping my arms to my side, irritated by the name, by his indifference. Balling my hands into fists, I stiffen and demand, "Remove the mask, Ary. I will have you without any secret."

At first, the skull mask stares unblinking back at me. My heartbeat stammers inside my chest, and I lose all breath before he finally acquiesces and permits me to look upon his face. His full lips harden, strong jaw clenches, and deep-hooded eyes breed with shadows. Otherworldly, beautiful, deathly.

"You stopped calling me little wonder," I address him, daring to step closer.

"You come all this way to my court to address a name change?" His tone darkens.

I roll my eyes and set my hands on my hips. "When I was in the oubliette, you sent the brides to me. You sent Finleigh to me. Don't deny it."

He doesn't flinch. He doesn't move a muscle. "Why would I?"

I lift a brow. Tilt my head, curious. "Why?"

"I owed Doom a debt. Now, why have you come?" He bows his head until our brows nearly touch.

I want to scream in his deathly face, but I take the deepest breath ever, inhaling his scent of black death roses, of ancient incense, of the sweetest and deepest of dreams. I lift my head until our breaths flirt with one another. The right corner of my mouth teases in a mischievous grin. "I've come to collect *my* debt, Ary. You will make good on your word tonight. You said you would trade your soul harem for one night. One night with *me*." I raise my hand then, touch his chest. "In all my blood, flesh, and *spirit*."

Aryahn Kryach seizes my wrist, seizes my throat in an attempt—one I smell from a mile away. Oh, he's seriously not trying to mimic Allysteir? I almost laugh at his desperate attempt to chase me away. But despite the icy trigger and my Nether-mark howling hoarfrost into my spine, I do *not* run. I stare at him dead on, on the verge of laughter, of mania.

"Don't you understand, little wonder? You cannot join with me without repercussions. Death takes everything. I will feed upon you. I will take your soul!"

And I rise, I posture on an invisible queen's throne. No...more than a queen. A human queen could not have climbed the gates. Or entered the realm of Aether. Or completed the trial. Because I am so much more than a queen.

"Ary..." Through tears, I lift my trembling hand to his face, to nestle my palm against his cheek. I smile when he relents, when he loosens his grip on my throat while his lips part in awe. He surrenders his face to my nurturing palm. It feels like velvet night. Closing my eyes, I stand on my tiptoes, lean in, and finish, "You cannot take what is given."

Overwhelmed by the raw emotions inside me and his shadows and smoke stroking my flesh, I sigh and buckle. The God of Death catches me, hauls me into his arms in a honeymoon hold, and crashes his mouth to mine. Hungering for me, he tastes me, savors me. I shiver, I shudder, I tremble in the arms of my greatest fear and my greatest temptation, determined he will be my greatest pleasure. At least for tonight.

"Little wonder." Ary pauses from my mouth to thumb my tears, to suck them from the tips of his fingers. "If you desire all of me, I will have *all* of you."

Devious, I tap his chest I long to explore beneath his depthless robes and hint, "Perhaps my soul will poison you, Aryahn Kryach. After all, you have fallen under my spell. Desire, lust, love itself...they are the greatest poisons not even Death has an antidote for."

"I will drink all your poison, little wonder. I will luxuriate in the wellspring of your heart, your mind, and...your flesh." He lists everything human. But not my soul. Only my soul is not human.

Ary cups my chin, fingers digging in. "Are you certain you wish to risk a night of martyrdom?"

I squint, playful, tapping his cheek. "Is your opinion of yourself so low as a lover, Ary? I could teach you if you'd prefer."

He growls low, kisses me again. Deeper this time. Cocking his neck to change the angle and the depth and probing past my lips, he tastes me in a single flick of his tongue. Leaving me gasping for breath.

"All night long, I will drive my organ so deep into you, little wonder, you will scream my name loud enough for Nathyan Ghyeal beyond the Nether-Void to hear. Is that quite clear?"

I gulp, resist a whimper, and nod. "Clear."

"Good girl."

First, the Death maidens prepare me. I don't object at all. I luxuriate in the bath of golden starlight. Hollowed into the ground of Death's domain, the bath is surrounded by an oasis of pomegranate trees which the Death maidens feed me to sweeten my breath. This bath tingles my skin with glitter kisses of the stars. I remember its familiarity. The oil of the Isles they gifted me on my wedding day. Except this is far grander, more potent. It kindles the heat between my thighs, so when the Death maidens help me out of the bath, the moisture does not forsake my core.

With a soft smile, I stand in the shadow of the Isle fruit trees while they rouge my nipples with pomegranate nectar. Their deft fingers braid my hair in an intricate design to mimic a corpus rose. Last, they dress me in a gown worthy of a mistress, of a goddess of Death. A transparent raiment of pure starlight and crystalline silk. I grow a single black death rose to fix in my hair.

Now, I am ready for the God of Death's chambers.

Heart pounding, thundering out of my chest, I follow the maidens through a labyrinth of gardens. Gardens of thorns, of a multitude of flowers, but I recognize them all. And catch my breath, touching my throat in amazement. Because Aryahn Kryach memorized the flowers I formed on my wedding night when I reclaimed myself. And their chaotic patterns. Tears glisten in my eyes.

Now, the maidens seem slower than ever. They lead me to the gardens' end where a great tent awaits me. Where the God of Death awaits me. No hesitation. I shove past the maidens, blowing them a grateful kiss on my way, but I don't stop until I've sprung through the air and into his waiting arms.

He catches me, bewildered brows rising from my action, but I wind my arms around his neck and whisper in his ear, "One night, Ary. And your harem of souls."

He grins. Strong hands glide to my hips while I close my eyes and breathe deep. His cock throbs against my inner thigh, and I gasp, suddenly eating humble pie from my earlier commentary.

"I will have you here," responds Ary. "I will chase you in the gardens. I will lick isle fruit from your flesh. And I will have you on my throne, little wonder, and worship you like the goddess you are."

Effervescent with the starlit oil radiating upon my skin, I rake my nails into the god's neck and ask, "What are you waiting for?"

FIFTY-THREE
"DEATH KNOWS THE BEST MOMENT FOR EVERYTHING."

ISLA

Breathless, I rush through endless rows of the garden, plucking Isle-fruit and starry flowers as I go. Raising the blooms to my lips, I sip their seductive, honeyed nectar. By some miracle, the black death rose still nestles in my hair. Picking another fruit, which glows luminous as silver pools, I bite into it, sampling the flesh and juice which tastes like moonlight on warm water. Every fruit is intoxicating and unique.

My pulse quickens with the memory of Ary's voice. Why I shouldn't stop.

I'll give you a head start, little wonder. But I will chase you. Would you like to know what will happen when I catch you?

When his shadows loom closer, I flush and swallow a squeak. Abandoning the fruit, I trample it under my bare feet and rush forward again, careless of where I'm going. Ultimately, he will catch me. This is his domain, and I am merely a willing trespasser...for one night.

So, when I round the next garden corner, which clears to a great tree of corpus roses, thousands of crimson blooms resplendent and shining as a sunset, I can't help but pause to gush, to fawn. In the burst of a moment, his hands descend to my hips and tug me back.

"Caught you," he whispers in my ear, and I close my eyes and breathe his midnight spice and gray death.

"How did you—"

"It's true, I cannot grow," Ary purrs in my ear and nuzzles the side of my neck, thrilling my blood to pulse quicker. "But I can *imagine*. Once you set foot in my realm, approached my throne, and came to collect, those fantasies came true from your spirit."

I smirk and bite my lower lip, turning to eye him. "Imagine! The God of Death is a dreamer."

Ary lowers his brows, gaze smoldering as he leans in to confess, "And you are my greatest dream, little wonder. The fulfillment of a vow to shatter stars so you may dance within their dust."

"And a poet," I add with a grin as he takes my hand and guides me to the tree.

Vines sprout from my bare feet to tease his shades as much as we have teased each other through this bewildering chase. But when the God of Death pauses, turns his whole body to mine, and closes the distance between us, I understand the teasing is at an end. I shiver when he deadpans, my lower lip trembling as he bathes my golden figure in his towering dark shadow. Underneath the corpus tree with my naked feet atop a curtain of petals shining like rubies, Aryahn Kryach lowers his head to kiss me for the first time.

"Wait..."

At my whisper, he hovers but a breath from my lips. I'm so tempted to simply tilt my chin to seal everything. His shades tread on my figure, curling icy wisps across my cheeks.

"Second thoughts so soon, little wonder?" Ary inquires, lifting a brow with a simper, but I pick up on his clenched jaw, teeth gritting in impatience.

I touch my palm to his chest, squeezing my eyes to defy the heated starlight oil enamoring my skin and warming my center. "Before anything else, I need to know: why did you help Morrygna?"

"I stood by when the lower gods ravished her, branded her with infinity fire." He swallows hard and lowers his head. "Call it a debt, restitution, or opportunity. Regardless, through centuries, I'd never taken the opportunity to repay her. Until *you*, little wonder."

I smile, but my smile fades when I can't help but question, "Why? Why me? After centuries of brides?"

"Centuries far too late."

Reading the hidden meaning, the way his shoulders lower in remorse because it should never have taken him this long, I lick my lips and point out, "You sent Finleigh and the bride souls. You are willing to release them all. But the wedding morning, what you did to me..."

Ary clenches his fists, growing an abundance of shadows around him. His veins throb through his dark skin, and I understand he's battling a growl when he responds, "I was indeed the monster Allystier spoke of, the reaper of all fear, and the nightmare you came to defy. Just as I was the monster who stood by and agreed to the games of the lower gods, to the Curse. I reaped thousands of bride souls. Some faded to the oubliette e're forgotten." His voice darkens as he gazes to the left, shades shrouding his eyes with deeper remorse.

"But when *you* volunteered as bride tribute, when you accepted my mark and sought me beyond *his* mask, I believed, for the first time, someone could choose *me* over him. Over all the Corpse Kings past. But that morning..." he pauses to brush a chilled hand across my cheek. Raw emotion wells up inside my throat, and I choke and close my eyes, remembering. I lean into his hand as he continues, "My pride was my downfall. When you gave me access but taunted me, I resented your strength, how a human could challenge the God of Death. Other than Finleigh, you were the first bride to never fear me. But she resented me. You played with me. I believed I could break you. And you—"

"Did not break." I shake my head and open my eyes with a smile.

"Nor did you break with Allysteir. Hatred, anger, and most importantly...passion. Such passion led to your growth. All night long, I watched you grow, knowing you would never again seek me as you once did."

"But you changed!" I protest, the heat rising as I welcome my vision blurring from tears.

Ary shakes his head with a soft smile and weaves his hand into my hair. "No, Death does not change. But...it can grow. Consider yourself inspiration *and* motivation."

My breath catches. "Motivation for what?"

He deadpans, smile transforming into a grin. "Motivation to kneel on the border of the Aether and plead an audience with the Highest God and Goddess who created us all from its womb. To learn how a human could possess such strength and life and growth. Only to learn, you are not so human after all."

I part my lips, a breath of awe escaping. "Why didn't you tell me?"

He plucks the rose from my hair and taps my nose. "I cannot disobey the laws of the Highest Ones, my Isla. They have plans for you. And it did not include me revealing the identity of your divine soul."

I huff but purse my lips in understanding while the heat cloys at my insides. Just a little longer, I hold out. "So, what stopped your motivation?"

"The night you discovered the secret to Master Ivory and the mines. I recognized the fire in your eyes. I offered my soul harem, but it was too late. And when you screamed my name during your consummation, I knew then if there was any hope whatsoever, I needed…" he pinches the bridge of his long, aquiline nose before dropping his hand to the side to conclude, "to let you go."

I wrinkle my nose, lifting my chin. "You let go too much!"

He sighs and kneads his brow. "I believed you were happy with Allysteir. You were finally his true bride."

My laughter blows through my cheeks, and I almost double over. Above me, Ary rolls his eyes, and without another word, sweeps me into his arms. I inhale a sharp gasp. Heat swarms my cheeks with a fresh blush, but I somehow recover and coil my arms around his neck. "Allysteir is a lovesick boy. But I want—"

"A lovesick God of Death?" he teases while carrying me closer to the tree.

"I want *you*, Ary. For one night."

His mouth crashes against mine. Cold and bitter enough to cause me to shiver, but my warmth counteracts his. My blood ignites from his delirious mouth plundering mine. Ary's tongue traces my lips, delving inside to taste me deeper while his hands roam along my neck, my arms, the sides of my body. Gasping and moaning into his mouth, I lift my fingers to his robe, only for Ary to set me on the ground. Before I may protest or try to touch him again, the God of Death seizes my wrists and pins them above my head to the tree. I inhale deep, licking my swollen lips, but I thrust my hips, my only struggle beneath his dark force.

Hovering a hair's breadth above my mouth, Aryahn Kryach murmurs, "I warned you I would catch you, little wonder. You wooed me and taunted me for months." His eyes deadpan with mine as he grins with a secret revelry. "Now, it's my turn."

"Oh!" I gasp when he binds my wrists with his shades, tender but unbreaking. Tiny bolts of lightning tingle my spine, prickling the hairs on my body to static.

Heat rockets my core from Ary's words, the image of the God of Death wooing me, seducing me. Now, the shift on my body suffocates me. Flushed warmth spreads to my bosom. My nipples turn erect to strain against the thin shift.

When Ary reaches up to release my hair from its confining braids until all my waves waterfall down my shoulders, I arch my neck, leaning forward, lips starved for his. My rouged nipples peak through the transparent shift, and I know the God scents my arousal.

At first, he brushes the backs of his knuckles along my one arm. I clench my teeth and squeeze my eyes over tears, recognizing the taunt in his delay. He sniggers, but I don't open my eyes, surrendering myself to his control as he builds the tension, stroking me everywhere but where I truly desire. My arms, my neck, my hips, my feet, only lingering on my erogenous zones as light as his shades with those knuckles.

After what feels like eternity, it's too much. I twist my wrists against the chains and cry out, "For the love of Death, Ary!"

"*Yes*," he croons against my mouth, proud tongue invading to devour, swarming my head with dizzied heat. "Say it, little wonder. Say it now," he demands.

I moan and thrash again, leaning forward to capture his mouth. In vain when Ary steps back, beaming at me, assured of his control and my inevitable surrender. For all must surrender to Death.

So, I dip my head low, scrutinizing him under my lashes, eyes narrowing to sultry slits as I respond, "I, Isla Bandye, a human, love you, Aryahn Kryach, God of Death."

Ary steps forward and palms my heart. I whimper when the edge of his hand covers part of my breast, but he's not finished with me.

"Human flesh, human heart, human mind, but the soul of the Goddess of Life, of Rebirth, the Goddess of Spirit," he defines.

And I conclude, "Of Resurrection."

From neckline to my shins, he tears the shift in one long divide. I lurch from the action, my breasts thrusting out more.

Ary's deathly eyes sweep across my form, burning and searing until gooseflesh forms upon my skin. His gaze lingers on my breasts, then journeys to the soft plumpness of my belly, along the silvery thicket covering my mound, and finally my thighs. I flinch when his fingers stroke my mound first. I sigh and moan when he captures my mouth in his, tongue warring with mine. He devours my whimper when he cups my breasts. Slowly, he takes his time. He explores, fondles, palms admiring the flesh and pulling desire through my whole body until my center weeps from need. Without even knowing, I urge my hips toward him.

"So eager, my greedy, little goddess," he murmurs against my swollen mouth, tone playful, eyes glinting. "Tonight, I will teach you the art of patience, Bandye."

"Oh!" I gasp when Ary circles my nipples with his fingers, rubs his thumbs across them in slow brushes until I'm straining against his shades, choking back sobs. More heat, more tension builds inside me, and I embrace the need to unleash.

Ary chuckles, observing the scarlet heart rosebuds growing along my arms. "Patience, little wonder. I will bring you to full bloom."

I roll my eyes with a disbelieving huff from his poor humor, but Ary collars my neck, pressing my head to the tree. "Hmm...if you make such a gesture again, my sweet human goddess, I may need to do more than taunt you."

"How about this for a gesture?" I taunt him back, raising my sole middle finger into the air from my bound wrists.

A dark chuckle. Head bowing to my brow. "I will pay you back for that, Isla. But for now..."

I suck wind through my nose when he pinches my nipples, then dips his head to lick a trail down my throat and lower to close his mouth around one erect bud. Scarlet heart petals fall from their flower centers as he feeds on my left breast, tongue stabbing and circling the nipple to savor the pomegranate juice. My thighs part involuntarily, my sex starved for his fingers, his mouth, his...

All my thoughts muddle and my eyes roll to the back of my head when Ary rubs my nether lips with two fingers, parting the inner folds softer than a snowflake. The tension inside me grows, a fuse igniting, burning to its last thread.

"Already soaked for me?" Ary whispers in my ear, a solitary finger probing my entrance.

I slam my eyes shut and circle my hips, a cry catching in my throat. "Ary, I'm—I'm—"

And before it strikes, and I clench all my muscles in anticipation, the fuse is snuffed. As simple as a swift breath smothering a candle flame. He still caresses my sleek lips, fingers treading into the deep crease to circle the slit of an entrance, but somehow, the pleasure has spiraled from its peak.

"What?" My voice cracks when I protest and glance down to discover Ary's shades plunging deep into my center, forbidding my climax. "No..." I breathe in an exhale and tip my head back against the tree.

Ary brushes his lips across mine and hints, "Patience, little wonder. Death knows the best moment for everything."

FIFTY-FOUR
"LET IT BE MY TURN!"

ARY

I love the control she gives me.

Goddesses take far more than they receive, always owning their divine thrones. Our joining is far more to sate boredom. No passion. No lust. No...love.

While Isla's body belongs to her, she has chosen to gift it to me for one night. A body of heated flesh, a beating heart, and a spirit birthed of heaven and hell—beyond the womb of time itself, beyond the realm of Aether where the High God and Goddess originate.

Her gift is worth any price to me.

So, I bear with the torture and draw out her climax to worship her as I'd vowed. I lavish my attention on her breasts, nipping the aroused, little buds until they turn as red as the blood rubies of the Isles. I ravish Isla's plump, firm beauties until I've scrawled my death bites onto her flesh and injected my shadow essence into the imprints. Stroking my tongue along her fruitful belly while tangling my fingers in the fine silver hairs along her mound, I build the tension before finally parting her thighs even wider. She gives a little whimper when I hook my hands on their undersides and raise her until her legs rest on either side of my shoulders. I meet her eyes with a grin, then direct my shades to anchor her to the tree. They drape across her back to prevent the bark from chafing her skin. Then, I stare directly at her willing and whetted entrance. I study the mystery of her little, gasping sex. And smile, feeling a muscle throbbing in my cheek.

"Have you never—?" she wonders, and my eyes deadpan, the silver striking hers like lightning since she nearly shrinks from my predictive revelation.

In the deepest of voices, I reveal, "Never. I reaped their souls, Isla. Only Allysteir joined with them."

More tears glisten in her eyes and she freely unleashes a sob of emotion. I hear her heart thundering out of her chest. It's nearly enough for me to lose all control and drive myself into her now. But she deserves to be taken slow.

"So, I am the first?" she wonders in awe.

Cocking my head, I gaze at her vulva, fascinated. Goddesses have never allowed me to study, though they spend eternity doing so with one another. Now, I understand why. The feminine vessel is so intricate and complex, perfectly designed. A physical embodiment of the divine. Created for their pleasure and not for mine. I am simply honored to be a vessel to gift her pleasure as all men should be, especially when such a fleshy, warm inner chamber will suck my organ to the tautest delirium.

I love her glistening silver nether hair bowing to her dark, rosy lips. When I nudge her clitoris with one finger, and she bucks, I smirk to the side. "The first *human*, sweet wonder. Goddess forms are different. It's far more about energy. Not this sense of touch."

She holds her breath, presses her lips, then asks, "As good?"

Enjoying her sweet blushing cheeks, I smile and shake my head, roam my hand up to fondle her plump thigh before exploring her sex further.

"No. You are *better* and beyond any dream, *Spirit Rose*."

At first, her center reminds me of Isle-fruit cut open with its core exposed, aroma fragrant from the oil due to my Death maidyans. It's smokier, richer. But when I part her inner and outer folds and probe her opening with my tongue to lap at her juices, I taste musk with a hint of sweetness. I stroke my tongue along those fleshy lips to taste the spice of the Isle-fruits she's consumed along with the starlight oil. Isla's whole body shudders. She twists her hips, desperate for more.

Not the best moment yet.

I plunge one finger inside her, feel her vaginal muscles thrust and clench around me. Rising, I kiss her mouth, opening her lips to flick her tongue, so she may taste her sweet and spicy musk. Devouring her gasps and sighs of emotion, I bury another finger inside her and another. When she moans, I reap the pleasurable tone and memorize its sound, knowing I may relive it at any time as I have captured this night to relive for eternity.

Death never forgets.

Her hips ride up and down, and as I part from her lips, my little wonder whispers a mournful plea, "Ary..."

I kiss her brow and nod. "This is the moment."

She cries when I lower my head and bury my face inside her gasping sex. She writhes when I lift the clitoral hood, lick at her pearl of the divine, and stab it with my tongue, circling it until every last muscle constricts to her erupting climax. My shades surge to mirror her pleasure until her euphoria reaches its ultimate peak. With sweat pooling down the sides of her face to gift her an otherworldly glow, Isla throws her head back and screams. My eyes never leave hers even as I lick her to the fullness of her ecstasy, assured she is the most beautiful and transcendent creature to ever grace the realms of Death.

She comes with tremors rippling through her exquisite flesh. Her sex bursts with a sticky, feminine liquid I've never once experienced from a goddess. They baptize my mouth and cheeks as shades radiate through my god form in pride. Careless of the fluids, I don't stop my tongue's pursuit. Despite how Isla squirms and thrashes her hips through her tormented cries, she comes again and again, dripping all over me and down her thighs.

Breath cleaving and heaving with limbs quivering in the aftermath, Isla drops her head onto my shoulder. I release her wrists from the shade bonds. Her legs, limp from pleasure, slide down the sides of my robe, but I hook them over my hips to rest, fingers lingering on her sweet and buxom backside.

I tilt my head toward her and ask, "How was that for the best moment?"

Winded and breathless, Isla responds, voice muffled into my robe, "Wondrous, Ary. It was wondrous."

"The next moment is coming."

Isla looks up, eyes wide as though I caught her in the midst of the hunt. In a way, it's true. The moment I bury myself inside her, those royal eyes glaze over. Her neck arches. Her mouth parts. I capture her cries and slam my fist against the tree from the shock of her sleek sex enclosing me. Oh, gods, she is raw and warm and wild. So damn tight as my deathly member stretches all her luxurious flesh. And yet, she does not cry from my reaping. Instead, she clasps herself around me, her muscles clenching around me so much, I must lower my head to her shoulder, overwhelmed by her passion.

She's so fucking wet and tight, I want to bury myself inside her magical sex for eternity. And between the times of taking her hard and long, I'll bow before her to drink from her sweet fountain forever. I'd keep her flushed, aroused, heated, and wet for me always, for Isla Bandye would be worth more than thousands of my harems throughout all time.

Desperate, her hips circle and stab forward, her channel accepting and receiving me even deeper until I'm She pleads for me to move. She pleads for more! Goddesses never want more. They already have enough. They have everything.

So, I raise my head, brandish my eyes against hers, and lower my hands to grip her hips. In a brutal moment of Death meeting Life, I ram into her hard. The momentum causes countless flowers to waterfall from the tree. They shed onto her ethereal waves. My shades brew, growing to plunge inside her, propelling my cock inside her even deeper. Isla clenches, eyes slamming shut.

"Bandye..." I whisper her name in a concerned prayer.

"Do. Not. Stop," she hisses, shrill without opening her eyes.

I don't. Her thighs tighten around my hips. I love how her pulse thunders, her blood like thousands of crimson butterflies thrumming through those beautiful veins. I forge my way into her warmest depths, into her innermost chamber while her vulva seals around me. I'd live inside the eternity of this moment.

Without warning, I sink my teeth into her flesh beneath her collarbone, savoring her scream of pain as it ebbs into a moan of pleasure once I stroke my tongue to taste her blood. No barrier of a Corpse King between us, I luxuriate in the quintessence of the strongest heart and spirit locked within a shell of human flesh and blood. A shell I know she will shed one day and trade for her rightful goddess form—the most glorious goddess of all time.

"Feel me in your soul, little spirit goddess?" I tilt my neck to stare up at her, licking my tongue where her blood stains my lips.

Isla rocks against me in a silent plea. Her sweet passion undoes me. She buries her face in my neck, kissing the veins abounding with my spirit essence. While her lips rub along my neck, I lap at her sweet blood and flesh on the other side. In the second she bites my flesh, I growl and dig my teeth in her more.

Death and Life trade bites and scars and spirit. She licks at the black life force. No blood. For gods have no blood. Her desire drives me onward. I grind my hips against her. And feel those tight muscles clench. A sob rises in her throat, but she drinks at my deathly soul, taking me inside her in more ways than one.

In a moment of pause, she lifts her head to mine. "Ary."

I lose myself in her royal eyes, an echo of her goddess-hood. All her body quakes while my organ throbs for her.

She touches my chest, and I peer down where her hand seeks my heart beyond my robes. Smiling, I tip my brow to hers and breathe a secret across her face, "Gods have no heart, Isla. It's why we will always desire *blood*."

Ever so slowly, Isla arches her neck, presses her lips to my ear, and whispers her command, "Take mine tonight, Ary."

Her words drive my teeth into her flesh. I devour as much as I dare. Isle-fire. And the first dream of the heavens.

Isla shrieks, but I drive my member into her again and again. I fill her. I seal her closed while my shades nourish her, granting her icy ecstasy beyond the burning pain. I don't once look away from the color scalding her cheeks. Or her glassy eyes as the heated tension grows.

"Yes, Bandye. Ride me. Take your pleasure, sweet spirit."

Isla tightens her legs around my hips, rocks harder so my member rubs those inner walls. I groan deeply from the lust. I love the sight of her swollen lips mirroring the sweet, puckered pomegranate seeds of her nipples as her breasts jerk from her movements. Palming one, I lower my head to the other to suckle, to close my teeth around the one bud and pull tight to nick and take her blood.

Isla whimpers. But her insides, her entire body flutters, pulses, and quakes around me. Those legs tighten.

Before she may achieve rapture, I pull out.

"No!" she screams and locks eyes with mine, lips pressed to an incensed seam.

I stiffen. She glances *down* at me, eyes flying open vast from the sight of my thick and engorged cock. I tip it to her entrance in a gesture of what I want. And when she rakes her nails along my chest and pushes her hips forward in a moment of total surrender to receive me, I slide my crown along her folds. Beaming, I kiss her, dragging out the slow torment, consuming all her moans of lust.

The sound of her heartbeat, the taste of her blood, the touch of her flesh will forever be ingrained within me. Sealed like a burning goddess mark

With my mouth crushed to hers, I open my eyes to hers. Growling hungrily and darkly, I cover her breasts with both hands, pinching her nipples to fill her with the same needy hunger. As I bring my chest down upon hers to feel the pounding of her heartbeat, I stop edging. She rolls her hips.

"I'm going to show you what being fucked by the God of Death truly means, Isla Bandye," I whisper against her parted lips. "I'm going to reap all of you. Your soul is strong enough to take my death, little spirit goddess. Take it now, Isla."

I unleash the force of my Death member deep into her. Seizing the back of her neck, I crash my mouth to hers and capture her scream. I drive myself into her, thrusting hardest and deepest. She comes, burrowing her nails into my robe, trembling and shuddering from her feminine waves of pleasure. With the aroma of her arousal drifting all around me, stoking my desire, I fucking snap. I roar my release and spill my Death-seed into her in cold, icy bursts.

We fall onto the soft bed of flower petals. I gather her close, touching my brow to hers, smiling from how she gulps for breath while my god lungs never want for air. Her heartbeat pounds against her chest, thunderous in the wake of her delirium.

And I will forever love the way she turns her whole body to mine, grips my robe, and begs, "Please, Ary, let it be my turn!"

FIFTY-FIVE
"WHERE ARE YOU GOING, ISLA?"

ISLA

I circle him, wearing a playful smile.

Aryahn Kryach turns in my direction, centering his eyes on mine. The heat in my flesh grows along with more rosebuds on my arms as I survey him. By the time I finish my circle, I've closed all distance between us so my bare breasts brush his outer robes. His brows draw low, smile mischievous to mirror mine.

First, I touch his strong brow, then his statuesque cheekbones, thrilling when he closes his eyes and inhales. I smile from the muscles throbbing in his cheeks, his jaw clenching from the effort it requires not to touch me. Next, I touch his lips—full and soft as silk and shadows. I trace them with one finger, flinching when he opens his mouth to suck the skin. Sighing, I withdraw my finger, and before he can blink, I thrust the robe off his shoulders, shaking my head in disbelief when I discover another. And another. And another.

"Hells balls!" I snap, thorns growing from my fingertips.

Ary throws his head back and laughs. I thread my brows and hold my chin high, pulse rushing blood to my ears.

"Forgive me, little wonder," he chuckles and reveals, "Consider it my little Night of Masks trick. For the God of Death wears shades without number. All you need do, Isla, is *ask*."

I cross my arms over my chest, a little perturbed, but then, I sigh, tap my foot, and meet his eyes. "Will you—"

He shakes his head, simpering. "Not me. The shades."

I shake my head in disbelief, huffing before eyeing the shaded robes swelling all over his form. After studying them for a few moments, I find the perfect method to request, "Please let me see him?" Not quite a question or a command.

"Spoken like a true goddess," declares Ary, pride in his voice as he stretches his hands to the sides.

Awed, I part my lips, stepping back and hugging myself. Countless shades branch off into thin whorls to curl from his body. They travel to mine, transforming to thin, twirling bracelets to tingle my skin with chilled goose flesh. In midair, Ary hovers, eyes closed as more shades forsake him, flirting with my bare skin. As the shades billow wind into my hair, I fling strands aside, holding them in place, so I may rivet my eyes upon Ary's form.

At last, his everlasting shades surrender.

He descends to the earth, the naked soles of his feet disturbing the tree's petals while I gaze at him, eyes not knowing what to take in first. Breathless, with tears shimmering my vision from the shaded wind, I approach Ary, curving my trembling fingers to his godlike form.

The High God tilts his head, lips parting as I touch his snowfall-soft skin. If snow is black as midnight. Blood-fire whirls all over his body like scarlet ink, and I lick my lips, remembering the taste of him: of shadows and nightmares, of black death roses and the sweet peace of surrender, of transforming to a current of cold, dark water. His stalwart chest is strong as a dark citadel, his arms like mighty rods of obsidian. I station my hands upon his hips, lower myself, beaming when he inhales sharply, dilating his pupils.

Despite how I am a goddess, despite how he has not requested this, I appreciate this newfound power. This understanding: I am the *first* to ever kneel before the God of Death with utter desire—not by force.

"Little wonder..." he tips his head back and closes his eyes as I stroke his legs, beginning with his feet. I caress his muscular legs and thighs hard as black diamonded pillars.

My throat grows thick, mouth watering as my aching fingers capture his already swollen and turgid dark member.

"Isla!" He balls his hands into fists, pounding them against the tree behind him, He quakes, writhing with blood fire.

All my nerve endings flutter as if butterfly antennae tickle them. Warmth growing between my thighs until something oozes from my sex. Just as he lowers his head to open his eyes, I fold my mouth around the hard tip of him, his wide, silken crown. All my muscles soften, so I may take him deeper.

"Fucking goddess!" he growls, thrusting his hands into my hair. I grin around him, permitting the desperate touch. "*Spirit!*" he roars.

The moment my throat contracts around his thick member, Ary wrenches himself from my mouth, unable to bear with it. Instead, he folds his powerful arms around my body and engulfs me within a whirlwind of his shades. As he carries me, I press my cheek into his shoulder. I lean into the warm energy of his blood-fire ink before cold iron greets my rump. Or what feels like iron.

Once the shades clear, I understand where we are. I gasp from the wide berth of the God of Death's throne around me and under me. Alone, the width of the seat spans three of me. He has set me upon his throne. A position of the highest honor next to the thrones of Heaven and Hell themselves.

Formed of an otherworldly substance of hundreds of skulls and great wings soaring far above my head, the throne is the perfect embodiment of the God of Death. On each side is an enormous sickle—at least five times my height. All the hairs prickle on the back of my neck, and a bone-deep chill spreads through me when I realize those sickles are for dispensing justice to the souls. These souls gather around Aryahn Kryach's Court.

But tonight is not for justice.

I shiver when Ary turns to his Court and commands in a voice to rival time itself, "Bow to the Mistress of the God of Death: the Goddess of Souls!"

Thousands of shimmering souls fall to their knees, bowing before my nude form seated upon the throne. Trembling, I hold in a breath, skin flushing from the public proclamation. My heartbeat roars in my ears from so many eyes upon me—for I am arrayed in nothing but my human-born goddess flesh glowing from starry oil.

And then, Ary drops to his knees before me and spreads my thighs wide.

"Oh, gods!" I gasp and arch my neck, head falling back but without hitting the throne's backing. No, I cannot even spread my arms wide enough to grip each armrest. Instead, I stay on the edge of the great throne seat. I dig my nails into the skull heads beneath me. And breath gasps as Ary worships me upon the throne as he'd vowed.

With a host of twinkling soul eyes bearing witness, the God of Death licks my swollen pubic lips, tongue delving into my inner chamber before swiping up to my distended clitoris. I gulp, sucking in deep breaths. My chest heaves. A cry catches in my throat as my fluids discharge while I shudder from the pleasure rocketing through me. Before I can so much as nudge my hips, Ary's tongue flicks my enlarged nodule, the throbbing, rosy nub still thrumming and burning like a tiny, flaming heart. And my sex is the center of a flower prepared to burst its nectar.

I grip the sides of his neck. My nails rake his flesh as he cocks his head to change the angle and circles around and around, drawing a deep groan from within my throat. The bliss flourishes, so intense, I grow a multitude of wildflowers from my chest, my arms, my lower legs. They clench with the heightening pleasure. The blossoms soar into the air, climbing and climbing to dance all over the Court of Souls, poised on the edge of my rapture.

Just before I reach the edge, Ary rises.

I whimper from the loss of his mouth, his ravenous tongue. Legs too weak, I am powerless to do anything when the God of Death plucks me from the throne by my hips and seats himself upon its powerful base. He spreads my thighs until they are curved on each side of him. I gasp, blushing and burning in understanding of what is coming. That magisterial and mighty member like a great reaper entity in and of itself poises its crown at the heat of my sex. For a span of a moment, Ary brushes his knuckles across my cheek. I shiver, lick my lips, arch my spine, and tip my waves back.

Ary growls, draws my chin, my eyes back to his. As soon as they land, he brings me down, impaling me on that cock of almighty Death!

"Oh, Kryach!" I scream, slamming my eyes shut from the pressure of his shaft like an iron scepter penetrating me. "Oh hell!"

"And heaven," Ary whispers in my ear, arms surrounding my back, mouth lowering to capture my breast.

"Death!" I whisper, and then he grips my hips and raises me until he withdraws fully. I whimper in a fleeting moment of fear right before he spears me again, ripping me open. And I explode. A rip-roaring orgasm tears through my body. I ride him. I raise my voice, "Death!"

"Good little spirit. Ride my damned Death-hood. Unravel yourself on my cock, sweet Isla."

Elated heat spikes in my blood as he thrusts deep inside me. I churn my hips, desiring friction, and lean into him more so he may suckle my erect nipple, teeth closing around to tug on the rouged bud.

All the souls transform to wild blurred starlight as Ary pounds me upon his throne until my face turns scarlet. Shades gather around us, bowing to us to mirror the host gazing in stunned silence as we spiral closer to hellfire and heaven's light.

Ary raises his mouth to kiss my throat up to my lips. My mouth embraces his as he rocks me up and down, stabbing the secret spot within me again and again until my head dizzies from all the climaxes ripping through me. Moaning into his mouth of spice and my nether musk, I twist my hips to match his movements. I writhe in desperation as he hammers me hardest and deepest, striking and piercing me to the core. Just as he spills his Death seed into me, Ary reaches down to clasp my breast with one hand and to rub my pleasure knot with his other.

We fall over the edge together. Into shades and stardust. Into goddess light and god darkness. Into Death and Spirit.

Lightning and comets of ecstasy explode up my spine. Thorny vines

shoot from my heart, binding around his entire form. They pierce him. I bleed his liquid fire. I reap his essence. I suck it down. I draw his Death into my spirit as his shades wrap all around me. He reaps parts of my flesh and blood. I reap parts of his High God soul,
We tremble in the aftermath. Gasping for sweet air.

And when Ary pulls out of me, he chuckles, peering at my sex. I thread my brows low and gaze down with him, I giggle at the sprig of spirit roses sprouting from my vulva. Drops of blood speckle their insides.

Ary plucks the sprig, raises it to his nose, and scents the blooms, flicking his tongue across one to taste the blood. "I believe I will keep this. A memento as it were."

I nod and drop my head onto his shoulder, nearly swooning.

Chortling deep, Ary sweeps me into a honeymoon hold and declares against my mouth, "Come, little wonder. I will carry you to my chamber where you will rest. But only for a short time before I feast upon your sex like the fruitful banquet it is."

"Ary?" I murmur in question as he traces idle circles along my back.

"Hmm?" the God of Death dips his head to me. Millions of tiny tingles erupt all over my skin from our lovemaking. I've lost count, and yet, my sex seems starved for him, for his tongue, for his Death shaft still hard and draped across my side.

Pressed against his naked body from where we lie on his sumptuous bed, I lift my head, light my lips on his chin, and wonder, "All the bride souls are different here. They aren't...unhappy. They do your bidding. You even granted a boon to Allysteir's grandmother. So, why is Gryzelda so different?"

His sigh is heavy and deep like a dark cloak folding around me. As Ary strokes my hair, he murmurs, "It was not my intention to reap only a fraction of her soul. Gryzelda was the most hostile to me and even more to Thayne. Her path was carved for her, set in stone by her misguided parents. On her wedding night, she jumped into the River Cryth, crossed the portal, and sought me out, believing she could convince me to spare her soul. But she was doomed the moment she jumped in."

I trail my lips along his dark chest, already suspecting. "She touched the Gates?"

He nods, rubbing a thumb down my spine. "Regardless, if a mortal crosses into the spirit world, they are never the same. A certain *darkness* takes hold of the mind. I granted her a choice. I was willing to reap her soul immediately, and she could rest with her ancestors." He pauses, tilting his head down. And I peer up to meet his silver chamber eyes. As I purse my lips, he kisses my brow and reveals, "I warned her that her mind would never be the same if she returned to Talahn-Feyal. But I did make her aware she would survive her wedding night. And she was determined to go back."

I shift in his arms, nudge my hips toward him. "You didn't reap a part of her soul?"

He shakes his head and cups the back of my neck above my Nethermark. "I reap all or nothing. There is no in-between. Finleigh was…my only exception."

"So, why would she—"

"Her mind was poisoned, and I never sought to correct it," he sighs out while playing with my hair. "If it brought her meaning or comfort to hate me, for her hatred to grow and give her strength, however misguided, I was willing. In any case, I accept responsibility for my hand in the matter of the Curse."

I swing my leg over his hip, so I'm mounting him, beaming with my hair radiating along the side of his neck. "Mmm, and your penance has been exceptional...so far," I add and kiss my way from his throat, across his powerful chest, lower to his navel. A warmth engulfs me when his roused member nudges my center.

"So far?" he questions, playing with my hair with both hands now.

Grinning, I circle my hungry center around his godhood tip, revel in how his head tips back. And how he groans deep in his throat when I slam down on him, squealing from the pain and pressure...and pleasure. Ary grips my hips to steady me as I wince from the silken diamonded hardness. My eyes whirl to the tent canopy clothed in a multitude of vines bearing spirit roses like starry blurs in my vision.

At last, I breathe a deep sigh, lean over to press my breasts to his chest, and whisper in his ear, "Your soul harem, Ary."

One lightning bolt's worth of a moment, and he's shifted our positions, leaving me winded, breathless, gaping up at him. "Oh!" I cry from the intensity when he pulls out and plunges into me again, rooting deep to the hilt.

Sweat clings to my brow. All my muscles have weakened to a near boneless state. But I wrap my legs around him, clenching tight. He covers my mouth with his and thrusts my arms above my head so he may taste me again. A pure surge of lustful energy sweeps through my body right before I clamp my hardest.

As soon as my knees give out and I fall back against the bed, the God of Death shoves my thighs wide until I'm practically spread-eagled. Muscles bulging, Ary circles his hips to penetrate my deepest core until

I gulp for air, feeling the power in his upper thighs and lower muscles of his stomach as he pounds into me again and again.

Closing my eyes, I receive him, accept him...*reap* him.

And once he explodes inside me, pumping icy seed into my hot chamber, I thrash my hair. Then gasp, moan, scream into his mouth. Arching my back, I tighten all my muscles. Heated lightning currents shiver up my spine. My whole body trembles and shudders in pure goddess ecstasy as the currents violently splash my face with glory and paradise.

His shaft spasms, body shivering against mine. With a tender kiss upon my throat, Ary drags his mouth to mine and murmurs against it, "I will release all to their ancestral realm. Except for *one*." I snap my gaze to his, lower my brows, and open my mouth to protest, but Ary deepens his eyes, seeking mine. That member throbs inside me, giving little twitches to pump the last of his seed into me. "Will you trust me, Isla?" he questions with a new challenge and traces my lips with his tongue.

I moan.

Not once do his eyes blink. Just a steady, tranquil gaze of fathomless silver. A celestial sea of starlight. Finally, I heave my shoulders back, sigh, and offer him a soft nod.

"Good girl. Now...where were we?"

My mouth rises to greet his, and our desires unite once again.

History repeats itself.

At dawn after our long night is over, and all but one bride spirit has evanesced to their ancestral, eternity homes as Aryahn Kryach had vowed, I return to the Underworld of Nathyan Ghyeal.

Whatever pain in my body bows to the Isle-sent burning, divine pleasure.

This time, my determination is tenfold. Everything feels stronger as the Cryth River spirits vault me through the water and to the dais. This time, I land on my feet, not on my knees. Raw power courses through my figure as if my Nether-mark surges fire and ice through my skin, my muscles, my blood, my bones, my very heart, and my soul. My body judders from this new force.

It's too much power. Too much god-essence, and I understand the source. And what I must do with it.

"Isla!" a familiar voice exclaims before the Court.

I posture, lifting my eyes to my leyanyn as she rises from the throne to approach me while cradling the swell of her belly. All around me, countless stewards and servants work to repair the Citadel after the Sleeping Stallion's damage. But I don't have time to examine further when Franzy embraces me tight. My breath leaves in ragged gasps.

"I thought I'd never see you again," she says, her warmth seeping into my body. I battle the urge to wince because my lungs burn with heaven's light, and my blood burns with hellfire.

The moment she kisses me is when the vision soars into my mind:

Franzy is sitting upon the throne of bones. She is so beautiful wearing the crown, *my* crown I love so much, the crown of black crystal and diamond-tipped bones woven with golden vines. The crown of the Queen of the Underworld. The entire court kneels before her while she holds a babe to nurse at her chest. A daughter. The Princess of Talahn-Feyal. Half-Ith and half-human. The first sovereign to truly bring unity and peace—with the guidance of her half-born mother—to the Underworld, to all Talahn-Feyal is Franzy's daughter! Oh, gods!

And I am not there beside her. The throne next to hers is...empty. For Franzy is strong enough to rule without a King or a Queen.

When the vision wavers, I gasp and face my leyanyn. I clasp her face to mine and kiss her unrelenting and deep. Tears flow, burning down my cheeks because I know...somehow, I know this, *this* is our last kiss. Like a firebolt, my pulse hammers blood into my ears, heart ramming against my rib cage with the need to release this energy, this godly *power*.

"Where's Allysteir?" is my first question when I break free, gasping.

She cups my shoulder, concerned. "No one knows. After he defeated the Sleeping Stallion, he was knocked unconscious. But when he woke, he climbed upon Ifrynna, and they left the Citadel."

I rub my lips, knots forming in my stomach, my chest, my throat from the knowledge I may never see him again. But I can't deny the need inside me—this overpowering craving, the pull I've had all my life—magnified by a hundred-fold, no...a thousand-fold.

I know where I need to go.

"I'll always love you, leyanyn." I squeeze her hands with rivers of tears trickling down my cheeks. A firestorm roars up my spine, and I suck in a sharp breath while Franzy narrows her eyes.

"I have something for you." She summons a nearby steward who brings her the crown which she passes to me. "You left it in the catacombs."

Glancing at the mark upon her collarbone, I smile. Despite the crushing emotion, my heart is fuller than ever with love for her. Purple bell-heather bursts from my palms to shower her. Franzy flinches but smiles quickly, loving my gift.

I take the crown in my hands and place it upon her head, proclaiming, "You will be the greatest Queen of the Underworld. You are stronger than the Scarlet Skathyk, my leyanyn. Someday, I hope to be as strong and wise as you, but my journey will take much longer."

Her eyes deepen upon mine. An otherworldly perception rooted deep within her. Her intuition has served her and blessed her with love and wisdom. "Where are you going, Isla?"

I lean in and whisper in her ear, "Home."

Kissing her one final time, I plunge back into the River Cryth, crying out for Betha.

EPILOGUE
"MY NAME IS SARYA."

ISLA

The spirits carry me through the portal but not into the Nether-Void. No, they carry me where I've requested. Where everything began on the border of my given-family's farm.

I face the depthless, swarming shadow of the Void. Its Nether energy pulsates and throbs into me until the fire and ice inside me from my tryskelle mark swells, growing extreme.

On the other side of the Void are hundreds, if not thousands of refters, slamming against the barrier. Some plunge past.

Behind me, alerted by my sudden presence on the farm, my given-family gathers. "Go!" I bark the command. "Get away from here!"

With the one-year-old bundle bound to her chest, Mathyr scrambles for the little ones and ushers them inside the log farmhouse where I spent my first eighteen years. Only Fathyr remains. A single lift of his hand. A gleam of pride in his eye.

I nod in gratitude, thanking him and Mathyr in a silent gesture for caring for the little girl with a Nether-mark upon her back and corpus roses in her hair.

For them, for Franzy, for Allysteir, for all in Talahn-Feyal, I steel my spine and approach the powerful, swirling black orb.

For the first time, my hands do not tremble. My soul remains strong. Even with the refter growls growing near, I close my eyes, inhale through my nose, travel deep into my mind, my heart, my very goddess soul. My spirit reaped the power of the High God of Death—the power I'd bathed in when I'd plunged into the womb that defies time itself. An untamable tempest of goddess magic, it may rebirth any power.

The Goddess of Resurrection. The Goddess of Souls.

With the force thundering through my mortal body, I spread my arms to the dark energy. My Nether-mark explodes with hellfire and heaven's ice. Fueled by the memories of my time in the spirit world, of my true parents and their love strong enough to unite heaven and hell, I unleash wondrous spirit-power.

It erupts! In the form of thousands of shades and spirit roses, it twists into an omnipotent double helix to attack the Void.

And destroy it!

Refters cower. They wither. They shrivel into bones. Into dark spirits evanescing into nothingness—the otherworldly energy granting them existence fades. That Nether-energy, born of Cursed essence, bows to my double-helix of Spirit and Death.

Gasping as the force claws its way from my lungs, I drive myself onward. Command and push the helix to chain its double-bound power around the shadow valley.

My blood burns. My veins turn to ice. Though my knees falter, weakening, I close my eyes and channel the memories of my parents' embrace. Roused by my will, the helix climbs and soars miles to cover the Void, to encase it. Spirit roses hook their talon-like thorns into the Void. Shades multiply to a miles-long mantle.

My teeth rattle. My veins quake from fire and ice. Hot tears plague my vision to ooze down my cheek. But tears should not ooze. And these are *red*.

Pain and power surge through me. All my muscles throb. Bones crack from the pressure this goddess strength wreaks upon my mortal form. The helix slows its pursuit of the Void. I crash to my knees. More blood scrawls my vision like scarlet calligraphy. Despite my bloodstream slowing and my bones fracturing, I reinforce my heart.

This will not be my *redoing* but my glorious *undoing*!

Because I am the Mallyach-Ender. The Ender of Curses. The Un-doer of Curses.

So, I charge the spirit roses, the shades to this final proclamation, my last act as Isla Adayra Morganyach. As the helix streaks across the sky to span the entire length of Talahn-Feyal from the southern border of my given-family's farm, across the Five Ladies of Nathyan Ghyeal, and to the great border where Feyal-Ithydeir land ends and the Sythe forests grow, I proclaim in a diaphanous whisper, "Bandye."

In one ultimate, omnipotent roar, the united power of Death and the power of Spirit, of Rebirth obliterates Talahn-Feyal's Nether-Void.

I fall. But my head does not crash to the ground. Instead, a figure with hands as cold and soft as frost catches me. My breath is fragile. My heartbeat dwindles. My bones have shattered. Dread weakens my delicate bloodstream. This feeble mortal shell housing my goddess-birthright essence is *dying*. Somehow, I register the lustful tongue stroking my cheeks, licking my eyes, and lapping the blood. I open my mouth but can't muster anything beyond a whimper.

"H-how?" I wheeze, breath too shallow as I drink in her intoxicating image—a blur of carmine waves, golden skin, and crescent-moon fangs bared and ready.

"A blood tracker naturally." She sniffs. "And a little foresight from my High Goddess who waited for your little tryst with Death to finish. That hardly matters at present. You are dying, little lioness. But I may save you if you wish..." she purrs in my ear.

Narcyssa.

I bow my head and welcome her lustful heat curling around me. She ignites me with enough adrenaline to grant me consciousness despite how much I long to pass out. Pain thunders through my body, luring me to eternal sleep.

"But nothing comes without a price," she warns, voice lowering to a deep smoke. "After what you have done here in Talahn-Feyal, the gods will desire you more than ever, Mallyach-Ender. War is coming. And you will need to prepare. If you wish me to save you, you will take my goddess mark, and *we* will take a piece of you. A piece of your choosing." She hints at the High Goddess of Love.

My choosing? I manage the strength to nudge her chest, a slight brushing of my brow for her to continue.

"The memories of your life in Talahn-Feyal, your very name here," dictates Narcyssa. "Or your memories of your time in the gods' realm from the Gates to the Trial. And yes, even your long night with Aryahn Kryach."

"No," I whimper to the last, knowing I cannot lose those. I cannot lose my moments with my parents, my conquering of the gods and their marks, of...Ary.

But I understand the deep weight of the sacrifice. I will lose *all* memories of being Queen of the Underworld. I'll lose my memories of wooing Ary. I'll lose all my time with Allysteir. I'll lose my given-family, of my...Franzy. I blink back bloody tears, remembering the vision of Franzy upon the throne with her daughter. My leyanyn for this brief existence in Talahn-Feyal. And if I am the Spirit Rose, while our union of mind and body will fade, my soul will welcome her someday.

Regardless, she does not need me. Perhaps she never truly needed me. No. All this time, all these years, it was *I* who needed her. The bittersweet weight of grief crashes over me, drying my mouth, burning my throat, and strangling my heart. But it would be a deeper weight to forget my true identity—to lose my glorious redoing in the womb before time.

This is my undoing.

I nod, I bow my head in acceptance.

Narcyssa plunges her fangs into my throat. Whatever sharp flicker of pain bows to a liquid warmth spreading into my blood, into my veins. Of her venom. It rewrites the doom transcribed upon this mortal husk. This other Goddess' force of mind and body is stronger than mine. She reaps those memories I'd surrendered.

Triggered by the sense of *forgetting*, my mind returns to the oubliette. I shiver with bitter adrenaline bleeding onto my tongue. That fog of nothingness clouds my vision, and I tip my head back. Now, I choose to forget. I embrace the sensation of Narcyssa sucking away the memories of Talahn-Feyal. Of my past becoming *nothing*.

Bones repaired, muscles gaining strength, blood pumping in my veins quicker, I cling to Narcyssa, arch my neck, and print my lips to her jawline. It only feeds her thirst since she sucks harder, deeper.

Her venom engulfs my body in a heated flame to command my blood to flow, to kindle my heartbeat until it practically hammers against my rib cage. Renewed. Revitalized. Rebirthed.

I knot my brows. Because something is missing. A sense of loss plunders all my nerve-endings, but I hardly care. It bows to the thickening fire of lust as the chilled, supple lips fold mine back, her tongue imparting the taste of blood and iron. Bitter but not unwelcome. Her tongue flicks my teeth, lowers to stroke mine. I moan into her mouth.

Once she breaks from my lips, I squint, pinch my eyes to behold her captivating face. Her eyes are deep and dark as chasms pinpointed by blotted scarlet. Her cheekbones are sharper than uncut diamonds. Lips red as blood with bronze skin and fiery hair, she is quite possibly the most alluring and intoxicating creature I've ever laid eyes upon. When she smiles, revealing her fangs, I flinch, understanding she's a...a—

"A vampyr," she concludes, straightening, shoulders pushing back, lithe neck lifting regal high. "I am Narcyssa, Queen of Mortya-Tereyn. And you are coming with me, my pet."

"Where?" I wonder, baffled. All my memories are hazy. Images of golden gates of hellfire glimmer in my mind. A boundless, whispering fog. I remember swimming inside a host of stars. A beautiful tree and an aged throne. Roses shatter my thoughts. The memories are too overwhelming, I can't piece them together.

Narcyssa pulls me to my feet and binds a hand around my waist, so her claws needle me when she responds, "To Orys a Crypta. The City of Crypts."

ALLYSTEIR

Ifrynna pounds her paws upon the ground, her spirit form traveling the hidden passages of Nathyan Ghyeal. Vitalized and renewed by our victory over the Sleeping Stallion, we press onward. And hope expands in my chest. True, unbridled hope for the first time.

When Betha alerted me how Isla passed into the god realms, I laughed. Laughter rippled through my chest and up my airway. Not out of disbelief but from my sheer idiocy not to recognize the essence of her blood, why it was new and exquisite every time—the essence of the gods.

And why she was drawn to Kryach more than any bride in history.

It's how I may release her with pride, relief, and jubilation. Well, jubilation came the moment Betha informed me of the great tidings from the spirit realm. Of rebirth and resurrection. While hope swelled in my chest for the first time, Ifrynna beckoned me to ride her.

Now, she carries me through the web of tunnels and to the secret passage only I know of with its keyhole in the molded shape of my wishbone. A wishbone I'd vowed to only ever break with my truest bride. Breaths deep, my heart jolts in my chest, prompting me into the back passage. I lick my lips, cautious, fearful of hope, fearful after five hundred years of waiting. Of my heart as ruined and rotted as my corpse body.

But I am whole now.

First and foremost, I hear the chains rattling.

As I step into the dome-like cavern nudging the Cryth shoreline, she tosses golden hair like streams from the sun onto the curve of her delicate shoulder—bare on account of the flimsy and ragged lace dress I'd clothed her in. My balled hands open to awed palms. All my tense muscles liquefy at the sight of *her*.

She turns to me, rolls her perfect midwinter blue eyes, her heart-shaped lips grinning mischievously as she says, "Really, Ally, I know I teased you about using chains in our relationship, but this was hardly what I expected."

Oh, gods! Heat radiates inside me, thoughts so elated, so scattered. I lose my breath even as I barrel to her side to gather her in my arms. I trace the warm, raw tears streaming down her cheeks. They mirror the ones glistening in my eyes. Once sunken in, her angular cheekbones have returned. The once ashen skin from its corpse state has renewed to warm gold.

Heart thundering in my chest, adrenaline like a shooting star in my blood, I speak my first, my *truest* bride's name, "Finleigh."

She kisses me. Seals her lips to mine. Without another second, I use the last remnants of shade power to break her chains, lift her into my arms, and spin her again and again. I open her mouth beneath mine to taste her. Not one trace of rot or ruin. Only the familiar scent of herbs and the musk of the cavern upon her dress.

Next, she relieves me of my robe. I follow with her dress, capturing the sight of her nude form I haven't beheld in five hundred years! Her slender and lean frame, her proud neck, small but high and round breasts with small areola and tiny pink nipples always hard for me. Finleigh scrambles to rid me of my tunic and breeches, her mouth falling open. I roar laughter as she practically pounces on me, springing into my arms and wrapping her slender legs around my waist. Tenderness will come later.

Heat raging through my member, I penetrate her. Not once have I lost the memory of plunging into her silken heat all those centuries ago. How her sex nourishes me, her breath restores me, and her heart heals me.

Thumbs digging into her lithe back and rubbing her spinal cord, I pound her hard, savor her mews of pleasure. I kiss her mouth, her neck, lower to capture her breast, rubbing my lips to suckle the pink stone of a tip. Finleigh clenches, throws her head back, and shrieks my name. I snap, burying deep inside her.

Here, I stand. My gasps mingle with hers. After several minutes of my mouth and nose pressed to her collarbone to inhale her scent, I don't move, don't retreat. Too afraid this is all a dream. Too afraid if I let go of her for one moment, she will disappear to the spirit world.

"Finny," I murmur, printing a kiss to her chin. "Finny."

"Allysteir." She tilts her neck to the side. "You can put me down now. I've been waiting five hundred years to do more than just *that*!"

At first, I want to ask her how, but I hardly care right now. Only the Mallyach-Ender could fulfill such a dream. Nor do I care about the lie Isla told me about our "child" when she urged me to help Ifrynna. Not with my golden treasure of Finleigh standing before me.

"A moment, my bride," I say and turn without releasing her hand.

Dragging her flustered, blushing form to my fallen robes, I retrieve the object I carry with me always. The first time I will ever show such an object to another living soul.

Finleigh smiles when I present it to her. Pulling in a deep breath, I take one end of the wishbone at the same time she takes the other and proclaim, "We break this now. Whoever claims the largest side chooses."

"Chooses what?"

I lean closer, brows bobbing with the reply, "Whether we will remain in Nathyan Ghyeal. Or where we will travel to first."

That conniving, crooked smile I fell in love with the night she opened the portal to the Unseen Section returns. I offer her a knowing grin.

"On the count of three..." she trails off, closing her fingers around the wishbone. "One."

"Two." I hold my breath.

She squeals, "Three!"

We snap the bone.

SARYA

"Come along now, my pet," Narcyssa says to me as we await the next coach in the center of the square within Cock-Cross. Everyone gives her a wide berth, including the Feyal-Ithydeir as I've learned they are called. No one would ever test the Queen of Mortya-Tereyn.

I huddle closer to my host. Her mark upon my throat stings me with her urging command, and I can't help but trace the raised flesh. By now, she's purchased travel clothes for me, but the form-fitting black bodysuit—however ornate with its gold trimmings, decorative bodice, and sweeping gray cloak—seems awkward. It smothers my skin. But the gold band housing precious stones she'd crowned my head with is a sharp contrast and feels more like a...a secret. A missing piece. That sense of loss crawls below my skin with a bone-deep chill.

Regardless, Narcyssa frowns and traces a claw across my knuckles in a warning. "Stop playing with your mark."

My breath heaves, and I swallow a knot in my throat, wishing her smoke and silk voice did not stir the longing in my chest, or my mouth to dampen. I drop my hand but glower. The opposite extreme of fear and contempt roils heat in my belly as if she's stolen something.

Narcyssa grins at my defiance and taps my cheek with her claw. "Don't look so glum, my pet. Trust me, you will be my honored guest in my realm."

"A guest or a pet, Narcyssa? Perhaps you should make up your mind."

She grins, feral and feline, fangs peeking beneath her lips. "There's the spirit I admire so much."

"Isla?" A masculine voice, a warm baritone, mentions before a cool hand cups my shoulder.

Flinching, I spin to face the invader, almost expecting Narcyssa to hiss at the handsome young man with rich, cinnamon hair bound in a knot at the base of his neck. His blue eyes are kind, deep, and soulful. Next to him stands a lovely, young woman with hair like a river of gold and skin a darker, gilded shade.

I shake my head. "I'm sorry. You have me confused with someone else. My name is Sarya," I tell him.

The young man threads his brows, eyes narrowing in on the mark at my throat. I wince when it lashes heat to my skin while he snaps his eyes to Narcyssa.

"It is good to see you restored and at peace as your land is, Allysteir," the Queen expresses. "Thanks to the Curse-Ender."

I swallow, uncomfortable with the missing gaps, the slithering feeling of how I should know the man before me despite not recognizing him. A shadow needles my thoughts, imparting a vision of my arms spread before a great shadowland of a Void, of spirit roses and shades.

"Yes." This Allysteir nods, responding to her, but his eyes don't flee from mine. "And now, Franzyna Mordhya will rule all Talahn-Feyal as High Queen while I and my bride take a real honeymoon." He folds his palm into the golden-haired woman's, smiling softly at her.

"Fair journey across the sea and to the southern lands, my lord," Narcyssa declares as a gold coach drawn by several winged black horses arrives.

"Thank you. And..." he clasps my hand in his. I shiver from the touch. So *familiar*. I can't fathom why tears form in my eyes at the presence of this...stranger. Or why my chest aches and my body feels cold with a melancholic heaviness as he rubs his lips across my knuckles and finishes, "Safe journey and fare thee well, dark rose."

I nod in gratitude but say nothing as Allysteir drops my hand with a smile. His lips crease at the corners as if wistful. My world slows as he turns and departs with his golden bride.

But the moment Narcyssa pulls upon our bond, heated energy surges inside me. I follow her toward the waiting coach.

Just before I enter alongside her, a wizened, crackly voice utters behind me, "Care for a fythdel bone to take as a memento, sweet champion?"

I turn, screwing my brows low at the weasel-faced man hunched over while offering me a little rectangular bone with a child's game rune marked upon it. And whatever compels me to accept the gift, I can't fathom. My heart lurches, and I snatch the token before he changes his mind.

"You may want to fly over the Nathyan Ghyeal Pass. I believe you will find it most...riveting."

"Thank you, Mr...?"

"Ganyx," he responds, bony hand touching his chest. It's all he says before he turns and lowers himself to the ground to play with more bones.

Shaking my head from the awkward encounter, I follow Narcyssa into the coach, clutching the little bone token.

When the horses stride into a canter and then a gallop before finally lifting to carry the coach off the ground, a lovely lightness overtakes my limbs to mirror their wings.

The landscape of Talahn-Feyal transforms into a whirling blur of dramatic mountains, deep green glens, forests, and moors. And as the coach sails across the Nathyan Ghyeal pass of the Five White Ladies, I peer down to behold a beautiful river. A *new* river, sparkling and swirling all around the crest of the highest mountain peak.

I inhale a sharp intake of breath when a new vision drifts into my mind. Ice engulfs my core at the image of the Goddess of Doom weeping, weeping this same beautiful river. But as the vision fades, a smile tugs at my lips. Hope flutters in my belly, and my heart grows wings to soar in my chest.

The coach flies onward, and we leave the river of tears and Talahn-Feyal far behind.

THE END

*(For now. Please see **Author's Note** and enjoy the **Bonus Scene**!)*

AUTHOR'S NOTE

Bride of the Corpse King was written within the darkest year of my life. To give some background: the end of 2020 brought revelation, awakening, and life to my spirit! In October of 2020, I wrote the most significant book of my life--*Courting Death and Destruction*. After writing thirty two books in many genres, this heart and soul work could not have stunned me more. Within three weeks, I'd written 120,000 words. Something long-suppressed in my heart rose up.

Courting Death and Destruction featured my first queer protagonist and cast, my newfound dark humor, a trauma-healing arc to parallel my own, sex positivity, goddess energy, and the first steamy scenes I'd ever brought to explicit life in a book. Immediately following book one, I wrote 120,000 words of book two in November followed by 145,000 words of book three in December. When people ask how I accomplished this, I tell them how I am still in awe, knowing I barely ate or slept, encountered dreams and visions, and pretty certain I traveled to an alternate dimension--just kidding on that last one (maybe). I finished book four in February.

Due to this heart and soul work, I stopped suppressing my identity and came out as bisexual. What was more amazing was how my husband, Kevin, had taken his pansexual awareness journey at the same time. We came out to each other that fall/winter.

However, 2021 brought crushing rejection as countless literary agents said no to *Courting Death and Destruction*. Early 2021, I was diagnosed with PTSD due to my early childhood trauma. Unfortunately, new medication made my depression and anxiety worse. In April, when I learned about Kindle Vella, I took a break from my *Death and Destruction* Series and started writing *Bride of the Corpse King*. Little did I know how necessary it would be.

Late June, Kevin, needed emergency cancer surgery. With him being so young at only 34 and us having two little girls, this rattled our little family. Shortly after the surgery, Vella launched. I'd already written 80,000 words and had several episodes publising. Despite being out of work for a month and needing to heal, Kevin was very supportive, though I worked 15 hour days to claim a spot in the Top Five out of 10,000 authors on Kindle Vella.

Due to how rare, fast, and aggressive the cancer was, Kevin required chemo in the fall. By this time, our family had been in quarantine for 1.5 years. Chemo took a harder toll on Kevin than the surgery and therefore much stress on our girls. At the beginning of October, chemo was done, but Kevin had contracted two nasty infections and needed to go back to the hospital. Thankfully, the antibiotics brought him back to normal by Wednesday, as normal as anyone can be following chemo.

What rattled us more was when I needed to go to the ER that same week for what turned out to be a blood clot. I have a history of them due to a blood clotting disorder. Unfortunately, due to the ER doctor prescribing me the wrong medication and his refusal to consult with a hematologist, I ended up in the ER several times that month with worsening conditions, including a pulmonary embolism I.e a blood clot in my lung. I also required two hospital stays. I'm on perma-blood thinners now.

During this time, I clung to writing *Bride of the Corpse King* to keep me steady. I remained as Top 8 in the charts, determined for one thing in my life to go right when everything else was dark. My sweet, therapeutic two cats also helped. Because I'm their mommy and due to my health issues, they became very territorial--to the point where one bit off a part of the other's tail, requiring emergency surgery. I almost lost my favorite companion and fur child.

By December, I was buried in the final stages of writing *Bride of the Corpse King* while marketing the hell out of it. But 2021 had dealt too many wounds, and I'd nearly reached my breaking point.

For 2022, I was determined to manifest rainbows. Out of the thunderclouds of 2021 has emerged these rainbows. My new work, *Bride of Lucifer,* has sparked a viral FB reader interest and new fans, who have truly become encouraging friends and anchors. I couldn't be more passionate or grateful for these new beginnings. I have also become the only Kindle Vella author with three books in the Top 250. *Bride of the Corpse King* has retained a slot in the Top 15 since launch. It's taken years to get here.

But due to all of 2021's dark trials, I now associate much of *Bride of the Corpse King* with pain and struggle and depression. I still have plans for this series. But I apologize to those who want more immediately. I must get some distance until those wounds have healed, or at least have scarred.

In the meantime, I hope you will read my other spicy fantasies with badass, magical heroines, dark alpha men, and trauma overcoming books. The first two books of *Bride of Lucifer* will release this October along with *Bride of the Shifter King*, my BDSM Beauty and the Beast. These and all my works can be found on Kindle Vella (for USA fans) and

Radish or my Patreon (for international).

Please consider voting for any of my books on Kindle Vella and supporting my author journey. The minimum to vote aka Top Fave is literally less than $1.99 a month. I love to treat my supporters to special art postcards and exclusive super fan group perks like helping me vote on names, fashion, and even getting access to advanced chapters!

Please follow my TikTok @authoremilyshore and be sure to join "Emily's Vella Verse" on Facebook: a public group where I share fun memes, teasers, games, and even a monthly giveaway.

Thank you so much for picking up *Bride of the Corpse King*. And to anyone who supports me on Kindle Vella with "thumbs ups" and "Top Fave" votes.

P.S. If you're wondering about Courting Death and Destruction, I would do a rapid release of this series. But it's my baby. So, I *ahem* require much begging to shine its light to the world.

OTHER ACKNOWLEDGEMENTS

To my original fans who've read my work throughout the years and have witnessed its evolution: Belinda, Laura, Jenny, and Lisa, your loyalty and support means the world to me!

To my new super fans who faithfully Top Fave every Sunday or support my Patreon (damn--I hope I include all the names I need to, yes I'm doing this--HERE WE GO!):

Mary, Alyssa, Allison, Chandra, Kitty, Mashalla, Quarnisha, Nicole (can't wait for our girls-weekend trip up north), Angela (thank you for being my spiritual momma), Jennifer C., Rosa, Ashley A., Amber C., Cristal, Carrie A., Stephanie, Hailey, Danielle A., Angela C., AC (I can't enough amazing things about you!), Jamie, Desiree, Natalie, Hilary, Hydra, Katy, Nalley, Blanca, Sabrina, Nicole, Teresa, Sio, Kim, both Alexas!, all the Ambers, Danielle C., Cordelia, Cera, Amiy, Elisha, Emily E., Kristi C., Sheila, Charity, Renee, Maria Cristina, Elisa, All the Amandas, both Heathers., Dava, Cera P., Mona, Melissa T-S, both Alexis's., Cheyanna, Isabella, both Aprils, Kat, Candace, Banchia, Alexandra, Toby, Samantha, Savvy, Angel, Cristina, Taylor C., Christina V.,Crystal A., Marissa, Melaney, Jennifer M., Madi, Brianna, Symothy, Dandee, Emily C., Brooke, Sarah, Tiffany, Teagan, Tessley, Kayla, Kaila, Holly, Lexi, Destiny, Tara, Brandi, all the Brittanys!, Kaylin, Courtney A., Magikal, Suzanna, both Rachels, all the Megans, both Ivys, Griselda, aaaaaand anyone and everyone who has Top Faved me. I definitely can't do this for each book! PHEW!

Molly Phipps of We Got You Covered: That skull and roses and pomegranates cover is truly epic and the formatting is gorgeous! I love how we started with *The Lord of the Rings* and our friendship has continued. You are still my #1 go-to for all my covers. Thank you for putting up with my OCD updates and too-many gifs.

RFK Designs: For the first cover of *Bride of the Corpse King* which I still love.

Amanda S: Thank you so much for composing this beautiful melody to the song at the beginning of *Bride of the Corpse King* and enlisting your musician friend to bring it to life.

Jennifer Corry: For recommending so many awesome horror/slasher/thrillers that helped me get through 2021 with my PTSD.

All the support we received during our darkest year. Manuscript Academy and the agents who helped me grow through critiques and lectures. The Vella Community because so many authors there have been so sweet and nice to me. (Audrey Carlan for liking my blog post about how writing and this business is a marathon.) The cast of Schitt's Creek, of course!

Kevin: for always supporting me through everything we've been through over the past seventeen years we've been together, including thirteen years of marriage. If we made it through 2021, we can make it through anything.

CAST OF CHARACTERS

Isla Adayra — the Persephone of Bride of the Corpse King

Allysteir Morganyach aka The Corpse King of Talahn Feyal — Original Character

Aryahn Kryach — the God of Death — loosely based on Hades and Thanatos

Franzyna Mordhya aka Franzy — Lifelong friend and sweetheart to Isla

Aydon Morganyach — Prince of Talahn Feyal and husband to Franzy

Elder Kanat — High Elder of Talahn Feyal and antagonist

Gryzelda Morganyach — Queen of Talahn Feyal

Morrygna — The Goddess of Doom — loosely based on the Morrigan

Narcyssa —- The Sythe Queen

Betha — Ban-Sythe to Morrygna

Finleigh — First Bride and lover to Allysteir

BONUS SCENE
IN ARYAHN KRYACH'S CHAMBER

ISLA

Upon Ary's sumptuous chamber bed, I sprawl my body out, arms over my head and ease a sigh of deep contentment. Yes, my sex is sorer than ever while my nipples sting as if thorns have pierced them, but all my flesh tingles. Turning to my side, I press my cheek onto the silk weight of the cool pillow, loving how great and deep and wide Ary's bed is. Low to the floor, all of it is black as a winter storm and surrounded by translucent, dark sheets to canvass us.

I suck in a deep breath as my skin sings the moment the God of Death's hands massage my back. My smile spreads when I realize he's caressing the Isle oil into my skin. It reawakens my desire for him. My pulse to thrum and my arousal to quiver my limbs.

"I thought you said we were here to rest," I murmur, shifting until I'm on my stomach, so he may gain more access to my back. Flutters swirl into a butterfly tempest in my belly as his hands lower to cup my bottom, to dig his fingers in the plump flesh.

His breath deepens above me, and I love how it curls across the back of my neck through my waves. "Do you not feel at peace, my sweet, little wonder?"

I moan when he massages oil into my thighs, his fingers embarking deeper to curve at the edge of my sex. Already, my fevered fluids have begun to ooze. I know Ary can scent them. He flares his nostrils but somehow manages to lower his hands. A moan loosens from my mouth at how he pays close attention to the backs of my legs, soothing the overworked muscles of my calves after our lovemaking, our fucking. Warmth, delicious and heady, seals across my entire back from neck down to my feet where his fingers linger.

"Oh!" I groan at the pleasure in his hands as he kneads my sore feet. After a few moments, a finger dips between my toes, and I jerk. An uncontrollable giggle sprinkles from my lips.

"Hmm...did I touch a nerve, Isla?" he goads.

"Don't!"

My warning is useless. Fits of laughter bubble from my chest and into the air from his fingers wiggling in between my toes and tormenting their backs. Instinct has me kicking and pulling back, but Ary is too strong. I laugh until pangs throttle my lungs, until my throat aches, and my legs surrender to his tickle torture.

"No more, please, Ary! You win!" I plead, gazing at him through my strands caked to my sweat-clad cheeks.

"Such fascinating mortal wonder at work," he muses, pausing to tap a finger to my large toe before trailing it down the arch of my foot. I squeal from the act. "Never before have I made a goddess laugh from torment. Their laughter is mocking. Yours is full and ripe and precious."

More curling heat knots my belly. I tremble when he releases my foot and turns my body until I'm lying on my back. He hovers directly over me, and my breath hitches at his powerful organ when it rubs my upper belly. Eyes dark and glowing, Ary leans in. Sharp desire tears through me. My pulse bursts as he rubs his lips across mine and whispers, "I will cherish your laughter like a sacred constellation, my little wonder. It will feed my loneliness for a century. I could spend an eternity listening to it and the sound of your moans as I buried deep inside you. I fear I'll never want to leave your warm mortal chambers."

Heart bursting, I cradle one side of his beautiful face. Heart-crushingly beautiful with those half-lidded dark eyes gleaming with a carnal hunger. A deathly villain in all the ancient tales. But he is my tortured villain. He tilts his head, kisses my palm while my other hand cups his shoulder until the other follows on the opposite side. So broad and large while his waist sweeps into a lithe, well-muscled, and flawless V-shape. Skin of pure moonless, black silk.

A knowing smirk spreads on one side of his face. I hold my breath, tensing when he grips a nearby bottle and pours more oil into his palms. His hands coiling around my throat and sliding lower hypnotize me. A touch so sensual and yet so starved for warmth and pleasure. His cock on my belly twitches. Lightning frissons engulf my skin when those palms gather my breasts, kneading starlit oil upon the mounds while his thumbs and fingers imprison my nipples. I clench my thighs and writhe on his bed. His labored breath only heightens my arousal.

And then, those hands forsake my breasts to glide across my belly and lower to where he spreads my thighs. And peels apart my pubic lips. "So velvet and pink, Isla. You are silk and sweetness, my dark rose." My breath hitches from his pupils dilating to depthless pools. "The sight of your sex and how its soaked heat grips me will forever haunt my dreams. You are blood and flesh and life. A precious jewel to be cherished. Like these…"

I inhale when he reaches for an Isle fruit sliced in half. A few rubied pearls drip from its center, tumbling onto my chest. Dipping two fingers into the fruit, Ary lowers those two fingers to my lips, offering me the tart seeds. I smile and fold my lips around his fingers, sucking greedily while my sex clenches and spasms with need. All my skin tingles, glistening with the gold and silver oil of the Isles.

And then, Ary pushes my legs up to my shoulders, commands his Death shades to bind them. Tears shimmer in my vision, and I groan from the heated fever burning within me as the God opens my folds to place several of the soft, ripe seeds within my throbbing sex. Oh, gods, my clitoris hardens and pulses! More fluids spill from me, disturbing the seeds, but Ary merely chuckles from deep within his throat and smears more of the fruit within my sex. He doesn't stop with one. He feeds the seeds through my narrow slit until I swear my vagina gasps, ready to burst from the delicious fullness.

Plumping my breasts with his hands, Ary finishes by rolling two halved fruits over my nipples until the seeds riddle my breasts and the juice drips in hearty globules all over the mounds.

"Now, you are ready. A sweet feast fit for the God of Death."

My eyes water. Gasping and heaving, I moan as he lowers his mouth to tongue my breast, lapping up the juice and flicking the flushed golden buds until he arrives at my nipples. A scream lodges in my throat as he suckles on each one, tonguing and feasting on them as surely as if they were pomegranate seeds themselves.

Heart panting, I gaze at him as he descends to between my thighs and studies my sex nearly bursting from the pomegranate fruit. First, he rubs my labia, squeezing some seeds to split and cascade their juice to mix with my fluids. He groans and puts his nose to my sex.

"Fuck, Isla, your fragrance is delirious. Your spirit scent overwhelms the ripe seeds."

"Oh!" I moan as he sucks at my folds. I clutch at the sheets when he tantalizes the inner folds with his tongue in long, languorous strokes. Maddening when he does not touch the fattened nub.

"How do you feel, little wonder? All your beauty exposed to me? Your luxurious scent in my lungs?"

"Aryahn, please!" I use his full name and dig my nails into my palms as his shades strengthen around my wrists.

He burrows his nose at the border of my entrance, tormenting me further. "Say it again," his voice darkens to a velvety heat that rolls across my body like a fever.

"Aryahn," I whisper, closing my eyes.

"Louder," he commands.

"Aryahn."

"Louder!" he snarls and sinks his teeth into my clitoris.

I buck and arch my back, screaming, "Aryahn!"

The God of Death spears my insides with his tongue. He shifts the seeds and extracts them from my slick heat. Lapping, licking, and savoring and following with deep, roving kisses to my vagina. I become his cherished and honored feast. Tortured beyond the point of sweat and tears, my insides shudder and quiver. When he dips one thick finger inside, my desperate core sucks him, squelching, and soaking him with my cream.

"So beautiful. So warm," groans Ary. "My desire is already hot and swollen and hard for you. You undo me, Isla. I will lose myself in the gift of your sweet, succulent sex."

He teases with his tongue, with his finger. Teeth lightly scraping the raw flesh, Ary sucks and kisses and licks at my lips, swirls and stabs his tongue at that entrance until I'm groaning and gasping and writhing in wet, liquid need.

He sinks deeper, fingers and tongue, and I fear I will become his mistress forever beyond this one night. That I will become his spirit mistress since mortal flesh cannot last in Eyleanan. Would I risk the lower gods waging war for my higher soul if it means surrendering myself to the God of Death's forevermore pleasure, knowing he could ravish me for eternity?

At one point, I glance down to meet his eyes, to behold the maddening silver fire within them as he feasts upon my swollen, satiny flesh. Lost within this frame of moments, time itself ceases to exist. As if we are together within that dark womb. He devours me until my flesh turns to liquid and flames, until the backs of my thighs bear his fingerprints, my entire being shakes from his ravenous essence. In the span of moments, my spirit spreads wings to lift from my restrictive, mortal shell to sagging so deep into Ary's bed, it becomes a black hole to swallow me whole.

Finally, his hands roam to caress my hips and sweep across my stomach, gifting me a reprieve even as his tongue continues its worship. I inhale and arch my neck, mouth watering when he fondles the flesh of my mound and rolls his thumb across the nipple. He torments the taut bud as much as he torments my lower, turgid flesh spread like an unraveling flower.

"My little wonder. My sweet Spirit Rose. My *Goddess*!"

When he squeezes my breast and draws my clitoral nub into his mouth to suckle, to nibble, and finally to lick, all the tension mounts to an insurpassable peak. With his mouth as hot as stars, he reduces all my muscles to liquid pools. All my mortal flesh wilts into a puddle of soaked, warm desire as his fingers revere every curve, and his tongue praises my sex.

Every nerve loses itself to that rhythmic throbbing pulse between my thighs until lightning hums inside my blood, building to a gushing, roaring crescendo. My inner muscles mirror the rhythm of his fingers, sucking them as he thrusts in and out, in and out. With his very soul arresting mine, Aryahn Kryach trains all his attention to twirling his tongue around that clitoral nub while his fingers curve deep into my drenched chamber. And my spirit heats and tightens to the unbearable edge. It grows. It bursts! Constellations of heartbeats rupture beneath my skin, each one brighter and more inflamed than the last. I scream and scream through a sea of raw tears from the explosion of fire. I shatter into the longest and most powerful climax. I fall into a shower of stars birthed from the God of Death's eyes.

Only my breath interrupts the silence. And a dark chuckle. Warm dust covers my face, drifts onto my naked body. At first, I believe it's the tingling aftermath of the unforgettable orgasm I just had. But when I open my eyes, Ary hovers above my face, grinning before lowering a finger to dip into the fluff of golden pollen covering my belly. I give a damp laugh, covering my lips from the sight of the floral dust sprinkling his mouth saturated from my juices.

Without warning, he covers my mouth with his and stabs his organ into my sex. And groans long and deep into my throat. Boneless and limp from pleasure, all I can do his kiss him back and give him nothing but my willing thighs and hips spread as he penetrates and pounds into me hard and heavy. Heavy as a tomb. Triggered by all his attention upon me, his girth has swelled, thickened and grown until he's stretching my moist walls to the point where they burn with sharp pain and lustful pleasure. Seated to the barest tip of the hilt, his cock is a deadly carnage, smoldering me from the inside out. His eyes stray once to where he may glimpse at where we are joined before they return to a commanding deadpan.

"I'm fucking you now, little wonder," he vows, lips hovering above mine. "Slow, deep, and hard. Feel all of me inside your warm, nectar pool. Give me your trembles, your moans, your tears, your screams. Give me your rapture."

The intimacy of his words destroys me, but he cannot kill me. Because I am the Spirit Rose. I am the High Goddess in mortal form—-higher than him. He still shreds me until I'm nothing but scraps of white, ripe flesh melting and receiving his burning, dark Death form. My delicate nerves are still holding onto the tailends of my pleasure.

Ary's demanding lips fold mine back for his tongue to fuck mine. He rolls his maddening hips, powered by the pillars of his thighs, to stir my inner cream. He stokes the tension. And ignites my blood. My nerves sing and soar, nearly detaching from my body, hanging on like floating ribbons. I'm floating outside my body once more while the rippling flames and twisting tension spiral through my body. This time, he meets me there. His terrifying energy and deathly form of shades and bloodfire to dance around my spirit roses in a precursor. This...*this* is what I felt from his Death mark upon my skin but multiplied a magnitude.

I hear a low growl from beyond this soul cocoon. And somehow, I feel it when Aryahn drags my legs up and up until my calves press to his shoulders. I feel his monstrous power leaving bruises on my flesh. Then, he thrusts into me. He fucks my soul, my mind, and my body in a dominating, all-mastering, omniscent triune to feed me his power. I devour it. I suck and swallow it all down, embracing the dark shades to chill all my flesh. Because it's not just my arousal that coats his unconquerable storm of a Death. It's blood.

"More!" I ascend higher in this soul cocoon, holding onto those threads of nerves for dear life because I've ever felt more alive. As if I've been dormant all my life with mere rumblings and murmurs that gift me a taste of the wonder and pleasures of the gods!

"My greedy, little wonder." He kisses me, and I feel the beat of his soul and taste bloodfire burning my tongue.

He doesn't stop. Charging and ramming, nearly crushing my sex. He pushes me into that soul cocoon, then pulls me deep into his soul and mouth, straining the nerves holding me to my mortal body. With his spirit thundering like a torrent of shades to meet the whirlwind of white petals of mine, the God of Death drives himself so deep into me. I bow to his power, his supremacy, addicted to the dark purity of his energy.

His jaw hardens to stone. He jerks and pumps into me, sovereign and prevailing. Commanding my pleasure. His very God face melts before me. Desperate, I grip the sides of his neck and press my lips to his, tasting the trail of silent tears trickling into his mouth from the incomparable rapture of this triune fuck. He lowers his hand to feel where we are joined and to seize my bloated clitoris. My protest is a squeal lodging in my throat. But he's groaning, releasing the depth of his breath to unite with mine in my lungs. And I'm sobbing and moaning as I come again and again. And again.

Nerves connecting once again, my spirit folds itself back into my body. Ary pulls out to show me his length soaked in our combined fluids. And though tears of raw emotion shimmer in my eyes, I don't marvel at the thickness I'd felt down to my core, into my very womb.

Eyes drifting across my flushed and sweat-soaked body to contrast his flawless one with not so much as a hair out of place, Ary shifts us onto our sides. He pulls me close until my back is against his chest. Sore and smoldering but soaring on the echoes of his elysium, I press my cheek to his arm draped under me, close my eyes, and fall into a blissful slumber, knowing he will fill my dreams with paradise. And wake me, my spirit rebirthed and ready for more.

ABOUT THE AUTHOR

EMILY SHORE is a best-selling author Kindle Vella author where her books have routinely made the Top Five out of 15,000 authors as well as #1 in Fantasy Romance, Urban Fantasy, Dark Fantasy, and Enemies to Lovers categories. As of 2022, she is the only Vella author to achieve three crowns (i.e three books in the Top 250).

Her small press dystopian, *The Aviary*, is a Top 100 Kindle ebook.

Emily has worked as a teen fiction awareness speaker all over Minnesota, including the annual Minnesota Educator's Academy conference.

As a bisexual feminist and a mother of two daughters, Emily is dedicated to empowering and inspiring the next generation of girls while offering spicy fantasy romance for adults. All her 2020 and beyond work features badass, queer heroines who take on dark alpha love interests.

Identifying as queer/polyamorous, Emily bridges the gap between LGBTQIA+ and cishet audiences. She goes beyond fetishized stereotypes by showcasing positive sexuality and sex-positivity while normalizing the beauty of queer/poly relationships because #whychoose?

Please subscribe to Emily's newsletter at **www.emilybethshore.com** to keep up with her series projects, author promos, and contests to receive fun prizes. Join **Emily's Vella Verse** on Facebook and learn how to become a supporter and receive a free signed paperback.

Made in United States
North Haven, CT
10 September 2022